Praise for *Th*

"Fast-paced action propels
versial plot."

—*Publishers Weekly*

Praise for *The Messiah Secret*

"An entertaining, hunt-and-chase thriller that races from
the English countryside to a hidden valley in the Middle
East . . . appealing and clever protagonists coupled with
intriguing history."   —*Publishers Weekly*

In Close Quarters . . .

The Walther kicked in his hand, but the only sound the
weapon made was a flat slap, followed by the metallic
noise of the slide being forced backward by the recoil, the
ejected case clattering onto the stone floor, and a fresh
round being loaded into the breech.

He had no idea whether or not he'd hit his target, but
because the man made no sound, Bronson assumed that
he'd missed. Semi-automatic pistols are notoriously inaccurate, even in experienced hands.

But then there was another shot, the crack of a small-
caliber weapon, and immediately Bronson heard a howl
of pain from the intruder, followed by the sound of
something heavy and metallic falling to the floor. No way
was he going to stand up to see what had happened, but
he still needed to know the situation. He reached up and
placed his flashlight on top of the metal control panel,
aimed it more or less at the door of the room, and
switched it on. At the same time, he ducked down again,
aimed the Walther around the corner of the control panel
directly at the lantern, and squeezed the trigger.

ECHO OF THE REICH

JAMES BECKER

A SIGNET BOOK

SIGNET
Published by New American Library, a division of
Penguin Group (USA) Inc., 375 Hudson Street,
New York, New York 10014, USA
Penguin Group (Canada), 90 Eglinton Avenue East, Suite 700, Toronto,
Ontario M4P 2Y3, Canada (a division of Pearson Penguin Canada Inc.)
Penguin Books Ltd., 80 Strand, London WC2R 0RL, England
Penguin Ireland, 25 St. Stephen's Green, Dublin 2,
Ireland (a division of Penguin Books Ltd.)
Penguin Group (Australia), 250 Camberwell Road, Camberwell, Victoria 3124,
Australia (a division of Pearson Australia Group Pty. Ltd.)
Penguin Books India Pvt. Ltd., 11 Community Centre, Panchsheel Park,
New Delhi - 110 017, India
Penguin Group (NZ), 67 Apollo Drive, Rosedale, Auckland 0632,
New Zealand (a division of Pearson New Zealand Ltd.)
Penguin Books (South Africa) (Pty.) Ltd., 24 Sturdee Avenue,
Rosebank, Johannesburg 2196, South Africa

Penguin Books Ltd., Registered Offices:
80 Strand, London WC2R 0RL, England

Published by Signet, an imprint of New American Library, a division of Penguin
Group (USA) Inc. Previously published in a Transworld Publishers edition. For
further information contact Transworld Publishers, a division of Random
House, Ltd., 61–63 Uxbridge Road, London W5 5SA, England.

First Signet Printing, October 2012
10 9 8 7 6 5 4 3 2 1

ALWAYS LEARNING   PEARSON

Any novel is a joint effort, and I'd like to thank my brilliant agent, Luigi Bonomi, for his unswerving support and encouragement, and Simon Thorogood and his talented and dedicated team at Transworld for all their work on this book.

And Sally, of course, just for being there.

PROLOGUE

It was the sound of boots on concrete that puzzled him.

Footsteps were always echoing through the labyrinth of passageways and laboratories in the perpetual gloom of the mine, but these sounded different, organized almost—a squad of men marching with purpose rather than a handful of scientists ambling along. And as far as Georg Schuster knew, there were no soldiers based in the facility.

The Komplex Milkow was located in the Wenceslas Mine, a bewildering network of tunnels and chambers, some natural but others hacked from the rock, which covered an area of almost thirty-six square kilometers. It was the home of *Der Riese*—"The Giant"—an SS research facility and one of the most secret bases ever established by Nazi Germany. The research project being

conducted there—it bore two project names: *Der Latern-*
enträger, meaning "the lantern bearer," and *Kronos*, or
"Saturn"—possessed the highest possible category of
both secrecy and funding priority within the Third Reich.
No other research of any sort, in any country, had been
allocated the classification *Kriegsentscheidend*, "decisive
for the outcome of the war."

Schuster had no idea why soldiers should be inside the
complex. Then an appalling thought struck him. Surely it
couldn't be the Russians? Not so soon? No, that was ridiculous, because if the Russians had arrived there would
have been yelling and shooting, and the explosions of
grenades.

Schuster opened the door of his laboratory and peered
out hesitantly. Then he relaxed, reassured by the sight of
the familiar uniforms of Wehrmacht soldiers.

Even so, the appearance of a uniformed German officer, accompanied by about a dozen soldiers, was unexpected, and Schuster stepped out into the corridor.

"Who are you?" he asked.

The officer leading the soldiers stopped and looked at the
man who'd just appeared. The questioner was a middle-
aged man wearing a white coat and a puzzled frown.

"I'm SS *Hauptsturmführer* Wolf," the new arrival replied politely, proffering a document that bore the distinctive signature of *Reichsleiter* Martin Bormann. "I'm in
charge of the SS Evacuation Kommando, working directly
under the authority of General Kammler. And you are?"

The scientist shook his head. "I've never heard of an
Evacuation Kommando," he said, glancing at the order
before handing it back.

"That's because you don't have a sufficiently high security clearance," Wolf responded, with a slight smile that vanished almost as quickly as it had appeared. "And I still need to know your name."

"It's Schuster. Georg Schuster."

Wolf took another sheet of paper from his uniform jacket and studied the list of names printed on it.

"You're one of the electrical engineering specialists?" he asked, and Schuster nodded. "Good. Just wait over there, in that chamber," Wolf ordered.

"What's going on? What do you want?"

"What I want to do is complete the task I've been given. In case you haven't noticed, Engineer Schuster, the Russian forces are almost upon us, and it's vital for the future of the Reich that they don't get their hands on the equipment you've been working on here. That's what I've been sent here to achieve."

"So you're going to evacuate us?"

"There's a Junkers Ju-390 heavy-lift aircraft waiting at Bystzyca Klodzka airfield just a few kilometers away," Wolf replied, not quite answering the man's question. Then he strode further into the complex, his men following on behind.

In less than an hour, Wolf had completed the first part of his assignment. He had identified all of the scientists and engineers at work within the facility, and these men and just a handful of women were now waiting in two separate stone chambers ready to leave the mine, one way or the other. But it wasn't just the personnel that Wolf had been ordered to take care of. Far more important than them was the device itself.

The double doors to the test chamber were massive—heavy steel frames lined with copious layers of what looked like insulating or soundproofing material. Wolf ordered his men to swing them open, and then he strode inside and for a few moments just stood and stared at the object in front of him.

General Kammler had told him in broad terms what the device was supposed to do, although neither Wolf nor, probably, Kammler himself understood more than a fraction of the science involved. But they both knew that Hitler's dream of a thousand-year Reich now lay in tatters. Not even the development and deployment of the V1 and V2 terror weapons, nor the latest generation of combat aircraft powered by jet engines, had been enough to hold back the armed forces of Germany's enemies. Forces that Wolf knew would soon be baying at the very gates of Berlin itself.

What was left of the German army was being squeezed between the British and American forces advancing from the west and the rapidly approaching Russian army. It was now apparent that the Soviet forces were going to reach the area of Ludwikowice first, and that was the worst-case scenario by far. It would be a disaster if the Americans or the British got their hands on the device, but if the Russians took possession of it, that would be a catastrophe of global proportions.

The orders from Berlin had been unequivocal. It was essential that *Die Glocke* remained in German hands. There was a chance, just the faintest possibility, even when defeat seemed both imminent and inevitable, that the device could be used to snatch victory, or at least serve to prevent the total destruction of Germany.

It didn't look like much of a weapon, Wolf thought as he stared across the chamber, though he could see exactly why it had acquired its nickname *Die Glocke*: what it resembled more than anything else was a bell. A big bell, almost three meters in diameter and over four meters high.

"What's that?" one of his men asked, pointing at a number of objects positioned around the perimeter of the largely circular chamber.

Wolf walked across to the wall and looked down, then prodded one with the toe of his boot. They were small blackened lumps, largely shapeless and with a jellylike consistency. But a couple of them had appendages that gave a clue as to their origin.

"I think they're plants," Wolf said, "or they were plants, anyway. I can see a couple of leaves and a bit of stem on that one."

"Quick! Over here," another of his men said, walking around to the opposite side of the vast device.

What he'd found clearly weren't more plants. Lying slumped against the wall, their wrists secured to chains attached to the wall, were two bodies. Both were male, both naked, and both very obviously dead. The numbers "3" and "4" were painted on the wall above the two corpses, and further over to the left were two more sets of chains and the painted numbers "1" and "2."

"Test subjects," Wolf commented. "I was briefed that we might see some of these. They're of no consequence, just Jews from the Gross-Rosen camp."

"So what killed them?"

"This, obviously," Wolf said, gesturing at the metallic object that almost filled the chamber. "*Die Glocke*."

He stepped forward and looked closely at the bodies. Whatever had killed them, whatever lethal force was generated by the Bell, their deaths clearly hadn't been pleasant. The faces of both corpses were contorted into expressions of absolute agony, and although their arms and legs were stick-thin, as would be expected of an inmate at Gross-Rosen, their torsos were bloated and lumpy in appearance, the skin discolored by reddish-purple blotches.

One of Wolf's men placed the sole of his boot against the stomach of one of the corpses and pressed downward. With a faint tearing sound, the skin on the side of the body ruptured and a foul-smelling black substance splashed down onto the rough concrete floor. A rank odor filled the chamber, and both the soldier and Wolf stepped quickly backward.

"What the hell?"

"Don't touch the other one," Wolf ordered, turning away.

But the soldier stayed where he was, staring down at the corpse with horrified fascination. "How could that, that thing," he almost stammered, "how could it do that to a human being?"

"It's only a Jew," Wolf snapped, "and I've no idea. Right," he went on, ignoring the two bodies and consulting a list of names, "we know what we have to do. Find Major Debus and bring him here to unhitch *Die Glocke* from the power supply and the other connections. Then we can load it onto the truck."

Getting the device out of the test chamber was far from easy, because of its bulk and weight and also because of the myriad connections that needed to be detached before they could even begin the removal process.

Eventually, Wolf ordered his men to back a truck through the main entrance to the Wenceslas Mine. The driver maneuvered it carefully down the narrow corridor until it was within a few meters of the test chamber. Struggling with the object's bulk and inconvenient shape, they used a pair of trolleys to haul it over to the truck, finally transferring it to the back of the vehicle.

As well as the device and the people who had been developing it, Wolf had also been ordered to remove the most vital sections of the reams of documentation that had been generated during the testing process. In all, it took nearly five hours to complete this part of the operation and transfer everything to the trucks waiting outside. The scientists would be easier to deal with.

Wolf consulted his list of names again. In fact, he had two lists, which corresponded with the two groups of scientists now waiting in the different chambers to leave the facility. He nodded to two of his men and led the way down the corridor. He opened the door of one room, stepped inside and carried out another roll call. It didn't take long, because there were only three people on his list: SS Major Kurt Debus, the engineer who'd shown his men how to detach the connections and prepare *Die Glocke* for removal from the test chamber; Elizabeth Adler, the specialist mathematician who had previously worked with Professor Walter Gerlach, the founder of the project; and the scientist Dr. Herman Obeth. As soon as he was satisfied that he had correctly identified these three individuals, he stepped outside again and ordered his men to escort the scientists out of the mine and into one of the waiting lorries.

Only then did he instruct another group of his soldiers to place the demolition charges that would be used to collapse the roof of the main tunnel and seal the mine for all eternity. Finally, he turned his attention to the large group of men and women in the second chamber.

Wolf stepped inside the room and duplicated his earlier action with the first group, taking a careful roll call to confirm exactly who was in the room in front of him. The twenty-eighth name he called out was Georg Schuster. Nobody was missing. He nodded, replaced the paper in his pocket and gestured to two of his men who were standing just behind him.

"Unfortunately," he began, "although the Junkers is a very big aircraft with an impressive carrying capacity, I regret that it is not big enough to take the device and all of you as a single load. But the Führer has decided that your knowledge of this project is so detailed and so important that we have to take elaborate precautions to ensure that you will not be captured by the advancing Russian forces. I wish there was some other way, but my orders leave me with no choice."

Wolf stepped out of the chamber, ignoring the puzzled expressions on the faces of the thirty-seven men and women who were standing there, as the first questions were directed toward him.

The two soldiers who were still standing just inside the room each removed a stick grenade from their belt, primed it and tossed it into the midst of the crowd of people in front of them. As the first terrified screams echoed through the chamber, they stepped outside, slammed the heavy door closed, and threw home the two massive steel bolts to secure it.

The grenades exploded within half a second of each other, the double explosion echoing through the tunnels and bringing down a scattering of small rocks and dust from the stone ceiling above.

The loud screaming inside the room had stopped, but neither Wolf nor his two men believed that just two grenades would have been sufficient.

"Go inside and finish them," he ordered crisply, then strode away toward the main entrance of the Komplex Milkow.

Wolf waited outside the entrance to the Wenceslas Mine until the last of his men emerged, then gave orders for the explosives to be blown. Seconds later, there was a dull rumble from inside the mine as the dynamite completed its work. He waited a couple of minutes to ensure that all the charges had detonated, then crossed to the entrance to check that the inner passageways were no longer accessible.

He glanced at the narrow-gauge railway that linked the Wenceslas Mine with the airfield at Bystzyca Klodzka and for a moment wondered if that would have been a better way to transport *Die Glocke*, but then shook his head. It would have meant transferring the device from the truck onto one of the railway carriages, and then repeating the process in reverse at the other end of the journey, and all of that would have taken time. Time which he really didn't have.

Only when he was completely satisfied did Wolf climb

into his staff car and lead the small convoy of three trucks containing his men, the device they had extracted from the testing chamber, and those three scientists whose work, knowledge and ability was of the highest caliber and who were vital for the eventual success of the project.

At Bystzyca Klodzka airfield, which lay in a valley within the Eulenbirge Mountains, to the west of Opole, the flight crew had already removed the tarpaulins that had concealed the huge six-engined Junkers Ju-390. They'd carried out the necessary preflight checks on the aircraft and the rear cargo door was wide-open, waiting for loading to begin.

The device was heavy, bulky, and awkward to handle because of its shape, and maneuvering it inside the relatively confined space of the fuselage was difficult. But eventually they got it secured in place, and Wolf then ordered the three scientists to climb on board the aircraft. The expressions on their faces reflected their conflicting emotions. They'd expected to be evacuated from the area, simply because of the importance of their work to the Reich and the vital knowledge they possessed, but what had happened at the mine clearly showed that there was more than one way for their masters to ensure that they kept their mouths shut.

When they had taken their seats in the cabin, Kurt Debus—the only one of the three with any military training—leaned across to Elizabeth Adler, who was visibly shaking.

"Don't worry," he murmured. "If they were going to kill us, they'd have done it back at the mine. We're safe, because we're too important to Hitler."

"Where are they taking us?" Herman Obeth asked. "Not Berlin, surely?"

"I've no idea, but somewhere out of the Fatherland, I think we can be sure of that. What we've achieved can still change the course of the war. We just need a little more time to perfect it."

"I hope you're right," Adler replied, her voice quivering with emotion. "I really hope you're right."

Hauptsturmführer Wolf was the last to take his seat, and only did so after carrying out a final check that nothing had been left in any of the vehicles that might compromise the project.

One of the engines on the port wing of the Junkers spluttered into life, then settled down to a steady reassuring roar. Then the second engine started, and the third, and in less than a minute the flight deck crew had all six running. The Junkers, which had been painted light blue and illegally wore the markings of the Swedish Air Force—a rudimentary disguise that might make an enemy pilot pause before opening fire with his cannon— began to move, and the massive aircraft started to taxi across the short distance to the end of the runway.

Moments later, the pilot pushed the throttles fully forward and the huge aircraft began gathering speed. It lifted into the darkening sky and swung around toward the west.

It's reasonable to assume that the paint job was a success, because no units of either the Russian forces or the Western Allies reported seeing a Swedish aircraft at any time that day or evening. They were too busy watching out for enemy aircraft, and it seems likely that the Junkers managed simply to slip through the front lines, perhaps seen but certainly not noticed.

The Junkers' ultimate destination was never recorded in any of the surviving documentation, and it's quite possible that the flight was so highly classified by the Nazis that no details of it were ever committed to paper.

After the war, various places were suggested as the location of the aircraft's final landing. One of the most cogent and believable reports states that a multi-engined German aircraft was seen touching down at an airfield in the Entre Rios Province of northern Argentina in May 1945.

Another report describes various witness sightings of a six-engined aircraft, provisionally identified as a Junkers Ju-390, being dismantled on a German-owned farm in Paysundu Province in Uruguay at about the same date. Some of the local residents also reported that the parts of the aircraft were then taken to the River Uruguay, which is over a kilometer wide at this point, and thrown into the water.

A third report suggested that the aircraft had a very much shorter flight, and landed near Bodø in Norway, though this might of course have simply been an interim or refueling stop as part of a much longer flight, and it seems probable that if the aircraft had remained in Norway it would have been seen and reported by somebody, and most probably seized by Allied forces.

What is certain is that at the end of the Second World War nobody knew where either the aircraft or its unusual cargo had been taken, or exactly what the secret device constructed in the Wenceslas Mine was intended to do.

Current researchers believe the project designation implied that it was a weapon of some description, probably a very early type of weapon of mass destruction, but since 1945 no definite information has been recovered about *Die Glocke* and nobody had any real idea of its function or its purpose.

Until now, that is.

1

"Can I just say something?" Chris Bronson asked. "I dislike sport to the extent that if you gave me a Cup Final ticket, I would rather pay you money than have to go and watch the match."

"Is that right?" The Met inspector looked distinctly unimpressed. He was sitting in a battered swivel chair behind a large but extremely cluttered desk—files stacked in piles on both sides of it—in a glass cubicle at one end of a squad room in a police station in east London's Forest Gate. Bronson was standing in front of him. He had no option—there was no other chair, not even enough space for one, in the tiny office.

The walls behind the desk were plastered with the usual selection of notices and leaflets, everything from Health and Safety directives—which looked noticeably clean and unread—to part of a faded page of newsprint apparently cut from the *Evening Standard*, the print too tiny for Bronson to make out the story. Other notices were attached to the glass walls of the office, but Bronson guessed that their principal purpose was less to convey information than to provide the inspector's tiny sanctum with some slight measure of privacy.

In marked contrast to the cluttered and untidy office, the inspector was impeccably dressed in a light gray suit, the material of which shimmered slightly every time he moved his tall, slim frame. Bronson didn't have to glance down at the floor to know that his black shoes would have a mirror-polished sheen; the man exuded an almost palpable aura of elegance. His features were even and regular, with a neat and slightly aggressive mustache that conveyed a military bearing.

Bronson was supremely conscious that he cut a rather less than impressive figure by comparison in his crumpled suit, slightly grubby shirt and black loafers. Nor could he blame the state of his attire on the train and tube journey up to Newham; he hadn't, he realized, looked all that smart when he had left Tunbridge Wells that morning.

"Well, let me tell you something, Detective Sergeant Bronson. I don't give a damn about your views on football or any other sport. You've been sent here by that bunch of yokels who laughably call themselves the Kent Police Force to help us out. Not that we can't manage by ourselves, but we do need a few extra bodies on the ground while the Olympics are on, and you've been selected as one of them."

"Yes, but—"

"Don't interrupt when I'm talking. I couldn't give a toss whether you like sport or not. I've got any number of coppers queuing up to be on duty in a stadium when some of the events are being held. But we need other bodies."

The Metropolitan Police inspector—the name on his door was S. R. Davidson—paused for a moment and glanced down at a note on his desk. Then he looked back at Bronson and smiled. "To be specific, I need somebody with certain talents and abilities, and I'm told you're the ideal man for the job."

"What talents?" Bronson asked suspiciously.

"You're big and bolshie and nobody here knows you. Now open the door."

"What?"

"You deaf or something? Open the bloody door."

Bronson turned round and pulled open the glass door he'd closed behind him three minutes earlier.

As it swung wide, Davidson bellowed: "Curtis! Get in here."

"Jesus," Bronson muttered, temporarily deafened by the inspector's impressive vocal capability. "Can't you use an intercom or something?"

"Broken," Davidson replied shortly, as a heavily built man, whose appearance and dress sense seemed closer to Bronson's casual scruffiness than the inspector's sartorial elegance, got up from his desk and ambled over to the door of the cubicle.

"Boss?"

"Remember that SLJ we discussed the other day, Bob? Detective Sergeant Bronson here is going to take care of it for us."

A smile spread across Curtis's face as he looked Bronson slowly up and down.

"And what shitty little job is that, exactly?" Bronson asked.

"Bob will explain everything," Davidson replied, looking slightly miffed that Bronson had recognized the acronym he'd used. "Take him away, Bob, and fill him in."

"A pleasure."

Curtis led the way across the squad room to his desk.

"Grab one of them," he said, pointing to a stack of dark gray metal-framed chairs with plastic seats.

"Popular man, your boss, is he?" Bronson asked, taking the top chair from the pile and sitting down in front of Curtis's desk.

Curtis grinned at him. "Not so's you'd notice, no. He's one of that new breed—fast-track coppers. Gets a degree in knitting or something and then joins the force, aiming for a chief constable slot before he's fifty. Frightening thing is, he'll probably make it. His initials stand for Steven Richard, by the way, but round here everybody calls him Shit Rises." Curtis paused and glanced across at Bronson. "Been in long, have you?"

Bronson nodded. "A few years, yes. But I was in the army on a short-service commission before I joined the force."

Curtis smiled again and looked to his left, toward the officer sitting at the adjacent desk. "That's a tenner you owe me, Jack." He swung back to face Bronson. "Had a small wager running," he explained. "Jack figured you for another graduate fast-tracker like Davidson. But I reckoned he was wrong because you look like you've been around the block a few times."

Bronson thought that worked out as a compliment.

"I hadn't planned on making chief constable," he replied. "For one thing, I'm not a Mason, and in any case I don't think I could handle the bullshit that comes with the job. Talking of jobs, what's this nasty surprise you've got planned for me?"

"It's not that nasty," Curtis said. "In fact, you might even enjoy it. But it is really important, because we're running out of ideas." There were about half a dozen files sitting in an irregular pile on one corner of his desk, and he reached across and pulled out the bottom one, which was also the slimmest. He flicked through the first couple of pages before looking up at Bronson again.

"Let me give you the background. Pretty much ever since London won the bid to hold the twenty twelve Olympics, there've been cases of sabotage and malicious damage at the various venues. At first, we thought it was the usual mindless vandalism that you get in every major city, but over the last three months or so it's become clear that we are looking at a concerted plan. There seems to be a definite objective to the damage. It's not just a case of breaking a few windows or daubing graffiti around the place, though there's been a fair amount of that as well. But these guys, whoever they are, seem to be targeting the machinery on the building sites, doing their best to ensure that the work won't be completed on time."

"Hang on a minute," Bronson said. "The Games start in exactly ten days' time. I thought that everything was pretty much finished—and all the construction work was completed ages ago."

"Dream on. The government and all the other talking

heads are just saying what they think the public wants to hear. Most of the building work has been completed, that's true, but there's still a hell of a lot of finishing-off to do before the opening ceremony. I reckon that the paint inside some of the buildings will still be wet when the athletes arrive."

Bronson nodded. "I hadn't realized that. But what do these vandals want? What's their motive? I thought most people believed that the Olympics would be a good thing for London, not just because of the income that'll be generated during the Games themselves, but also because of all the redevelopment of the East End. Surely everyone will benefit to some extent?"

"Yeah, you'd think so, wouldn't you? But this bunch seems to have a different agenda."

Bronson glanced at the thin file in front of Curtis. "From the look of that," he said, "you haven't got very much to go on."

"You got that right. We know that they usually work at night, but so far we've made no arrests. In terms of evidence, about all we have got are the damage reports from the construction companies, and statements from our own people about how they broke into the sites."

"But surely the Olympic sites are guarded? There must be cameras, nightwatchmen, patrols by security companies? And this close to the event, the work will be going on twenty-four hours a day, won't it?"

"All true, and when the work stops the nightwatchmen are posted, but these people have a knack of knowing the odd corner or length of fence where the surveillance cameras don't have total coverage, that kind of thing, and there are so many sites involved that they've got plenty of choice about where they hit each time."

"Have you got any leads at all?" Bronson asked.

"A few whispers on the street, but that's about it. We think the gang is based somewhere in this area, because on the odd occasions when any of them has been spotted and chased, they've always managed to slip the net down alleyways, side streets and so on. That suggests detailed knowledge of the area."

"Or it could just mean that they've done a thorough reconnaissance of the target area beforehand," Bronson said, "or even that they've invested in a bunch of really good quality GPS units."

Curtis nodded. "I can't argue with any of that. We think they're a local bunch, but we really don't know. And we've no idea what their objective is."

Bronson shook his head. "I can see how frustrating this must be," he said, "but surely it's only an irritant? Why can't you just double the number of nightwatchmen and CCTV cameras and increase the regular patrols around the sites? Surely that would be enough to neutralize this bunch of idiots."

Curtis smiled at him. "Until about a week ago, I'd have agreed with you. Then two things happened. First, we got a lead on the name of the man who seems to be the head of the group, and that does tie up with some of the graffiti we've found. At several of the sites they hit, we found fresh graffiti that looked a bit like a capital "M" with a lowercase "u" directly underneath it. In fact, we'd started referring to them as the "Mu Gang," though we had no idea what the symbol was supposed to mean.

"Anyway, one of our informers finally came up with the name Wolf, spelling uncertain. He thought that was the man's surname, and that his first name might be Mark or maybe Marcus, but he wasn't sure. He also told us that the graffiti, the "Mu" symbol, was meant to represent a wolf's head, the "M" being the ears and the "u" the snout, so that all seemed to hang together."

"Interesting, but not particularly helpful," Bronson commented. "What was the second thing?"

"The second thing changed everything. Five nights ago, what we believe to be the same gang launched an attack against one of the stadiums. They got in undetected by cutting through the boundary fence, and made their way over to where some construction equipment was still being stored. They did a fair amount of minor damage to some of the most expensive equipment they could find, cutting diesel fuel lines, putting sugar in petrol tanks, all that kind of thing, because there isn't much else you can do to a bulldozer or a crane to stop it working. Unless you've got a wrecking ball or cutting equipment, that is.

"Then it all went wrong. We think the nightwatchman on the site saw something on the CCTV cameras or maybe heard the gang. Whatever happened, he dialed triple nine and then headed out to try to stop them. He was by himself, and from the recordings we've looked at, there were at least six of them."

Bronson had a horrible feeling he knew what was coming.

"He tried to tackle one of them, but he was set upon by the gang and beaten up. That was bad enough, but he wasn't that young and his heart gave out during the attack. By the time the first patrol car arrived, he was already dead and the intruders were long gone. So what started out as just a bloody nuisance has now turned into a full-scale murder inquiry."

"I presume you don't want me to help out with that?" Bronson asked.

"No. We've already got a full Murder Room running, not that they've got very much to go on because of the lack of any useful forensic evidence. But Shit Rises has got a better—or at least a different—plan in mind, and that's where you come in. He's under a hell of a lot of pressure from the top to get this sorted. The clock's ticking, and we absolutely have to find this bunch of thugs and get them off the streets before East London is flooded with athletes and spectators. He's been looking for a volunteer for this for a few days, pretty much ever since the killing of the nightwatchman."

"I'm not exactly a volunteer, am I?"

Curtis grinned again and shook his head. "No, not really. But he needed somebody from out of the area who wouldn't be recognized as a police officer. And he also needed a man with certain talents and experience, so he checked all the local forces and the name that popped up at the top of the list was yours. So you'll have to do."

"So this really isn't just a shitty little job then? I mean, it actually matters?"

"Oh, it matters. It really matters. That was just Shit Rises trying to be funny. As all of us working here know, he has a well-developed sense of humor," Curtis added, with a perfectly straight face. "This is important, and you'll get whatever help and support you need. Make no mistake about this. As you said, the Games will be start-ing in exactly ten days, and we have to take this group of vandals off the streets before then. Between you and me, I think the powers that be are worried that there's some-thing else planned."

"Like what?"

"I have no idea. But if there was any kind of attempt to disrupt the opening ceremony, for example, that would be really embarrassing for London and Britain, with a worldwide audience of billions, and the Met would be so deep in the shit that we'd probably never be able to dig our way out."

"So no pressure, then?" Bronson said.

Curtis shook his head, and his expression remained grim.

"I'm not trying to con you, Chris. This isn't going to be easy, and to make it worse, you're going to have to work alone. We can support you, and provide backup if it's needed, but basically it's all down to you."

Then Curtis passed the slim file across the desk, leaned forward and explained precisely what Davidson wanted Bronson to do.

2

19 July 2012

"Got another one here," the uniformed constable announced, as he and his colleague made their way somewhat erratically toward the desk.

The reason for their unusually halting progress was the
man between them. He was dark haired, unshaven and
wearing stained jeans and a leather jacket. He was big and
solidly built, and it was immediately clear that subduing
him would not have been easy. He was still struggling and
mouthing abuse, and it was taking all the efforts of the
two officers to keep him heading in the right direction,
despite the handcuffs that secured his wrists in front of
him.

Two other suspects were already standing beside the
desk, accompanied by three uniformed officers, but these
two men were not giving anybody any trouble.

"What's the charge?" the desk sergeant asked, eyeing
the approaching trio.

"The usual," the constable replied. "Malicious damage, resisting arrest and abusive behavior. And once we've shut him up and got a Breathalyzer mouthpiece between his lips, I'm pretty sure we'll be able to add drunk and disorderly to that lot."

After a couple of minutes, while the sergeant completed the processing of the other two men, the dark-haired man seemed to calm down a little, possibly realizing that he had no chance of getting out of the police station, at least until his handcuffs had been removed.

"Where did you find him?"

"He was cutting his way through the boundary fence around the new hockey stadium," the constable said. "We were coming down the street in the car and saw him doing it. Had a crowbar and a club hammer with him as well as a set of bolt-croppers, so he obviously intended to do some damage once he got inside. Oh, and a couple of cans of spray paint as well. They're all in the car outside— we'll haul them in here as evidence as soon as he's been processed. He's a big bugger. Took us all our time to keep him quiet until the van arrived to take him away."

"Open-and-shut case, then," the sergeant remarked, looking at the third suspect, who had now fallen silent, but was glaring at him with naked hostility. "This joker say why he was doing it?"

The constable nodded. "Didn't shut up about it, even when we were sitting on him. Pretty much what you'd expect. He told us the Olympics were a sham, some international conspiracy organized by big business simply to make money, and had nothing at all to do with sport. You know, I think he might have a point about that. He also seemed to know quite a lot about the costs involved. He reckons London will take years to get out of debt because of the Games."

"He's got a couple of soul mates over there, then," the sergeant said, aiming the point of his pen toward the two men who had already been processed and were now sitting in a couple of chairs that lined the wall near the desk. "I don't suppose he has any idea how getting into the site and breaking a few windows is going to help the situation? And if he was targeting the hockey stadium, I suppose that proves he knows sod all about sport, 'cause there'll only be about a dozen people who'll want to watch the matches.

"Right, then. Name?" The sergeant paused and looked expectantly at the dark-haired man.

The man shrugged. "You choose," he snapped.

"I just love comedians." The sergeant turned back to the uniformed constable. "Any ID on him?"

"Nothing useful. When we checked him at the scene, all we found in his pockets were twenty quid in fivers, a day ticket for the tube, a comb, a handkerchief and a door key. No wallet, driving license or car keys. Probably stashed them somewhere while he did his bit of amateur B and E."

The sergeant glanced back at the suspect. "Come on, mate," he said, "don't mess me around. You're only making things more difficult for yourself. What's your name?"

The dark-haired man shrugged again. "Alex," he said finally. "Alex Cross. No 'e,'" he added.

The sergeant looked at him somewhat questioningly. "I've heard that name somewhere before," he said, "somewhere recently. Is that your final offer?"

"It'll do for now."

"Right. If that's the way you want to play it, that's fine by me."

Just over an hour later, the three men walked out of the Stratford police station together, Cross having apparently convinced the sergeant that he had given his real name and address, or maybe the middle-aged police officer really didn't care too much about the veracity of the information he was writing down, as long as he'd completed the paperwork and ticked all the appropriate boxes. Although all three men had been arrested, their actions had not been deemed sufficiently serious for them to be detained. Cross had even passed the Breathalyzer test, despite the smell of alcohol that the constable had noticed.

For a few moments, Cross glanced around him, up and down the street, then he zipped up his leather jacket, stuck his hands in his pockets and strode away.

A couple of seconds later, a voice rang out down the street. "Hey! Hang on a minute."

Cross stopped in his tracks and glanced back to see the two men walking swiftly toward him.

"What?" he demanded.

"You fancy a drink somewhere?"

Cross hesitated, then nodded. "Sure, why not? Get rid of the taste of that cop shop."

They walked the short distance to the nearest pub, its rough and battered exterior a perfect reflection of the appearance of most of its clientele. Cross pushed open the door and the three men stepped into the saloon bar.

It's a familiar cliché that when a stranger enters a particular kind of bar, all conversations stop as the locals assess the new arrival. But like all clichés, it contains more than a grain of truth because there are places like that even today, places where any new face is a potential source of trouble or perhaps of opportunity. The East End of London has more than its fair share of such establishments—pubs that the tourists never visit, where the only bar food on offer will be packets of crisps and pork scratchings, and where anyone asking for a drink as suspect and effeminate as a glass of wine is likely to be thrown bodily out into the street. These are places where deals are discussed and concluded, where a man wishing to obtain a weapon for a robbery can lease a pistol and a fully loaded magazine for a day or a week, where a contract for the permanent disappearance of a business rival or an enemy can be negotiated, and the price agreed, and where strangers are at best tolerated for the money they hand over, but are always discouraged from paying a return visit.

As Cross pushed his way in, the buzz of conversation didn't stop, but it certainly diminished as most of the men—and there were no women in sight—glanced at him and his two companions. Then, apparently seeing nothing particularly threatening or of interest in the new arrivals, the faces turned away again, and muttered conversations were resumed.

Four men were just getting up from a scratched and battered circular table in the far corner of the bar, and another three men were heading that way to commandeer the seats. But Cross got there first, and just stood beside the table, staring at the approaching trio.

All three were big and bulky, their knuckles and faces scarred from past disagreements. They were clearly men used to getting their own way, and not afraid to resort to physical persuasion if other negotiating tactics failed. But it was as if they saw something in Cross's eyes that warned them off, something that told them that the man they were looking at was more than capable of matching them blow for blow and that, whatever they started, he would be quite capable of finishing.

And as they stared at him, Cross's two companions walked across to the table and flanked him, one standing either side of him. The conversations in the bar died away again, as the locals switched their attention to the silent tableau in their midst. After a few seconds, the biggest of the three men in front of Cross shrugged, then turned round and walked away, the other two following him.

As Cross sat down at the table, his two companions looked at each other, and one of them nodded. Then they both strode across to the bar to order a round of drinks. Pints, obviously.

"Time for introductions, I suppose," the man who'd bought the drinks said, after taking a sip of his beer. "My name's Charlie Williams, and my mate here's called John Eaton. Is your name really Alex Cross?"

The third man shook his head. "No," he said, "but I've got a very good reason for using an alias, so if it's okay with you two—in fact, even if it isn't okay with you—I'm sticking with it."

"We can live with that. So you're not happy about the Olympics either?"

"I don't give a toss about the bloody Olympics. That's just a good target. I've got my own reasons for doing what I do."

"And they are . . . ?"

"Personal, mate, that's what they are. Let's just say I was shat upon from a great height, just for trying to do my bloody job, and this is one way of getting some kind of payback."

Williams nodded. "Okay. So you've got a grudge against authority. But we couldn't help overhearing what that young copper said about you. Were you really targeting the hockey stadium?"

Cross took a sip of his beer and grinned at him. "To be perfectly honest with you, I had no idea what was on the other side of the fence, except that it was a part of the Olympic complex. That was good enough for me."

"And what were you going to do once you'd broken in? That's stadium's finished, as far as we know."

"The usual. Break some windows, smash up anything I could, spray a few slogans on the walls. I know I can't do anything to stop these Games from going ahead—there's nothing one person can do about an operation as big as this—but I wanted to hit out, do some damage."

Cross took a swallow of his beer and then looked sharply at Williams.

"So what were you picked up for?" he asked.

Williams smiled briefly. "Much the same as you, actually," he replied, "with one big difference. You said it yourself. There's bugger all one man can do, but it's completely different if you're part of an organized group."

"So there's more than just the two of you?"

"Exactly. We were just a diversion, something to keep the coppers on their toes and chasing us, while the rest of our people got inside a completely different part of the site, and set to work doing some really serious damage."

"Like what?" Cross asked.

"You'll read about it in the papers tomorrow," Eaton interjected. "And that's the other thing you've been doing wrong. There's no point in breaking a window or spraying a wall. They just get the glaziers in the next day and replace the glass, or use industrial cleaner to remove the paint. It's just a nuisance—hardly slows them down at all. So what we do is target the equipment. We hit the bulldozers and the cranes and generators, all that kind of stuff. You can do a lot of damage to a diesel engine with a hammer, if you know what you're about, and a few bags of sugar poured into a fuel tank really screws them up. That can pretty much write off an engine."

"And why are you doing it?"

"There's more than one reason why we're involved."

"Yeah?" Cross looked interested.

But Williams just shook his head and turned his attention back to his pint of beer.

"You'll get nowhere by yourself," Eaton said. "But you look as if you can take care of yourself, so maybe you should think about coming in with us. We could use someone like you."

Cross shook his head. "I'm not really into organized groups, thanks all the same. I normally work alone—only myself to worry about, you see."

"We're not a group like that, really. We always arrive at the target site individually, and find our own way home after the event. But what we do is we meet beforehand and organize the target, and the timing, and what everyone involved is going to do. That way, we cover every aspect of the attack, and each of us can then focus on his own particular job. Last time, like Charlie said, we were the decoys. We showed ourselves, did a little bit of damage and made sure the coppers spotted us, and then we legged it, leaving our mates with a clear run."

"And we never resist arrest," Williams added. "That just gives them another charge to slap against you if they feel like it. Quiet and cooperative is the best way in the end."

Cross took another sip of his drink and nodded.

"You're probably right, but sometimes that's easier said than done. You get treated like shit by the coppers, and all you want to do is hit back at them somehow."

"You are, by doing what we're doing," Eaton said. "Because we're organized, we've been running rings around the rozzers for weeks. They never know where we're going to hit next, or when."

"Look," Williams said, "John's right. We really could use you, and you'll achieve a hell of a lot more working with us than you ever will out there by yourself. Why not give it a try? Come along on one raid. After that, if you still want to go off and do things your own way, that's fine. Otherwise, join us."

"Just like that?" Cross asked. "Please can I join your gang?"

"Not quite. We're a small group, and we need to be really sure about each other because of what we're doing, so if you do want to be part of our operation there'll be a vote, once we've seen you working."

"Like a trial period," Eaton added. "But if you do okay, that shouldn't be a problem."

*   *   *

Just over an hour after they'd walked into the pub, the
three men stepped out the door and strode off down the
street. At the first junction, they went their separate ways,
Williams and Eaton heading in one direction, the man
calling himself Cross in the other.

He walked quickly down the street, took the first left
turn that he came to, then immediately crossed the road
and strode down an alleyway on the right. At the end he
stopped, flattened himself into a doorway, and waited for
five minutes. Nobody else came down the alleyway—in
fact, he saw no one else in the street beyond.

Satisfied that no one was following him—or if they
were, they were really good at their job—he continued
down the street. At each corner he glanced behind him,
but nobody appeared to be taking the slightest interest in
him or where he was going.

He walked for almost twenty minutes, taking a circu-
itous route along unfamiliar streets and roads, but always
heading toward the east, looking out for one of the land-
marks that he had memorized. Finally, he saw a street
name that he recognized. He again checked that nobody
was behind him, did a complete circuit of a block of ter-
raced houses to flush out anyone who might have gotten
in front of him and be keeping him under surveillance,
and only then headed for his objective: a small area of
waste ground between two buildings.

A confusion of tire tracks close to the street suggested
that the vacant ground was used for unofficial parking
during the day, but at that time of night there were no
vehicles on it. The back of the lot was overgrown, rough

grass and a handful of stunted bushes struggling for su-
premacy among the detritus of urban living: a couple of
abandoned shopping trolleys and a crop of plastic bags,
empty bottles and cans. On the right-hand side were a
handful of empty paint tins; it looked like they'd been
dumped there by some builder.

He stepped over to them, checked again that he was
still unobserved, then lifted up one of the tins. Under it
was a tatty plastic bag, which he picked up and opened.
Inside it was a pay-as-you-go mobile phone, a cheap model
from an obscure manufacturer that no self-respecting
thief would go anywhere near. Cross slipped the phone
into his pocket and walked away.

A few hundred yards down the street, he again checked
that no one was anywhere near him, then switched on the
phone and accessed the contacts list. Only one number
was listed, and no details were given of the identity of the
recipient, who was listed solely as "A." He pressed the
appropriate key to dial the number, which rang only twice
before being answered.

"Yes?"

"It's me," Chris Bronson said. "I think I'm in."

3

The pub sat on a fairly quiet street corner just northeast of Gallows Corner, where the A127 split off from the A12 and speared down to the southeast to intersect with what the locals called the world's biggest car park, London's orbital road, the M25.

Bronson had met Eaton and Williams as planned the previous evening and had arranged to meet them again that lunchtime. He parked his car—a nondescript five-year-old Ford saloon supplied by the Forest Gate police station—in a side street about a hundred yards away from the pub, facing away from the building, and on the last parking meter of a short line, where it couldn't easily get boxed in by other vehicles. He wasn't expecting any trouble, but it never paid to assume anything.

He was early, over two hours early, in fact, because he wanted to walk around the area a couple of times to familiarize himself with the layout of the streets, just in case he had to make a run for it. And he had another appointment in a backstreet café that he needed to keep first.

As far as Bronson knew, Eaton and Williams had bought his story about having a grudge against society and trying to take it out on the forthcoming Olympics. But there was always the possibility that they were smarter than they looked, and had somehow guessed that he wasn't exactly what he seemed. And while the mobile phone tucked into his jacket pocket could call in reinforcements, Bronson knew that if he had to make the call, it would probably be too late. He could handle one or two of the group without much problem, he thought, but against half a dozen angry men armed with baseball bats—or worse—and a good reason to use them, he would stand little chance. He was acutely aware that this group were responsible for the death of the unfortunate nightwatchman. If they found out that he was a police officer trying to infiltrate them, he guessed that he could expect to meet the same end.

And this time, it wasn't just Eaton or Williams he was going to meet. As a prospective new member of the group, Bronson knew there would be other people checking him out. Curtis had claimed that there was no chance anyone in the group could possibly know who Bronson really was, but sometimes the cosmic joker rolled the dice in a certain way and the long arm of coincidence stretched out, tapped you on the shoulder, and the impossible happened. Bronson firmly believed that Sod's Law had just as much force and validity as any other rule of life, and frankly wouldn't be surprised if half the members of the group he was trying to infiltrate had met him before. Sometimes, that was just the way things worked out.

And that was why he'd taken another precaution before coming to this meeting. Bronson had told Curtis that he'd never been to this part of London before, and that was true, but it didn't mean that he didn't know anybody in the area. For years, he'd kept in sporadic contact with a man he'd gotten to know while he was in the army, a former sergeant named Dickie Weeks, but who everybody in the unit knew as "The Fixer."

Weeks had finally been thrown out of the army after one of his more optimistic schemes had been uncovered by a senior officer who couldn't be persuaded—or bribed—to look the other way. The only reason he had avoided prosecution was probably simple embarrassment on the part of his superiors—in open court the full extent of his various wheeler-dealings would have been exposed to public scrutiny, and the reporters from the tabloids would have enjoyed a serious feeding frenzy. Because Weeks had managed to spirit away the better part of a quarter of a million pounds' worth of army gear and dispose of it for cash to people who appreciated having access to that kind of equipment.

The man was, by any definition, a treacherous thief, but that didn't stop almost everyone who met him from enjoying his company because Weeks was, whatever his faults, a thoroughly likable man, with a ready smile and quick wit. Bronson had never commanded him, but on a couple of occasions he had appreciated the rogue sergeant's ability to obtain precisely the right equipment at precisely the right time, no questions asked. And that morning he had arranged to meet Weeks before his lunchtime rendezvous at the pub.

The café Weeks had suggested—in a parade of shops on the west side of Straight Road, north of the main Gallows Corner intersection—was easy enough to find. When Bronson pushed open the door, accompanied by a melodic tinkle from a small bell attached to the door frame, he immediately spotted Weeks sitting at a table for two in the far corner, his back to the wall and the remnants of a full English breakfast on the plate in front of him. It was counter service only, so Bronson ordered a mug of black coffee and a bacon sandwich before walking across to join his former comrade in arms.

"Diet going well?" Bronson asked, gesturing to the congealing fat and bits of bacon rind decorating the plate in front of the other man.

"You know me, Chris. Eat like a bloody horse and I never seem to gain an ounce."

That was both true and irritating. Weeks was a big man—almost as bulky as Bronson—but despite having a prodigious appetite for all the wrong food, he never seemed to put on weight. If there was a scrap of divine justice in the world, he would have weighed a quarter of a ton and be suffering from a variety of digestive-system-related maladies. As it was, he radiated health and was, Bronson knew, extremely strong.

Bronson, in contrast, did have to watch what he ate, steering clear of what had become the traditional diet of most Britons—pizza, pasta, curry and fish and chips—because he knew that all the excess calories made straight for his waistline and took up permanent residence there. On the other hand, he had the frame to take it. He stood over six feet tall and was, in a word, wide—heavily built with broad shoulders. He exuded an air of barely restrained menace that he'd found useful in his early career as an army officer, and even more useful as a policeman. As his encounter in the pub he'd visited with Eaton and Williams had demonstrated, his physical presence could be quite intimidating.

Bronson sat down opposite Weeks and took a bite of his sandwich.

"Before we start, Chris," the former sergeant said, keeping his voice low and taking a quick look around the interior of the café to make sure that nobody could overhear their conversation, "just so you know, I'm wearing a wire and that's linked to a recorder in my car that's already running. Miracle of modern technology, really. In this business, I don't trust anybody, not even you. If I even think there's any sign of entrapment, if you've been set up to try to take me down, I'll be out of here real fast, but you won't be following because you'll have a bullet through your leg. And that's if I'm feeling generous. Piss me about, and it'll be in your gut instead. Do we understand each other?"

Bronson nodded. "No entrapment, Dickie, no funny business. I'm here because I need help, and you were the only person I could think of who could get me what I wanted. And I don't blame you for being suspicious. In your position, I'd be just as paranoid."

Weeks allowed himself a brief smile. "Yeah," he said. "And just because I'm paranoid, it doesn't mean some bastard isn't out to get me. Anyway, those are the rules. If you're straight with me, there won't be a problem."

"You have my word," Bronson replied.

"So you're in trouble again?"

Bronson shook his head and chewed his sandwich for a few moments before he responded.

"Not exactly. I've got a bit of a nasty job on, and I just thought I needed an insurance policy."

"And the powers that be didn't think you needed to be tooled up?"

Bronson shook his head again. "I didn't even ask them because I know what they'd say."

"And that would be 'no,' I assume."

"You assume correctly. They get very sniffy when it comes to firearms. You wouldn't believe the number of forms you have to fill in before they'll issue you anything more lethal than a bloody truncheon."

"But you did the course, didn't you? I mean, you're an Authorized Firearms Officer, right?"

Bronson nodded. "Yes. Because of my army training I did the AFO course quite soon after I joined, and I'm also a qualified SFO—Specialist Firearms Officer—which means I have the dubious privilege of being able to enter premises known to be occupied by armed criminals. Not that there's a lot of call for that kind of thing in Tunbridge Wells. But that's not the point. This op I'm on means I'm going deep undercover, and at the moment the only thing I can do to protect myself is take my mobile phone out of my pocket and hit the number nine three times. By the time an Armed Response Vehicle could get to me, the chances are I'd just be a mess on the floor. And I'm not wild about that possibility."

"I take your point," Weeks said. "So you want something to give you an edge, just in case the shit hits the fan. And that's why you called me."

Bronson grinned. "I could tell you I was pining for the pleasure of your company, Dickie, but you and I both know that wouldn't be true. What I'd like from you is something small so that I can hide it easily, but with enough power that I can use it to finish any argument that anybody else starts."

"Always happy to oblige an old comrade. I brought along a selection, actually. They're outside, in the motor. And it'll be cash, Chris—you know the rules."

Bronson nodded. "Just remember I'm only a struggling copper, not some wealthy East End villain. I can't afford to pay top dollar for what might become a throwaway weapon."

"I was rather hoping you might bring it back when you've finished whatever you're doing. If you do, I'll give you half what you paid for it."

"Half? That's not much of a deal, Dickie."

"It's the recession, mate. Affects every business, even mine. But as it's you, I'll lop a bit off the price and you can have two-thirds back. Can't say fairer than that. Oh, that assumes you don't use the weapon in a killing. If you do, you'll be keeping it, because I can't move it on."

"I bloody hope it doesn't come to that."

"Getting squeamish in your old age?" Weeks asked with a smile.

"Not really. I was just thinking about all the extra paperwork I'd have to do."

About five minutes later, the two men walked down Straight Road, turned left into Colchester Road, the A12, and immediately crossed to the south side. The Gidea Park shopping center was located on the corner of the road, and Weeks led the way into its car park.

Bronson looked round. The parking area was fairly long and narrow, with spaces for about two hundred cars, but bordered by a row of bushes on the side adjacent to the main road.

"You parked here?" he asked.

Weeks caught his glance and shook his head. "No. Too bloody confined for my liking," he replied. "Never know what nasties somebody could have hidden away over there. I like the wide-open spaces. Like Tesco."

Weeks turned right into the car park and then continued walking diagonally across it, toward the exit into Bryant Avenue. With Bronson keeping pace beside him, he crossed the road and walked on into the much bigger car park that lay behind the Gallows Corner Tesco store. Standing by itself at the far side of the car park was a late-model Range Rover, a deep lustrous black in color and with heavily tinted windows, that probably cost nearly as much as Bronson earned in a year.

"Nice motor," Bronson said, as Weeks pressed the remote control to unlock the doors.

"Tools of the trade, mate. All the windows are bulletproof, and there are Kevlar panels in the doors and behind most of the bodywork. That wouldn't stop a serious attack, but I've had the engine breathed on a bit and the tires are run flat, so if the shooting started, I hope I'd be able to use it to get the hell out of the way."

When they were still about fifty yards from the car, Weeks raised his hand to stop Bronson getting any closer.

"Not so fast," he said.

"What?"

Weeks didn't reply, just selected another button on the larger-than-normal remote control unit. As he pressed it, the Range Rover's engine started with a throaty roar, then settled down to a steady idle.

"Just in case somebody managed to wire a lump of plastic into the ignition circuit," Weeks explained. "I never sit in the thing and turn the key, not even if it's in the garage at home."

Bronson stood still and stared across the car park at the vehicle. Then he glanced at Weeks and shook his head.

"For a few minutes there I was starting to envy you your lifestyle, but if this is how you have to watch your back every day, I think I'll stick to what I do."

"You get used to it," Weeks replied shortly, and led the way over to the Range Rover.

The two men climbed into the front seats. Weeks immediately checked the open expanse of the car park ahead of him and the view behind the vehicle visible in the rearview mirrors. Shoppers, mainly women, some by themselves and others with children reluctantly in tow, were pushing trolleys to and fro, while cars were arriving and departing all the time. There was movement all around them, but none of it appeared in any way unusual or suspicious.

"Looks okay to me," Weeks said. "No sign of any of the thin blue line lurking about either."

"I told you, Dickie," Bronson replied, "I'm here by myself. This isn't a sting operation or an entrapment. Though if it was, I doubt if you'd spot any of the watchers."

"It's not just your lot that I worry about. I'm in a competitive industry, and sometimes people decide that a bit of direct action might be the easiest way to make sure I don't get the business."

"You make it sound almost legitimate," Bronson remarked. "Selling guns, I mean."

"That's the funny thing about the arms business. It's one of this country's biggest industries, and Britain sells everything from pistols to aircraft and warships to other nations, knowing bloody well that some two-bit dictator in the middle of Africa will use the weapons to make his program of genocide that bit more efficient. And the people who run the British arms industry get invited to tea at Number Ten and are given knighthoods and all the rest. But if a freelance businessman like me gets caught selling a twenty-two-caliber target pistol to someone, he'll end up in the slammer for a few years, and so will the buyer. Makes no sense to me."

Bronson guessed that Weeks was treading a familiar path, though what he was saying was undeniably true— yet another demonstration of the arrant and arrogant hypocrisy of most politicians. Ever since Tony Blair had famously "banned handguns," the only people who owned weapons in Britain were criminals, and the Labor Party had somehow managed to spin this obvious lunacy into a piece of good news for the public.

"Okay, you want a pistol, right? And some ammo, obviously. I've brought three along, but it all depends on what you want to spend and if you think you're going to bring it back to me."

"I'll try, but I don't know how this is going to pan out."

"Then you probably won't want this one," Weeks replied.

He reached over to the backseat of the car, where a couple of coats had been draped, apparently casually, and pulled out a wooden box secured with metal catches. Weeks snapped them open and lifted the lid. Inside, set in a shaped recess, was a small black semi-automatic pistol. He lifted out the weapon, showed Bronson that there was no magazine fitted, then pulled back the slide and handed it to his companion—basic safety precautions to ensure that the weapon was unloaded.

"Smart. A subcompact Glock," Bronson said, recognizing it immediately. He turned it over in his hands. The butt was very short, allowing the weapon to be held by two fingers, the third finger nestling in a recess at the front of the magazine when it was in place. "A nice piece of kit, but I don't know if I can afford this. Which model is it, and what's it chambered for?"

"It's a Model Twenty-six, so nine millimeter, with a ten-round magazine. I've got a Model Twenty-seven as well, to take the forty-caliber Smith and Wesson round, but that's a bit more expensive, and really that cartridge is a bit of a handful in a pistol this small. I've got a standard magazine, as well as one of the factory plus-two models that gives you twelve rounds altogether, and a spare mag from a Glock Seventeen that'll fit. That holds the usual seventeen rounds, but it sticks out a hell of a long way. If you wanted that, you'd probably be better off with just the Model Seventeen right from the start."

Bronson nodded, looking down at the compact pistol. "It's ideal, Dickie, but these are expensive little buggers. How much are you asking?"

"That weapon's virtually new, and they are pricey. But for you, as a deal, you can have it for six hundred, plus twenty for a box of Parabellum. And I'll give you four hundred if you bring it back when you're done."

Bronson shook his head and reluctantly handed back the weapon. "Too rich for me," he said. "I was hoping you'd got something for less than half that."

Weeks nodded. "I have," he said, "but you won't like it as much."

He replaced the Glock in the box, closed the catches and returned it to the backseat, then rummaged around under the coats and took out another box, bigger and more battered, showing signs of its age.

He opened this box, took out the pistol and did the usual safety checks, then handed it to Bronson.

"It's another Glock," Weeks said. "This one's a Model Seventeen, with two standard magazines. It's been around for a while, but it works well. Dead reliable, these pistols."

Bronson nodded as he inspected the weapon. It was a bit battered and there were several smears of what looked like paint on the polymer grip, but all the damage was cosmetic and the firing mechanism itself seemed in good working order as far as he could tell. There was really only one problem with it, apart from possibly the price.

"I'm not bothered about the way it looks, Dickie, but

this is a full-frame pistol, and I don't know if I could keep a weapon this size hidden in my pocket or wherever. I really need something a bit smaller."

Weeks smiled at him as Bronson handed back the Glock 17. "Well," he said, "if the Twenty-six is too rich for your tastes, I've only got one other option."

"And this is the one I'm not going to like," Bronson suggested.

"Exactly. This is the cheap and cheerful option, this week's special offer."

He returned the box to the backseat and this time reached into the pocket of his jacket. He pulled out a small black pistol, pressed the release, which dropped the magazine out of the butt, and then worked the slide. A small cartridge flew out of the weapon and landed in his lap; clearly the pistol had been loaded. Then he passed it over to Bronson.

For a few moments, he didn't recognize it. Although it was small and compact, the pistol bore more than a passing resemblance to the venerable Colt Model 1911, for many years the standard sidearm of the American military, albeit scaled down.

"What is it?" Bronson asked.

"It's a Spanish-made Llama XV, chambered for twenty-two Long Rifle." Weeks held up the ejected cartridge so Bronson could see it, then fed it into the top of the magazine. "It's not exactly a man-stopper, but it'd probably be enough to win any argument you're likely to get involved in. Most people who own these guns seem to like them. And it's cheap, so if you have to throw it away, it won't matter."

Bronson nodded. The fact that it was Spanish didn't bother him. Decades earlier, Spanish pistols had been something of a joke, badly made Astras and other makes proving unreliable and sometimes as lethal to the person firing the weapon as to whoever it was pointed at. But all that had changed, and modern Spanish pistols—and, okay, the Llama was a few years old—were as good as anything available anywhere. And the Spanish also made one of the best pure combat pistols ever designed, the SPS.

The .22 Long Rifle cartridge was a little small, certainly a lower caliber than he had hoped to find, but in the right hands it was still lethal. Bronson knew that Israeli assassination teams routinely used weapons in that caliber, because it could be silenced more effectively than full-bore weapons—meaning those of nine-millimeter caliber and above—and as long as the target was engaged with a head shot, the bullet was as deadly as anything else out there.

He looked across at Weeks. "How much?"

"For you, my friend, a century, and for that money I'll throw in a couple of boxes of ammo as well. Bring it back, and I'll give you sixty for it."

Bronson hefted the weapon and racked the slide back a couple of times, checking the tension in the spring and getting the feel of the pistol. He could easily hide it in his clothing—he'd had breakfast with Weeks and walked around the streets for several minutes, and he'd never even guessed the man had the weapon in his pocket—and it was certainly cheap enough. And, he hoped, he wasn't going to get involved in a firefight. What he needed was a weapon to get him out of trouble, to end a confrontation that he wouldn't otherwise be able to walk away from. And for that, almost any working pistol, of any caliber, would probably be enough.

He looked across at Weeks. "I'll take it," he said.

Weeks nodded. "Good choice. It's clean, as far as I know, and for that money you can ditch it if you have to and walk away."

Bronson pulled out his wallet and handed over five twenty-pound notes, which Weeks slid into his jacket pocket before handing over the fully charged magazine.

Then Weeks gestured to the dashboard in front of Bronson. "The boxes of ammo are in there."

Bronson opened the glovebox and looked inside. There were two boxes of twenty-two-caliber cartridges there, along with boxes for a number of other calibres, all the way up to 357 Magnum.

"That's kind of my ready-use locker," Weeks said. "Never know when I'll need a box of something."

"I'm sure," Bronson replied.

Keeping his finger outside the trigger guard, he slid the magazine into the butt of the Llama, pulled back the slide and chambered the top round. He pulled it back again, ejecting the cartridge onto his lap, and repeated the sequence of actions until the magazine was empty and the slide locked back. Then he reloaded the magazine, replaced it in the pistol and again chambered the first cartridge, making it ready for use. He set the safety catch and slid the weapon into the pocket of his leather jacket.

"Thanks, Dickie. I hope I don't need it, but it's good to have it, just in case."

"Drop you somewhere?"

Bronson glanced at his watch before replying, then nodded. "Yes, be a help if you could."

Moments later, Weeks steered the Range Rover out of the Tesco car park and followed Bronson's directions, heading back toward Straight Road and his second rendezvous of the day.

4

The first car arrived early in the afternoon and parked inside the large underground garage that formed part of the basement of the house. Within twenty minutes, two other cars had parked beside it, and three more were standing on the graveled driveway outside the double garage doors.

The last car to arrive, a black BMW, drove quickly along the ruler-straight Röthen Road to the north of Spreenhagen, a large village to the southeast of Berlin, then slowed and made the right turn off the road, bordered on both sides by thick woodland, and down the driveway leading to the house. The driver was the sole occupant of the car, and he was a few minutes late because he'd been held up by a minor traffic accident en route.

He parked the car, nodded to the two men who were standing by the double doors, and strode quickly into the garage. As soon as he'd done so, one of the men pressed a remote control and the doors closed behind him with a metallic clatter.

Inside the property, the man walked briskly, tracing a familiar route. At the end of the corridor leading from the garage was a flight of stairs he took two at a time; then he walked down a corridor to a large formal dining room. But there was neither food nor cutlery on the long polished walnut table, around which half a dozen men in dark suits were seated.

Apart from the absence of laptops, briefcases and writing pads, it could have been a typical board meeting. It had been their rule from the first that no writing or recording materials of any sort were allowed in the room, and the room itself was swept for bugs at least once a day.

The new arrival muttered his apologies, then took the last remaining seat.

"Let us begin," said the man at the head of the table.

He was just over fifty years old, slimly built, with fair hair, a pale complexion and light blue eyes. Apart from his height—he was well under six feet tall—he could have been cast from the classic Aryan mold, and he was clearly the dominant personality in the room. That was immediately obvious from the way the other men looked at him and had refrained even from chatting among themselves whilst they'd waited for the last member of the group to make his appearance.

"Not all of you will be aware of the progress we have made and how close we are to achieving our goal," the man went on, his voice surprisingly deep and resonant, his German formal and grammatically correct. "*Die Neue*

Dämmerung is on track and on time as I speak, though we do have one problem that I will address at the end of our meeting. First, and to ensure that you are all thoroughly familiar with all aspects of our operation, I would like Klaus to outline what we have achieved so far."

The man sitting on his right, a solid-looking, dark-haired individual with craggy features, nodded and sat up straighter in his seat. He had acted as second-in-command to Marcus for the last twenty years, and was just as dedicated to ensuring the success of the operation.

"Thank you, Marcus," he began. "I will start with a bit of history. Most of you are aware of the events that took place in Poland at the end of the last war. You will know that the SS Evacuation Kommando—which was, of course, under the command of Marcus's grandfather—successfully retrieved the device upon which so many of the hopes and dreams of the Third Reich rested. You may also have heard that it was successfully transported to Bodø in Norway and then flown on to South America to ensure that none of the enemies of the Fatherland could take possession of it. The few scientists deemed essential to the project traveled with the device, and all other people with any significant knowledge of what we were trying to achieve were eliminated."

Klaus Drescher looked swiftly around the table. Several heads nodded knowingly. "At that time, the regime in Argentina was sympathetic to our cause, and work was able to continue on the device without hindrance. Great strides were made both in increasing the effectiveness of *Die Glocke* and in the process of miniaturization, though there remained a number of significant technological hurdles to be overcome. In fact, it took over half a century before a new generation of our scientists was able to create a fully functioning and reasonably portable version of the device. That triumph was finally achieved only five years ago, and we now have six weapons concealed in secure locations here in Germany."

He paused for a moment, and then smiled slightly.

"In fact," he went on, "that's not strictly true. We actually only have five weapons in storage, because the sixth one is about to be deployed, and where we position the other five devices will largely depend upon what happens after this first, live test. If we have to take further action, most of the targets are fairly obvious: Paris, Madrid and Rome, certainly, and probably Brussels as well, and that will still leave us with one weapon in reserve. And as you all know, because of our recent activities, the first weapon of our arsenal will be triggered in London. The Olympic Games is simply too good an opportunity to miss."

A heavily built man on the opposite side of the table shook his head. "You know there will be reprisals. If the British discover that we were responsible, military action against Germany is possible, perhaps even probable. And the United Nations and America might also become involved."

Drescher shook his head, the smile still in evidence.

"We have taken steps to ensure that that will not happen. The vehicle to be used for the transportation of the device will have no connection to Germany whatsoever, and we are also employing measures to suggest that the real culprit, the author of the atrocity, is a much older and far more dangerous enemy than Germany."

He smiled more broadly as he looked around at the other men.

"It is just possible that our action could rid the world of a contagion that has existed since the beginning of recorded history." He paused again, and then continued. "Because, gentlemen, we are going to make it clear that the perpetrators of this attack have made their home a long way to the east, on stolen ground. We are going to blame it on the Jews."

There was a brief silence, and then another of the men spoke: "How?"

"The details are not important, but rest assured we can achieve it. Once the attack is over, we will make absolutely certain that the Jews are identified as the perpetrators. The international backlash against the Zionist state should be enough to finish the task that the Führer started."

"And what about the effectiveness of the London weapon? What degree of lethality are you anticipating?"

Drescher shrugged his shoulders.

"That is very difficult to predict because we do not know how many people will be within the lethal radius when the device is triggered. But the weapon will be activated during the opening ceremony, so we anticipate that at the very least there will be thousands of casualties, possibly tens of thousands, in addition to the long-term effects caused by radiation damage—effects that are, of course, impossible to predict."

Klaus glanced back at Marcus, who nodded.

"Thank you, Klaus." Marcus now turned to the man

seated on his left. "Hermann, can you bring us up-to-date with the situation regarding the vehicle?"

"Of course. Our people have already identified a suitable organization that will be sending a team to cover the Olympics, and we have our own vehicle prepared. We have agents watching the company, and as soon as they are ready to dispatch their lorry, we will move into position. We do not anticipate any difficulty with the substitution."

Marcus nodded again.

"I have personally overseen the testing of the weapon," he said, "up to a very low power setting, of course, and it worked exactly as we hoped."

"Did you use test subjects?"

"That was the only way we could confirm its effectiveness. We picked up a handful of vagrants and used them. The results were entirely satisfactory."

"Unfortunately," Klaus Drescher interjected, "there were no Jews available."

All the men smiled at that remark, and a couple of them laughed.

The meeting continued for another half an hour as various members of the group reported on their particular aspects of the operation, and then Marcus moved on to the other matter that he felt they needed to know about.

"And now," he said, "we have a small problem that I am in the process of resolving. One of our recruits was discovered attempting to pass information to the police here. Fortunately, he was detected and stopped, but it is clear that we need to know if he was acting alone. My men will start their questioning in the cellar in a few minutes, so we have just got time for a drink beforehand."

Five minutes later, Marcus led the way into a subterranean whitewashed room. Four men armed with pistols stood just inside the doorway, their attention focused on a man whose arms and legs were lashed to a stout wooden chair, the legs of which were bolted to the concrete floor. He was blindfolded and gagged, and was tugging frantically at his bonds, but to no avail. The leather straps were pulled tight, and held him immobile.

Two rows of seats had been placed along one wall of the room and, with the exception of Marcus, the new arrivals walked over to them and sat down. Most were still carrying small glasses of schnapps, and a couple of them had coffee as well.

Marcus gestured to one of the armed men, who moved across and stood beside the wooden chair, awaiting further orders. When he was satisfied that everything was ready, Marcus nodded his first command.

Without hesitation, the man leaned down, seized the little finger of the captive's left hand and in one swift and brutal movement bent it backward. The snapping of the bone was audible to everybody in the room, and was immediately followed by a muffled but agonized howl of pain.

"That is just the start, my friend," Marcus said, "just a taster to show you that we are serious. You *will* tell us whatever we want to know. Every time we think that you are lying or not telling us the whole truth, I will instruct my associate to break another of your fingers. When we run out of fingers, we will begin amputating your toes. It can take you days to die."

Marcus glanced at the seated men along the wall. Every one of them appeared eager for the show to begin, their eyes fixed on the bound man.

"So now we'll start," Marcus said. "Take off the gag."

The moment the gag was removed, the captive screamed his agony, then began sobbing, his desperation obvious to every man in the room.

And then the questions started.

5

20 July 2012

Chris Bronson pushed open the door of the pub and stepped inside. He spotted Eaton immediately. He was standing at one end of the bar, deep in conversation with two other men, both of them showing the kind of muscular development that comes from hard physical work, not time spent in a gym somewhere.

Bronson nodded to them, stepped up to the bar to order a pint and then walked over to the three men.

Eaton gave him a brief smile of welcome, then turned to his companions.

"This is Alex Cross," he said, "or, at least, that's what he says his name is. We met him at Stratford nick a couple of days ago. I reckon he could be quite useful to us."

Bronson didn't respond, and nor did Eaton's two companions, who simply stared at him in a faintly hostile manner, looking him up and down.

The man on his left glanced round the bar and finally

spoke. "John tells me you've been doing a bit of damage at the Olympic sites."

Bronson nodded and took another sip of his beer.

"Don't talk a lot, do you?"

"No."

"So what's your real name?"

"Alex Cross'll do for now."

"There some reason why you won't tell us?"

Bronson nodded again. "Yes."

Eaton grinned. "I told you, Mike. Man of very few words, is Alex here."

The man he'd addressed as "Mike" glanced at Eaton, then back at Bronson.

"Thing is," he said, "we're just a small group of people trying to make a difference, and that means we have to trust each other. And if we're going to trust each other, we have to know who we are. And we definitely have to know about anybody who wants to join us."

Bronson shook his head. "I don't want to join you." He gestured toward Eaton. "John here thought I might be able to tag along on one of your jobs, but I'm not bothered. You want a CV from me, forget it. Go and find someone else."

The three men stared at him, then Eaton gave a short, mirthless laugh.

"Jesus, Alex, we don't want your life story. We just want to find out a bit more about you."

It was, Bronson thought, almost like the start of a sexual relationship, each party probing the other, showing interest but not wanting to appear too eager, and he remembered an old quote about courtship he'd heard somewhere: how a woman always begins by resisting a man's advances, and ends up by blocking his retreat. This situation was different, obviously, but the principle was the same, though he had no intention of allowing his retreat to be cut off. As soon as he'd found out enough about the group for "Shit Rises" and the team back at the Forest Gate prison to pick them up, Bronson intended to return to the relative sanity of Tunbridge Wells.

"Look," he said, "I've done a lot of stuff in the past, been in plenty of different jobs. The longest was in the army. Right now, I'm just a pissed-off citizen, pissed off for a bunch of different reasons, in fact. I'm fed up with the money this city is throwing at these bloody Games, and I'm trying to do something about it. That's all you need to know."

"What did you do in the army?" Mike asked. "Ever use explosives, anything like that?"

Bronson shook his head. "I was infantry, not a sapper. I know about weapons and grenades, and I did some work with explosives for a while. Give me some plastic and a detonator and I can blow a hole in something, but I'm not a fully qualified demolition specialist."

"Pity."

"Why?" Bronson asked. "Don't tell me you've got a stash of C4 or Semtex?"

He watched the faces of the other men closely. If this group had access to plastic explosives, that made them infinitely more dangerous than Davidson and Curtis had expected. The detective sergeant had told Bronson that the activities of the group were a nuisance, and that the death of the nightwatchman was more likely to have been manslaughter rather than deliberate murder. But if they possessed high-grade military explosives like C4—Composition Four—then he knew they were looking at serious terrorists. Perhaps that was what Curtis had been hinting at when he'd said there were fears that the group posed a more serious threat than simple vandalism. Suddenly, Bronson was even more thankful that he had bought the little Llama pistol from Dickie Weeks.

Mike took his time before he replied.

"Might have," he said finally. "We've got contacts, people who can get us what we need. And we've only just started."

Those words sent a chill through Bronson.

"Listen," he said, "I don't mind painting slogans on walls and smashing up a few machines, but if you're serious about having access to plastic explosives, that's a whole new ball game. When I was in the army, I saw the damage that just a few ounces of explosive could do to a vehicle or even to a building. If you go that route, you'll lose any public support you've got, and when the police come after you—which they will—they won't be carrying truncheons. They'll have Heckler & Koch MP5s and they'll be happy to use them. That's a dangerous game you're playing."

Mike looked at him for a few seconds, then smiled slowly.

"So you can talk," he said, in a tone of mild surprise. "I didn't say we had explosives. I didn't even say we could get explosives. I just said we had contacts who could get us what we need. I've no idea if we'll end up trying to bring down one of the buildings in the Olympic village using a few lumps of plastic—that won't be our decision—but if we do go that route, it's good that you know something about demolition."

Eaton looked from Bronson to Mike and back again.

"I told you that we could use you, Alex. I just didn't guess you knew anything about explosives."

"Hang on a minute," Bronson said. "I haven't said anything about joining your group, and after what he"—he pointed at Mike—"has just said, I really don't think I want to. Sounds to me like you're getting into dark and dangerous territory." Bronson switched his attention from Eaton back to Mike. "And what did you mean when you said that if you used explosives it wouldn't be your decision? If you don't decide things like that, just who is pulling your strings?"

Mike grinned at him. "We're just a small part of a much bigger group, and they call the shots."

"And they are . . . ?" Bronson demanded.

Mike shook his head firmly. "You've just walked in off the street," he said, "and we still know sod all about you, so there's no chance of me saying anything else. You could be an undercover cop for all I know."

"Do I look like a bloody cop?" Bronson demanded, feeling the first faint stirrings of unease. Did they know something about him? Had he said something to blow his cover?

"No, but you wouldn't, would you? That's what it means to go undercover. You try to blend in with your targets." Mike took a step forward, moved closer to Bronson and stared straight into his face. "I don't trust you," he said, "and I don't think I'm going to like you. The only reason we're here at all is that John reckoned you might be useful. In my book, there's only one way to find out whether he's right. Either you piss off out of it right now or you do something to prove who you are. We're doing a job tonight, and you can tag along, if you want to. If you do, you'd better do exactly what we tell you, how we tell you, when we tell you. If you do okay, then we'll think about letting you work with us. If you don't, well"—he smiled unpleasantly—"let's just say you won't be seeing any of us ever again. In fact, you might not see anybody ever again."

It was hardly a veiled threat.

"And if I don't want to play your games?" Bronson asked.

"Like I said, you just turn around and walk away and hope that none of us see you again."

For a few seconds the two men stared at each other in silence, the tension in the air almost palpable.

Finally Bronson nodded, because he had absolutely no option if he was to stand any chance of penetrating the group.

"Okay, *Mike*," he said, "you've talked me into it. I'll play your game. Where and when do I meet you?"

Mike shook his head. "It's not quite that easy. We'll be ready to roll at about seven, so John'll call you at around six. He'll give you the rendezvous position and tell you what we want you to do. After that, we'll see what happens. If you do turn up, we'll be watching you."

He reached for his glass, drained the remainder of his

beer, nodded to Eaton and then strode out of the pub, his bulky companion—who'd said not a single word the entire time—following behind him.

Bronson watched them leave, then glanced back at Eaton. What he'd learned from the man called Mike was both interesting and disturbing, but in reality he wasn't really that much closer to finding out what was going on. Everything depended upon him being accepted by these people, and on him then being able to identify the ringleaders.

"You didn't tell me your lot was part of a bigger group," he said.

Eaton shrugged. "You didn't ask," he replied, "and I don't think it really matters. We act pretty much by ourselves, but they just pay the bills. And us," he added.

"You mean they pay you?" That was a wrinkle that Bronson hadn't expected.

Eaton grinned at him. "You might be in this because you're running some kind of one-man crusade against the Olympics, but most of us are involved because there's money to be made."

"How much money?" Bronson asked. He didn't think displaying a little avarice was a bad thing.

Eaton's smile grew broader. "You'll find that out a bit later on, if Mike and the others decide you can join us."

Bronson finished his drink. "You'll call me, right?"

Eaton nodded. "Yeah. Just make sure you can get back to the right area within about an hour. That time of the evening, the traffic can be a bitch."

6

Getting back to his car took over half an hour, partly because it was parked some distance away, but mainly because Bronson wanted to ensure that nobody was dogging his footsteps. But he knew he couldn't just run straight evasion tactics because that would immediately alert anybody who was following him to what he was trying to do. And if he really was just an angry citizen who objected to the Olympic Games being held in London, there would be no obvious reason for him to worry about being followed.

So he spent some time browsing in a bookshop, staying near the door so that he could look out into the street, and another few minutes sitting at a round metal table outside a small café where he drank a cup of coffee that he frankly didn't need, or even like very much. Then he did a bit of window shopping. And he saw absolutely nobody who took the slightest interest in him or what he was doing. So either they weren't following him—which was very good news—or they *were* following him and they were really good at it, which was obviously extremely bad news.

When he reached the car he took a final look around him, then unlocked it, climbed into the driver's seat and drove away, keeping one eye on his mirrors. He maneuvered the vehicle through the side streets until he reached a junction with the A127, the Southend Arterial Road. He turned left and followed that route until he reached the junction with the M25, where he turned right and headed south toward the river.

Again, Bronson watched his mirrors very carefully, and wound the speed up to a little more than eighty-five miles an hour, just to see if anyone would try to keep up with him. Then he slowed right down before the next junction and swung the Ford east into the Lakeside shopping center at Thurrock. There were car parks everywhere, all fairly full, but he had no difficulty in finding a space at the southern end of the trading estate outside the IKEA store. There his blue Ford was just one more anonymous car. Bronson sat for a few moments in the driving seat of the Ford, looking around him. As before, nobody seemed to be taking any interest in him. And then another car—a dark green Vauxhall with two passengers—pulled up a couple of spaces behind him. Two men got out and started walking directly toward his vehicle.

Bronson tensed and wrapped the fingers of his right hand around the butt of the little Llama pistol as they drew nearer. But when they reached his car, they simply continued walking, heading toward the store entrance.

Only when they'd vanished from sight did he relax, take out his mobile phone and press the speed-dial button for the number—another mobile phone—that he wanted. Curtis answered almost immediately.

"It's me," Bronson said. For obvious security reasons, just in case the group they were trying to infiltrate had obtained scanners or other ways of hacking into either of the mobile phones, it had been agreed that neither man would ever mention their respective names. The previous year the newspapers had featured little other than phone-hacking stories.

Both men knew that hacking a mobile was far more difficult than most of the papers had made out. Many of the reported hacks had not only occurred several years earlier, when mobile network security was much less efficient than it was today, but most had also involved attacks on a user's voice mail messaging system, and now the commonest way of communicating apart from simply making a call was to use text, and that was far more difficult to break into. Nevertheless, they were determined not to take any chances.

"How'd it go?" Curtis asked.

"I think you could say that I'm on probation. They're doing some kind of operation this evening, and they've invited me along. But they're cautious. I don't know where it is, or exactly what time it's going to be starting. John Eaton will call me on my mobile at six and tell me where to go, and I have to be within about an hour's drive of the site. But I've got no idea when the action will kick off. I'd have thought they'll probably wait until dark."

"What are you going to do? Turn up, or do you want out now? If you call me as soon as you've been given the rendezvous, we could bust in and grab the lot of them."

Bronson shook his head as he replied. "I'd love to walk away from this, but I don't think that would work," he said. "All I've been told is that I'll need to rendezvous somewhere, presumably close to the site, at seven this evening. What I don't know is whether I'll be meeting the rest of the group there, or just one or two of those I've already seen. If I was a betting man, I'd say they were still suspicious of me, and the rendezvous position that I'll be given will be nowhere near where the rest of them will be assembling. So if you do send in a team of officers instead of me, you'll be lucky to grab one or two of them."

"And that will spook the rest and blow your cover completely," Curtis finished for him.

"Exactly. And one of them—he was introduced to me as Mike, no second name and I've no idea if that's really any part of his name—actually said to me that I could be an undercover cop trying to penetrate their operation. I think I talked him out of the idea, but that's still a bit worrying."

There was a short silence while Curtis digested this unwelcome piece of information. "You sure about that? I mean, do you think he was being serious, or was it just a kind of throwaway remark?"

"I don't know. But if I'm going to get inside this group, I can't see any alternative to my turning up to-night."

"Well, just be careful, that's all. And if it looks as if it's all turning to rat shit, get the hell out of there and call for backup. I'll make sure there are a few extra patrol cars and a couple of ARVs in the general area from about eight o'clock onwards, so if you do blow the whistle, we can have officers with you in just a few minutes."

That was some comfort, but Bronson knew that a lot could happen to him between the time he raised the alarm and the first car arriving.

"Thanks," Bronson said. "I hope it won't come to that."

"Right," Curtis said briskly. "I'll brief Shit Rises on your progress so far. Anything else you need to tell me?"

"Yes, three things. First, if what John Eaton told me at lunchtime today is correct, then this group working in London is just a small part of a much bigger organization. But before you ask, I've got no idea what it is, where it's based, or what its agenda is. I got the feeling that we're not just talking about another bunch of low-lifes doing malicious damage in Edinburgh or Cardiff or somewhere. I think this other organization is directing the London group, telling it what targets to hit and when to hit them, which suggests a high degree of control. That's interesting, maybe even surprising, though I don't know much about this kind of criminal activity.

"The second point's related to that one. According to Eaton, the superior group, for want of a better expression, actually pays this London mob to carry out their attacks. They're acting as mercenaries, or maybe even paid employees, of this other lot."

"That's a new one, no mistake," Curtis said. "I don't think we've ever met that before. I'll pass it on. A couple of years ago we found a group of vandals—nothing very violent, mainly daubing slogans on buildings, that kind of thing—who had all paid into a fund so that if any of them were caught and fined, the fund would pay it. That was unusual enough, but I've never encountered what you might call vandals for hire before. And the third thing?"

"This is what worries me most of all. They were quizzing me about what I'd done in the past, and I told them I spent a few years in the army. The first question they asked me was if I knew anything about explosives, and they hinted that they had access to plastic explosives, through this other group."

"Shit," Curtis muttered. "That's all we need."

"'Shit' is an understatement. Most terrorist groups—and I think we have to consider them as terrorists rather than vandals—have to manufacture their own explosives. They use something like potassium chlorate or ammonium nitrate, which is a major constituent of most fertilizers, and mix it with a fuel like diesel oil. It can produce a hell of a bang—"

"You don't have to remind me," Curtis interrupted. "I was in Docklands when the IRA Canary Wharf bomb exploded back in 'ninety-six. That was a fertilizer bomb, and when it went off you could hear the bang over most of East London."

"I remember it, too. Most of the estimates suggested it was about a half-ton device, about eleven hundred pounds, and I think it did about ninety million pounds' worth of damage and killed a couple of people. But military-grade plastic explosive is about five times more powerful than a fertilizer bomb."

"So do you think these comedians could get their hands on plastic explosive?"

"I've no idea. The trouble is that C4 and Semtex— that's the civilian equivalent, if you like, used in quarries and so forth—are readily available if you know where to look, and especially in Europe. There are supposed to be literally tons of Semtex unaccounted for, so if these people can locate a source, I suppose they could get some into Britain."

Curtis grunted. "This is sounding a bloody sight worse every time you open your mouth," he said. "And you know how urgent this is. We've got a matter of days to get it sorted. But you're right. You have to meet these people tonight and try to find out as much as you can about them. But the moment you get any definitive information about their identities or where we can find them, and especially if you get a firm lead on this plastic explosive, you blow the whistle and get out. Understood?"

"You've got it," Bronson agreed, and ended the call.

He sat in thought for a couple of minutes, then took a different mobile phone from the glovebox, inserted the battery and dialed another number, one he knew from memory.

"Hello?"

"Hi, Angela; it's me."

"I've been trying to call you, but your mobile is permanently switched off. Where are you?"

"Sorry, it's a long story. The short version is that I've had to go undercover, and that means no phone calls to anyone who could identify me. I'm taking a risk calling you now, but I wanted to tell you what was going on."

"I thought you were just going up to London to be an extra body in the run-up to the Olympics."

"That's what I thought, too," Bronson replied, "but I was completely wrong. I can't go into any detail, but it does actually have something to do with the Games. Anyway, I'm stuck with it for the moment, but with any luck I might be finished in a few days, maybe a week at the most, because the timescale's really tight."

"I suppose this means that I won't be seeing you for a while?"

"Not until this is over, no."

Angela was silent for a few moments, then Bronson heard a deep sigh.

"Well, just be careful," she said, then rang off.

Bronson switched off the mobile and removed the battery, replacing the unit in the glovebox.

He didn't like to think what his former wife would say if she knew he was sitting in a car with a loaded—and completely illegal—pistol in his pocket, waiting to be summoned by a gang of putative terrorists to join them in engaging in some serious vandalism in London.

But he didn't think she'd be too happy with the idea.

7

He got the call he was expecting at ten minutes past six, and the man who phoned him—Bronson thought it was probably John Eaton, but he couldn't be sure—simply gave him a time and a place, and then rang off.

Fifty minutes later, Bronson parked his Ford in one of the side streets close to the West Ham Cemetery. The street was quiet and largely deserted—parked cars occupied most of the available spaces, but very few people were visible. Lights were on in the majority of the houses that lined both sides of the road.

He was sure that nobody had followed him to the rendezvous, but he still sat in the car for almost five minutes, checking his surroundings. Reassured, he took out the Llama pistol, dropped the magazine out of the weapon, unloaded it and then reloaded it with its maximum load of ten rounds of ammunition. He left the box of cartridges in the glovebox, because if he needed more than ten bullets he reckoned he was going to be dead anyway. Then he clicked the magazine back into place. He was very aware that semi-automatic pistols, unlike revolvers, are prone to jamming, and that the commonest reason for a stoppage is a cartridge not feeding properly into the breech from the top of the magazine. Unloading it allows the magazine spring to fully extend, and many people believe that that helps to reduce the possibility of a misfeed.

Then he bent forward and slid the pistol under the driver's seat of the car, because at that moment he'd had a change of heart, deciding it would not be wise to carry a weapon, not to that meeting.

His logic was simple enough: if Eaton and his cronies were still unsure about him, it was likely that he might be searched, just in case he was wearing a wire or another type of recording device. And the last thing he wanted was for any members of the group to discover that he had a weapon. That was his ace in the hole.

Bronson opened the door, stepped out onto the pavement and glanced around him; nothing he saw or heard gave him even the slightest twinge of concern. He took out his A to Z of London, located the street he was standing in, and where he needed to get to, which was literally just around the corner, memorized the layout of the immediate area, and slipped the book back into his pocket.

The rendezvous was another pub, the Lamb and Flag, but this time Bronson had been instructed to wait in the car park behind the pub, rather than go into the building. He could, of course, have parked his Ford in the car park, but he was concerned about being boxed in if he did so, not to mention one of the group somehow being able to trace the Ford's registered owner. So he'd decided that his best option was to leave the car nearby instead.

He was also unsure about who he would be meeting but, because he'd been told to wait outside the building, he guessed the pub was just a first point of contact, and that he would be given further directions by whichever members of the group were there.

As he turned the corner, he spotted the pub on the right-hand side of the street, about seventy yards in front of him, and slowed his pace slightly. This road was noticeably busier—cars and vans driving along it, pedestrians walking along the pavements and milling across the street. Several people were clustered outside the front of the public house, sitting at the handful of metal tables or just leaning against the wall of the building, almost all of them smoking furiously.

He waited until the traffic flow eased and then crossed the road so that he could walk past the building on the opposite side of the street as a final reconnaissance, not that he expected to learn anything from doing so—it was just a pub, significant only because of the man, or perhaps the men, he was supposed to be meeting there—but this served as a final check, a last reconnoiter.

The pub looked as if it dated from the early part of the twentieth century, the lower half of the structure built from red brick, some parts of which needed re-pointing quite badly, while the upper story had been rendered and painted. Originally it had obviously been white or maybe magnolia, but the years had not been kind, and several sections of the render had fallen off to expose poor-quality masonry underneath, while the paintwork that remained was faded and discolored. It had the appearance of a building that nobody loved, or even liked very much, but the truth was probably simpler: the important thing about a pub was the location and the interior, the ambience, the food, and the quality and price of the drinks it served, not what the exterior looked like. And judging by the number of people Bronson could see inside through the windows, as well as those he'd already noticed standing outside, this pub was popular.

Bronson walked about fifty yards beyond the public house, waited for another gap in the traffic and then crossed back to the opposite side of the street to retrace his steps. He walked past the main entrance and turned left down the roadway that led to the car park.

Almost as soon as he left the street, the sounds of traffic faded, replaced by the buzz of dozens of separate conversations that floated out through the pub's open windows, voices rising and falling, and punctuated by the occasional shout of surprise or burst of laughter. All very comforting and normal.

The car park at the back of the building was, in fact, more like an area of waste ground. There were no parking bays or markings, and the dozen or so cars left there had been positioned around the perimeter, allowing just enough room for each to maneuver and get back to the road when the owner returned to the vehicle.

Bronson walked slowly, checking the interior of each car as he did so, but they were all empty. Whoever had been sent by the group to meet him had yet to arrive. He glanced back down the access road, but nobody was visible.

At that moment, he heard the sound of an engine and glanced round to see a white Transit van driving down the access road. He moved over to one side of the parking area and watched as the vehicle braked to a halt a few feet away from him.

The passenger door swung open and John Eaton climbed out, a kind of wand with a circular sensor in his hand. He nodded to Bronson and beckoned him to walk over toward the van.

"Sorry about this, Alex," he said, sounding not the least bit contrite, "but we still don't really know you, so I have to do this. Orders," he added briefly.

"What, you think I'm carrying a weapon?" Bronson asked.

Eaton shrugged. "Maybe," he replied, "but actually Mike is far more worried that you might be wired for sound. He still thinks you could be a cop."

"If he really thinks that," Bronson snapped, deciding that going on the offensive was probably his best option, "why doesn't he just tell me to get lost?"

"Simple. He thinks your army training might be useful to us, what you know about explosives, that kind of thing. So he's cutting you a little slack while he decides what to do. Mind you, if it turns out that he's right and you *are* a cop . . . Well, let's just say he's got a nasty temper, Mike has."

Without a word, Bronson raised his arms sideways to shoulder height, assuming a crucifixion pose while he waited for Eaton to carry out his check.

The other man clicked a switch on the wand, which emitted a single beep to show that it was active, and

Bronson silently applauded his forethought in leaving his pistol in the car.

But even as the thought crossed his mind, he realized something else. He had half expected to be searched, but what he had anticipated was a pat-down, a physical search of his body and clothes, not this type of high-tech procedure. Metal detectors of various sorts were common, readily available and comparatively cheap, but the instrument Eaton was holding was different. It was expensive, highly specialized and rarely seen except in the hands of qualified security personnel, and usually only at sensitive locations like airports. The fact that the group Bronson was trying to infiltrate possessed one was yet another indication that it was well organized and had access to expensive equipment. That told him a little more about the organization he was facing, but it was hardly good news.

Eaton ran the detector over Bronson's torso, front and back. When he passed the wand down Bronson's right side, it emitted a series of rapid beeps and Bronson reached into his pocket and pulled out his car keys. Eaton nodded and continued his scan. When it beeped again, Bronson produced his mobile phone, but Eaton found nothing else.

"Okay," he said, "you're clean, so get in the van and we'll get this show on the road."

"Where are we going?" Bronson asked.

Eaton tapped the side of his nose and shook his head, then swung open the rear doors of the vehicle. "You'll find out when we get there."

Bronson nodded, climbed up into the Transit's loading area and sat down on a thinly padded wooden bench seat screwed to one side. The back doors slammed shut and he was left alone in the darkness of the vehicle. Moments later, the engine started, the driver reversed the van a few feet, and then drove it back down the access road.

At the end, it turned right onto the street and accelerated, and after that Bronson had no idea at all where it was going.

8

Bronson didn't know the area at all well. He'd driven around it a couple of times and studied the relevant pages in his A to Z, but as the van pulled away he knew he had no chance of working out where it was going. If he had been driven around his old stamping ground of Tunbridge Wells, there was a good chance that he would have been able to visualize the route the vehicle was taking, and even have a decent guess at its ultimate destination. But the best he could do in the present circumstances was to time the journey.

He glanced down at his watch, the luminous hands faintly visible in the darkness of the Transit's rear section, then shook his head as he realized he was just wasting his time. He wasn't a kidnap victim dragged off the street and trying desperately to work out where his captors might be taking him. When the vehicle stopped, Bronson would be let out, he assumed, and he would probably find himself somewhere near one of the sites of the Olympic complex. Knowing where he was, or where he was going, was unimportant. All that mattered was what happened when he reached his destination and found out what mayhem the group had planned, and what part he was supposed to be playing in the operation.

As it turned out, the journey was quite short—about seventeen minutes by Bronson's watch, that was all. The van's speed dropped considerably; then it bounced a couple of times as it went over a curb, or perhaps hit some potholes. The driver reversed the vehicle, probably maneuvering it into a parking space, and brought it to a halt. The diesel engine rattled into silence, and Bronson heard both front doors of the vehicle open and then close, and a few seconds later the rear door swung wide.

"We're here," John Eaton said unnecessarily.

Bronson stepped down out of the Transit and looked around. Another two vans were standing near the one in which he had arrived, and he now saw that they were parked in the forecourt of a garage that had obviously closed some time ago, possibly months earlier. All three Transits were facing out into the road, presumably to enable them to drive straight off the forecourt if they needed to leave in a hurry. The curb adjacent to that part of the forecourt had not been lowered, which explained the bumps Bronson had felt just before the vehicle finally came to a halt.

The garage was located in a wide street that seemed to contain mainly commercial properties, all of which were closed at this time of the evening. There were no other vehicles or pedestrians visible.

A few feet away, Bronson saw Mike giving orders to about a dozen men, all wearing heavy boots, jeans and either jerseys or jackets. They looked a tough bunch. A large map was resting on the hood of one of the Transits, and the men clustered around Mike were all listening intently to what he was saying.

"Just hang on here," John Eaton said. "As soon as Mike's finished, he'll tell you what he wants you to do."

That didn't take long. In a couple of minutes, most of the men dispersed, striding away purposefully in twos and threes, and Mike walked over to where Eaton and Bronson were waiting.

"You decided to come, then?" he said by way of greeting.

"Looks like it," Bronson replied. "So what's the plan?"

"You only need to know your part of it. I've decided that you can act as one of our diversions tonight. There's a building site two streets away. It's not one of the Olympic sites, but some of the machinery there has been used in the construction of the athletes' village, so it's a legitimate target. John knows where I mean. You two can get over there right now and take a look at the site. Decide what you're going to do, but don't start until exactly eight fifteen, so that you coordinate with the rest of what we'll be doing tonight."

Bronson looked at him. "What do *you* want me to do?" he asked.

Mike shrugged. "I don't care. According to John here, you think you're fairly tough and you've been running a one-man campaign opposing the London Olympics. Personally, I'm not sure about you. So here's your chance to prove me wrong. You do whatever you want to do, but if you want me to take you seriously, I'll be expecting a bit more than just a few slogans painted on some wall. I want to see damage, real damage, the kind of damage that will keep their machinery out of action for weeks. There are tools in the back of the van over there. Take whatever you think you'll need."

Bronson nodded. "Okay. I'll see what I can do."

He strode across to the vehicle that Mike had indicated and opened the rear door. Inside was a large wooden box containing a selection of hand tools and equipment, the kind of stuff you'd expect to find in a vehicle owned by a jobbing builder. There were hammers, chisels, saws, screwdrivers, crowbars and bolt-croppers, all entirely innocent within their present context, but not exactly the kind of thing most people would expect to see being carried through the streets of London in the middle of the evening.

Bronson glanced at Eaton. "You know this site," he said. "What will we need to get inside?"

Eaton didn't hesitate. "There's a chain-link fence all round it that would take too long to get through, but it's got steel gates secured with a length of chain and a padlock, so that's how we'll get inside. We can use the bolt-croppers to cut the chain, no problem. I don't know what we'll find inside the site that we could use against the stuff that's stored there, so I suggest we take a couple of club hammers as well. You can do pretty serious damage with one of them."

"Fine with me," Bronson replied. He reached into the tool box, picked up a set of bolt-croppers, a large chisel and a heavy hammer, and then a pair of heavy-duty gloves, and waited while Eaton selected his own tools of choice. Eaton picked up a canvas bag, the kind sometimes carried by a carpenter or plumber, put all the tools inside it and closed the rear doors of the van.

He nodded to Mike, and then he and Bronson strode away from the garage, heading down the street toward their target.

Mike watched them go, a thoughtful expression on his face. Then he turned and walked back onto the garage forecourt, toward the two other men who were still standing there, waiting by the Transits. They were the drivers—Mike himself would drive one of the vans away from the garage when the others returned.

"You know what to do?" he asked. "And you're sure you've got everything?"

The man nearest to him nodded. "Yeah, no problem. Be a piece of piss. Used one of them before, see."

"Good. Right, you'd best get moving, then."

The man he'd been speaking to reached into the cab of the Transit next to him and took out a small gray bag made of a soft fabric, and nodded to Mike. Then he set off down the street, following exactly the same route Bronson and Eaton had just taken.

9

"It's not far now," Eaton said, turning the corner and heading down another street principally occupied by light industrial and commercial premises. Like the other roads they'd walked down, this street was virtually deserted, devoid of both cars and pedestrians. They walked on for about a further thirty yards, then Eaton nodded in the direction of a yard on the opposite side of the road.

"That's it," he said.

A pair of tall steel gates, painted dark blue but showing the inevitable scrapes and bumps caused by the movement of heavy machinery in and out of the yard, marked the entrance. The gates were supported on steel columns on either side, and heavy-duty steel-mesh fencing was attached to the other side of each post and, as far as Bronson could see, completely enclosed the yard. Parked inside, and clearly visible through the fence, were several pieces of construction equipment, including a low loader, presumably used for transportation, three bulldozers, a number of cranes of various sizes, several machines that looked a bit like tractors but which were fitted with digger attachments, and dozens of cement mixers of various types and sizes.

Bronson was feeling increasingly uncomfortable. He'd broken rules in the past and cut corners when he thought he could get away with it, both during his time in the army and later as a police officer. From a legal point of view, the most dangerous act he'd ever undertaken was probably buying the Llama pistol from Dickie Weeks, because he knew better than anyone that unauthorized possession of a firearm in the United Kingdom attracted a mandatory custodial sentence. But what he was about to do now disturbed him more than that, or any other act he had ever performed. What he and Eaton were planning to do was nothing more than mindless vandalism, impossible to justify on any level.

Except, of course, that the only way he could possibly be accepted as a member of the group was to live the lie that he had created, to do for real the kind of things that he claimed to have been doing already.

But he really didn't like it.

Eaton glanced both ways, but the street was empty. He checked his watch, nodded, and then led the way across the road, stopped beside the double steel gates and opened the canvas tool bag.

"You're stronger than I am. You cut the chain," Eaton ordered, leaving Bronson no choice.

As Eaton had done, he checked that there weren't any pedestrians anywhere near them, or anyone watching.

Then he reached into the tool bag, pulled on the gloves and took out the bolt-croppers. He fitted the jaws around one of the links in the heavy-duty chain and forced the handles together. It was harder than he'd expected, and he changed his grip a couple of times until he felt the steel starting to give. Once the jaws started to bite, the chain began to part, the link finally giving way with a sharp crack that sounded uncomfortably loud in the quiet of the street.

Cutting through the other side of the broken link took less time, now that Bronson knew the level of force he had to exert, and in less than a minute the steel gave way and the chain fell to the ground.

Eaton pushed open the right-hand-side gate and they stepped into the yard, pushing the gate closed behind them to retain the appearance of normality.

"What now?" Bronson asked.

Eaton shrugged. "It's your show," he said. "Do what you like."

Bronson nodded. Essentially on trial, he knew he had to make it look good. But for the sake of his own conscience, he was going to try to do as little damage as possible.

He grabbed the hammer and chisel he'd put in the tool bag and walked over to the closest bulldozer. He rested the blade of the chisel against the pipe leading to one of the diesel injectors on the side of the engine and rapped the end sharply with the hammer. The pipe fractured instantly, a trickle of diesel fuel weeping out of the broken end. Then he repeated the action on the other injector pipes. He wasn't doing any lasting damage to the bulldozer—to do anything major would require far more powerful tools than just a hammer and chisel— and he knew the construction company would only have to replace the pipes to get the vehicle working again. But he was taking it out of action for a day or two, and he hoped that was the kind of thing Eaton was expecting him to do.

It wasn't.

"Come on, Alex, that's just fiddling about. They'll have that dozer running again in a few hours. You need to think bigger. Get into the cab, smash up the instrument panel. Do something that'll take it out of commission for a few weeks."

"Don't worry," Bronson growled. "I'm just getting started."

He pulled himself up onto the side of the large yellow machine and grabbed the handle of the door. It was locked, but he had more or less expected that. He looked round once more, then swung the hammer in a vicious arc that connected solidly with the window set into the door above the handle. The glass shattered with a crash, covering the floor of the cab with a myriad of jewel-like but worthless blue-green glass beads.

Bronson reached through the opening, released the lock and swung the door open. He brushed the glass off the seat and sat down on it. Conscious that Eaton was watching him from the yard below, he knew he had to make it look good. He raised the hammer and smashed it down on the top of the instrument panel, where it left an impressive dent even if it did nothing else. Then he swung the hammer into the center of the group of dials. Glass shattered as he destroyed the instruments, for the first time doing real, serious damage. He hit the instrument panel a couple more times, then climbed down from the cab.

As he had expected, Eaton climbed up just a few moments after Bronson had stepped onto the ground.

He nodded his satisfaction. "Good job, Alex," he said. "Now smile for the camera."

"What?"

Eaton pointed toward the metal gates, one of which was now standing slightly open. In the gap stood a man, a camera held in both hands, the lens pointing directly at Bronson.

"Who the hell's that?" Bronson demanded, taking a step toward the newcomer.

"Relax, Alex. He's one of our people, just capturing your exploits on celluloid—or rather one of those bloody memory chip things—so that we've got a bit of a lever if you ever decided to roll over and try to turn us in to the plods. He's just filmed you doing about three or four grand's worth of damage to that dozer—easily enough to put you away for quite a while."

"Clever bastards," Bronson said, realizing he'd been set up. "I suppose that was Mike's idea?"

"Pretty much, yeah. Anyway, you've proved you're on our side—at least you have to me—so let's get the hell out of here before the pigs turn up. There's an alarm system here, so they should already be on their way."

And as if to underline his remark, Bronson heard, faintly but quite distinctly, the sound of an approaching siren.

"I wish you'd bloody well told me that before," Bronson snapped, dropped the hammer. Then he turned and ran for the gate.

The man with the camera had already disappeared when Bronson wrenched the gate open and headed off along the road, back the way he'd come. But even as he reached the road, a police car turned into it, traveling quickly and heading straight toward him, roof lights flashing but with the siren switched off. Not all patrol officers were obliging enough to give an audible warning of their approach.

Bronson glanced to his right, where Eaton had just appeared, running beside him.

"Split up," Bronson ordered, and ran across the road ahead of the police car, which was now only about fifty yards away. He ducked down a narrow alley between two of the industrial units, where the car couldn't follow, and sprinted toward the opposite end.

Behind him, he heard a squeal of brakes as the police car slammed to a halt, then the sound of running feet and shouted commands to stop. He ignored them, concentrating on putting as much distance between himself and the pursuing officers as he could.

He took a quick glance behind him when he'd covered perhaps eighty yards, and then immediately stopped, because the alley was deserted. Obviously the two patrol officers had gone after Eaton, not him.

For a moment he just stood there, then turned round and ran back toward the road. He stopped at the end of the alley and looked out before he showed himself.

What he saw was unexpected.

Eaton was about seventy yards away from him, and over to his right, running back toward him, the two officers a few yards behind him, and apparently gaining on him. He must have doubled back, hoping to shake them off. And it clearly hadn't worked.

It went against every fiber of Bronson's being, but he knew what he had to do.

Eaton saw Bronson standing at the end of the alley, changed direction and ran past him down the narrow passageway. As he did so, Bronson shifted position, tucking himself out of sight, waiting for the first of the two patrol officers to follow.

The moment the man appeared, Bronson stepped forward, crouching slightly and bracing himself, his left arm bent at the elbow to act as a ram. The running policeman had no time to react or change direction. He simply ran straight into Bronson's immovable figure, and more or less bounced off, tumbling backward, gasping for breath.

Almost immediately, the second officer rounded the corner, running hard. Bronson stepped aside, then kicked out with his right foot, catching the policeman's left leg beside the knee. The man let out a howl of pain and crashed forward onto the ground.

Bronson didn't hesitate. He knew both men would be on their feet again in a few seconds, and he couldn't afford to be caught. So he turned tail and ran, ran as hard as he could, retracing his steps down the alley, Eaton about thirty yards in front of him.

At the end, both men slowed down and looked back.

The two police officers were more or less where Bronson had left them, but both were standing and one was clearly speaking into his radio, probably relaying a description of Bronson and Eaton and calling for reinforcements.

"Thanks for that," Eaton said. "Now let's get out of here."

Seconds later, the two men jogged out of the far end of the alley and turned left, away from the construction yard, then slowed to a walk as they made their way down the street. They heard the sounds of a siren from the road they'd just left, but saw no sign of police officers or vehicles anywhere near them.

"There's no linking road between these two streets," Eaton pointed out. "The pigs'll have to go all the way back to the main road to get down here."

"With a bit of luck they won't bother," Bronson said.

"Did you hurt them?"

"Not really. One of them'll have a sore knee for a few days, but the other was just winded."

"Well, thanks again. That was a good job," Eaton said, as they headed back to where they'd left the Transit van. "I think Mike'll be happy to have you join us now. You might even get to meet Georg."

"Georg?"

"All in good time," Eaton replied with a grin, "but between you and me, he's the one who gives Mike his orders. He's the money man, if you like."

Bronson filed away this piece of information: another new name and perhaps a glimpse of the hierarchy. He hoped he'd done enough to gain proper access to the group, so that he could identify the key players and then walk away, get back to doing something that didn't leave quite such a sour taste in his mouth.

*   *   *

Back at the construction yard, once they'd caught their breath, the two-man crew of the patrol car conducted a rapid search of the premises and found nobody there, which was what they'd expected. When the alarm had been triggered, the principal key-holder had been alerted as well as the police, and only about fifteen minutes after the patrol car had skidded to a stop, a balding, middle-aged man arrived in a Jaguar saloon and introduced himself to the two officers as Jeremy Heaton.

He inspected the damage to the bulldozer and expressed his irritation—he knew it would be a long time before that vehicle would be back in working order—but he was happy that only one piece of equipment had been targeted.

"Thanks for getting here so quickly, lads," Heaton said as he walked back to talk to the patrol car crew. "You probably scared the bastards away before they could do any real damage."

"We saw two men here, but we couldn't catch them," one of the officers said, declining to explain what had actually happened. "That dozer's a bit of a mess, though, isn't it?"

"Yes, but it's an old one, and it was coming up for a major service anyway, so it's no great loss. The insurance company won't be happy, but that's their problem. I've already called one of my people to come out here and sort out that gate," Heaton added. "Get the place secure again, until the next time some comedian decides to have a little fun in here."

"Right, sir," the second officer said. "If you've got everything in hand, we'll be on our way."

"Thanks again. Oh, we've got a new security system here. If it recorded anything useful I'll leave a copy at the local nick."

Heaton watched the car reverse out of the open gate and head off down the street. Then he walked across to the locked office at the back of the yard, feeling in his pocket for his keys.

The new security cameras had been installed only a few weeks earlier, and Heaton still wasn't sure they were in the right places and were working properly. He decided he'd look at the tapes—sorry, the solid-state hard drives, as the installer had emphasized to him several times—on-site before he handed over the pictures, if the system had done its job and taken any, to the police.

The security company had fitted two cameras, both tucked neatly out of sight. One covered the main gates, the obvious place for any intruder to effect an entrance, and was linked to the alarm system, so it would have started recording the moment the gate swung open and broke the contact. The second camera provided a wide-area view of the yard, and would show exactly where any intruders went and what they did. It was, the security company had claimed, state-of-the-art equipment, and would provide the best possible chance of identifying and apprehending anyone who entered the premises illegally.

In his office, Jeremy Heaton sat down at his desk, switched on the LCD screen that hung on the wall opposite his chair and somewhat uncertainly negotiated his way through the various menus that controlled the security system. He finally found what he was looking for and settled back to watch the video sequences.

The pictures were incredibly clear, the faces of the two men in sharp focus. The system actually seemed to be working far better than Heaton had expected, even better than the installer had promised, in fact.

One of the menu options offered Heaton the ability to make copies of the video recordings. He clicked the appropriate key, then followed the on-screen instructions that told him where to insert a blank DVD disk. He'd deliver that to the local police station, as he'd said he would, not that it would help much. Heaton had no illusions about the likelihood of the two criminals being apprehended, unless they already had records and could be identified from the images.

Once the copying process had finished, he extracted the disk and slipped it into a case. Then he opened his drawer again, took out a second blank disk and inserted it in the machine. He'd make another copy, he decided, and this one he wouldn't hand over to the police.

He had a much better idea what he could do with that recording.

10

The moment Chris Bronson followed Eaton into the office at the back of the old warehouse situated at the edge of a trading estate in Essex early the following afternoon, he knew something was badly wrong. He'd been expecting to see one or two other members of the group there, probably Mike and maybe the man Eaton had referred to as "Georg." In fact, Bronson found himself staring at Mike and half a dozen tough-looking men with unfriendly expressions on their faces.

But that wasn't what worried him the most. Bronson's attention was caught and held by a plasma TV set in the corner of the room, the picture frozen, but perfectly clear. It was a remarkably sharp image of his face, and below that the caption: "Police officer implicated in act of vandalism."

And even as he registered that, Bronson was grabbed from behind by two other men who'd been hidden behind the door of the room. He twisted and turned, struggling to free himself from their grasp, but they were too strong. They hustled him across to a stout wooden chair positioned near the center of the room and forced him to sit down. Then, assisted by two of the other men there, they tied his wrists and ankles to the arms and legs of the chair, completely immobilizing him.

"I knew there was something that didn't smell right about you," Mike began. "We caught this on the news this morning. I recorded it, because I thought you might want to see it. Your fifteen minutes of fame, so to speak."

He turned round, picked up a black remote control from the desk behind him and aimed it at the digital receiver mounted just below the television set.

The screen sprang into life as the announcer's words filled the room: ". . . caught on a security camera at a construction equipment yard not far from the site of the Olympic stadium."

The picture changed—two men entering through the gate, heading straight toward the camera. Then it altered again, to a view of the yard from above this time. The two figures could be seen approaching a bulldozer, and then one of them, the bigger of the two men, began hammering at something on the side of the engine.

The newscaster continued explaining the sequence of events, just in case any of the channel's viewers were too dense to grasp what they were seeing.

"The two men were recorded by the security system as they broke in through the locked gates, carrying heavy hammers and other tools. Once inside, they made straight for this bulldozer and caused several thousand pounds' worth of damage to the engine and controls, according to the company's owner. Sky sources have positively identi- fied this man"—the image shown on the screen returned to the still picture of Bronson's face—"as Christopher John Bronson, a police sergeant living in Kent. The iden- tity of his companion is so far unknown, but—"

Mike clicked a button on the remote control. The re- corded program vanished and the live news feed was dis- played. He pressed another control and the sound was immediately muted.

"When I first met you," Mike continued, his tone con- versational, almost friendly, "I thought you could be an undercover cop, but then I decided I had to be wrong, because not even the Metropolitan Police would be that stupid. Well, guess what? They really are that stupid, and now here you are, up shit creek without a paddle. Or even a canoe, for that matter. You've got no way out of this, my friend."

"I'm not your friend," Bronson snapped.

"You got that right," Mike sneered.

Bronson's mind was racing, figuring the angles as he tried desperately to find some way out. The only asset he had was the Llama pistol, tucked into the rear pocket of his jeans and under his leather jacket. Nobody had searched him, probably because most British police were still rarely armed, and even undercover officers seldom carried weap- ons. But to get to the pistol he needed at least one of his hands free, and right then he didn't see how he was going to achieve that.

What he did know was that there would be no point in appealing for mercy. From what little he knew of the man, Bronson guessed that compassion wouldn't be very high on Mike's list of qualities. If indeed it featured at all.

He hadn't had the radio switched on in his car when he drove out to this rendezvous, the time and location specified in a telephone message from John Eaton, and neither Curtis nor anyone else at the Forest Gate police station had called his mobile. He'd walked into the situation cold.

"So, Mr. Policeman, now we have to decide what to do with you."

Bronson said the only thing he could think of that might turn the situation around.

"You said the Metropolitan Police force was stupid, *Mike*. Well, from where I'm sitting, the only stupidity being shown in this room is what's coming out of your mouth."

Mike crossed the room in three quick strides and smashed his fist into Bronson's face.

"Shut up," he snapped. "You'll have plenty of time to talk when we put the screws on you. Until then, just keep quiet."

Bronson's cheek was numb from the blow, but he still seemed to have all his teeth, which was something.

"Do all your thinking with your fists, do you?" Bronson asked. "Easier to hit than use your brain?"

Mike spun round and raised his right hand again, but then a single voice cut across the office and he stopped instantly.

"Wait."

Bronson had not even noticed the man until he spoke, probably because he was sitting in a chair against the far wall, rather than standing in a group with the other men. He had a thin, pinched face and a somewhat straggly beard that seemed barely attached to his chin, like some badly applied theatrical prop. He was slightly built, and although he was sitting down Bronson guessed he was well under six feet tall. But despite his unimpressive appearance, he exuded authority and seemed to be the dominant personality of the group. Certainly, his single word of command had stopped Mike in his tracks.

"You're not going to listen to him?" Mike snapped.

"Sit down and shut up," the seated man said, his eyes never leaving Bronson. Mike glared at him for a couple of seconds, then slunk over to one side of the room, dragged a chair forward and sat down on it.

"Right, Bronson—and I assume that really is your name, not 'Alex Cross'—you've got sixty seconds. Give me one good reason why I shouldn't let Mike take you apart."

"Simple, and I would have thought it was obvious. I'm not an undercover cop, and what's just happened proves it."

"Fifty seconds left. I'm not convinced."

The seated man had a faint accent that Bronson couldn't place. It wasn't French or Italian, because Bronson spoke both, Italian fluently and French reasonably well, but it could have been German, or possibly he was from one of the Eastern European nations. The man's English was fluent, but it clearly wasn't his first language.

Bronson knew he had only the one chance, and his best bet was to tell the truth as far as he could, admit some things and hope they swallowed the big lie at the end.

He'd discussed the possibility that he might be unmasked with Curtis before he went undercover, and between them the two men had concocted a story, a story that Bronson knew he was now probably betting his life on.

"My name *is* Chris Bronson," he said, "and I *was* a police sergeant. But I left the force months ago. To be exact, I was thrown out."

"Why?" the seated man asked. "Thirty seconds," he added.

"If I've only got thirty seconds left, I'd rather skip the details."

"Fair point. Go on."

"I've done undercover work in the past, and to protect the identity of officers involved in that kind of operation, there's a standard procedure that is followed by the media. Before any story is run that might identify a police officer, in any context, the Home Office has to be informed, just in case that officer *is* working undercover. If I was still in the force and trying to penetrate this group, that story"—Bronson nodded his head toward the TV set in the corner—"would never have been broadcast. And that proves I'm not who Mike thinks I am."

In fact, Bronson had not the slightest idea whether any such procedure was followed, though he thought it would probably be a good idea if it was. But it sounded plausible, and that was what mattered. He guessed that Curtis would have been just as surprised by the contents of the news broadcast as he was, and he hoped he was even then doing something to mitigate its effects.

"Okay. You've bought yourself another minute. Why were you thrown out of the force?"

"I got a little carried away when I was questioning a suspect. He ended up with concussion and a broken arm and I got charged with grievous and actual bodily harm. And then they threw me out for good measure. That's why I gave a false name when I was arrested at Stratford nick. If they'd known who I really was, they'd never have let me out—there's an outstanding warrant for my arrest because I skipped bail after they charged me."

The man with the straggly beard nodded.

"That's a good story," he said, "but we've got no way of verifying it. What we do know is that you were—or are—a police officer, and we have no wish to get involved with the forces of law and order here in Britain. Or anywhere else, for that matter."

"Georg." One of the other men in the office was looking at the television set, pointing at the screen, at the live program being broadcast.

Along the bottom edge a ticker was running, saying "Breaking News," and Bronson's picture was again displayed on the screen.

"Turn up the volume."

Somebody grabbed the remote control and pressed the "mute" button, and immediately the announcer's voice filled the room.

". . . now understand Sergeant Bronson was dismissed from the force some months ago following an incident, and that there is an outstanding warrant for his arrest on charges of assault. Members of the public are advised not to approach this man under any circumstances, but to contact the nearest police station immediately if they believe they've seen him. Also in London, a council official in Lambeth has—"

As the man again muted the set's volume, Bronson looked across at the seated figure. "Now do you believe me?" he asked.

Georg shrugged: "That depends on how much credence you give to what they tell you on television."

"You were ready enough to believe the first report about me," Bronson pointed out.

"That's another fair point, but I'm still not convinced."

Bronson tried one last gamble. "Right. Untie me, and I can show you something that might help you make up your mind."

"What?"

"Untie me, and I'll show you," Bronson repeated.

The seated man glanced round at the other men in the room, presumably assessing the chances of Bronson being able to overpower them, then nodded. The two men standing behind Bronson bent down and removed his bonds.

"Thanks," he said, as his arms were freed.

For a moment he rubbed his wrists, getting the circulation going again. Then he stood up, turned to his right and smashed his right fist into the face of the man standing beside him. Before anyone else could react, he twisted around to his left and did exactly the same to the man there.

"Touch me again, you bastards," he snapped, "and I'll blow your bloody heads off."

Then, as three of the other men started to move toward him, he whipped his right hand behind him, pulled out the Llama and aimed it straight at them, clicking off the safety catch as he did so.

"Just give me a reason," he snarled.

All three men stopped in their tracks, mesmerized by the sight of the pistol.

"Still think I'm a cop, Georg?" Bronson asked, glancing momentarily toward the seated figure.

"Right now, I'm not sure," the man replied, apparently unfazed by the sight of Bronson's Llama. "But that doesn't look much like a police-issue pistol, so that's one point in your favor. Now, unless you think you *are* going to start shooting, I suggest you put the weapon away. Then perhaps we can talk."

11

Bronson hadn't put the pistol away, but he had sat down again, clicked the safety catch back on and lowered the weapon to his lap, keeping it within easy reach of his right hand.

"So who are you, exactly?" he asked.

"You don't need to know that."

"I do if I'm going to work with you."

Georg shook his head. "We're a long way from deciding that," he said.

"Fine," Bronson replied, and stood up. "Then I'll go."

Georg lifted a restraining hand. "No, not yet. I think you could be useful to us, but we have to be sure where your loyalties lie."

"And how are you going to find that out?"

"There are ways," Georg replied calmly. "But having a former policeman in the group makes sense. You know police tactics; you might even have friends on the force, people who could be persuaded to supply information that would be useful to us."

Bronson laughed shortly. "You obviously know nothing about the way the police force works. For what I did, I became an instant pariah. None of the people I worked with would cross the street to piss on my head if my hair was on fire."

"A colorful metaphor, but I understand what you mean. Still, your knowledge of police tactics and procedures could help us, especially when we put the last pieces in place. And we already know you're handy with your fists."

Georg glanced at the two men who'd grabbed Bronson when he walked into the office. One was still rubbing his jaw while the second sat on a chair in the corner, holding a handkerchief to his bleeding—and possibly broken—nose.

"I can take care of myself, yes."

Georg looked at him for a few seconds, apparently considering. Then he nodded, as if he'd just come to a decision.

"Right, Bronson," he said. "It's not my decision, and obviously we'll have to run a few checks on you, but my feeling is that you're probably telling the truth."

Bronson inclined his head, but didn't respond.

"That pistol, for one thing, is a giveaway," Georg continued. "If you *were* undercover and your masters had decided you should be armed, I'd expect you to be carrying a full-bore pistol, probably a Glock or perhaps a Walther, not some piece of Spanish crap that you picked up in a dodgy deal somewhere."

"So if you don't decide, who does?" Bronson asked. "You mean you take a vote on it, something like that?"

Georg shook his head. "No. Something much simpler, a kind of test that you'll either pass or fail. You'll find out later. For now you can go."

Three minutes later, Bronson was sitting in the driving seat of his car and heading away from the industrial estate, back toward London.

Once he was sure nobody was following him, he turned off down a side road, looking for a quiet spot where he could park up for a few minutes. He found it in the form of a roadside pub that had just opened for business, and which had a large car park, already half full of parked vehicles. He slid the Ford into a space at the far end, where he had a good view of the road, then opened the glovebox and took out his mobile phone.

Curtis answered on the second ring.

"Hello?"

"Yes, but it bloody nearly wasn't," Bronson snapped. "What the hell happened with that news broadcast on Sky? That could have killed me."

"I'm really sorry about that. The first we knew was when somebody here saw it—in the canteen, actually. We checked with Sky immediately. It turned out that the owner of the equipment yard where you had your bit of fun last night made two recordings. He gave one to the local police station and sent the other to them. They ran it first for what it was—footage of two unidentified men doing a bit of damage to a bulldozer. But then one of your former colleagues from Tunbridge Wells rang the station and identified you. Sky checked him out, and then ran the revised footage once they were satisfied that he did know who you were. You must have really pissed off somebody down there, Chris."

Sitting in his car, Bronson nodded. He knew exactly who it must have been. "Detective Inspector Harrison," he growled. "Known to one and all as 'SOS Harrison,' and about as popular as a dose of clap."

"'SOS'?" Curtis asked.

"'Sack of Shit,'" Bronson replied. "He's slimy, greasy and overweight, and he's hated my guts ever since the day I first walked into the station. He finally retired this year."

"Sky wouldn't say who it was," Curtis replied. "Protection of their sources and all that, but they did say it was a former senior police officer, so I guess that fits. Anyway, as soon as we explained the situation, they agreed to run the update, the story we cooked up about you being kicked out of the force. So what happened?"

It only took a couple of minutes to give Curtis the edited version of what had happened in the industrial estate, leaving out all mention of the Llama pistol, of course.

"What really saved me was Sky, oddly enough," he said. "If they'd turned off the TV set none of them would have noticed the update to the bulletin, which of course confirmed my story. By itself, they'd never have taken my word for it, and I might still be there, but probably not still in one piece."

"They're that dangerous?" Curtis asked.

"I don't know. Mike is a thug, pure and simple. He

thinks with his fists, and I was expecting him to beat me up as he tried to get information out of me. Most of the others are heavies with the same sort of attitude—they're really just muscle for hire, dangerous but not too bright—but the one who worries me most is this man Georg. And by the way, he sounds German to me."

Bronson described the man he'd seen at the warehouse.

"We can get a squad out there in an hour or so," Curtis suggested. "Will they still be in the building?"

"I doubt it. It looked to me as if they were planning on leaving soon, so they've probably already gone. And there's another reason, too, why hitting them now wouldn't be such a good idea."

"What?"

"John Eaton told me that Georg was the man who pulled Mike's strings, the one who gave the orders. He also told me he was the money man, the financier who paid the members of the group for what they did. I assumed that he was the boss, but it's clear that he isn't. There's some larger organization that Georg reports to. If you mop up this group now, you'll take one bunch of men off the streets, but my guess is that Georg or whoever replaces him will just recruit a new team from the fringes of the underworld. You'll probably grab the people who killed that nightwatchman, but I'm certain there's something darker and more dangerous at work here."

"Like what? And don't forget, infiltrating the group is the whole point of the exercise. We need to get them off the streets before the Games start."

"I know," Bronson replied, "but I get the distinct impression that what these people are doing is just a nuisance: smashing up a machine here, breaking a few windows there, that kind of thing. It's just a kind of diversion tactic, something to focus our attention on the wrong area, while something else, something much bigger and more destructive, goes down elsewhere."

"What's your evidence for that?"

"That's the problem. I haven't got any. Only something Georg said, almost a throwaway remark about putting the last pieces in place. There's something about him that I don't like. He's too calm, and too bright for the company he's keeping. There's no way he'd be involved with these people at all unless there was a bigger picture, something we're not seeing at the moment."

After Curtis rang off, Bronson sat in silence in the car for a few minutes, trying to work out what he should do next.

The trouble was, there was almost nothing he could do. His relationship with the group, such as it was, was reactive and responsive: they had his mobile number, but he had no way of contacting them. The only person who ever called him was John Eaton, and he had configured his mobile so that the sender's number was blocked. Apart from the warehouse on the small industrial estate he had just left, the only other physical points of contact he'd had with the group were a couple of pubs.

He would just have to wait until somebody—Georg or Eaton or another member of the group—called him and arranged another rendezvous. And then he'd have to decide if that was the right time to let Curtis loose the dogs to roll up the group. Or not.

Bronson frowned, started the Ford's engine again, pulled out of the pub car park and turned back onto the road.

12

"And bring your passport," the voice on the mobile instructed, then rang off.

For a second or two, Bronson stared at the handset, then shrugged and replaced it in his jacket pocket. Why the hell did he need his passport? Did Georg or Eaton want to confirm his identity by looking at the document? Or was there some other reason?

It was the day after the meeting at the warehouse, and Bronson had just been summoned to another rendez-vous, this one back in London, in Stratford. It was a residential address, maybe a safe house, which might mean that the group was beginning to trust him. At the very least, it was the first meeting place that wasn't either a pub or a warehouse, so it was progress of a sort.

For the duration of the operation, he had taken a room above a pub in Epping, a cheap and anonymous lodging from which he could come and go as he wished, because the first-floor accommodation was approached by an outside door that was independent of the pub's entrances. He had traveled up to London with the bare minimum he thought he would need—half a dozen changes of clothing, his washing kit and a couple of paperbacks—but he had brought along his passport. In fact, he rarely traveled anywhere without it.

The decision he had to make was whether to tell Bob Curtis about the meeting. On the one hand, if most of the major players from the group were going to be there it would offer an excellent opportunity for the Metropolitan Police to grab the men involved in the killing of the nightwatchman. But if a squad of officers kicked down the door and found only John Eaton, for example, then Bronson's cover would be comprehensively blown and there would be no chance of identifying the other members of the gang. And, from Bronson's point of view, no possibility of finding out what else Georg had planned for London, because he was still sure that the German—and he thought he'd identified the man's accent now—had a much more dangerous agenda planned than the mindless vandalism that had taken place so far.

Realistically, there was only one option that made sense. Bronson looked at his London A to Z, spent a couple of minutes studying one page of it, then took out his mobile phone again and pressed the now familiar speed-dial combination.

"It's me again," he said when Curtis answered. "I've been summoned to another meeting this afternoon, but I think they're still checking me out, so there'll probably only be one or two of them there."

"You said there were a whole bunch of them waiting for you at that warehouse yesterday," Curtis pointed out.

"I know, but then they thought they were confronting an infiltrator, an undercover cop, which is why they were there mob-handed. That's also why they told me to drive out into the wilds of Essex, so that if they decided to beat the crap out of me, or worse, there'd be nobody around to hear, or to interfere."

"No witnesses."

"Exactly. You knew where I'd gone, but if they'd decided that I was a liability they could do without, I'd have been dead and buried long before you could have got a team organized and out there to find out what had happened to me."

"So why are you sure you won't be walking into a bullet or a knife this time?"

"Mainly the location," Bronson replied. "The meet's in a residential district. One of the neighbors would be bound to notice any unusual noise, so I think I'll be safe enough." He paused for a moment. "But if you could keep a car or two, or maybe an ARV, in the vicinity until I call you afterward, I'd appreciate it. Just in case I've read it completely wrong and I do need to call the cavalry."

"No problem. Give me the address and the time."

Bronson read from the brief notes he'd made during his earlier conversation.

"Right," he finished, "I'll talk to you later today, once I leave the meeting. And it might be worth checking out who owns or rents that property."

"Already doing it," Curtis replied.

Ten minutes before the time specified, Bronson parked his Ford in a neighboring street, checked that the Llama was secure in his pocket and fully loaded, then climbed out of the car and walked along to the address he'd been given.

He was still about twenty yards away when the door of a dark gray Vauxhall saloon car swung open in front of him and John Eaton leaned out.

"Hop in, Chris, we're going for a ride," he said.

Bronson stared at him for a moment.

"I thought we were meeting in that house," he replied, pointing up the street.

Eaton shook his head. "No. Georg picked that address at random, just to provide a location where we could meet you. The meet's a couple of miles from here."

Bronson nodded. "Right. Well, no offense, John, but I'm not getting in the car with you, not after what happened at the warehouse. My car's parked about a hundred yards away. I'll go and get it, and then I'll follow you."

"Mike said you had to be in this car."

"You really think I give a toss what Mike says? No way am I getting in that car. You want me at a meeting, I'll drive there myself. If you don't like that, I'm walking away right now."

Eaton nodded in resignation. "Okay, if that's the way you want it. I'll stay here. What kind of car is it?"

"Blue Ford Focus, on a fifty-seven plate," Bronson told him. "I'll be no more than five minutes."

As soon as Bronson turned the corner and knew he was out of sight of Eaton's car, he pulled out his phone and called Curtis.

"Really quick," he said. "Forget that address because it's nothing to do with the group. They just picked it as a location for me to get to. I'm going to get my car and follow John Eaton to the actual site for the meeting. You've still got the GPS tracker on the Ford?"

"Yes, and I know that it's working."

"Good. Make sure you keep an eye on my position, and keep an ARV close behind me. And if I call this number but don't say anything, it'll be because it's all turning to rat shit and I need help, fast."

Bronson reached the Ford, unlocked it and dropped into the driver's seat.

"Right. I'm in the car and about to move off. Talk to you later."

"I hope so. I really hope so."

13

Eaton's estimate of a couple of miles wasn't too far out. Bronson followed about fifty yards behind the Vauxhall as Eaton threaded his way through the afternoon traffic. Their route was toward the east, through districts Bronson had never visited before, moving steadily away from the congestion of the city and deeper into the suburbs.

Eventually, Eaton turned into another small industrial estate—the group was obviously fairly consistent in its choice of rendezvous locations—and pulled up outside a unit that either had been abandoned early in the life of the estate or had simply never been used at all. It was impossible to tell which, and it really didn't matter.

Bronson pulled the car into a parking space on the cracked concrete forecourt of the unit. Grass and stunted weeds sprouted from the cracks, evidence of the time that had passed since the unit had last been occupied, by either builders or tenants. He climbed out of the vehicle and locked the doors. The GPS tracker unit, he knew, was powered directly from the battery, and had its own independent battery pack as a backup, so now that he had finally stopped moving, he assumed Curtis would already have passed his position to the crew of the Armed Response Vehicle he hoped had been tasked to follow him. He realized there were rather a lot of assumptions in his situation, and absolutely nothing he could do about any of them.

There were already half a dozen other cars occupying slots on the unit's forecourt, but as the commercial premises next door had a full car park, Bronson wondered if the vacant lot was simply used as an overflow car park by the people who worked there. Whatever the case, the presence of so many cars was a comfort, because that meant there had to be a number of people in the vicinity— inconvenient witnesses if the group intended to do him any harm.

The structure was typical of many small industrial units. There was a small door on the right-hand side beside a large window, perhaps intended for a receptionist, while the majority of the front of the building was occupied by a wide metal roller-shutter door, the opening big enough to allow a small truck to enter. The paint on both doors was faded white and peeling, and the window beside the office entrance was cracked in one corner. The whole building exuded an air of dereliction.

About halfway down the side wall of the building was another door, dark gray this time, already standing open, and Bronson spotted a set of keys in the lock. He took a last glance behind him, then followed Eaton inside and found himself in a short corridor with three doors—one at the end, which presumably led to the main open area of the unit, and the others on either side of the corridor, both of which obviously opened into internal offices. Bronson followed Eaton into the office on his left, and wasn't entirely surprised to see Mike leaning against the far wall, naked hostility radiating from him, and Georg sitting quite comfortably in the only chair in the room.

Georg glanced round the empty office. "I would ask you to sit down, but the facilities here are a little limited, so I'm afraid you'll have to stand. But this won't take long."

Bronson nodded, and mirrored Mike's pose, leaning against the wall beside the door.

"You bother me, Bronson," Georg began, "precisely because you used to be in the army and then, as we found out later, served as a police officer. The kind of people who follow that career path tend to have clear and rigid ideas about right and wrong. When John Eaton first told me about you, I was prepared to bet that you were working undercover, trying to infiltrate our organization, simply because you told him you'd been in the army. I assumed that your talk of vandalizing sites to do with the London Olympic Games was just a smokescreen, boastful bravado to hide your true purpose."

Bronson shrugged, uncomfortably aware of the accuracy of Georg's analysis.

"Not everyone in the army has a 'clear and rigid' concept of what's right or wrong," he replied, "and bent coppers aren't exactly a rarity."

"I know. And I saw the way you attacked that bulldozer. I watched the two videos—the one my man took and the one shown on Sky. It looked to me as if you were enjoying yourself, and you clearly did a good job on it, maybe even wrote it off, in fact. The way you did that didn't seem like you were an undercover cop trying to establish some credibility. There seemed to be real rage in what you did."

"I still don't trust the bastard," Mike growled from his perch against the wall.

"Shut up," Georg snapped, without even turning round, then turned his attention back to Bronson. "That, and the fact that you're walking around with an unlicensed pistol in your pocket, could mean that you're exactly who you say you are. But there's still a nagging doubt in my mind."

Bronson shrugged again. "That's your problem, not mine. You don't like me, you don't want me around, just say the word and I'll walk."

He took a couple of steps forward, then turned toward the door.

"I didn't say that," Georg murmured. "You still have the potential to be very useful to us. You've only recently left the police, so you'll know the kind of operations they'd be likely to mount against us. Information like that could be very valuable, and we'd pay well for it."

Bronson stopped in the doorway and looked back.

"How much?"

"That depends. First, we need to be sure about you, be certain that you won't betray us."

"Yeah? And how do you do that?"

Georg shook his head. "I won't. It's not my decision. Did you bring your passport?"

Bronson nodded and produced the document from his trouser pocket.

"Good. I don't need to see it, but you'll need it later today." Georg stood up and reached into his jacket.

Bronson tensed instantly, his right hand closing around the butt of the Llama. But Georg simply pulled out a thick buff envelope and tossed it across the room to him. Bronson caught it with his left hand, flicked up the flap with his thumb and glanced at the contents. Banknotes.

"There's one hundred pounds in twenty-pound notes in that envelope, plus five hundred euros. There's also a piece of paper with an address on it. It's in Berlin. They're expecting you by tomorrow evening. That should be enough for the ferry crossing, petrol, autobahn tolls and so on. If there's any change you can keep it."

"Hang on a minute," Bronson said. "Why the hell am I driving halfway across Europe? And who am I meeting in Berlin?"

Georg shook his head. "Berlin is hardly 'halfway across Europe,' Bronson. It's about a day and a half's drive from the French Channel ports, about twelve hundred kilometers or seven hundred and fifty miles, that's all."

"And I'm meeting who, exactly?" Bronson asked again.

"My colleagues. They want to see you, and then they'll decide if we want to involve you in what we're doing." Georg leaned forward, to emphasize what he was about to say. "Let me be frank, Bronson." He flicked a glance toward Mike. "Hiring muscle is easy. We pay them well, and they do as they're told. You're different. You've got brains as well as brawn, and your background and the knowledge you have would make you invaluable to our cause, and especially at the end."

"What do you mean, 'at the end'?" Bronson asked.

"That doesn't matter. All you need to know is that what we're doing now is just a prelude to the main event. A distraction, if you like. You'll be told exactly what we're doing once we're certain where your loyalties lie."

"And how are your colleagues going to establish that?" Bronson asked again.

Georg smiled for the first time since Bronson had walked into the disused office.

"I'm sure they'll find a way," he replied.

14

As he followed Eaton out of the office and walked down the short corridor, Bronson realized just how little he really knew about this group. They had already caused tens of thousands of pounds' worth of damage, killing a man in the process, and that, according to Georg, was simply a "distraction." Whatever the group's final aim, it could be catastrophic for London, something that could rival, maybe even surpass, the carnage caused by the suicide bombers who'd struck the city on "7/7."

And the only way he could find out what they intended was to do exactly what Georg had told him. He had to travel to Berlin and hope he'd be able to worm his way inside the group there. Handing Georg, Mike and Eaton to the police would achieve nothing useful. He had to wait until he knew far more before he could order an attack on them.

But as he reached the end of the alley between the two

adjacent buildings and was about to head across the fore-court toward his parked car, he saw something he really didn't like.

He watched an unmarked white Transit van turn into the entrance road to the industrial estate and then stop, the front of the vehicle pointing toward him. That wasn't unusual—vehicles of that sort were ten a penny through-out the area during the working day—but the wire mesh that covered the windscreen *was* unusual. The only group of people who routinely operated vehicles protected in that way, Bronson knew, were the police.

Something had gone wrong. Perhaps Curtis had mis-understood what he'd said, or maybe a more senior offi-cer had decided to take the opportunity to make an early arrest, despite what Bronson had told them. He didn't know, and it didn't matter. What was important was try-ing to retrieve the situation, because he had to get to Berlin, had to find out what the group was planning.

"John," Bronson said urgently, just as Eaton reached the end of the alley. "Back inside."

"What?"

"That's a police van. It's a raid."

Eaton followed Bronson's glance and nodded, then turned on his heels and swiftly retraced his steps.

"What is it?" Georg asked, as Eaton and Bronson stepped back into the office.

"There's a van-load of coppers outside," Eaton said urgently. "Chris spotted them."

"You mean he bloody brought them here," Mike shouted. "He's a plant—I told you that."

"If I brought them here, why the hell would I warn

you?" Bronson responded. "I don't know how they found the place. Maybe somebody in the unit next door recognized me or John and called the cops—our faces have been splashed all over the news. The how doesn't matter. What we have to do is get out of here."

"What will they do?" Georg asked, standing up. "How will they approach us?"

"That depends on what information they have. If they know we're in this building, they'll cover the exits, then use an enforcer—a battering ram—on one of the doors. Then they'll swarm inside. If they just followed my car or John's, then they won't have our precise location, and they may wait where they are until they spot one of us."

"So what do we do?"

"First we watch," Bronson replied, and stepped out of the inner door of the office into the open central area of the building. The floor was littered with debris, mainly small items but interspersed with a few empty cardboard boxes, while fluorescent light fittings were suspended from the ceiling, most of them missing their tubes.

Bronson strode over to the front office, beside the roller-shutter door. When he tried the handle, he found that the access door was locked.

"I don't have a key for that," Georg said from behind him.

"No problem."

Bronson took a step back, then kicked out hard with the sole of his right shoe. The blow connected with the internal door directly alongside the lock. The wood creaked, but didn't give, but on the second kick, the jamb splintered with a crack, and the door crashed open. He walked straight across to the window and peered out cautiously, keeping his body out of sight behind the wall that ran between the window and the outside door.

The white van didn't appear to have moved, and was still parked in the road, two shadowy figures faintly visible in the cab, but Bronson had no doubt there were at least half a dozen other officers sitting in the back of the vehicle waiting for the signal to disembark.

"What do we do?" Georg asked, for the second time. He sounded only mildly concerned. Mike, in contrast, was clearly very agitated.

"Come on, Mr. Ex-copper. Sort this out."

"I can't 'sort this out,' you idiot," Bronson snapped. "All I can do is try to work out how the hell we get out of here."

He turned away from the window.

"Yeah, well do that, then," Mike snarled.

Bronson ignored the remark and looked at Georg.

"Are you known to the police?" he asked. "I mean, if you stepped out of here and walked past that van, would anyone inside it recognize you?"

Georg shook his head. "No. As far as I know, I've never come to the attention of the authorities here."

"Good. That's something."

"They might know my face," Mike interrupted. "There've been cameras at some of the places we've hit."

"Brilliant," Bronson said, irritation lacing every syllable of the word. "So there's a good chance the three of us would be recognized." He paused for a moment, then glanced at his three companions. "The bad news is that there are probably eight officers in that van, maybe more," he said, "so there's no chance of us being able to fight our way past them. But unless there are other vans or cars parked out of sight, they've only got one vehicle here, and that gives us a chance. John and I came in separate cars. How did you two arrive?"

"Mike drove me," Georg replied.

"So we've got three cars. They can't follow all of us, so I suggest we scatter. Get to the vehicles and just go for it." He turned to Georg. "Have you got a key for the roller-shutter door?"

"It doesn't need one. It's bolted on the inside."

"Good, that means there's something else we can do. The police don't know you, you said, so you go outside, get into Mike's car and back it inside here when we open the main door. Then Mike can duck down in the back of it, or maybe get into the boot, so that he's out of sight, and you should be able to drive right past that police van. And while you're driving out of the estate here, the police will be looking at your car, hopefully, so they won't be watching this place. Then John and I will get outside to our vehicles and take our chances on the road."

It wasn't much of a plan, and Bronson knew it, but it was the best he could come up with in the circumstances.

"Good enough," Georg said, and turned to Mike. "Keys," he said shortly, and the big man pulled a bunch out of his pocket and handed them over.

As Georg walked out of the office, to leave the building by the side door, Eaton and Bronson crossed to the roller-shutter door and released the locking bolts. The moment they heard a car engine start outside, Bronson hauled on the chain that operated the door, and with a series of loud protesting creaks the metal shutter slowly began to rise.

As soon as the door was fully open, Georg backed the car inside the building, and climbed out of the car as the roller-shutter descended again. The vehicle was another Vauxhall saloon, the side windows slightly tinted.

"Boot or backseat?" Georg asked.

"I don't want to get in the boot," Mike said. "No way of getting out if there's a problem."

"I agree," Bronson said. "If you are stopped, for any reason, if you both run for it in different directions that'll split the police pursuit."

Mike nodded, opened the back door and climbed in.

"Crouch down on the floor, and don't look up as Georg drives past the van," Bronson instructed, and watched as Mike complied.

Bronson stepped back into the office and looked out of the window again. The police van still hadn't moved, and he wondered if they were just observing, or waiting for other vehicles to arrive.

As he stepped out of the office, he saw that Georg was already back in the driver's seat and just buckling his seat belt, the engine of the car still running. Bronson stepped over to the chain, gave Georg a thumbs-up, then pulled it down to start the roller-shutter door moving again.

Georg waved at the two men standing beside the door as he drove out of the building.

As soon as the car had left, Bronson lowered the door again, slammed the bolt into position, and strode back to the side corridor, Eaton following just behind him. They left the unit by the open door, and jogged down the alleyway at the side of the building, slowing as they approached the end, while they were still effectively invisible to the occupants of the white van, parked some seventy yards in front of them.

Then Bronson slowed his pace even further. He'd noticed something, something in the alleyway that was only now registering on his conscious mind.

The adjacent building was essentially a mirror image of the one he and the other men had just left, with a side entrance door. In fact, it was identical in most respects except for one thing. Perhaps because of what was stored in the other building, or the work that went on there, or maybe simply to protect the employees, a fire alarm system had been installed. And right next to the side door was the small red box that contained a manual alarm switch, tucked safely behind a sheet of glass.

"Let's see if we can cause a little confusion around here," Bronson muttered, a bleak smile on his face.

He strode back down the alleyway, took the Llama out of his pocket, reversed it so that he was holding the weapon by the slide, and smashed the butt into the glass.

Instantly, an atonic wailing filled the alleyway as the building's sirens screamed into action. And by the time Bronson had reached the front of the building again, all the doors on the front of the adjacent unit were open and men and women were streaming out, most of them glancing back at the structure, presumably looking for some evidence of what had triggered the alarm.

In moments, the forecourt was a mass of people milling around, some with their hands over their ears in an attempt to muffle the noise of the sirens. Others were running for their cars, clearly intending to move them away from the building in case the fire really took hold and spread outside the structure.

Bronson looked at the confusion and nodded in satisfaction.

"Okay, John," he said, "I'll go first. When we get out of here, turn left and keep your eyes open for me. I'll stop about a mile down the road. When you see me, stop the car because I'll need a ride." He checked the scene in front of him again. "Now we can go. And run, don't walk. You're worried about the fire, right?"

15

When the sirens were triggered by the fire alarm, Georg's car was already approaching the white van, driving along the exit road from the industrial estate. Bronson knew that the men in the cab of the van would be confused by what was going on. They'd be trying to study the car as it drew near them, and at the same time wondering what was happening in the industrial unit in front of them.

Bronson ran over to his car, unlocked it and started the engine. Then he dropped the driver's side window and put the Llama pistol on his lap. Despite the activity around him—several of the cars on the adjacent forecourt had already driven off, the drivers parking some distance away—he had a feeling he might have to use more than his natural charm to get past the parked vehicle. If Davidson had ordered the raid, which was the most logical explanation for what had happened, the officers in the van would at the very least know the make, model, color and registration number of the Ford, and they'd certainly stop him as he tried to leave. Or attempt to, anyway.

Bronson had hoped that some of the vehicles might have been driven out of the industrial estate, but that didn't seem to be happening, so the attention of the police officers was likely to be on his and Eaton's cars as they attempted to leave.

Eaton was just starting the engine of his car as Bronson drove off the industrial unit's forecourt and headed toward the exit road.

Ahead, he saw that Georg's car had already turned left onto the road outside the estate, so obviously the police officers hadn't spotted Mike in the back of the vehicle.

He accelerated toward the parked van, but even as he did so, the passenger-side door swung open and a black-clad figure emerged, wearing the kind of combat gear used by police assault teams, the word "POLICE" prominently displayed across his chest. The man strode around to the front of the van and waved his arms to attract Bronson's attention, then stepped directly in front of the Ford and held up his right hand.

Stopping wasn't any part of Bronson's plan, but clearly he couldn't drive over the officer. He veered left, away from where the man was standing, then braked hard and came to a standstill. He couldn't drive past the man—there was simply no room—but he knew he had to get away from the trading estate. If he was arrested, there was no chance of him finding out the group's hidden agenda.

So he had to do whatever was necessary to get away. He had to take the risk. And what he had in mind would, he guessed, cement his relationship with Georg and his colleagues.

The police officer nodded—perhaps he thought the driver had just seen his signal a little late—and started walking over toward Bronson's Ford. Then he stopped dead.

Bronson extended his right arm out of the car's window, took careful aim with the Llama, and pulled the trigger. The pistol jerked in his hand, the spent cartridge case spinning out of the breech and carving a transient golden arc in the afternoon sunshine. The right-hand-side front tire of the Transit blew with a satisfying bang, and the vehicle lurched to the right.

Bronson didn't wait. He'd disabled the police vehicle, and that was all he'd intended to do. He tossed the Llama onto the seat beside him and lifted his left foot off the clutch pedal, accelerating the car hard down the road. In his rear-view mirror he saw the rear doors of the Transit swing open and more police officers clamber out. But there was absolutely nothing they could do to catch him now.

But Bronson had no illusions about the efficiency of the Metropolitan Police. He'd burned his bridges when he waved the pistol, and destroyed them completely when he fired at the Transit van. By now, there'd be an alert out for his car, and because of the GPS tracker fitted to it, they would know exactly where to find it. That was why he'd told Eaton to pick him up. He would need to dump the car as soon as he could, before a couple of ARV gunships were vectored onto it.

Just over a mile down the road was a turnout, but

there were two cars already parked in it, and Bronson needed an absence of witnesses when he changed vehicles, so he drove on. He kept checking his rearview mirror, hoping for a sign of Eaton, but he couldn't see the other car. But the road was fairly busy and he guessed Eaton would be some distance back. He hoped he was somewhere behind him, anyway. If the man had been arrested by the police, or had forgotten what Bronson had told him and turned right, it would make everything a lot more difficult. Not impossible, but certainly very difficult.

Then he spotted another place where he could pull off the road. It wasn't a proper turnout, just a patch of rough ground on the left, barely large enough to accommodate more than a couple of vehicles. But it was ideal for what he wanted. There were no houses on either side of the road, so the only possible witnesses would be anyone driving past when he climbed into Eaton's car.

Bronson pulled off the road, the Ford bouncing over the rough ground, and stopped the car at the far side of the patch of earth. Then took out the mobile he'd been given by the police and removed the battery—he didn't want Curtis ringing him while he was sitting in the car beside Eaton and that also disabled any tracking chip the Met might have placed in the phone. He pocketed the Llama and his own mobile phone, checked he'd left nothing else in the vehicle, and got out of the car, watching out for John Eaton as he stepped closer to the road.

Every second car seemed to be a Vauxhall, and after three or four minutes Bronson started to worry that Eaton wouldn't appear, for whatever reason. But then he saw a car indicating left, and stepped out of the way as

Eaton swung the Vauxhall to a stop a few feet away from him.

Bronson waited a couple of seconds, until no other cars were passing, then walked over, pulled open the passenger-side door and sat down.

"Go, John," he instructed.

Eaton nodded, pulled the Vauxhall back onto the road and drove away.

"What took you so long?" Bronson asked.

"The bastards stopped me," Eaton explained. "They were right pissed off at what you'd done, and as soon as I drove up, they made me stop. I told them I'd been in the other building, the one where the fire alarm went off, and they couldn't prove that I wasn't, so they let me go. Checked all the documents, of course, but the car's straight, and I don't have a record or nothing, so there wasn't anything they could do. None of 'em recognized me from the TV, like." He paused and grinned at Bronson.

"Never thought you'd blow their tire like that. Bloody good shot."

"I didn't want to," Bronson replied, "but they were going to stop me as well, so I had no choice. If I'd stopped and they'd got a good look at me, I'd be in the slammer by now."

"And you had to dump the car because they'd seen you driving away in it?"

"Exactly. One of them would have got the number for sure, and there'll be an APW out for it by now, so I couldn't take the risk of driving it any longer than I had to."

"Your motor, was it?"

"Yeah," Bronson replied, "though I hadn't finished paying for it. I was going to sell it anyway, so it's not a great loss."

"And they'll know it was you in the car, waving that gun around?"

Bronson nodded. "The car was registered in my name, and I'd be amazed if one of them didn't recognize me."

"So now they'll be after you for firing a pistol at them, as well as the other charges?" Eaton indicated left and took the next turn, moving them away from the main road and the industrial estate.

Bronson nodded again. "You got it. I was aiming for the front tire of the van, obviously, but I've no doubt the Crown Prosecution Service could spin that into a charge of attempted murder if they wanted to. Then there's possession of a firearm, discharging a firearm in a public place, attempting to endanger life, malicious damage, failure to stop, evading arrest, and even littering because the pistol ejected the cartridge case onto the road. About the only charge they won't be able to stick me with is assaulting a police officer, because the cop who climbed out of the passenger door didn't come any closer when he saw the pistol. But the book, as they say, will be thrown at me.

"And all that lot does leave me with a problem," he continued. "I have to get to Berlin by tomorrow, and because of what's just happened my face'll be on a watch list at every port and airport and there'll be a stop order against my passport."

"How would the pigs know you were planning to leave the country?" Eaton asked.

"They wouldn't. It's just standard procedure, part of the All Ports Warning. So I'm going to need a new passport—or rather a different one—and a new set of wheels, preferably today, so you need to talk to Georg as soon as possible. Fill him in on what's happened and see what he can come up with."

"Right. I'll just put a bit of distance between us and the scene of the crime, so to speak."

That suited Bronson, and for the next fifteen minutes he sat in silence in the passenger seat as Eaton steered the Vauxhall down a succession of largely unmarked roads. He knew they were still somewhere in the tangle of suburbs that lay to the northeast of London, but exactly where, he had no idea. He just hoped that Eaton did.

"You know where we are?" he asked eventually.

Eaton nodded. "My old stamping ground," he said, "though it's changed a bit since I was a kid. We're on the edge of Epping Forest, near Loughton."

A couple of minutes later, Eaton pulled the Vauxhall off the road and into a long and wide turnout, in the middle of which stood a mobile canteen van, painted dark blue and with the legend "Joe's Lite Bite" written in somewhat shaky and uneven white letters on the side. He took out his phone and dialed.

Eaton's call was answered quickly, and he explained what had happened at the industrial estate after Georg and Mike had driven away.

"You should have seen it," Eaton said. "He pulled up

beside the coppers' van, stuck his pistol out of the window and shot off their front tire. Bloody marvelous."

"It was only one round from a twenty-two caliber pistol," Bronson pointed out. "Not the bloody Gunfight at the OK Corral."

"Anyway," Eaton continued, getting back to reality, "now he's got a problem because the pigs know he's carrying a weapon and he says there'll be a watch out for him at all the ports. So if you still want him to go to Berlin, we're going to have to find him a different passport and another car."

Eaton listened for a few moments, then spoke again.

"Yeah, but does he still have to go to Germany? I mean, after what he did today?"

Another silence, then Eaton glanced across at Bronson and nodded.

"Okay, I'll tell him. Where do you want to meet?"

Eaton ended the call and slipped the phone into the pocket of his leather jacket.

"Georg still wants you to go to Berlin. He said it's all set up. He'll sort out a passport—there are a couple of blokes in the group who look a bit like you, probably close enough for you to get out of the country—and he'll find you a car as well."

"We'll meet him, then?"

"Yes. Don't know where or when yet, but he'll call me back."

Bronson nodded. "So what do we do now?"

Eaton shrugged. "Georg said you should just keep out of sight."

"Right. Then you can do me a favor. My mobile's given up the bloody ghost, so can we drive to a shop somewhere so you can buy me a new one? Nothing fancy, just a cheap pay-as-you-go."

Eaton nodded. "Sure."

Twenty minutes later, Eaton walked out of a large newsagent on the outskirts of Epping carrying a plastic bag that bulged around the shape of the box inside it. He passed the bag to Bronson, who opened it and pulled out the box.

"I got you a car charger as well, just in case," Eaton said, pointing at the second, smaller packet that the bag contained.

"Thanks, John; good thinking."

Bronson opened the box and took out the basic Nokia it contained and plugged the car charger into the cigarette lighter socket to make sure the battery had a good charge before he started using it.

"There's thirty-five quid on the SIM," Eaton said. "The phone came with ten, but I asked the bloke in the shop to add on an extra twenty-five. Thought that would do you for a while. I've got a note of the number, as well, so we can reach you."

"Thanks again." Bronson reached into his pocket and took three twenty-pound notes out of the envelope Georg had given him. "There you go, John," he said, handing them over. "Thanks for the phone. And for picking me up. Been a bit poorly placed if you hadn't."

"No need for that," Eaton said, but Bronson insisted, thrusting the notes at him, and finally he took them.

"One last favor," Bronson said. "I'm staying here in Epping. Can you take me about a quarter of a mile down this street and then drop me off? I'll need to sort out my stuff for this trip to Germany. Then I'll be ready to go as soon as Georg does his bit."

16

22 July 2012

They'd followed the dark blue articulated truck ever since it had pulled out of the industrial park on the southern outskirts of Prague. Three cars, two men in each, swapping places at irregular intervals. It hadn't been a difficult task. The truck was simply too big, and too slow, to miss.

The complicated bit came after it had crossed the Czech Republic border near Waidhaus and headed west into Germany. The Germans knew they had two options: either they had somehow to divert the truck off the autobahn onto the quieter country roads or they had to wait until the crew stopped for fuel, or a break, or whatever. In the end, it proved to be easier than they'd expected.

A few kilometers to the west of the Schönschleif interchange, the truck had pulled into a service area. The three cars had followed, the drivers getting out and topping up their tanks just in case the truck pulled out again immediately. But it hadn't. After filling the tank with diesel, the driver of the truck had pulled away from the pumps and driven the vehicle over to the truck parking area, where he'd stopped and switched off the engine. Then he and his companion had climbed down from the cab, locked the vehicle and walked over to the cafeteria for a meal.

If the men in the cars had scripted the events themselves, it could hardly have worked out better for them. Forty minutes after the truck had pulled off the autobahn, it was on the move again, this time with two different men in the cab. The stiffening bodies of the original crew were locked in the cargo section behind, each wrapped in heavy-duty plastic sheeting sealed with tape, because it was important that the smell of decomposition shouldn't be detected for some time.

As they drove away from the service area, the passenger in the cab of the truck made a thirty-second phone call to a Berlin number to arrange the rendezvous for the next phase of the operation.

Six hours later, in a busy industrial park near Erfurt, where dozens of trucks arrived and departed every hour throughout the day and night, they made the switch, uncoupling the trailer from the Czech Republic truck and leaving it in a line of other unhitched trailers. Two hours after that, the sides of the trailer had a fresh coat of paint to conceal the original markings, and new heavy-duty padlocks had been fitted to all the external doors. It would be days, probably weeks, they hoped, before anybody took any interest in the vehicle.

One of the men attached the tractor unit to an entirely different trailer, which had been positioned in the park over two weeks earlier, the sides of which had already been painted with the appropriate logos, but which contained equipment of an entirely different nature to that loaded into the other trailer. It was now fitted with the registration plates from the Czech Republic trailer to complete the deception. The articulated truck drove out of the park as soon as all the phases of the operation had been finished, its route and destination preplanned and fully understood by all those involved.

It would actually take only a couple of days to make the journey, but the drivers knew they'd have to spend quite long periods parked en route because the arrival time had already been determined, and for several reasons it was very important that the vehicle didn't arrive too early or—far worse—too late.

17

Bronson didn't immediately walk toward the pub. He'd asked Eaton to drop him some distance away because he wanted to be sure that there were no nasty surprises waiting for him in or near the building. With both his own mobile and the phone Curtis had given him disabled, he was reasonably sure that the police wouldn't know where he was at that precise moment, and he'd never told Curtis or anyone else where he was staying.

But if there *was* a tracking chip in the police mobile, and the Met had been following his position over the last few days, it was possible that they could have worked out where he'd taken a room. So he wanted to be sure of the position before he opened his front door, and that meant checking that there were no surveillance units in the area. He hoped he'd be able to spot them—after all, he'd been involved in enough operations of that sort himself while he'd been in the force.

Then another thought struck him. An old trick, but it might work, or at least serve to muddy the waters a bit.

He glanced down the street. A bus was just approaching him, perhaps a hundred yards away, and there was a stop fairly close to where he was standing. He ambled across the pavement and joined the end of the short queue. While he stood there, he reinserted the battery in the police mobile, snapped on the back cover and switched it on.

When the phone played the slightly irritating melody to indicate that it was working, the elderly lady directly in front of him swung round to stare at him in a hostile manner. Bronson shrugged and smiled at her, and she turned away again.

He accessed the menu system and selected "silent" for incoming calls and texts. That suited him perfectly.

When the bus arrived, Bronson bought a ticket and then moved to the back of the vehicle, to an area where no other passengers were sitting. He sat down, then bent forward and felt under the seat. There was some kind of a mesh under the seat itself, and metal struts forming the frame. On one side was a kind of pocket formed by the base of the frame; it was just about the right size. He checked that nobody was watching, then bent forward again, slipped the phone into the space and sat back up. A cleaner or somebody would eventually find it, he supposed, and if the bus braked hard it might well fly out and clatter across the floor, but he really didn't care what happened to it. If there was a tracking chip inside it, that would divert police resources away from where he would actually be.

He got off at the next stop and walked back in the direction the bus had come from, back toward his lodging. There was a small café, more accurately a greasy spoon, about two hundred yards away from the pub and on the opposite side of the road. Bronson walked inside, picked a table right beside the window, which offered a clear view down the street, and ordered a coffee and a slice of Madeira cake, which looked like the safest thing on the menu. Then he settled down to watch.

Half an hour later, he stood up and walked out. He'd seen no sign of anything that looked even slightly like a surveillance operation. In fact, the only sign of a police presence at all was a patrol car that had driven slowly down the road after he'd been sitting at his table for about ten minutes. That didn't bother him, because he supposed the street was a part of a regular police patrol route. But he'd seen no parked vans—or none that didn't stop, load or unload something and then drive away again—and no indication at all that the pub was the subject of anyone's scrutiny but his own. But still Bronson was cautious. He walked past the pub on the opposite side of the road, checking everywhere as he did so, then crossed the street lower down and headed back the way he'd come. And again he saw nothing suspicious.

Then he walked steadily around to the rear entrance of the building, a part of the pub that wasn't overlooked from any of the adjacent buildings or any possible vantage point that he could identify, opened the door and stepped inside. He walked quickly up the stairs to his room, unlocked the door and stepped inside, relocking the door behind him.

The room was untouched, as far as he could tell. It took him only about ten minutes to pack all his possessions into a soft-sided bag fitted with a long shoulder strap. Then he walked down the steps and out of the back door. He'd paid for a week in advance, so there was no need for him to see the landlord or any of his staff, and he wouldn't have done so anyway, precisely because of the publicity he'd had. To be recognized by one of the bar staff and arrested in the pub would have comprehensively ruined his plans.

So he slipped away quietly, out of the back door and away down the street.

Epping lies at the edge of the forest of the same name, and he had no trouble finding an open area where he would easily see anyone approaching. There were a couple of wooden benches on one side, and he strode over to the nearest one and sat down.

Bronson still had two mobiles: his personal phone and the new cheapie Eaton had bought for him. He daren't use his own phone because there was a good chance the Met would have obtained the number by now, so he took out the chip and worked it between his fingers until it cracked in two, then discarded it in a nearby rubbish bin, along with the phone itself. He'd planned to buy himself a new one anyway. Then he took the new mobile out of his pocket, checked the settings to ensure that his number wouldn't be displayed on the recipient's phone, and then called Angela.

He was feeling more than a little guilty. For the last month, they'd been talking about taking a holiday while the Olympic Games were being held in London, on the reasonable grounds that the capital would be hell on wheels during that period, and neither of them had the slightest interest in any form of organized sport. Angela had to work in London—she was a ceramics conservator at the British Museum—and the prospect of battling not only the regular London traffic and pedestrians but also the anticipated tens of thousands of spectators for the Games had been moderately daunting.

They'd discussed going abroad—any country would do, but France or Italy seemed to have risen to the top of the list—and just sitting in the sun by the sea and doing pretty much nothing. It was an enticing prospect, and Bronson had been on the point of making the booking when his superior had given him the bad news about his secondment to the Metropolitan Police.

Bronson and Angela had had a short and somewhat stormy marriage, and their separation and divorce had been almost entirely Bronson's fault. The reason for their breakup had been a classic romantic novelist's cliché, but like all clichés it was both common and fundamentally true: Bronson had actually been in love with Jackie Hampton, his best friend's wife. Or at least, he thought he had been. But then Jackie had been killed—murdered, in fact—in Italy and since then Bronson had been doing his best to convince Angela that they should be together again. He'd also come to the conclusion that his feelings for the dead woman might have been, at least in part, simply a desire for the unattainable, though he also realized that could have just been him trying to rationalize his conflicting emotions.

Angela, quite understandably, was very cautious about committing herself again, and she had told him she intended to take things slowly this time, to wait and see what the future held for them both. Bronson was quite certain about her feelings for him—he knew that she loved him, that she had always loved him—but he was also keenly aware that she couldn't stand the thought of being hurt again if he suddenly switched his affections elsewhere. Not that that was going to happen, Bronson was positive. So they had spent a lot of time together while she tried to come to a decision.

They had been very close over the last few months, and Bronson had already decided that it was the right time to propose to her again, although he still wasn't sure what her answer would be. He had hoped that a holiday would help Angela clarify her thoughts, but obviously that wasn't going to happen.

"Hi," Bronson said, as soon as she answered.

"You've been on TV," she replied immediately. "And not in a good way. What the hell's going on, Chris?"

"I can't explain it right now, but it's all a part of this undercover operation they've shoved me into."

That statement had the benefit of being almost true, as long as you excluded the most recent events from the explanation.

"You might even see more stuff about me over the next few days," Bronson went on, "but none of it will necessarily be true. Now, as part of this, I've got to go away for a day or two."

"Where to?"

"Germany, actually."

"Germany? Why? I thought this operation was something to do with the Olympics?"

"It is, kind of, but it would take too long to tell you about it. I've got to go to a meeting in Berlin."

Bronson paused for a moment, choosing his next words with some care.

"There's something else," he said. "You might be contacted by the Metropolitan Police about me, asking if you know where I am. Don't tell them anything. Just say you haven't seen me for several days."

Angela snorted. "That's not a problem, because I haven't seen you, not for about two weeks. But why would they talk to me? Surely they know where you're going and what you're supposed to be doing?"

"Not all of them, no. This operation has been cleared at the highest level, but to maintain security they're going to treat me as a wanted man, so the police in London will be looking for me. It'll all help to establish my cover."

That sounded almost believable, but Bronson doubted if Angela bought it for a second. And her next words proved it.

"You're in trouble, aren't you?" she said.

"Only a little," Bronson replied reluctantly. "And I really can't tell you any more at the moment. As soon as I have a better idea what's going on, I'll let you know."

"Promise?"

"I promise."

"Good," Angela said. "I'll hold you to that. And be careful. I worry about you."

Bronson ended the call and then dialed the number he'd memorized: the number for Bob Curtis's mobile.

"What?"

"Hi," Bronson said.

"Where the hell are you? We've been trying to reach you for hours."

"I'm sure you have."

"What number are you calling from?"

"That doesn't matter," Bronson said. "Have you got anything to tell me?"

There was silence for a moment, and when Curtis spoke again, his voice sounded almost resigned.

"I suppose you mean why did a van-load of coppers turn up at your meet?"

"Sounds like a good place to start."

"Look, you know the way the system works. The sergeants tell the constables what to do, and the inspectors take the credit, just like any other big organization, right?"

"Yeah. Oh, and just so you know, I'm in a bus, so there's no point in trying to triangulate where this call's coming from."

"I wasn't." Curtis sounded indignant. "Anyway, chain of command and all that, so I had to keep Shit Rises informed. After your last call, I told him what you'd said, specifically that you'd blow the whistle if you needed close support, and he decided it was a good time to roll up the group."

"Just like that, despite what I'd said?"

"Just like that. He even called it an 'executive decision,' the pretentious prat. He forbade me from telling you what he'd planned, because he wanted your reaction to be natural when our blokes hit the meeting. The team used the GPS tracker to follow your car, but when they got to the site they didn't know which building you were in, and that was why they were still waiting on the road when you drove out. I did try calling your mobile to warn you, but you never answered."

"It was switched off," Bronson replied. "I didn't want it ringing when I was talking to those people and having to explain who was calling me."

"Right," Curtis said. "Well, you may not need to explain anything to them, but now you sure as hell need to explain things to us. Why the gun? Where did you get it? And why the hell did you fire it at those coppers?"

"Lots of questions."

"Yeah, and I'm hoping for lots of answers. Good, solid, honest answers."

"First, I didn't fire it at anyone. I shot out the front tire on that van just so I could get away from the industrial estate. Nobody was in any danger, and it cemented my relationship with the group, that's for sure."

"That's one point of view, certainly. Unfortunately, Shit Rises has a rather different slant on what happened. He thinks you've gone renegade, some kind of odd variation of Stockholm syndrome. There's a warrant out for your arrest—a real warrant, not something intended to help build your cover—and it's gone countrywide. With your picture plastered all over Sky News, and every copper in Britain with a copy of your photograph, you've got no place to hide."

Bronson felt a cold shiver pass down his back. Despite what he'd told Eaton and Georg, he had hoped that he would have been able to continue what he was doing with official support.

"That's bloody ridiculous, and you know it."

"What you know and I know won't make any difference," Curtis replied. "Davidson has made the decision,
and he's sticking with it. He figured you'd probably call
in, and I've been ordered to pass you the official line: you
should surrender yourself and the weapon—I gather it's
only a twenty-two-caliber pistol—to any police station.
The fact that you were operating undercover will be a
mitigating circumstance at your trial, but I think you can
be certain that your career as a police officer is over as of
now."

Bronson was silent for a few seconds, his mind racing.
He tried one last appeal.

"Listen, Bob, you know as well as I do that that's not
going to happen. If I was going to turn myself in, I'd make
bloody sure the weapon never saw the light of day. There
are a thousand ways I could lose it—even if I chucked it
into a skip you'd never find it—and any halfway competent
defense barrister would be able to convince a jury that
there was no proof I'd ever had possession of it, or that I
was the person who fired the shot."

"What you've just said is almost an admission of guilt.
How do you know I'm not taping this call?"

"Taping a mobile isn't as easy as taping a landline
phone. That's why I called you on this number. And it
probably wouldn't be admissible as evidence in a trial
anyway. So are you taping it?"

"No," Curtis conceded.

"Good. Now listen. I still think this group is just a
front for something else, something much more deadly.
If I can just have a few more days, I'm certain I'll be able
to find out what it is."

"You're back on that conspiracy theory kick, Chris, and it won't wash. I ran it by Davidson, put the best spin on it I could. No dice. Because of what happened today he thinks you're just trying to save your own skin by inventing some kind of a terrorist plot. Take my advice. Get rid of the pistol, yeah, that's a good idea, but if you walk into a police station of your own free will that'll help your case. If we find you and arrest you, that'll be completely different."

"You know I won't do that."

"I didn't think you would, but I had to tell you. You'll do what you have to do, I guess. Oh, I presume you've picked up a different mobile, which is a good idea. There's a tracking chip on the motherboard of the one we gave you, so I suggest you lose it."

"Gosh, I wish I'd thought of that," Bronson said, and rang off.

18

Ten minutes after he ended the call to Bob Curtis, Bronson had watched two police cars traveling at speed down the main road through Epping, blues and twos on, following the same route as the bus he'd taken about an hour earlier. He guessed that the driver and passengers on the vehicle were about to have a fairly interesting encounter with the thin blue line.

John Eaton rang about half an hour after that, by which time Bronson had moved to an entirely different location in the town, staying off the main streets as much as possible.

"Where are you?"

Bronson had already noted the name of the street he was closest to, which was just off the main road. "Epping. North end of the town," he said, "near the main drag. Where do you want me to be?"

"That'll do," Eaton replied. "I'll be there in ten minutes. Same car. Watch out for me."

"Got it."

Bronson waited seven minutes by his watch, then got up from the bench he was sitting on and covered the short distance to the main road. There was a fairly long and relatively straight length of road in front of him, and he reckoned he'd see the Vauxhall easily as it approached.

As it turned out, Eaton drove along the road almost by himself, a white van about fifty yards in front, and only a lone motorcyclist following behind him. The moment Bronson saw him, he stepped to the edge of the pavement, waited for the car to stop and climbed in.

Eaton pulled smoothly away from the curb.

"Any problems?" he asked.

Bronson shook his head. "Nobody took any notice of me," he said. "Just shows the power of TV advertising. Maybe a dozen people looked right at me, but none of them recognized me."

"Bloody good thing, too. Right, with any luck you'll be on the road in half an hour. Georg has sorted out a car for you, and he's got a couple of passports as well."

"Genuine ones? Because when I get to Dover they'll probably scan it, and a fake'll show up immediately."

"As far as I know they're the real deal, but you'd better ask him yourself."

Fifteen minutes later, Eaton pulled the Vauxhall to a stop on a concrete drive outside a very ordinary semi-detached house, a typical three-bed, two-recep, large garden, deceptively spacious, early viewing recommended, so beloved of estate agents everywhere.

It wasn't exactly the kind of place Bronson imagined Georg using, but he supposed it was the sort of location the German would occupy briefly and then move on. Maybe it belonged to one of the members of the group, or perhaps they'd rented it for a month or so to use as a safe house.

As the two men approached the front door, painted classic suburban blue with a large brass knocker in the shape of a dolphin, it opened and Mike peered out.

"You made it, then," he said, his tone suggesting that he, personally, would rather Bronson hadn't gotten away, or was at the very least indifferent to his fate.

"Looks like it."

Mike stepped back and Bronson walked in, closely followed by Eaton. There was a narrow hallway, a staircase with a wooden handrail ascending on one side, and three doors opening off it. The nearest one stood open and as he stepped forward Georg appeared and beckoned him inside.

The room was a lounge, white paintwork and magnolia walls, a settee and a couple of easy chairs in cream leather the principal furnishings. A wide-screen plasma TV dominated the far wall, a Sky box sitting on a shelf underneath it, alongside a DVD player. Below that was a gas-effect electric fire where fake flames flickered slightly, though the heating elements weren't switched on.

"Eaton explained what happened at the industrial estate," Georg said. "Thank you for your quick thinking, and for what you did to get the two of you past the police van."

"It was self-interest as much as anything," Bronson

replied. "If they'd managed to make me stop, I knew what would happen to me."

"Well, thank you anyway. Now . . ." Georg turned away and picked up a couple of British passports that lay on the glass-topped coffee table in front of the fire. "Two members of the group bear a slight resemblance to you, and have agreed to loan me their passports."

"For a fee, presumably?" Bronson asked.

Georg smiled at him. "This lot don't do anything unless they get paid," he said.

He handed the passports to Bronson, who opened both at the page showing the holder's photograph and studied each in turn. Georg was quite right. Superficially, there was a resemblance, in that both men were about Bronson's age, roughly his height and had dark hair, but in truth neither man looked very much like him.

"Would one of those do?" Georg asked, sounding slightly worried.

Bronson nodded slowly. "The checks at Dover—when they bother doing them at all—are really designed to check the validity of the passports being presented. There's only the most superficial attempt to ensure that the person presenting the passport is the same as the man or woman whose picture is in it. So my guess is that either of these would probably do." He looked at the two documents again, then made his decision.

"I'll take this one," he said. "He's a couple of years older than I am, but I think he looks more like me than the other guy. I'll memorize the information on that page before I get to Dover. John said you had a car for me as well."

Georg nodded. "In fact, I have two, registered to the owners of these two passports. To keep things simple, I suggest you take the vehicle owned by"—he glanced at the name inside the passport Bronson was still holding—"Charlie Evans. It's parked a few meters up the road. It's a gray Hyundai. The registration number's on the label attached to the key ring."

Georg reached into his pocket and produced two sets of car keys, and handed one to Bronson.

"The tank's full, and there's a Green Card in the glovebox to cover you for driving in Europe. Charlie would appreciate the return of the car in one piece."

"I'll do my best."

Georg slipped the other set of keys back into his pocket, then took a folded sheet of paper from another pocket and handed it to Bronson. "This is the rendez-vous," he said. "It's a few kilometers south of Berlin, but it should be easy to find. You need to be there by seven tomorrow evening. Don't have your pistol or mobile with you at the meeting, because they'll be taken away from you. Any questions?" he asked.

Bronson shook his head. "No. I'll get on the road."

"One suggestion before you leave. The pictures that were broadcast on television showed you with an un-shaven face and the beginnings of a beard. You might be less recognizable if you were clean-shaven. You can use the bathroom upstairs if you want to do something about it."

"That's a good idea." Bronson picked up his soft bag and headed for the stairs.

He was down again in less than ten minutes, and sitting in the front seat of the Hyundai three minutes after that.

The car was about three years old, judging by the registration plate, and it was immediately clear that Charlie Evans was a heavy smoker. The ashtray overflowed with cigarette ends, and the entire car smelled of tobacco smoke. It was the kind of rank odor that Bronson knew no amount of cleaning would ever entirely shift. He opened the two front windows as he drove away, which helped a little, and as soon as he found a quiet spot he stopped the car and dumped the contents of the ashtray on the ground.

While the car was stationary, he also checked the trunk, making sure that there was a spare wheel, jack and wheelbrace. In the glovebox, as Georg had promised, there was a Green Card insurance document and also a satnav unit. That would make things a lot easier. Bronson knew the way to Dover, having made the Channel crossing many times before, but he'd never driven anywhere in Germany.

He attached the sucker to the windscreen, plugged the charging cord into the cigarette lighter, and clipped the satnav unit into the holder. He switched on the unit and the software asked him to select the appropriate country, so it obviously had European mapping included.

Bronson nodded in satisfaction, chose the United Kingdom and settled for the Dover ferry port. He'd input the address in Germany once he reached the other side of the Channel. The female voice in the unit sounded disconcertingly like one of his teachers from years ago, but otherwise he didn't think he'd have any problems with the satnav.

He picked up the M25 within a few minutes, drove around it until he reached the junction with the M2 motorway signposted to Dover, and then turned east. He had no ferry ticket, of course, but he knew he could buy one for cash on arrival at the port.

Just over two and a half hours after unlocking the doors of the Hyundai, he switched off the engine on the car deck of a P&O ferry, locked the vehicle and followed a crowd of people heading for the stairs. He'd grab a bite on the ferry, he decided, and that would set him up for the first part of the drive he had in front of him.

But at least he'd gotten out of Britain with no problems. As he'd expected, the officer behind the glass of the booth had barely even glanced at him, just scanned the passport, handed it back and then told him to carry on. And the French immigration post a few yards further on was completely deserted, as usual.

So now he was on his own. Sitting in a quiet corner of the restaurant, Bronson stared out of the window at the choppy gray waters of the English Channel and ran over the events of the last few days in his mind. What had started out as a fairly simple infiltration operation, just a matter of him identifying a group of violent vandals who'd been causing such aggravation in East London, had turned into something much darker and more dangerous. The death of the nightwatchman had been unfortunate, but probably accidental, a question of manslaughter, not murder, and Bronson was reasonably certain that it had been Mike and some of his cronies who had attacked the man.

With hindsight, maybe Bronson should simply have given them up to the Met as soon as he'd gotten a few names and memorized their faces. But he had been seriously disturbed by the man who called himself Georg, a man who seemed as wholly out of place in the group as a piranha in a tank of goldfish. He was clearly working to a very different agenda, and Bronson knew without a shadow of a doubt that he was extremely bad news. Bronson had never been directly involved in an operation against terrorists, but he had read enough about the kind of people who moved in that world to recognize the threat, and the type.

His biggest problem had been the complete absence of any form of proof that he could offer about what Georg was planning. That, and the autocratic attitude of Inspector Davidson, of course. If Shit Rises hadn't decided to ignore what Bronson had said and roll up the undercover operation so quickly, there would at least have been a chance that Bronson could have gone to Berlin, obtained whatever information he could, and that might have led to the capture of the entire gang before they could complete their operation.

As it was, Bronson had been abandoned—or actually rather worse than that—by the British police. He was armed only with a pistol that most people familiar with handguns would consider a joke rather than a serious weapon, and he was on his own, heading for a rendezvous with a group of people he knew nothing about, except that he was quite certain they posed a mortal danger to London and its citizens.

It was not, on the whole, a comfortable position to be in.

19

Klaus Drescher ended the call on his mobile phone and looked across at Wolf with a satisfied expression on his face.

"The pieces are coming together precisely as we planned it, Marcus. That was Lutz, the leader of the group from the Czech Republic. There were no problems in the substitution of the two vehicles, so now the device is on its way to London with all the correct documentation. I've reminded him of the importance of the timing, and he and his team will get the vehicle across to the Calais area fairly quickly, and then wait there for the optimum time to cross the Channel. Even then, they'll still have time in hand, and will be able to park on the road between Dover and London to ensure that they arrive precisely when we want them to."

Wolf nodded, and glanced down at the screen of the laptop computer that was open on the table in front of him.

"Excellent," he said. "Now, before you leave, there's one other matter you need to be aware of. I've received another e-mail from Georg in London. As we discussed, he's sending this former policeman—Bronson—to see us here. He thinks he might be useful to us because of his knowledge of British police tactics and so on. I'm not convinced, but I do respect Georg's judgment."

"That has worried me ever since Georg mentioned it," Drescher replied. "I gather that Bronson was an army officer before he joined the police force, and that implies that he might have a strong loyalty to his native land. If he somehow managed to find out exactly what we are intending to do, I'm convinced that he would go to the authorities."

"Then we have to make sure that he doesn't find out," Wolf said. "And we also need to establish such a strong hold over him that he would find it impossible to tell anybody about us."

"How can you do that?"

Wolf smiled, but it was the kind of smile that conveyed no amusement whatsoever, only cruel anticipation.

"I think I know a way that we can do so. In fact, I think I can provide a foolproof guarantee that he will do exactly what we tell him, when we tell him."

"How?" Drescher asked again.

"Trust me on this, Klaus. I will brief my men here to check him at the rendezvous and ensure that he is unarmed and not wearing any kind of transmitter. You arrange for everyone else to come here tomorrow evening, to arrive no later than seven o'clock. Then we will all see what this man Bronson is like, and you will be able to satisfy yourself that we have him entirely within our power before he leaves here."

"And if we're not satisfied? If your guarantee somehow fails to work?"

Wolf smiled again.

"Then the Englishman will leave this house feetfirst, and we will dump him somewhere in the forest. We've come too far in this operation for there to be any doubts, any doubts at all, about the final phase. If Bronson won't join us, then he will die. It's as simple as that."

20

23 July 2012

Bronson pulled into the station car park at Rangsdorf, about twenty miles south of the center of Berlin, at twenty past six the following evening. The town was probably a good location for a rendezvous, being easy to find even for a stranger, and very close to the Berliner Ring, the city's ring road, which offered easy access to the autobahn system. And the station car park was also a good choice, with plenty of parking spaces when Bronson arrived. He guessed that most of the vehicles belonged to local residents who commuted into Berlin; by the time of the rendezvous—seven o'clock—the area would be almost deserted.

He was right. The car park emptied around Bronson as men and women emerged from the railway station, climbed into their cars and drove away, and by six forty-five there were only a handful of vehicles left.

At six fifty, two cars—both dark-colored BMWs—

drove into the car park and stopped, one at either end, their occupants remaining inside the vehicles. Watchers, Bronson presumed, there to make sure that the meeting would be neither observed nor interrupted. It looked to him as if there were at least two men in each of the cars. He guessed they already knew he was there, because his was the only vehicle in the place with British registration plates.

Precisely at seven o'clock, another car, this one a light gray Mercedes saloon, entered the car park and stopped in a space close to Bronson's car. For a few seconds, there was no movement from any of the new arrivals, then both front doors of the Mercedes opened. Two heavily built men got out and strode across to Bronson's vehicle.

As they approached, Bronson climbed out and stood waiting.

The two men stopped a couple of paces away, motioned him to take a step forward, and then to lift his arms up to shoulder level. Bronson complied, and one of the men stepped behind him and expertly frisked him. Then the man opened Bronson's jacket, checked the inside pockets and then his shirt, presumably to make sure he didn't have a miniature microphone taped to his skin.

"I'm not wearing a wire, and I'm not armed," Bronson said, assuming the men would speak English.

The second man nodded. "We still have to check. Nothing personal."

Then the searcher stepped away from Bronson and nodded.

"So far, so good, Mr. Bronson. You're in the right

place at the right time, and you seem to have followed Georg's orders accurately. Welcome to Berlin."

"Thanks. What now?"

"Now we take you somewhere else." He gestured to the Mercedes. "Get in the car," he said.

Bronson looked at the two men, now standing side by side near the car, and shrugged. He didn't like the idea of getting into the Mercedes with two men he was quite sure were armed and extremely dangerous, but he had no option. Or, rather, the only options he had were either to go with them or to get back in his car and return to Britain and whatever uncertain welcome might be waiting for him there.

So it wasn't really a choice. He was certain, beyond a reasonable doubt, that these men were involved in something deeply, deeply dangerous and injurious to his native land, some kind of a terrorist act, and whatever happened he was determined to stop them, or at the very least find out enough about their plans to pass on the information to somebody who *could* stop them.

"Okay," he said, walking over to the Mercedes. "You'll bring me back here later?" he asked.

"That depends on what happens."

It wasn't quite the reassurance Bronson had been hoping for, but it was too late to argue.

"In the front seat," he was instructed.

Bronson changed direction slightly, pulled open the front passenger door of the car and sat down. One of the men took the backseat directly behind him, and the other got into the driver's seat. The man in the back reached over Bronson's shoulder and handed him a pair of sun-glasses with black, impenetrable wraparound lenses.

"Put these on, and make sure you keep them on."

"No problem," Bronson said.

With the sunglasses in place, Bronson could see almost nothing; obviously the lenses had been treated somehow to make them virtually opaque. The interior of the Mer-cedes was barely visible, and the view outside the win-dows was completely obscured.

The driver started the car and slipped it into "drive," and moments later the vehicle began to move forward. With his eyes essentially useless, Bronson tried to use his ears to work out where the car was going, though he real-ized this was a fruitless exercise unless the vehicle hap-pened to drive past some local feature that emitted a really distinctive sound. But there was one thing he could do. Although the sunglasses obscured his vision ahead, the lower part of the lenses didn't quite touch his face, and there was a thin sliver between the glasses and his cheek that was unobstructed, and that was just wide enough for him to be able to look down and see his watch.

He noted the time: nine minutes past seven. When they finally stopped, he would at least know how long the journey had taken, and that would provide a rough search area, though, of course, the longer the drive, the larger that area would become.

Bronson remembered the route he had taken to get to the rendezvous position, and at first he believed they were retracing his steps, but when they reached the Ber-liner Ring they turned right not left, and from that point on he had no idea where he was going. Judging solely by the sensation of speed in the Mercedes, he guessed that for some time the car stayed on the autobahn, but he didn't know if they were still somewhere on the Berlin ring road or had turned off it.

Just over thirty minutes after the journey had started, he knew he'd been right, as the big saloon car slowed down virtually to a walking pace, and he caught just the briefest glimpse of the shadow of a barrier lifting ahead of the Mercedes, which meant they'd just passed through a toll booth. And because they hadn't come to a complete stop, he guessed the car was equipped with one of the electronic devices that recorded the date, time and place where the vehicle entered and left the toll road system. That might be a helpful piece of information to identify where he was being taken, and he memorized the exact time on his watch.

After that, the vehicle drove for a further fifteen minutes or so on the normal roads, negotiating roundabouts and stopping at traffic lights, and then finally came to a halt. The noise of the engine echoed strangely as the car slowed down, and Bronson was aware of a sudden darkness outside the windows. He wondered if the Mercedes had been driven into a garage or a warehouse, or something of that sort. He glanced down again at his watch, and memorized that time as well.

The doors opened and the other occupants of the vehicle stepped out.

"We're here," one of them said, and tugged on Bronson's arm to show that he should get out of the car.

As Bronson complied with the instruction, he heard a

banging sound from somewhere behind the Mercedes, and guessed that the outer doors of whatever building they were in were just being closed.

"You can take off the glasses," he was ordered.

Bronson slipped the glasses into the breast pocket of his jacket and looked around. It wasn't a warehouse—which he supposed made a change after his recent experiences—but a large garage, perhaps forty feet long by thirty wide, with four other vehicles parked neatly against one wall. It obviously wasn't a public parking facility, and he guessed that it was either part of the customer parking area of a commercial garage or maybe even a garage for a company or a large private house. The floor was concrete, painted light gray, while the walls and ceiling were made of the same material but painted white. Fluorescent lights were evenly spaced across the ceiling, and provided stark illumination.

He glanced behind him and saw that one of the two BMWs from the station rendezvous had followed them into the garage and had parked directly behind the Mercedes. Two men had just climbed out of it, and one of them was aiming a remote control at a pair of wide metal doors through which the vehicles must have driven. The second door was just swinging closed. At the other end of the open space another metal door, presumably a fireproof door, was set into the wall between two of the parked cars.

"This way."

The man opened the fire door and led the way down a short passage, again fabricated from concrete, painted white and lit by another pair of fluorescent ceiling lights.

At the end was a small lobby, a concrete staircase as-

cending on the left-hand side, while on the right were the
unmistakable steel doors of a lift. The man walked across
to the control panel and pressed one of the buttons,
which immediately illuminated. Bronson heard the sound
of an electric motor, and a few seconds later the doors slid
to one side to reveal the interior of a small lift, probably
intended to hold only five or six people. The three of
them stepped inside it, and moments later the doors slid
closed and the lift began to go up.

Bronson guessed they'd only ascended perhaps two or
three floors when the lift stopped and the doors opened
again.

They stepped out into another small lobby, about the
same size as the one they'd just left, but that was where
the resemblance ended. This room was paneled in
wood—Bronson thought it might be mahogany, but he
frankly didn't know—with a thick carpet on the floor and
a high ceiling featuring ornate cornices and a single crys-
tal chandelier in its center. A handful of easy chairs were
dotted about the room, perhaps so that people waiting
for the lift would have somewhere to sit. Opposite the lift
was a short flight of steps, at the top of which two tall
wooden double doors stood open, and beyond them another room beckoned.

The man who seemed to be in charge led the way up
the stairs and through the doors. The new room was
much larger than the lobby, about three times its size, but
shared the same ornate decoration and comfortable-
looking furniture. Three chandeliers cast a clear light over
the room, which reminded Bronson of pictures he'd seen
of Victorian withdrawing—the name later shortened just

to "drawing"—rooms, with easy chairs grouped around low tables where people could gather after formal dinners and enjoy a coffee or a liqueur.

He wasn't sure what he'd been expecting, but it certainly wasn't this. He could have been a guest in a country mansion somewhere in England, rather than in a house—he assumed that's where he was—on the outskirts of the German capital.

"Good evening, Mr. Bronson," a cultured voice said from somewhere in the room, the greeting sounding uncannily similar to the way the villain always seemed to address the hero in the James Bond films. The man's German accent was unmistakable, but his English was perfectly understandable.

Bronson looked around, and as he did so a slight individual, probably no more than five feet seven or eight, and with a very slim build, stood up from an easy chair a few feet away. He was wearing an immaculately tailored dark brown suit and gleaming black shoes. He had a fair complexion, his hair an indeterminate shade of blond, and very blue eyes. Bronson estimated the man's age at something over fifty, though he guessed he could easily be ten years out either way. But the overwhelming impression was one of youth. Somehow he seemed much younger than he looked.

The man stepped forward briskly to where Bronson was standing and extended his hand.

"My name is Marcus," he said, giving Bronson's hand a vigorous shake, "and Georg has told me quite a lot about you. He said you'd actually shot your way out of a police ambush. Not the sort of behavior one would expect to witness in the Home Counties, Mr. Bronson, but perhaps indicative of the kind of man you seem to be. Georg was very impressed."

Bronson shook his head slightly. "It was actually a lot less dramatic than it sounds," he replied. "All I did was shoot out one of the tires of the police van, just to immobilize it."

Marcus looked at him for a moment, then smiled slightly. "If you say so," he replied. "Anyway, Georg seems to be quite satisfied that you are who you say you are, but for me there's still something of a question mark above your head. As you might have guessed, our organization operates below the surface, shall we say, of polite society. We take extreme care that none of our personnel ever come to the notice of the forces of law and order, though of course our work is on display for all to see."

It was a somewhat surreal conversation. Bronson knew, perfectly well, that the German was talking about acts of terrorism, or acts of sabotage at best, but he could have been the director of a legitimate company discussing its products and public image with a fellow businessman.

"And that, you see, is the problem with you. As I said, we avoid the police as much as we can, but you are a former police officer, which puts us into something of a quandary. You wouldn't be here at all without Georg's strong recommendation."

Bronson shook his head. "Look," he said, "Georg sent me to meet you here in Berlin. It wasn't my choice, though it did suit me to get out of the country for a while, just because of what had happened at the industrial estate. If you're unhappy with my being here, I can just go back. That's no problem for me."

Marcus smiled, but there was no humor in his expression.

"It might not be a problem for you," he said, "but it certainly would be for us. You know my name, you've seen my face and those of several members of this organization, and you've been inside my house, so it's far too late for you to just go back, as you put it. You will be leaving here, but what we have to decide is whether you walk out or if it would suit our interests better to ensure you never walked or talked again."

It was neither more nor less than a casual death sentence, delivered in the same urbane, conversational manner as everything else Marcus had said, and Bronson felt a chill run through him. He was acutely aware that he was completely unarmed, surrounded by a group of men, all of whom were probably carrying pistols, and that nobody outside the building had the slightest idea where he was.

If Marcus decided to have him shot down there and then, Bronson knew there was almost no chance that anyone would ever find out about it or discover his body. His corpse could be stripped, loaded into the trunk of one of the cars, driven out into the countryside and dumped down a well or mineshaft or just left deep in the woods to rot. And if they cut off his head and hands, identification would be virtually impossible.

Even Angela—who was absolutely the only person he was sure he could trust—only knew that he had been intending to travel to Germany, and Germany was a very big country. All Bronson had been able to tell her was that he had a meeting in Berlin. If he didn't call her within about a day, she would raise the alarm, certainly, but that probably wouldn't do any good. By that time he would simply have vanished without trace.

Despite these extremely unpleasant thoughts coursing through his brain, Bronson remained outwardly calm and unruffled.

"You're right," he said, "I was a police officer, but I was kicked out of the force months ago."

"I know," Marcus replied. "Georg checked."

That was a small comfort. Obviously somebody in the Met had faked the records to show his dismissal when Davidson had decided to send him undercover. Whether those records would be altered to reflect the truth of his situation now that there really was a warrant out for his arrest on firearms charges was another matter entirely. All Bronson could hope was that Georg wouldn't decide to probe any more deeply.

"So you'll know that I have no love for my former employers," he stated. "And Georg should also have told you how I came to meet his group in the first place."

Marcus smiled. "Yes," he said. "Doing a bit of minor vandalism at the Olympic sites. Hardly the Great Train Robbery, Mr. Bronson, was it? And then you attacked that bulldozer with a hammer, a somewhat inadequate weapon if you were being serious."

"That was about all we had to hand," Bronson said defensively. "And you can do a lot of damage if you know how. I probably smashed it up enough to write it off."

"Bravo," Marcus muttered ironically, "so the sum total of your efforts to disrupt the London Olympic Games amounts to the possible financial destruction of one piece of earthmoving equipment that might at some point have been used on the site. Obviously there's no way of telling, because all the major construction work was completed some time ago. Not particularly impressive."

"I did what I could," Bronson replied, then decided that perhaps attack was the best form of defense. "And as far as I could see, Georg and his merry men weren't doing much better, and there were about a dozen of them."

Marcus nodded. "Actually, they were doing exactly what we wanted them to do. They were just providing a diversion, making the police think that the biggest threat to the Games was this kind of minor vandalism."

That tied up with what Georg had told Bronson earlier, and implied that the German was planning something else, something darker and much more dangerous.

"So you've got something else in mind?"

Marcus shook his head. "Before we decide to share that information with you—if we ever do, that is—we need to be sure exactly where your loyalties lie."

"I would have thought I'd established that by now. I'm wanted by the British police for assault and whatever other charges they've been able to drum up against me. If I go back to England, there's a strong chance I'll be arrested as soon as I get there and then spend several years in prison. I've no option but to throw in my lot with Georg and the rest of the group in their campaign against the Olympic Games, and that's why I'm here now."

Marcus nodded patiently. "I know, but what you don't understand is that we really don't care about the Olympics except as a convenient vehicle for what we intend to do. And if you are going to play any part, however small, in our operation, then, as I said a few moments ago, we must be certain of your loyalty."

"And how are you going to achieve that?" Bronson asked.

"A simple test, that's all. You'll be performing a small service for us, but one that will satisfy me that you can be relied upon."

Again, this echoed what Georg had said to him back in England, and Bronson didn't like the sound of it any more the second time round. But there was nothing he could do except go along with whatever Marcus had planned.

"Follow me," the German said.

Marcus gave a slight nod, then turned away and began walking toward a set of double doors at the far end of the room, the two men who had accompanied Bronson following on behind. Bronson was led down a flight of stairs, and then down another flight, by which time he was certain that they were below ground level. At the end of a short corridor was a steel door, standing partially ajar.

As Marcus approached, the door swung open to reveal a brightly lit room, the walls and ceiling painted brilliant white, in which about half a dozen men were standing waiting. But unlike the opulent surroundings Bronson had just left, this chamber was almost bare. The floor was gray-painted concrete, and the only objects in the room were bright lights—almost like floodlights—set in each corner, and a heavy wooden chair, the back, arms and legs fitted with leather straps, bolted to the floor in the center, the area around it scuffed and discolored with dark stains. A professional-looking movie camera was positioned at one side of the room, its lens pointing directly toward the chair.

Bronson was walking into what looked like a film studio intended for a very particular type of action, and he had a sudden, disturbingly clear idea about exactly what Marcus intended.

21

Marcus stopped inside the room and gestured for Bronson to approach him.

"The test we've devised is very simple, and will only take a couple of minutes. Afterward, as long as you've passed it, I'll decide exactly how much I should tell you about our operation."

He turned away and made a gesture to one of the men standing beside the wall. The man nodded, then strode across to another door a few feet away, opened it and barked a command.

Two other men appeared from the open doorway, half carrying, half dragging, a third figure, another man wearing only a pair of jeans and a T-shirt, both garments heavily bloodstained. His face bore the unmistakable marks of a severe beating, and even from where Bronson was standing it was clear that several of his fingers had been broken, and his arms were covered in what looked like acid burns. Whoever he was, he had clearly suffered appalling torture, either as punishment for some infraction or, probably more likely, to extract information from him. He was muttering almost incoherently, in great pain, and the only words Bronson could make out were *nein* and *bitte*.

The man was hustled roughly across the room to the wooden chair and forced down into it, the straps tightened around his waist, arms and legs to secure him in place. The two men then maneuvered a heavy wooden frame into position directly behind the chair. The front of the frame was fitted with long, wide and thick strips of heavy rubberized material that were attached at the top. Bronson knew exactly what the device was, though he'd never seen a mobile version before. A short distance behind the rubberized strips there would be a heavy-duty steel plate, or perhaps even a sheet of Kevlar.

Marcus looked on, a slight smile playing over his lips. "This organization is small but we try to be as secure as possible," he said. "We run what you British call a tight ship, and there are two things that we simply do not tolerate. One is failure, and the other is breaching our security. This man"—he gestured toward the bound figure—"was guilty of both. About a week ago we discovered from monitoring his phone calls that he was in contact with a member of the Berlin police force, and was preparing to pass information to him in exchange for a promise of immunity from prosecution and a substantial pay-off. Knowing the Berlin police as I do, I suspect he might have got the former, but certainly not the latter. So he breached our security, and you could also say that he'd failed, because he breached it in such a clumsy way that we were almost certain to find out about it."

Marcus glanced back at the bound man, then looked again at Bronson.

"We've managed to persuade him to disclose everything of value that he knew, and now he's of no more use to us. Or to anyone else, in fact. As you can see, our questioning had to be somewhat robust to persuade him to tell us what we wanted to know. He's obviously suffering and your test, your initiation, if you like, is to ease his pain. We want you to kill him. Right here, and right now, in front of the camera."

Marcus reached into his jacket and took out a clear plastic bag, much like the evidence bags used by the police, inside which was a semi-automatic pistol. He handed the bag to Bronson.

The weapon was an early model Walther P99, with the green polymer frame which was a characteristic of that pistol. He could tell immediately by the weight and balance of the Walther that either the magazine was empty or it wasn't fitted at all. He quickly glanced down, half turning the weapon in his hand until he could see the base of the grip, and the empty black oblong that showed that the magazine was missing.

Bronson looked at the man in the chair, and then back at Marcus. The German seemed utterly unconcerned that he was ordering the death of another human being. If anything, he seemed slightly amused, and for the first time Bronson caught a glimpse of the kind of dispassionate and callous efficiency that had characterized the German administrators of the horrendous concentration and death camps of the Second World War.

As far as Marcus was concerned, the murder of the anonymous figure strapped to the wooden chair was of absolutely no consequence. It was simply a convenient tool, a device to guarantee Bronson's loyalty, because the film of the execution would be all the proof that any jury, in any country, would need to convict him of cold-blooded murder.

"And if I refuse?" Bronson asked.

Marcus shrugged. "That's entirely up to you," he said, "but if you don't do the job, I or one of my men will do it, and then you'll replace that man in the chair."

The German's eyes betrayed no emotion whatsoever as he stared levelly at Bronson, the expression on his face unchanged. Despite the man's meek and mild appearance—he was one of the most physically unthreatening people he had ever met—at that moment, Bronson knew that he was in the presence of sheer, calculating and unremitting evil.

Bronson also knew that there was only one thing he could do in the circumstances. He was hopelessly outgunned and outnumbered, and he had absolutely no doubt that if he failed to carry out Marcus's instructions, he would be dead within minutes. He had killed before, in the heat and confusion of a fight, and in self-defense, which he'd always thought was justifiable, or at the very least excusable. But that was a lifetime away from the cold and clinical execution of another human being.

Bronson dropped his gaze from Marcus's face and

looked around the concrete chamber. Eight men stared back at him, their expressions ranging from simply neutral to overtly hostile. Three of the men, he noticed for the first time, carried pistols in their right hands, and he had no doubt whatsoever that, at the first sign of any aggressive move on his part against Marcus or any of his other men, he would find himself looking down the barrels of multiple weapons.

As far as he could see, there was only one way that he could get out of that chamber alive without killing the bound man, and it all depended upon what Marcus did next. If he handed Bronson a full magazine for the Walther—he thought the weapon had a maximum capacity of fifteen rounds, much like the Browning with which he was much more familiar—and then stayed within reach, there was just a chance. Bronson would have to insert the magazine and cock the pistol, grab Marcus and stick the gun to his head, and then use him as a human shield to get out of the house. It was a plan born of desperation, but it was the only one he had.

"So what do you want me to do with this?" he asked, taking the pistol out of the bag and hefting it in his hand. "Beat him to death with it?"

"Nothing so crude," Marcus said. He reached into his right-hand jacket pocket and produced a pistol magazine, also inside a clear plastic bag, the black shape unmistakable. He took a couple of steps backward and then lobbed the bag to Bronson, who caught it easily in his left hand.

"As you can see, Mr. Bronson, there's only one round in it, so you've got just one shot, and just one chance."

Bronson had been outmaneuvered, and he knew it.

Marcus was now about ten feet away, and the silent men lining the chamber like grim sentinels would be able to cut him down before he could cover even half that distance. Two more had now produced pistols, and they were all aiming their weapons at him. He opened the bag, removed the magazine and slid it into the butt of the Walther, racked the slide back and then let it go to chamber the single round he'd been given, then glanced back at Marcus.

"Suppose I miss?" he asked.

"You're ex-army and a former policeman, and it's quite obvious from the way you're handling the pistol that you've had weapons training. If you miss, we'll assume it was deliberate. And if you do miss, the man in the chair will still die, and so will you." Marcus made an impatient gesture. "The camera's running—in fact, it's been running ever since you walked into this room—so get on with it."

Bronson looked over to his right, toward the camera, and noticed the tiny red light illuminated on the front of it, showing that it was operating.

"So you've also recorded our conversation," he said, "including you forcing me to do this?"

Marcus smiled again. "Yes," he replied, "but that won't matter. My men will cut out those bits and produce a disk containing the edited highlights, as they say in the vacuous world of the media. Any more questions?"

Bronson shook his head. He was fresh out of options. There was only one thing that he could do.

Without even appearing to aim, he swung the pistol up toward the seated man and squeezed the trigger.

22

The noise of the shot was deafening in the confined space, the concrete walls seeming to concentrate and amplify the sound. The Walther kicked in his hand, the slide instantly locking back as the spent cartridge case was ejected, the glittering brass case spinning out of the open breech to land on the concrete floor with a metallic tinkling noise.

The bound man grunted once as the copper-jacketed bullet slammed into the center of his chest, then slumped forward, killed instantly by the single shot. The front of his T-shirt turned red as blood flooded out of the entry wound. Below the chair, more blood began to pool on the floor from the ruptured vessels and ripped flesh of the exit wound that Bronson knew the bullet would have torn in his back. Behind the chair, the rubberized sheets of the movable bullet trap swung gently backward and forward, having done their job in stopping the nine-millimeter slug after it had performed its deadly task.

Bronson's mind suddenly filled with images of Baghdad. He'd done two tours of duty in Iraq as an army officer, and had been involved in several firefights during that time. But that was a very different environment: contesting ownership of the streets of the battered city with heavily armed insurgents, clearing rebel-held houses using grenades and automatic weapons, the enemy dimly seen shapes flitting from one piece of cover to another as they fired long bursts from their Kalashnikov assault rifles. For a while, the whole city had become a single killing zone, and Bronson genuinely had no idea how many Iraqis had fallen to bullets fired from his SA-80 or his pistol. Anonymous men fighting for their country or for their leader, and dying in droves as a result. Urban warfare was perhaps the bloodiest and most unpleasant form of conflict.

But even that hadn't left the same kind of sick feeling in his stomach that Bronson was now experiencing. He'd just carried out an execution—the cold-blooded killing of a man he'd never seen before—and he'd done it as much as anything to save his own skin. Because he was absolutely certain that if he'd refused to pull the trigger, Marcus would have carried out his threat without a second thought. The man lashed to the chair would still be dead, and Bronson would have been lying beside him.

The only sliver of comfort Bronson could take from what had just happened was that at least the man had been killed instantly by the single bullet and hadn't suffered. And he, Bronson, was still alive, and that meant that he still had the ability to bring Marcus and his gang of thugs to justice.

"Good shot, Mr. Bronson," Marcus said, stepping forward and holding out the plastic bag for Bronson to drop the Walther into.

Bronson handed over the weapon—again, there was nothing else he could do because of the watchful armed men in the room, and the pistol was useless to him now that it was unloaded—as he stared across at the dead man in the chair. Even as he watched, a couple of Marcus's men stepped forward and began to release the leather straps that still held the corpse in place. Released from his bonds, the dead man tumbled untidily to the floor to lie facedown on the discolored concrete, the exit wound on his back now clearly visible.

Any vestige of hope that Bronson might have harbored that he was part of an elaborate theater, that the man's injuries had been faked and that the cartridge was a blank, was dashed in that instant. He'd seen dead men before, and the unmistakable limpness of the body as it thudded on to the concrete floor told its own story. He was in no doubt whatsoever that he'd just committed murder.

"Who was he?"

"What?"

Bronson pointed at the figure lying on the floor. "The man I just executed for you," he said. "I'd like to know his name."

Marcus nodded. "Yes," he replied, "I suppose we owe you that, at least. His name was Herman Polti, and perhaps I ought to clarify one small point. I told you that he was in contact with the Berlin police, and that was not entirely true. In fact, I should say it was wholly untrue.

Polti was actually an undercover police officer, much as Georg feared you might be when you first made contact with his group."

As Marcus's words sank in, another wave of revulsion swept through Bronson. Police officers everywhere were accustomed to putting their lives on the line and, rightly or wrongly, killing a policeman was always considered to be one of the worst possible crimes. And arguably the worst possible way for any police officer to die was at the hand of a fellow policeman. What just happened had put Bronson beyond the pale. Way, way beyond it.

The German smiled coldly at Bronson. "So now we have you on film shooting a bound and helpless police officer, and we have a pistol with your fingerprints all over it. When we dump Polti's body, we'll ensure that the bullet and the cartridge case are found with it. The Walther and the film from the camera will be stored away in a safe place, but the moment you do something we don't like, or we suspect that you might even be thinking of running off to the authorities, I'll make sure that all the evidence is handed to the police. As of this moment, Mr. Bronson, we *own* you."

And that, Bronson thought, was a pretty reasonable summary of the situation. But as he looked into the German's cold eyes, Bronson made himself a promise. No matter what happened, someday, somehow, he would come back, find Marcus and kill him.

For a few seconds, Bronson stared at the scene in front of him. One of the men had brought in a rigid stretcher, the top covered with a plastic sheet, and he and another man were in the process of placing the body of the dead man on it. A third man was standing near the chair, a bucket of some kind of granular material, possibly sawdust, in his hand, and he was sprinkling it over the bloodstains.

Bronson looked back at Marcus. "So what happens now?" he asked.

The German looked slightly surprised at the question. "You're one of us now," he replied, "but there's nothing for you to do in Germany. I have a full team here and in any case you don't speak the language, or so I've been told. I'll tell Georg that you passed our little test, and that he can trust you to do the right thing. And we both know exactly *why* he can trust you. Then it's up to him to decide how best to make use of your talents in London before the *Laternenträger* gets there."

Bronson's face reflected the confusion he was feeling. "The what?" he asked. "What are you talking about?"

Marcus shook his head, and for the first time looked a little uncomfortable. "It's just a German expression," he replied. "Forget I said it. Now," he continued briskly, "I'll get one of my men to drive you back to your car. By the time you reach London I'm sure Georg will have organized some jobs for you to do."

The German reached into his jacket pocket and took out an envelope, which he handed to Bronson. Inside were six five-hundred-euro notes.

"What's this?" Bronson asked. "Blood money?"

"No. You're now on our payroll, and so you can call that an advance of salary."

Three minutes later, having retraced his steps, Bronson was back in the garage, accompanied by two of the

Germans, neither of whom seemed inclined to speak to him, not that he was interested in holding a conversation. Marcus had told him that he'd be driven back to his car by one man, which had immediately suggested to Bronson the possibility of taking the initiative and overpowering him, and then somehow getting back inside the building to find the pistol and the incriminating film footage. But against two armed men, Bronson knew he wouldn't have a chance.

In the garage, one of the men stood opposite the double metal doors and used the remote control to open them, while the other walked over to one of the BMWs, opened the driver's door, gestured to Bronson to get in the back, and then sat down. As soon as the doors were open, to reveal the midevening gloom, he drove the car out of the garage, pausing to allow his companion to walk over to the car and sit down in the front passenger seat.

The second man waited until the car had driven out of the garage before again using the remote to close the doors. As he did so, he looked back at Bronson and gestured for him to replace the heavily tinted sunglasses over his eyes. They were clearly much more relaxed about their security now that he had been fatally compromised by Polti's execution. They knew that he daren't approach the authorities to inform on them—if that was his intention—because of the consequences to him personally if he did.

Bronson nodded agreement, removed the glasses from his pocket and put them on, because as before he had no other choice. But he'd already taken a long look around him as the car had pulled out of the garage. Lights were shining in various windows, and there was still enough natural light for him to get a good idea of the appearance of the property. The house looked smaller from the outside than the interior had suggested, but it was still obviously a substantial building.

The double garage doors were set in the lowest level of the structure, a few feet below ground level, and were approached by a well-tended gravel drive. These doors appeared to form the only opening to the house on that level, at least as far as Bronson could see, and it looked as if most of the lower-ground-floor area was given over to garaging, so presumably the occupants and their guests tended to arrive by car rather than on foot. Bronson guessed that there would be other entrances at ground level on the back or sides of the building, and he could see a wide veranda on the level directly above the garage, with a half-glazed door set in its center.

The property rose for two stories, probably built of brick, though the white painted walls made it impossible to be certain, under a roof that was notable for its shallow pitch and wide overhang at the eaves, clearly intended to cope with the heavy snowfalls the area experienced every winter. All the windows Bronson could see were fitted with shutters stained light brown to match the beams and trusses of the roof. It looked, in short, much like many of the other large houses he'd seen since entering Germany.

But in the few brief seconds before he'd been told to replace the sunglasses, Bronson had committed the appearance of the house to his memory, because knowing where to find the place again was now his highest priority. He had not the slightest intention of just trotting obediently back to London, as Marcus had told him to do. He believed that if he could find his way back, there was at least a chance that he could break in somehow and find what he needed.

And unlike the meeting places chosen by Georg in and around London, the house he'd just left was clearly a permanent residence for at least some of the people in the group—the room that had been used for the torture and execution of the unfortunate Polti demonstrated that clearly enough.

The last—and perhaps the most important—part of the puzzle was to find a street name or some indication of the district or town where the property was located, and Bronson hoped he would be able to do that as the car drove away, simply because he was sitting by himself in the backseat.

He had put on the sunglasses, as he'd been ordered, but as he'd done so he'd snapped off a tiny section of the plastic lens on the left-hand side, which gave him a small but usable window on the steadily darkening world outside the car.

The BMW drove slowly over the gravel and then crossed rougher ground before coming to a halt between a pair of stone gateposts. He heard the sound of an approaching vehicle—a car or small van, he guessed—which passed directly in front of the car and then continued on its way. As soon as it had passed, the BMW accelerated across the road and turned left.

Through the tiny gap that he had created in the lens of the sunglasses, Bronson tried to take note of the terrain the vehicle was passing. He had hoped he might see

a street sign or something else that would positively identify the location, but the car seemed to be driving along
a fairly straight but narrow country road bordered, at
least on the left-hand side, by woods and without any
turnings or junctions as far as he could see. That single
fact would help him find the house again, but only after
he'd somehow managed to identify the district where
it was located, and for that a road sign, a road number,
or a village name—something concrete that he could
remember—was essential.

The car had picked up speed, and Bronson guessed it
was traveling at fifty or sixty miles an hour as the road
continued straight. Just over four minutes after turning
onto the road, he felt the BMW begin to slow down, the
driver shifting down two gears as he applied the brakes,
and then the vehicle steered to the left at a Y-junction.

Without appearing to do so, Bronson shifted his gaze
and just caught a glimpse of a small sign that presumably
indicated the name of the road the car had turned into. It
was too dark for him to read the entire name, but he did
see—and, more important, he made sure he remembered—
the first part of the word: "*Kaupt.*" And he couldn't swear
to it, but he thought the second part of the name was the
German word for street: *straße* or *strasse*.

A few seconds after it had turned onto the other road,
the car drove past a group of buildings on the left-hand
side. At first sight Bronson thought it might be a farm,
but then changed his mind because, through his very restricted aperture, it looked more like a small estate of
upmarket houses, though it could also, he supposed, have
been a small industrial park. He was having to use only

his peripheral vision and that, along with the fading light, made discerning anything clearly very difficult.

A few moments later, the car again slowed down almost to a crawl but continued moving in a straight line, and it was soon obvious that the BMW was joining a major road. Bronson could hear the sound of other vehicles passing in both directions in front of them before the car pulled out onto the road. The driver swung left to cross the lane handling opposite-direction traffic, and then to the left, to continue in more or less the same direction that he'd been driving before.

Then Bronson had a stroke of luck as the car drove onto a bridge that spanned either a river or a canal, most probably the latter because the waterway seemed to have a very consistent width. That was an identification feature that should help narrow his search markedly. And almost before that thought had fully registered, the car slowed again as it entered a built-up area.

Bronson vainly searched for a village name, but saw nothing useful. The road appeared to continue more or less straight, but then he felt the car enter a sweeping curve to the left and a few seconds later begin a turn to the right that was almost as sharp. Moments after that, they were back in the open countryside. He didn't know how many villages or suburbs there were around Berlin that were near a canal and that had a main road running through them with an S-bend in the middle, but he hoped there wouldn't be too many.

He continued trying to build a picture of the remainder of the journey, but within a few minutes of leaving the village, the car turned onto an autobahn that was, like

most German main roads, devoid of unusual features. So
Bronson just concentrated on making sure that what he
had seen remained locked in his memory.

When the car finally turned off the autobahn, he
guessed he was near his journey's end, and a couple of
minutes later the BMW drew to a halt.

"You can get out now," the driver said, his English
heavily accented.

Bronson nodded, took the sunglasses off his face and
reached for the door handle. As he stepped out of the car,
he recognized the station car park once again, and saw his
Hyundai parked a few yards away. He didn't look back,
just strode across to his car, feeling in his pocket for the
keys, and when he did finally glance behind him, he saw
the BMW driving away from him toward the exit.

Bronson sat down in the driver's seat, turned on the
interior light, then reached across to open the glovebox
and took out a small notebook and a pencil. He flicked
through the book until he found a blank page and then
swiftly wrote down the identification features that he had
remembered: a straight road with woods on one side; the
street name *Kaupt*, possibly followed by *strasse* or *straße*;
a canal or river that ran under the road at right angles,
followed by a village in which the main road followed an
S-shaped path. Then, on the following page, he drew a
rough sketch of the house to which he had been taken.

When he'd finished, Bronson looked over what he'd
written, and added the two times that the journeys had
taken. It was little enough to go on, but it was all he had,
so it would have to do.

But before he even started trying to locate the house

and track down Marcus, there was something else he needed to do. He was alone in Germany, without easy access to the Internet unless he visited a cyber café or bought a laptop computer or netbook and found somewhere offering Wi-Fi facilities and, in truth, he didn't really know where his search should start.

What he was sure was that the word Marcus had used—it had sounded to Bronson like *laterntrager*—was significant for some reason, just because of the way the German had reacted when he let it slip. Perhaps it was the code name for the operation the Germans appeared to be mounting against London, or possibly even the name of a weapon they intended to use to disrupt the Olympic Games.

He shook his head. Actually, disrupting the Olympic Games was probably only a bonus as far as Marcus was concerned. When Bronson had looked into his eyes, he'd seen the pale and dispassionate stare of a true fanatic. Whatever the Germans had planned, he was quite certain that it would involve a massive loss of life, not just some attention-grabbing interruption to the Games.

Bronson shivered involuntarily. There wasn't, at that stage, too much he could do to investigate the meaning of the word—his first priority had to be to locate the house—but he had high hopes that Angela would not only know where to look, but would be able to find out its true significance.

Always assuming, of course, that he'd heard and remembered it right.

23

"Chris! I've been worried sick. Where the hell are you? Your phone's been switched off for days."

"That's a bit of an exaggeration," Bronson replied. "I'm just using a different mobile; that's why you couldn't call me."

"Well, why didn't you give me the number? So where are you now? Berlin?"

"Yes," Bronson replied. "I'm still in Germany, and I'm in trouble."

"And you need my help." It was a statement, not a question. "Do you want me to fly out there?"

"No. Or not yet, at least. Everything's a bit confused here at the moment." As he said the words, Bronson knew how lame that sounded, and just how big an understatement it was. But he had enough to contend with in Berlin without having to worry about Angela as well. The last thing he wanted was for her to get involved with Marcus and his gang of German thugs.

"So what can I do?"

"I just need you to do some research for me. The leader of the gang I'm trying to infiltrate used a German word that seems to be important. I've no idea what the word means, or even if I've remembered it correctly, but I'm sure it's something to do with this plot, because he talked about sending whoever, or whatever, this word means to London. And then he seemed to realize that he'd said too much."

"Okay. Go ahead then. What was the word?"

"I think it was *Laterntrager*." He spelled the word to her, or what he guessed was the spelling.

"It sounds German, I'll give you that," Angela replied, "but I don't recognize it. Of course, that's probably because I don't speak German, but luckily I know somebody who does. Have you tried looking in a dictionary?"

"I don't have a dictionary. Could you please just see what you can find out, and I'll call you again in the morning. Don't try to call me on this number, because I don't know where I'll be or what I'll be doing. In fact, I'll probably have the phone switched off most of the time."

"Okay. Leave it with me. And, Chris," she added, "whatever you're doing over there, just be careful, will you?"

"I'll do my best," Bronson said, then ended the call.

For a minute or so he sat in silence, his mind racing, then he came to a decision. He had no idea how seriously the British police were trying to trace him, but it was conceivable that they might have put an intercept on Angela's home and work telephone numbers, and on her mobile, just in case he called her.

They wouldn't know that Bronson was the person ringing Angela, but they might well guess it was him because she was being called from an unregistered British pay-as-you-go mobile phone located in Germany. That would probably be enough for them to request the assistance of the German police in finding out the identity and location of her caller. And Bronson was keenly aware that as long as a mobile phone was switched on, its position could be determined by finding out which radio masts it was in contact with.

It wasn't worth taking the chance. He unclipped the back panel of the mobile, took out the battery and put all three pieces of the phone in the car's glovebox. And, just in case he was right and the German police had been contacted by somebody in the Met, he started the car, drove out of the car park and back through Rangsdorf to the main road. There, he turned right and headed south until he reached a smaller settlement named Groß Machnow, where he took the first major junction on the left, following a road sign that directed him toward Mittenwalde. He had no particular destination in mind, and was working on the reasonable basis that if *he* didn't know where he was going, it would be extremely difficult for anyone else to predict his route.

The countryside was dominated by rich agricultural land, fields and patches of woodland extending on both sides of the road. A short distance outside Groß Machnow, the road—he knew he was driving along the Mittenwalder Strasse—bisected a wood where there were pull-offs on both sides of the road. He'd seen almost no traffic since he drove out of Groß Machnow, and could see no other cars parked in the wood. It was probably as good a place to stop as anywhere else he'd seen.

Bronson swung the car right, bouncing off the tarmac and on to the hard-packed earth of one of the turnoffs, and tucked the Hyundai behind a group of shrubs, where it would be virtually invisible from the road. He opened the two front windows, then switched off the engine and for a few moments just sat and listened. The only sound he could hear was birdsong—the evening equivalent of the dawn chorus—and the buzz of insects. He knew he would hear any approaching vehicles easily enough, and the chances of him being spotted were extremely slim. And even if somebody did see him, sitting there in the car, he wasn't actually doing anything illegal. Unless they found the Llama pistol under his seat, that is.

Bronson opened up the map book of Germany that he'd purchased en route from Calais to Berlin, and began studying the area to the southeast of the city, the area where he guessed the house was located. The problem, he saw immediately, was that there were a lot of waterways—rivers, canals and lakes—around Berlin. He remembered reading in a German tourist brochure on the cross-Channel ferry that the area was known to be marshy from the very earliest days of the settlement, and that the word "berl," which formed the first part of the city's name, actually meant "swamp" in some archaic European language. The terrain shown on the map to the southeast of Berlin was splashed with blue, and the rivers and canals were crossed at frequent intervals by roads, almost always at right angles. In many cases settlements had sprung up near the junction of the road and the waterway—rendering two of Bronson's remembered identifying features essentially useless.

And there was a further irritation because the map book was intended for motorists and so most of the roads were identified by numbers, not by names, and he could see no sign of a road named *Kauptstrasse* anywhere in the area. He knew he would need to buy more detailed maps, more like the British Ordnance Survey sheets, to find what he was looking for.

The only other option was the satnav unit, but before he could ask it to find *Kauptstrasse*, he had to be able to identify the town, village or district in which the road was located. He switched on the unit anyway, waited until it had locked onto the satellites, then selected Berlin as the city and typed in *Kauptstrasse*, but the result was more or less what he'd expected: the unit couldn't locate it, simply because the road wasn't in Berlin itself, but in some suburb or outlying village.

He glanced at his watch. It was already after nine, and Bronson was hungry and thirsty, but also physically exhausted and emotionally drained, wrung out by the events of the evening. He needed food and drink, and then somewhere to stay for the night.

But for now he needed to get some sleep.

24

Just over an hour after Angela ended the call to Bronson, the entry-phone in her apartment buzzed, and a couple of minutes after that she opened the door in response to a double knock. A tall, dark-haired man stood waiting outside on the landing, wearing an open-necked shirt, a light-colored pullover and a knee-length leather coat. He was strongly built, with the powerful arms and broad shoulders of a committed sportsman—he looked like a swimmer, or maybe a rugby player.

"Steven," she said, opening the door wide and ushering her guest inside. "I'm so glad you could make it. I really didn't know who else I could call."

Steven Behr stepped forward and gave Angela a kiss on each cheek. They'd known each other for years, ever since first meeting at university, and had always remained good friends. But they rarely saw each other simply because of their hectic but very different lifestyles. Angela knew Steven had a high-powered job in IT but had never really been sure exactly what it was. She just knew he was somebody she could rely on and, more important to her at that precise moment, his German was fluent.

The giveaway was his unusual surname. Angela knew that Steven had done a little research into its origins, and had discovered that it had most probably been derived from Bähr, and that name from the nickname Bär, meaning a "bear." And, she had often thought, rarely had any surname been more appropriate: Steven Behr was in many ways remarkably like his animal namesake. He was strong and courageous, but blessed—or perhaps cursed—with an impatient and highly competitive streak that meant he didn't suffer fools gladly. In fact, she knew he didn't suffer them at all, which was probably one reason for his success in business.

"You know you can call me anytime," Steven said. "I'm always pleased to help if you need a shoulder to lean on."

Angela led the way into the sitting room, where her laptop was open on the coffee table in front of the sofa. In the opposite corner of the room, her TV was switched on and displaying one of the satellite news channels, but with the sound muted.

"Take a seat, and I'll get you a coffee."

"Thanks. A cappuccino would be great. Got any biscuits?"

Angela smiled. Steven Behr's appetite was legendary, but he never seemed to put on any weight because of his incredibly active lifestyle.

"I thought you knew me better than that," she said. "The best I can do is instant with a dash of milk."

"Pretty much what I expected, actually."

Steven walked across to the leather recliner by the side of the sofa and sat down, drumming his fingers on the arm of the chair.

A minute or so later Angela reappeared, put the mug of coffee down on the table, along with a plate of assorted cookies, and resumed her seat in front of the laptop.

"I gather you've got a bit of a problem?" Steven asked, picking up a digestive.

Angela nodded.

"Well," she said, "it's not so much me as Chris. I don't pretend to know anything like the full story, but he's had to go over to Germany. Something to do with his work, with the police, but I really don't know what."

"The ideal choice, I suppose," Steven said, "because he doesn't speak a word of German, as far as I know. Typical of the bureaucrats who run the police these days. So what's his problem? Does he need a translator? I could go over there for a couple of days if that would help."

Angela shook her head. "Not a translator so much as a translation. The problem is that he overheard a German word, a word that could be important because of the circumstances in which he heard it, but it doesn't make any sense to me. I mean, it's not in any of the dictionaries I've looked at so far. That's why I thought of you, because you're fluent."

Steven nodded.

"So you think he might have misheard it, and I might recognize what the word should actually be?"

"Exactly."

"I'm all ears. What did he hear?"

"He thought it was '*Laterntrager*,'" Angela replied.

For a few seconds Steven didn't reply, just finished the biscuit and took a sip of coffee before replacing the mug on the table. Then he glanced across at Angela.

"You're right—he probably did mishear it. That's a fairly uncommon proper name in Germany, but as far as I'm aware it doesn't have any other meaning. Could it just have been someone's surname?"

"I don't think so. Because of the context, Chris seemed to think that it referred to an object of some sort, perhaps to a kind of weapon or even a machine. Something physical, anyway."

Steven nodded, and mouthed the words a few times. Then he nodded again and looked back at Angela.

"That changes the dynamic," he said. "I can think of one word that sounds quite like '*Laterntrager*' and it probably does refer to some kind of a mechanical device. But it's not '*Laterntrager*,' it's '*Laternenträger*.'"

Angela looked puzzled for a moment.

"I see what you mean," she said, "because the words are very similar. But what do you mean when you say it might 'probably' mean a mechanical device? If you know the word, surely you know what it means?"

Steven smiled and shook his head.

"It's not quite as simple as that, Angela, and it's a long and pretty confusing story. The easy bit is what the word means. '*Laternenträger*' doesn't really have an exact translation in English, but I suppose the closest would be 'lamplighter.'"

Angela's face reflected the confusion she was feeling.

"'Lamplighter?'" she repeated. "What on earth could that have to do with what Chris is investigating?"

"I don't know what he's investigating, obviously, and I wouldn't expect you to tell me because it's presumably some kind of undercover operation. But that word is archaic and you really wouldn't expect to hear any German today use it in conversation. Except in one connection, and that's a dark and disturbing story that began in Germany in the nineteen thirties, and ended in Poland in April nineteen forty-five as the Russians advanced from the east, mopping up the last pockets of Nazi resistance as they did so."

Angela stood up and walked across to the doorway leading to the kitchen.

"I'll make some more coffee," she said, "because you're right: this is going to take us a while. I know almost nothing about Nazi Germany and the Second World War, and I have a feeling it's going to take you some time to educate me. I'll bring a bottle of brandy as well," she added as an afterthought, "just in case you need some extra stimulation to keep going."

Five minutes later, Steven took a sip of brandy, then put the glass down on the coffee table and leaned forward.

"We don't know exactly when, or even precisely where or who, but at some time during the early nineteen thirties one or more German scientists began working on an idea so radical that it led directly to the most important and highly classified weapons project ever undertaken by the Nazi regime."

Steven Behr had Angela's full attention. She trusted

his knowledge implicitly. He knew more about the Second World War, and especially the events that took place in Germany during that incredibly turbulent period, than anyone else she'd ever met.

It was, she knew, going to be a long evening, but by the end of it she was certain that she'd have some kind of an answer to Chris's question.

25

Urgent pressure from his bladder awakened him just after six in the morning, by which time it was already quite light, and he immediately looked all around. There was nobody in sight, so Bronson stepped out of the car, relieved himself in a nearby bush, and did a quick circuit of the area, again checking that he was unobserved.

Then he started the car and headed out of the woods and toward Bestensee. When he reached the main road running east–west through the town, he turned left, toward the closest autobahn junction. As he cleared the western end of Bestensee, he caught a brief glimpse of a road sign, did a double take and almost immediately pulled the Hyundai to a stop at the side of the road. There was no traffic behind him—it was still very early in the morning—and he backed up the car a few yards until he could see the sign clearly.

The word written on it was *Hauptstraße*, and it suddenly dawned on him that perhaps, in the half-light of the previous evening, he could have mistaken the initial letter of the street name he'd seen. He'd thought it was a "K," but perhaps it had actually been an "H." Had he somehow just found the road he'd been driven down?

Bronson grabbed the map book and opened it at the correct page. He studied that section of the map for a few moments, then shook his head. The *Hauptstraße* he was driving along was the wrong shape—it simply had too many bends in it—and as far as he could see it didn't cross any stretch of canal or river. But maybe *Hauptstraße* was a common street name in German, like "High Street" or "Main Road" in English? Bronson already knew that *strasse* or *straße* meant "street," and it wasn't too big a leap of logic to guess that *haupt* could mean "high." If so, there could be dozens of roads with that name in the area.

But still that might help him track it down, because he could set the satnav to take him to every single *Hauptstraße* in Berlin, and then in each of the outlying districts. It would take time, but he'd find it in the end.

At eight forty local time, seven forty in the United Kingdom, he parked the car in a vacant space in the Am Kahlberg service area, put the battery back in his mobile phone, switched it on and dialed Angela's number. She answered on the third ring; Bronson knew she was always awake by half past seven.

"It's me," he said. "Any joy?"

"And good morning to you, too," she replied briskly.

"Sorry. Good morning. Any joy?"

"I suppose that depends on what you mean. I know my

limitations, Chris. I'm linguistically challenged, so I asked Steven Behr to come around last night and help me out because he speaks fluent German. The first point is that the word *Laterntrager* doesn't appear in German dictionaries, but Steven told me it's a fairly uncommon proper name. It has no independent meaning, just like—oh, Burdiss, for example—has no independent meaning. It's just a name, and not a very common one at that. So my first question is: could the person you were talking to have been referring to somebody by that name?"

"I don't think so," Bronson replied. "I can't remember the exact phrase he used, but it was something like 'before the *Laterntrager* arrives,' as if he was referring to an object of some sort. So maybe he was using the word as a code name or nickname."

"I suppose that's possible," Angela replied, not sounding particularly convinced by his argument. "Steven applied a bit of lateral thinking and suggested it could be another German word that sounds very like *Laterntrager*, but this word *is* in the dictionary: *Laternenträger*. Could that have been what he said?"

Bronson murmured the word a few times, trying it on for size, as it were.

"I suppose it could be. So what does that mean?"

"It's an archaic word, one that Steven wouldn't expect most Germans to have ever spoken, purely because of what it describes, though he was sure they would be able to tell you what it means. The literal translation would be 'lantern bearer' or 'lantern carrier,' and the English equivalent is most probably 'lamplighter,' the men who used to walk around the streets of London and other big cities lighting the gas lamps in the days before electricity. Is that any help?"

"I don't know," Bronson replied, "though I suppose it makes more sense. I've been thinking all along that Marcus—that was the man's name—was probably referring to some kind of weapon, and it's quite common in the military for weapons to be given nicknames, often names that relate to what the weapon is or what it does."

"Really?"

"Yes. There's a six-barreled Gatling minigun that's fitted to tank-busting helicopters and aircraft, and that's often called 'Puff the Magic Dragon' because of the effect it has on its targets."

"That's a bit sick, really, Chris."

"Blame the military's very basic sense of humor. Anyway, I'm just wondering if this is the same kind of thing, if this 'lamplighter' name describes what the weapon does, rather than what it is. It could be some kind of massive incendiary device, something that's designed to 'light up' everything around it when it's triggered. And from the way Marcus was talking, I think this weapon—assuming we're right, of course—is a device with a high yield, and the effects of it would be devastating, quite literally."

"Are there weapons like that?"

"There are lots of types of incendiary bombs, of course, but they're usually quite small because they're designed to start fires, not blow things apart. I'm not aware of any big incendiary weapons, apart from the really nasty stuff like napalm and Willy Pete. That's another really inappropriate nickname for the white phosphorus bombs the Americans used to have, but I've been out of the army for a long time now, so I'm right out of touch."

For a few moments Angela was silent, then she sighed.

"Then I suppose this is as good a time as any to explain what else Steven came up with. I told you what *Laternenträger* means, what the dictionary definition says. But there's another possible interpretation of the word which is much, much older than a nineteenth-century lamplighter. It could be a fairly literal translation of an ancient name, a name that's resonated down the ages, a name that's synonymous with death and destruction."

"You're sounding almost messianic, Angela. Or maybe apocalyptic."

"That's not a bad description, actually. The Latin phrase *lucem ferre* means 'the bearer of the light,' and that gave us an English name that means almost the same thing. 'He who carries the light' is the ancient name of Lucifer, the Devil. The Devil is supposed to be the author of all evil, the fallen angel who brought death to this world. If you're right, Chris—and I pray that you're not—then this man Marcus might be planning to unleash a weapon on London that would be far worse than the wrath of God; it could be the Devil's revenge."

26

"That tiny island is an anachronism that Europe simply doesn't need," Marcus Wolf said. "We came so close in the last war to utterly destroying it, and if the Führer had not turned his attention to the east and awoken the sleeping Russian bear, we could have—we should have—succeeded."

Klaus Drescher nodded. The leader of *Die Neue Dämmerung*—The New Dawn—was treading familiar ground but, as usual, Drescher didn't disagree with anything that Wolf said. They had both studied, in considerable detail, the history of the Second World War, and their analysis was unequivocal. If Hitler had pressed home his advantage, prevented the mass evacuation of Dunkirk that had been hailed as—and indeed was—an Allied triumph, and forced Hermann Goering to commit every aircraft he had to destroying the British Royal Air Force, Britain would certainly have been defeated in the winter of 1940. Then Hitler's Operation Sea Lion could have proceeded as planned, and would have resulted in an overwhelming victory for the Fatherland. Only after the war had ended did it become clear just how close Britain had come to ultimate defeat and inevitable surrender.

But now, thanks to the *Laternenträger*, Germany had a chance to redress the balance, though it had been a long wait.

When it had become clear to even the most dedicated and fanatical Nazi that Hitler's dream was over, and that Germany would be overrun by enemy forces within a matter of weeks, farsighted individuals began implementing the plans they had already drawn up. Some of these later became public knowledge. The Vatican, for example, had been perfectly happy to facilitate the transport of high-ranking Nazis out of Germany in exchange for financial donations, and even Red Cross officials knew that many of the so-called "refugees' they were processing were actually wanted Nazis. And the Odessa—the *Organization Der Ehemaligen SS-Angehörigen*, the Organization of Former SS Members—had established numerous "rat lines" to allow the escape of senior SS officers from Germany and Austria to other countries, primarily South America.

Marcus's grandfather hadn't needed to avail himself of any of these organizations, simply because he had been on board the Junkers Ju-390 that had spirited *Die Glocke* out of Poland and on to its ultimate destination in Argentina. There, he had found a number of like-minded former German officers, and within a fairly short time he had set up *Die Neue Dämmerung*: the group that would herald the new dawn of the Nazi dream.

They had hoped, even after the end of hostilities, to quickly regroup and re-arm and, allied with the threat of the devastating military capability promised by *Die Glocke*, to force the Allies to surrender. And then they would have returned to the Fatherland in triumph. But the destruction of Germany had been so complete, so devastating, and the work required on *Die Glocke* so complex and time-consuming, that they were never able to realize their dream. Until now, that is, when their scientists had finally perfected the weapon that was even then on its way to London.

Leadership of the New Dawn had been passed from father to son, to ensure that the organization never lost its focus or clarity of purpose, and now Marcus Wolf held the reins, and was preparing for the triumph that had eluded the group for so long.

"Eventually, the people of Germany will thank us," Klaus said now. "It was a mistake, a bad mistake, to have allowed Britain ever to become a part of the European Union. We have nothing in common with them, and they have been nothing but trouble, just as they were in the nineteen forties."

"You're absolutely right," Marcus agreed. "After we have succeeded with our mission, we will be able to ignore the United Kingdom, and that will allow Germany, the Fatherland, to again take its rightful place as the most powerful nation within Europe. The Führer failed to achieve that using tanks and soldiers and aircraft, but we are going to succeed. We will eliminate Britain as a political and economic force by the application of pure science, by the triggering of our weapon, and our nation will then go on to dominate the continent because of the power of our economy and our implacable political will. Within five years, my friend, I believe that Germany will be the fourth most important nation on Earth, and we can then, perhaps, begin making plans to topple America and Russia, and maybe even China as well."

"When they see what the *Laternenträger* can do, and they realize that there is no defense against it, the political climate will change dramatically," Drescher agreed.

"Exactly," Marcus said. "There is nothing to stop us now."

27

Bronson removed the battery from the mobile phone, placed the components in the Hyundai's glovebox, then started the car and drove out of the service area and back onto route 13, heading south.

As he pulled out into the light early-morning traffic, he glanced frequently in his rearview mirror. And what he saw confirmed his suspicions. He'd only just cleared the end of the slip road when he noticed two marked police cars heading south toward him, and traveling very quickly. A short distance behind them, a Mercedes van was matching their speed. As he watched, the two police cars slowed and turned into the service area, disappearing from view. The Mercedes van continued along the autobahn, slowing all the time, and then turned right onto the end of the slip road, partially blocking it.

It could, of course, have been some kind of exercise, or a mere coincidence that the German police had arrived in force at a location he had just left, but Bronson didn't believe in coincidences. He was now certain that his mobile phone was being tracked. If he'd spent just two more minutes on his call to Angela, he knew he'd now be in custody and awaiting extradition back to England to face whatever charges Detective Inspector Davidson thought he could make stick.

The phone would have to go, obviously, but he would still need to be able to contact Angela, and using public pay phones simply wouldn't work. He needed another mobile phone. And, just as important, so did she, because the only way the Metropolitan Police could possibly have worked out that he was using this particular mobile was if they'd placed a watch on Angela's home, office and mobile numbers.

He would have to risk one final call to her from that phone.

The next exit from the autobahn was the Groß Köris junction. Bronson took the slip road and then turned east toward Klein Köris. As soon as he found somewhere to park safely beside the road, he stopped the car, reassembled the mobile phone, and called Angela's mobile. She answered almost immediately.

"It's me again," Bronson said. "This is important, so just listen and please don't interrupt. My phone's being tracked by the police here, and they must have discovered the number by monitoring my calls to you. I'm getting a new phone this morning, and I want you to do the same. Just buy an ordinary pay-as-you-go mobile for cash and load the SIM card with as much credit as it'll take, but at least twenty pounds. Keep your present mobile with you,

and I'll text you the number of my new phone as soon as
I've got it."

"If you do that, won't the police also know your number?" Angela protested. "And you're in even more trouble now, aren't you?"

"No, I'm at about the same depth as usual, I suppose.
And sending a text should be safe. I'll explain why later.
Now, I've got to go. I'll talk to you this evening."

Bronson again removed the battery from the phone
and drove on. He hoped he was right about a text message being safe. It was one thing for the Metropolitan
Police to ask a mobile phone company to locate the position of a particular handset by checking which radio
masts the unit was in contact with, or even to obtain a
listing of the calls made and received by that mobile, but
it was quite another to monitor the calls and messages
themselves. That needed warrants or court orders, and
Bronson doubted if Davidson had enough evidence to
convince anybody that he needed to be able to listen to
what Angela Lewis, a respected ceramics conservator
working for the British Museum, a lady who had never
been given so much as a parking ticket in her life, was
saying, or what her texts comprised.

And unless they had obtained a warrant to record her
calls, there was no way they'd be able to track him once
he'd ditched his original mobile. After that, their conversations would just be from one unregistered mobile in
London to another unregistered mobile near Berlin.

That thought gave him some comfort as he continued
east toward Klein Köris. All he had to do now was find
somewhere to buy a new phone.

In fact, that didn't prove too difficult. When he reached the town, he easily found a parking place in a side street, locked the car and walked the short distance to the main shopping area. At the end of a short parade of shops, he found the kind of retail establishment that would be instantly familiar to any British shopper: smart and glitzy, staffed by bright young things, and with examples of all the latest handsets mounted in racks on the walls.

Bronson had no interest in the number of texts he could send at no charge, or the length of time he could spend pointlessly surfing the Internet on a phone with a screen the size of a large postage stamp. All he wanted was the cheapest pay-as-you-go phone the shop had to offer. And eventually, after a good deal of gesticulating, pointing and miming, and even trying out a bit of his French on the assistant, Bronson got what he wanted: a cheap phone with a mains charger and a SIM card in a colorful box, plus the largest amount of credit the unit would accept, all of which he paid for in cash.

He returned to the car, opened the box and checked the phone. All the instructions were in German, obviously, but mobile phones aren't complicated to use, and he didn't expect to have any trouble getting it to work, especially after he went into the menu system and changed the display language to English.

The owner of the Hyundai had helpfully left a universal phone charger in the glovebox, perhaps because he used several different phones for different purposes—a common trick employed by drug dealers—and Bronson quickly found the correct adapter for his new unit. He

plugged the other end of the charging lead into the cigarette lighter socket, and left the phone switched on. Now
he needed to send the text to Angela, and then lose the
old unit.

He checked the map book. He still believed that the
house he'd been taken to lay somewhere to the southeast
of Berlin, but he guessed he was too far south. The fastest
way to drive to the north would be along the autobahn
he'd recently left, but he was reluctant to do that just in
case there were any checks or roadblocks on it. He much
preferred the freedom of choice and multiplicity of routes
offered by the normal roads.

Bronson started the car again and drove straight
through Klein Köris to the T-junction with route 179,
where he turned left. About five miles north of the junction, he found a convenient turnout and pulled in. He
reinserted the battery in his old mobile phone and
switched it on.

He'd just entered the phone number of his new mo-
bile when a thought struck him: there was something,
something important, that he hadn't asked Angela to do.
After the mobile number he quickly added a few sen-
tences: REMOVE BATTERY FROM NEW PHONE
WHEN IN OR NEAR OFFICE OR FLAT. PHONE
CAN BE TRACED IF BATTERY ATTACHED. ONLY
SWITCH ON WHEN ABOUT TO CALL ME. ONLY
CALL ME FROM CAFE OR RESTAURANT OR
OTHER CROWDED LOCATION. UNDERSTAND?

He left the phone switched on for a couple of minutes
while he worked out the route he was going to follow,
just in case Angela replied quickly. And she did, just be-

fore Bronson was going to start the engine and drive
away. Her message was just as abrupt and terse as his had
been. I GET IT, she'd sent. Bronson grinned, pulled out
the phone's battery, and drove away.

Near Körbiskrug he pulled into a garage to fill the
car's fuel tank, and buy some snacks and a couple of cans
of drink. While he was in the garage, he looked at some
of the other items on display, and in what looked like a
"special offer" section—which was probably stuff the
owner was desperate to get rid of—he found exactly what
he wanted. And it was cheap, too.

A mile or so further up the road he pulled into a large
turnout to eat his scratch lunch before starting his search
for the house in earnest. There were three other vehicles
parked in the turnout, two cars and a pickup truck with
an open flat-bed rear, full of bits of furniture and other
stuff. Bronson pulled his car to a stop a few yards away
from it, and looked at it thoughtfully, a simple plan forming in his mind.

He reached over and opened the glovebox, put the
battery back in his old mobile and turned on the unit.
The driver of the pickup truck was sitting in the vehicle,
eating a large sandwich and chatting to his passenger. The
sound of country-and-western music was faintly audible
through the truck's open windows, and neither of them
seemed to be paying too much attention to their surroundings.

There were various bits of rubbish littering the floor of
the Hyundai, and a bin a few feet in front of the truck—to
Bronson this seemed like a good opportunity for a bit of
housekeeping. He picked up most of the rubbish, got out

of the car and made his way past the vehicle, watching the truck's side mirror carefully. When he was sure that the passenger was looking away from him, at the driver, he quickly tucked the phone into the back of the pickup, sliding it under a piece of tarpaulin and out of sight. Then he strode across to the bin, dumped everything in it, and retraced his steps.

About five minutes later, the truck's engine started, and the vehicle moved away, pausing for a second or two beside the bin so that the passenger could dispose of the remains of the early lunch the two men had been eating. Bronson watched it drive out of the turnout and cross the carriageway before accelerating away down the road, heading south.

A few minutes later Bronson finished his own lunch, started the car and drove out of the turnout, heading north toward Königs Wusterhausen. When he reached the town, his satnav guided him faultlessly through the center and steered him north, across the Berliner Ring on the L30, which would take him along the southeast bank of the V-shaped Großer Zug lake.

He'd studied the map and identified a couple of places that could be close to Marcus's house. The first of these was a small town named Wernsdorf, which, according to the map, did have a main road running through it that followed an S-shaped path, and two roads that crossed straight and narrow stretches of water. One of these was the river, which joined two larger bodies of water, the Krossinsee and the Wernsdorfer See, and the other was the Oder-Spree-Kanal. And the final clincher was that Wernsdorf itself lay very close to both the river and the canal. In fact, it was on the banks of both and, as far as Bronson could see, that town was the best match to what he had seen from the back of the BMW as he was driven away from the house.

But when, about ten minutes after he crossed the Berliner Ring, he entered Wernsdorf, nothing that he saw seemed in any way familiar. He drove slowly through the town, and in the center continued along the L30, which swung right onto the Dorfstraße, heading for the bridge over the canal. If Wernsdorf *was* the town he'd been driven through, that had to be the road he'd been on, because of his recollection of the way the main road had turned in the town center.

Bronson knew for certain that he was in the wrong place when he drove across the bridge over the canal. The waterway was a lot wider than he remembered, but, more important, the structure and design of the bridge was entirely different from the picture he was carrying inside his head.

The second place he'd identified as a possible location lay due east of Wernsdorf, a small town named Spreenhagen. A short distance north of the bridge over the canal, Bronson eased the Hyundai in to the side of the road and reprogrammed the satnav. Spreenhagen was only about twenty miles away, and he didn't think it would take him much longer than three-quarters of an hour to get there.

His rough estimate was fairly accurate, though as he got nearer the town, Bronson was concentrating only on what he could see through the windscreen. The L23 ran through the village of Latzwall and then straightened up as it approached Spreenhagen, and as soon as he saw the road junction at the end of the straight, a flood of recognition washed over him.

He hadn't been driven down the stretch of road he was on at that moment, but he was certain that the junction with the minor road on his left was where the BMW had emerged. As he passed the junction, he caught a glimpse of the small collection of buildings that he remembered seeing the previous evening. And as he steered the car around a gentle curve at the end of the straight, Bronson saw, on the left-hand side of the road, the sign that he had spotted in yesterday's twilight. Now, in full daylight, he could see quite clearly that it didn't read *Kauptstraße*, as he'd thought, but *Hauptstraße*. He was definitely in the right place.

Now he knew he'd be able to find the house. What he still wasn't entirely sure about was what he should do when he did so.

28

Bronson drove over the canal—the bridge looking precisely as he remembered it—and into Spreenhagen. He didn't need further confirmation, so as soon as he was able to do so, he turned the car around and headed back the way he'd come. Once over the canal, he eased the car to the right, down the minor road that joined the *Hauptstraße*. A short distance further on was another junction, where he again remembered that the BMW had slowed down to cross the carriageway. He checked for other traffic—there was none in either direction—and then continued north along the arrow-straight road that had been cut through the wood.

The trees grew densely on either side of the road, with no apparent breaks at first. But then he saw a cleared area on the right-hand side where a large building—some sort of industrial structure, he guessed—had been erected. That was obviously not what he was looking for, and he continued driving steadily down the road, a road that a sign had already told him was named Röthen.

Shortly after that building, the wood petered out on the left-hand side of the road, and fields and farmland extended out to the west. To the east of the road, the wood appeared just as dense as the other section he'd driven past, and Bronson guessed that the house he was searching for had to be somewhere on that side.

And then he saw the end of the driveway, and the gravel section of the drive running up to the garage doors. And beyond it, in the same instant, he saw the house itself, looking deceptively innocent in the sunlight, its exterior giving no hint of the horrors that had been perpetrated within.

Bronson didn't slow down. In fact, he did little more than glance over to his right—the kind of half-curious look any passing motorist might bestow upon a large secluded house. Instead he drove on, along straight stretches of road punctuated by gentle bends, until he estimated he was at least half a mile beyond the house. Then he stopped the car, did a swift U-turn in the road and began driving back, retracing his steps.

On his right now, where the trees gave way to open farmland, the fields were bordered by hedgerows, but were apparently uncultivated, at least for the moment. On the left-hand side of the road, the same side as the house itself, Bronson could see a small copse of trees, and beyond that a stretch of open land that ran all the way to the edge of the wood. As he drove along, Bronson spotted the end of a rough and rutted track that ran along one side of a kind of thin extension of the wood. At that end, a line of trees and bushes extended from the wood toward the road, the track running beside it.

Without hesitation, he steered the car across the carriageway and onto the track, the suspension working hard to cope with the ruts and furrows. Wide and deep tire prints, presumably made by tractors or other heavy farm machinery, were visible all the way along the track, and Bronson presumed that it was a regular route used by a local farmer to get from one of his fields to another. The ground was dry and hard, and the car's tires had little difficulty in finding enough grip to keep going.

He drove on, trying to pick the smoothest path that he could, while taking frequent glances at the line of trees beside him, so that he would know when he'd reached the boundary of the main part of the wood. Quite suddenly, the wood darkened, and he knew that he'd gotten to the right area, a good starting point for him to approach the house.

He picked a gap between two trees that was obviously wide enough to accommodate the car and stopped. Then he climbed out and stepped past the treeline, to make sure that there were no holes, boulders or other hazards lurking in there which could do serious damage to the vehicle. In fact, beyond the trees lay a small clearing, perhaps thirty feet square, which was largely open, just a few small bushes dotted here and there. More important, a line of bushy shrubs was growing on one side of the pair of trees, and Bronson knew that if he parked his car close to them, it should be invisible to anyone walking along the track.

He strode back out of the wood to the car and checked

all around him. On the road below, a small motorcycle appeared, traveling quite quickly and possibly heading for one of the houses at the end of the road, its exhaust note a belligerent rasp that shattered the quiet of the early afternoon. As the sound faded, Bronson concentrated on listening, as well as looking. From somewhere out of sight, perhaps on the other side of the low hill in front of him, he could hear the noise of a tractor engine, the sound rising and falling as the vehicle maneuvered. He checked the track again, in both directions, but there was still nobody in sight. No farmers out shooting, no couples walking dogs. Nobody at all, which was just what Bronson wanted.

He climbed back into the Hyundai, turned the car and then backed it between the two trees and into the clearing, positioning it close to the shrubs that he'd noticed previously. He wanted the vehicle to be facing in the right direction to get away from the wood, just in case he had to beat a hasty retreat.

For a few moments he sat in the car, trying to decide his next move. First, he switched off the interior light. It was full daylight now, but he didn't know how long it would take to find the house, let alone find some way of getting inside it. If he came back to the car after dark, opening the door and having the interior light coming on would be a particularly stupid way of betraying his presence. For the same reason, when he left the car, he would lock it with the key, not the remote control. The characteristic flashing of the hazard lights would act as a beacon to anybody searching for him.

He stepped out of the car and eased the door closed as

quietly as he could. Sound tends to travel in the country-side, although the trees around him would help to deaden the noise. He walked around to the trunk of the car and opened it. In a plastic carrier bag was the item he'd bought earlier in the garage—a pair of compact binoculars. He slung the cord around his neck and tucked the binoculars inside his jacket, so they wouldn't swing about. Also in the bag were two bottles of water and some chocolate bars, and he took one of each. He checked that he had his new mobile phone in his jacket pocket, with the vibrate function turned off and the ringer set to "silent." Finally, he slid the Llama pistol into the rear waistband of his trousers, under his leather jacket. The magazine was fully charged with ten rounds of .22 Long Rifle ammunition, and he had the remainder of the box in another pocket.

That was one advantage of carrying a small-caliber pistol. He had fifty rounds with him, and was barely aware of the weight. Fifty nine-millimeter Parabellum rounds would be bulky and heavy, as would the weapon used to fire them. And at close range, in a competent pair of hands, both weapons were equally deadly, as the assassins employed by the Israeli Mossad service had demonstrated on numerous occasions.

Bronson walked across to the twin trees and looked out of the wood again, checking for anyone who might have seen him, but the track was empty. The only sound was the noise of the distant tractor, but it was still somewhere out of sight.

He had no doubt that he could get close to the house quite easily. Approaching a target premises over open ground was always difficult and sometimes impossible to achieve without being spotted, but doing the same thing through a wood or forest was comparatively straightforward. Unless they'd surrounded the house with a network of antisurveillance and counterintrusion devices, such as tripwires and infrared sensors, he should be able to get close enough to observe whatever was going on, and hopefully find his way inside without being detected.

It all depended on what he found when he got there.

Bronson shrugged his shoulders, took a final glance around the clearing, and then set off in the direction he thought the house must lie. Finding it wouldn't be difficult; he guessed he could probably walk from one end of the wood to the other in about half an hour, and as long as he could see the sunlight through the branches of the trees, he'd have a reasonable idea about which direction he was heading. Locating the house, and finding his way back to the car, come to that, should be easy.

The ground was solid underfoot, the hard soil softened somewhat by a layer of leaf mold, which would serve to deaden the sound of his footsteps. The tree growth inside the wood was much less dense than it had appeared from the outside, a phenomenon Bronson had noticed before; quite often, the thickest growth of trees and bushes was at the very edge of a wood or forest. Somebody had told him that it was dictated by the amount of sunlight that penetrated the canopy to stimulate new growth, but he'd no idea if that was true or not.

At first, Bronson moved fairly quickly, taking care that he didn't step on a fallen branch that could break or make any other noise that could be detected by audio sensors in his vicinity. One of the most obvious sounds that sentries are taught to listen for is the regular tramp, tramp, tramp of a walking man, so he took care to vary his stride, to ensure that his footfalls were as silent as possible, and he paused at frequent intervals just to look and listen.

After he'd penetrated about fifty yards he stopped and again checked all around him. He was looking for any sign of human presence, obviously, but also staring at the trees, checking to ensure that there were no cameras or microphones visible, and at the ground, looking for tripwires. He saw nothing, and walked on, moving from tree to tree, and stopping beside each one to make a further check before proceeding.

It was slow progress, but by taking his time Bronson believed he had the best possible chance of reaching the house without being detected.

He was heading approximately southwest, and after he'd covered about a hundred yards, he saw the first signs of a break in the treeline over to his right. It looked like a clearing or perhaps a fire break, and he guessed that he'd reached the edge of the wood that surrounded the property.

Now he moved even more cautiously, checking absolutely everywhere, because if the house was protected electronically, this was where the first of the devices would probably be positioned. He'd only covered about twenty yards when he saw the unmistakable shape of a house roof almost directly in front of him, and stopped in his tracks.

For almost ten minutes, Bronson stood virtually motionless beside the trunk of a large tree, assessing the situation. He couldn't see very much of the house itself, only a section of the rear wall, the ridge of the roof and a part of one side, but he was satisfied that it was the right building. He worked slowly and methodically, carrying out a visual search of all the trees he could see between his position and the edge of the wood where the house was standing. He let his eyes roam slowly up and down each trunk and along the principal branches, looking for the telltale sign of a camera or sensor. He was looking for anything that looked either unnaturally round or equally unnaturally square—shapes not normally found in nature.

But he saw nothing, which surprised him. He had been expecting, at the very least, a PIR detector or surveillance camera. Then he thought for a few moments and guessed the possible reason. He didn't know what kinds of wildlife lived in this area of Germany, but he assumed that there were probably deer, maybe wild boar, and possibly even wolves and bears, any of which would have about the same heat signature as a man, and would trigger any electronic alarms they installed. It also meant that tripwires wouldn't work, because animals that size would simply walk through them, and Marcus's men would have to continually reset them.

Reassured by both his logic and the complete absence of any visible anti-intruder devices, Bronson crouched down and then began making his way slowly toward the edge of the wood. He stopped a couple of yards short of the side of the clearing, where several shrubs provided a natural barrier between him and his objective, and lowered himself onto his stomach. He eased himself slowly forward, sliding his body under the lowest branches of the bushes, until he had a clear and unobstructed view of the house.

He was about twenty yards from the back wall of the house, and the first thing that struck him was how quiet it was. There were no people visible in the grounds and no signs of movement within the property—though obviously all he could see were the curtains on those windows where the shutters had been opened. There was no way of telling whether the house was occupied, because any cars would presumably have been parked in the large garage that lay on the side of the property closest to the road.

Bronson pulled the binoculars out of his jacket, and for several minutes just studied the building in front of him, making sure that his face was always in shadow to eliminate any chance of a stray reflection from the lenses of the instrument. Although they'd been cheap, the binoculars weren't bad quality, and he was able to see the property in sharp detail. But even without anything to enhance his vision, it would have been immediately clear that entering the house would not be easy. There were seven windows in the back wall—three on the lowest level, another three directly above them, and one at the top, underneath the ridge of the roof—and each of them, except the very top one, had been fitted with a steel grille between the panes of glass and the wooden shutters. At least, that was Bronson's assumption, because only one of the windows on the lowest level and two on the middle level had the shutters folded back, but it was a reasonable guess that what had been done to one window in a row would also have been done to the others. The very top window had neither shutters nor a steel grille, but its height above the ground made reaching it almost impossible without a very long ladder. And Bronson didn't think Marcus and his men were the kind of people who would leave a long ladder somewhere in the grounds for the convenience of any passing burglar.

Bronson tucked the binoculars away again, eased himself slowly backward, away from his vantage point, and retreated about five yards into the wood. Then he began moving around to his left, taking extreme care not to do anything that might attract the attention of anyone watching from inside the house. Now that he was closer to the building, he was also even more alert for the presence of tripwires or sensors, because they might have installed them close to the building, where wild animals would be less likely to roam.

It took him another fifteen minutes of slow and cautious progress, but finally he was able to look at the left-hand side of the house. Unfortunately, it wasn't a much more encouraging sight than the back of the building had been. Over half of the windows had the shutters open, but each one had the same kind of metal grille fitted to it.

The only possible entry point he could see was a single door positioned more or less in the middle, but which through the binoculars he could see was fitted with two locks: a Yale or its German equivalent, and some kind of a dead bolt, to judge from the shape of the keyhole. The Yale, like most locks of that type, would probably yield to a bit of gentle pressure against the latch from a credit card, but the dead bolt was an entirely different proposition, and Bronson had neither the tools nor the skill even to attempt to open it.

He lowered the binoculars from his face and considered his next move. He dismissed the idea of working his way around to the other side of the building; he'd seen the level of security on two sides of the house; he doubted very much if he'd find an easy way in anywhere else. Whoever had designed the property's passive defenses—the openings that formed the doors and windows—seemed to have done a good job, and they would certainly not have left the remainder of the house unprotected.

Although he'd still seen nobody, he knew he daren't risk walking across the open space around the house and trying the door. It would be locked, he was certain, but there was also a good chance it would be alarmed, so even if by some miracle it had been left unlocked, the moment he stepped inside, the siren would go off. The previous evening he'd noticed a square box on the front wall of the house bearing a three-letter legend, which he was almost certain belonged to a monitored alarm company. He had much the same system in his own home back in Kent.

He hated to admit it, but it looked as if his plan to get inside the house wasn't going to work. About all he could do was observe, and unless somebody appeared soon, that wasn't going to achieve any results either.

Then another thought crossed his mind, something that gave him a glimmer of hope for the first time since he'd arrived at the house.

There was one door to the property that definitely wasn't secured with a dead bolt, and that would probably be opened wide at some point during the day: the electric garage door. There was a chance he might be able to force it, but even if that proved impossible, if anybody arrived or left the house, the door would have to be open long enough to allow them to drive in or out of the garage. And when the door was opened, there was at least a chance that he could sneak inside undetected.

That was a kind of a plan, he supposed, and it was the only one he had, so Bronson slid backward away from his observation post and slowly, with infinite care, began to work his way around the perimeter of the clearing toward the front of the house.

When he reached a spot from which he could see that part of the property clearly, he wriggled into position in the undergrowth and began his observation. As he'd expected, the garage door was shut, and there was still no sign of activity anywhere in the property. He focused the binoculars on the box he'd noticed on the front wall, and could clearly see the logo. It showed the company trigraph inside a stylized fortress wall, and there was a small red light flashing regularly in the center, which just confirmed his suspicions.

He guessed that showed that the system was armed, and that probably meant the house was empty, because most homeowners would set their alarms only when they left the premises. And if it *was* empty, with any luck somebody would be coming back to it during the afternoon—or the evening, if he was unlucky. If it was a single man, Bronson hoped he'd be able to overpower him, and force him to hand over the Walther and the recording made by the camera.

He was aware that there were a rather large number of

variables and uncertainties in the scenario he'd envisaged, but he was optimistic. He also knew it was probably going to be a long afternoon, so he made himself as comfortable as he could, placed the binoculars to one side, and rested his head on his crossed arms.

It was a hot day, the sun was warm on his back, and the sound of buzzing insects and birdsong was gently soporific. Ten minutes later, Bronson was sound asleep.

29

A metallic clattering noise woke him, and for a few seconds Bronson had no idea where he was or what he was doing. He'd fallen asleep with his head lying across his folded arms, and his neck ached abominably. Then realization returned. Moving slowly and carefully, because the human eye is particularly well adapted to detect movement, he lifted his head to face the house.

The air was noticeably cooler, and the sun had almost set. The front of the house was now illuminated by the last of its rays, giving the wood a golden glow, and infusing the building with an appearance of benign and rustic comfort that Bronson knew was entirely illusory.

He raised the binoculars to his eyes, although he had already guessed the cause of the sound that had awakened him: the garage door was wide-open. The garage's interior lights were still switched off but he could just make out the shapes of two men standing together on the left-hand side of the open door. The odd word of German floated into the quiet of the evening, but even if Bronson had been able to speak the language, he doubted if he could have followed their conversation, because he was simply too far away.

It looked to Bronson as if they were waiting for something, or someone—perhaps for Marcus or one of the other men to arrive, which wasn't good news. He could have tackled one man, perhaps even two using the threat of his pistol, but it was clear that that window of opportunity had now passed. To implement his very sketchy plan, he would have needed to be standing somewhere near the garage door when it opened. Now, it would be impossible to cross the seventy or so yards of open ground between his present position and the garage without being seen.

And then he heard the sound of a car approaching, and guessed that this might be the vehicle the men were expecting. He glanced to his left and saw through the trees the irregular flickering of a set of headlights, the note of the engine changing as the car slowed down. Moments later, a vehicle turned off the road and drove down the track toward the property, its lights shining into the interior of the garage and revealing the presence of four other cars already inside.

That changed the odds considerably. Even if each car had been driven there by a single individual, that still meant there were at least four people in the house, and possibly as many as sixteen. Adding to that number the occupants of the vehicle that had just arrived, Bronson knew he could be facing up to twenty men, many of them armed if his past experience was any guide. To approach the building now would be suicidal. The best he could hope to do was wait until at least some of the men had left. Assuming, of course, that they would be leaving. He would just have to wait, and watch, and see what happened.

He'd been expecting the car to drive into the garage, and had assumed that was the reason why the two men were waiting by the open door, but then he realized that the number of cars already inside would have made maneuvering somewhat difficult. Instead, the car swung around to the left and parked on the gravel drive. Its lights were extinguished, the sound of the engine died away, and then the car doors opened.

Four men climbed out and walked around to the vehicle's trunk. Each man reached inside and took out a bulky bag, about the size of the weekend bag that Bronson had locked in the trunk of his car; then they strode across to the door of the garage. As they did so, the interior lights flickered into life.

Two things struck him immediately, both unexpected. The first was the way that the two men waiting there were dressed. Despite the warmth of the evening, both were wearing long and heavy overcoats that came well below their knees, and apparently had on some kind of boots, because Bronson could see the glint of black—presumably leather—below their coats. The second was what they did as the four new arrivals approached. They stood rigidly to attention and nodded deferentially as the other men stepped inside the building. Whoever the guests were, they appeared to be people of some importance.

But it was the overcoats that puzzled him. Now that the sun had gone down, the evening was getting cooler, but the air was still warm, and presumably the house had a central heating system, so why were the two men dressed in that fashion? It couldn't be because they were cold; that didn't make sense. In fact, Bronson could only think of one possible reason for what they were wearing, and he didn't like the idea at all.

He switched his attention back to the events unfolding in front of him. One of the men was still standing by the open door of the garage, while the other was escorting the four guests to the door at the rear of the garage, and in a few moments all five men had disappeared from view.

Bronson toyed with the idea of trying to get across to the house and into the garage while there was only one man on duty, but he guessed there was only one logical reason for the second man to remain by the open door, and that was because additional visitors were expected. Moments later, he was proved right when a second car turned into the driveway and parked near the first. Again, four men emerged from the car, collected bags and then disappeared into the garage. The only difference this time was that as soon as all four men were inside, the garage door closed behind them and the thin sliver of light visible under the door was extinguished.

Bronson lay still, the binoculars still clamped to his face, studying the building, but no lights went on anywhere in the property, and in any case, every set of shutters that was visible to him was now firmly closed.

He tried to make sense of what he'd just seen. The only reason he could think of for the two men to be clad in heavy overcoats on such a mild evening was because of what they were wearing underneath. That, together with the gleaming black leather boots they both had on, suggested a uniform of some sort, and presumably a uniform that they did not want any casual passerby to see. And that thought generated a host of different, and distinctly unpleasant, possibilities.

From the first, Bronson had assumed that Marcus and his band of men had formed a terrorist organization, and terrorist groups did not tend to wear uniforms or anything else that would enable them to be easily identified. That, in fact, was the point. Terrorists lurked in the shadows, forming their plans, delivering their weapons, and then making their escape, if at all possible, completely undetected. Wearing a uniform would never be a part of their agenda.

He still had no doubt that Marcus had planned some kind of terrorist-style atrocity against London, but now Bronson wondered if the German had formed a sort of private army. Could this gathering at the house be a meeting of the principal officers of that army, a meeting that required the attendees to wear full uniforms? That would explain not only what the two men in the garage had been wearing, but also the bags that the eight visitors had carried into the house.

And there was yet another, even darker, possibility, suggested to Bronson by those gleaming black boots. What if Marcus hadn't created a private army? What if he had simply re-created an older one? Maybe what was happening inside the property at that very moment was a neo-Nazi revival, a re-creation of a part of one of the most evil and ruthless regimes the modern world had ever seen. The thought sent a shiver down Bronson's spine.

One thing was now perfectly clear to him: there was no way he could get inside the property that evening. There were simply too many people in there for him even to attempt it. And if his theory about a neo-Nazi group was correct, if he was apprehended on or near the property, he had absolutely no doubt what the outcome would be. If he was lucky, they'd simply shoot him. If he was unlucky, he'd be strapped to that hideous chair in the concrete room and worked over for a day or two by some of Marcus's men to extract whatever information they wanted, and then they'd kill him.

The one thing he wasn't going to do, he decided, was get any closer to the house. He considered returning to his car and simply driving away, but he was loath to do that for the moment. In any case, he had no idea where he'd go or what he should do. He couldn't simply walk away from what he'd been forced to do inside that house. He had to try somehow to retrieve both the pistol he'd used to kill the man in the chair and the film Marcus had taken of the event. For the moment, that must be his goal. The bigger, and ultimately far more important, problem of the threat to London had receded somewhat in his mind, taking second place in his list of priorities.

The best thing he could do, he decided, was wait. And watch. When the garage door finally opened again, he might see something that would help him decide his course of action, and perhaps he could even memorize some of the faces of the people as they emerged to return to their cars. A decent camera with a telephoto lens would have been extremely useful at that point, but Bronson hadn't gotten one, and he had no way of obtaining one at that time in the evening.

For the next two hours, the house remained still and silent: no lights showing in any of the windows, no sign of any activity. The winking, telltale light on the burglar alarm box had been extinguished, because the system had been disarmed, and the property looked completely deserted. The moon was the faintest of crescents high in the sky above him, but it cast sufficient light for Bronson to see the shape of the house, even if he could no longer make out any of the details.

The noises of the wood had changed after nightfall. The birdsong had ceased, the buzzing of insects was no longer audible, and a silence seemed to have fallen across the land, disturbed only by the sounds of the creatures of the night. Somewhere over to his right a vixen screamed, the howl of a tortured soul, and some distance behind him a snuffling and grunting sound suggested that he'd been right about the possibility of wild boar being found in the area. He heard plenty of noises, but actually saw very little. A fox wandered across the clearing in front of him, between him and the house, and paused briefly to stare in his direction before moving on, following its usual patrol route. Several times he heard bats, their high-pitched squeaking unmistakable, and once a large owl, uncannily silent on its massive wings, flew slowly over the house, heading north on its nightly search for prey.

Just before midnight, the light in the garage snapped on again, dimly outlining the closed door, and moments after that, with a faint click and the whirr of an electric motor, the door began to open and light flooded out across the gravel drive.

Bronson focused the binoculars on the garage. As the door clicked up into the fully open position, one man appeared, striding across to the wall on the left-hand side of the door, then disappeared from view. Moments later, three floodlights mounted on the garage wall were switched on, illuminating the two parked cars outside the building. Then the man reappeared, stepped outside the garage and looked round, then walked back inside and across to the internal door, which was standing open.

Before he reached it, another figure appeared, quickly followed by about seven or eight others, most of them carrying bags—Bronson guessed they were the men he had seen arriving earlier. As far as he could tell, they were dressed in the same clothes they'd been wearing before, but as he stared through the binoculars at the group, now standing and talking more or less in the center of the garage, one figure immediately stood out.

Bronson knew that he would never forget Marcus's face. It wasn't simply that he recognized the man who'd forced him to kill a helpless human being, it was what the German was wearing that gripped his attention.

The black jackboots, black breeches and tunic were chillingly familiar, as was the peaked cap bearing the eagle insignia with the skull symbol, the *Totenkopf*—Bronson knew that much German—mounted below it. On the left-hand side of the uniform hung a chained black ceremonial dagger, and the lapel bore a rank badge bearing four square pips above two parallel bars. Bronson remembered military ranks from his days in the army, and that, he was sure, was the German rank *Obersturmbannführer*, equivalent to a British lieutenant colonel. The only splash of color was the blood-red armband displaying the all too familiar black swastika in a white circle.

Then Marcus turned slightly to his left, and for the first time Bronson could see his right lapel. There, gleaming in the overhead lighting, he could clearly see what he'd been expecting ever since the German had stepped into the garage: the twin lightning-bolt runes of the SS.

Two of the men then raised their right arms toward Marcus in rigid salutes, salutes which he returned. Then the two men turned on their heels and walked out to the cars.

He'd been right. The German hadn't created his own private army. Instead, he'd revived the most feared and detested military unit of all time, the SS or *Schutzstaffel*, the black-uniformed thugs responsible for running the concentration camps and perpetrating the vast majority of the atrocities recorded during the Second World War. The SS had fielded almost one million men, and had managed to enslave, torture, experiment on and eventually kill some twelve million people, most of them Jews. But they'd also directed their lethal attentions toward other "undesirables" who might in some way contaminate the purity of Hitler's ideal of an Aryan race, such as Poles and Slavs, the mentally and physically handicapped, political dissidents, clergymen and homosexuals. Of all the forces, of all the nations, involved in the global conflicts of the twentieth century, the SS had been by far the most chillingly efficient as a killing unit, and by far the most reviled.

Bronson knew that what he was staring at wasn't some toothless neo-Nazi revival, a bunch of deluded socialists wearing shirts with silly badges. From what he'd already found out about Marcus, he guessed that he was as close as possible to the real thing.

Not neo-Nazi. Just Nazi.

And that worried him more than anything else.

30

Just under half an hour later, once the two cars had departed and the house was again still and silent, Bronson moved back from his observation position below and behind the bushes and stood up, his joints and muscles protesting.

He had two choices about getting back to his car. He could retrace his steps through the wood, but that meant passing close by the house again, and in the dark he wasn't sure he could do that without tripping over something or making enough noise to be detected. Or he could work his way down through the wood, moving away from the house all the time, until he reached the road. Then he could simply walk along it, turn right up the rough track and get to his car that way.

It wasn't a difficult decision.

He took a last look at the house and turned away, moving slowly and carefully and keeping inside the wood itself. The further away he got from the property, the quicker he felt able to move, and in less than five minutes he stepped over a narrow ditch and onto the tarmac surface of the Röthen road.

When he reached the open area in front of the house, Bronson crossed to the opposite side of the road, just in case there were any watchers positioned. His rubber-soled shoes made almost no sound on the tarmac, but as a precaution he stepped onto the grass verge and walked along that, where his footsteps would be completely silent.

The house still looked empty in the faint moonlight, the only light the steadily blinking telltale on the external alarm box, which meant that somebody had armed the system again, presumably after the occupants—and he had counted at least four men plus Marcus still in the house—had retreated to their bedrooms.

Beyond the house, Bronson crossed back to the east side of the road. The beginning of the track was easy to find because the gap in the undergrowth was wide, though the track itself was barely visible in the moonlight. He checked the road, but saw no vehicles in either direction, then began making his way along the track. Bronson was fairly sure he was alone, but he still took his time and exercised caution as he headed toward the clearing where he'd parked his car, keenly alert for any noise that would indicate the presence of one of Marcus's men, or anyone else, for that matter.

In the end, it was something he smelled that alerted him. The faint whiff of tobacco smoke was unexpected but unmistakable. Somebody had smoked a cigarette on or near the track in the last few minutes.

It could have been one of the locals out walking his dog last thing in the evening and enjoying a cigarette. Or it could have been somebody a lot less innocent, and Bronson wasn't about to take a chance.

The instant he detected the smell, he stopped moving. Then slowly and silently he moved over to his right, toward the trees and bushes that bordered that side of the track, removing the Llama pistol from his waistband as he did so and clicking off the safety catch. He knew that there was already a round in the chamber, so the weapon was ready to fire.

For several minutes he stood motionless by the trunk of a large tree, concentrating with every fiber of his being on looking and listening for any movement or noise from the wood in front of him, anything that would show him where the armed man—and Bronson was sure that the man who had smoked an incautious cigarette would be armed—was positioned. He heard no movement, but he did hear a low murmur as somebody spoke, the words indistinct. Then another voice, clearer and probably closer, replied with a single syllable: *"Ja."*

That changed the odds; there were at least two of them waiting for him in the darkness of the wood ahead.

Still Bronson didn't move, his mind racing as he considered his options. He could walk away, abandon the car, but that really wasn't much of a choice. He needed a form of transport, but hiring a car wouldn't work because his passport didn't match his driving license, and if he stole a vehicle that would set the German police on his tail within hours. He needed the car, and that meant somehow getting into the clearing and incapacitating the men Marcus had positioned there.

For a moment he wondered how he'd been detected. He could only assume that before one of the clandestine meetings of the "new" SS in the house, Marcus probably ordered his men to do a quick search of the surrounding area. That would have been carried out while Bronson was asleep, and he guessed he was lucky that they'd only found the car, not him. And when they told Marcus it was on British registration plates, they'd know exactly who it belonged to.

Because he'd heard no movement, only the two brief snatches of conversation, Bronson still didn't know exactly where the men were waiting for him, so he did the next best thing: he tried to work out where he would have positioned his men if he'd been told to set up an ambush in the clearing.

With two men, he'd probably station one in the undergrowth directly opposite the opening between the two large trees, and the second man over by the car. That way, both of them would see the intruder at about the same moment, as he stepped into the clearing and, if the intention was to eliminate him, they could cut him down in their crossfire.

And the other thing Bronson would have done was to position a car or other vehicle some distance further up the track so that, if by some miracle the target was able to incapacitate the men waiting in ambush in the clearing, the third man in the car would be able either to follow him when he drove away or, more likely, to ram him and attempt to stop him as he headed down the lane.

In fact, that was something he could check, he hoped. Bronson gripped the binoculars and took two cautious steps to his left, moving just far enough to enable him to see up the track, while keeping most of his body hidden in the undergrowth. He raised the binoculars and started looking at the land in front of him. In the dark, the instrument was less help than he had hoped, and at first he was unsure what he was looking at; everything just appeared to be different shades of gray.

Then he managed to identify the edge of the wood on the right-hand side of his field of view and slowly moved the binoculars to the left, looking for the more or less straight line of the track. Then a faint glint appeared in the eyepieces, and Bronson immediately focused his attention on that. There was a dark square shape just about visible some distance away, and what he'd seen was the faint reflection of the moonlight off one of the headlamps. He had no idea what type of vehicle it was, or how many people were inside it, but it was definitely some kind of car, and just as definitely it hadn't been there when he'd arrived.

That was at least a confirmation, albeit an unwelcome one, that his tactical analysis had been fairly accurate. What he had to decide now was what to do about it, and as far as he could see, only one option made sense. There was no point in trying to sneak into the clearing to tackle the men hiding there while another group was sitting in the car in the lane, waiting for him to make a move.

He had to sort out the people in the vehicle first. And

as he decided that, another thought struck him. Something that could actually turn the situation around in his favor. The only question was what he should do about it.

What he couldn't do, quite obviously, was to continue walking up the track. That would just ensure that he was either captured or killed within a matter of minutes. Instead, he had to make use of the large open field that lay over to his left.

But for several minutes, Bronson just stood beside the tree and waited, because there was one other factor he'd noticed that might give him a tiny advantage. There were a few small and more or less circular clouds in the sky, all drifting slowly northeast, and a couple of them were soon going to obscure the moon.

The moment the first cloud blotted out the faint light, Bronson stepped back onto the edge of the track, keeping as close to the trees and bushes as he could without actually touching them, and began retracing his steps.

He didn't go all the way to the end of the track, because he was very aware that the moon would reappear any moment, and he needed to get into the large field as quickly as he could. As soon as he reckoned he was out of sight of whoever was waiting in the car, he turned to his right and started jogging toward the center of the field. The ground rose toward the north, and he was reasonably certain that he was now effectively over the horizon as far as the people waiting for him were concerned.

Then he started heading east, this time much more slowly and cautiously, trying to get his bearings and, more important, hoping to spot the position of the waiting vehicle before the watchers inside it could see him.

A brief wash of pale white illumination swept across the field as the moon reappeared from behind the clouds, and Bronson immediately stopped moving. From his different perspective, looking across at the track from one side rather than along it, and from the slightly higher ground near the middle of the field, the vehicle was clearly visible.

It was a dark-colored saloon, possibly one of the BMWs he'd seen previously being driven by members of the group. It was less than a hundred yards in front of him, facing down the track, but in the poor light he had no idea if the car was empty or filled with armed men. That was something he needed to find out before he got too close to it.

The moon vanished again, this time behind the larger cloud, and the landscape was plunged into darkness once more. Bronson knew he had perhaps four or five minutes before the cloud moved away, a brief enough timescale for what he had to do.

He moved quickly down the gentle slope, angling slightly over to his left so that he would be able to approach the car from the right rear quarter. All mirrors have blind spots, and he hoped that the car's occupant—or occupants—would be concentrating on the view in front of them, straining to see their victim as he walked up the track toward them. They probably wouldn't be expecting him either to carry the fight directly to them or to approach them from behind.

He stopped moving the moment he could discern the bulky shape in the darkness in front of him, and eased slowly down to lie full-length on the ground. He guessed the car was only about twenty-five yards away. He still had no idea how many men were inside it, and that was vital information. He raised the binoculars to his face, adjusted the focus and stared at the car.

It was too dark to see anything clearly through the windows and obviously no lights were switched on in the interior of the vehicle. But as his eyes grew accustomed to the darkness, he saw a faint movement in the front seat, on the driver's side, but no sign of anybody sitting in the other front seat, or in the back of the car. And that, he supposed, made sense. It looked like there was just a single occupant. The ambush in the clearing was where they expected to trap him; the man with the car was just an insurance policy in case something went wrong.

And if Bronson's plan worked, it would certainly go wrong for them.

He slowly rose into a crouch, and then backed away until he could no longer see the car, which meant that nobody in the car could see him. The field was hard-packed earth mostly covered in grass and presumably used for grazing cattle or maybe sheep. But there were a few low stumpy bushes dotted around the edge of the track, and one of those might help him.

Bronson moved about fifty yards behind the car, staying inside the field, and began tugging on the stems of the small bushes he found growing there. Most were firmly anchored by their roots, but within a couple of minutes he'd found one right at the edge of the field that wasn't. The stem moved slightly when he pulled it.

He reached around to the belt on the right-hand side of his trousers and snapped open a small holster that contained the folding multi-tool that he never traveled without. He opened it and, working by feel, selected the knife blade and locked it into place. Then he worked the blade around the base of the bush, digging it into the ground to cut through some of the roots. It gave way suddenly, and he found himself holding the bush with a couple of pounds of earth still attached to the roots. It was just what he needed.

He folded up the multi-tool and replaced it in his holster, then walked cautiously back toward the car, approaching it at an oblique angle, hopefully staying out of sight in any of the rearview mirrors.

He stopped about twenty feet behind and to one side of the car, measuring the remaining distance by eye, then acted. He swung the bush back, and then lobbed it underarm toward the vehicle. It was another BMW, as he'd guessed, this one a 3-series.

The bush with its cargo of earth described a parabola, landed with a dull thud almost directly in the middle of the trunk lid, then slid off it and fell to the ground behind the car. The impact wasn't enough to damage the vehicle, but Bronson was sure the man inside would have heard and felt it. And would want to investigate the cause.

For a few moments nothing happened, and he wondered if he'd been wrong, if the car was empty, if he'd been tricked by a shadow and hadn't seen anyone in the driver's seat. Maybe the car had simply been used by the men waiting in the clearing as a means of transport.

Then he heard a click, and immediately closed his eyes to preserve his night-sight, because the driver's door of the BMW had just swung open, triggering the interior light. Bronson knew that the bulb was very low powered, just a few watts, but in the blackness of the night it was like a searchlight snapping on.

He stared down at the ground before he opened his eyes, but then the light was extinguished as the man closed the door again. Bronson looked up and watched as a dark, bulky figure stepped around to the back of the car.

As soon as the man looked down at the bush, he muttered a single word—"*Scheiße*"—which Bronson didn't need to be a linguist to translate.

But by then, he was already moving.

31

Bronson covered the dozen or so feet to the other man in a few swift and silent strides, then stopped right behind him. He reached forward over the man's left shoulder and wrapped his hand around his mouth. At the same moment, he hit out with his right fist with all the power he could muster. The blow connected with the other man's back beside his right kidney, exactly where Bronson had been aiming. It was an incapacitating, not a killing, blow. The man loosed a sudden muffled grunt of surprise and pain as he arched backward.

Bronson was already pulling him in the same direction, and the man tumbled helplessly to the ground, cracking the back of his head on the hard-packed soil as he did so. But Bronson hadn't quite finished with him, and swung his right fist again, this time aiming for the solar plexus, driving every vestige of breath from the man's body. And he followed that with a sharp uppercut to the jaw to complete the process. The man's head snapped backward as unconsciousness claimed him.

It was a rapid and brutal demolition job, and had offered the man no possible chance of responding, which was precisely what Bronson had intended. For about half a minute he stood where he was, staring down the track into the darkness and listening intently. He doubted if the noise of the assault could have been heard more than a few yards away, but he needed to be certain nobody was approaching him. But he heard nothing, no sound of movement.

Then he bent down and quickly searched the unconscious man. He found a Walther pistol—this one a PPQ model, very similar in appearance to the smaller Glocks—in a shoulder holster and with two spare magazines in a belt pouch. A metal tube in one of his pockets turned out to be a suppressor for the weapon.

Bronson shrugged, pulled off the man's jacket, and took the lot. He took off his own jacket, donned the shoulder holster and the belt pouch, and screwed the suppressor onto the threaded barrel of the Walther. He pressed the magazine release and hefted it in his hand. It felt full, but he had no time to check it. Bronson replaced the magazine in the pistol and eased the slide back just far enough to confirm that there was already a round in the chamber.

That was the first part of his plan completed. Now all he had to do was get past whoever was waiting for him in the clearing further down the track.

Bronson still needed a car, and had realized that it might make sense to "borrow" the BMW, rather than even try to retrieve the Hyundai. BMWs, after all, were as common on the roads of Germany as Fords were in Britain, and he would stand out less driving that than the British-plated vehicle.

There was nothing in the Hyundai he needed to recover, and it couldn't be traced to him because he didn't own it. And despite the addition to his armory, Bronson still wasn't happy about tackling the men in the clearing. He knew there were at least two of them, and even they would be a handful. If there were three or four waiting there, he'd almost certainly come off worst. In all respects, taking the BMW and getting the hell out of Dodge made sense.

He walked round to the driver's door, slid into the seat and closed the door. The keys were in the ignition, and he immediately started the engine and switched on the lights, selecting main beam. There was no point in trying to be sneaky, because not even Harry Houdini could have managed to spirit a four-door saloon car past the men waiting in the clearing.

He lowered the door window and placed the Walther on the seat beside him, where he could easily reach it. Then he engaged first gear and began driving slowly down the track.

He was watching where he was heading, making sure he kept the saloon on the track, but most of his concentration was directed toward the wood on his left, waiting to see what would happen when he reached the entrance to the clearing. Would one of the men step out to stop him and ask where he was going, or would they just assume he'd been recalled to the house by Marcus?

A squawk from the dashboard made him look down, and he spotted a small two-way radio on the front of the transmission tunnel. The noise was followed by a short burst of German, so he guessed that somebody, presumably one of the men in the clearing, wasn't waiting for him to reach them, but was asking him what he was doing.

Clearly he couldn't reply to the question, so he just kept on driving, but picked up the Walther in his right hand and rested it on his lap, just in case they tried to stop him. Then he saw the two large trees on his left, and knew he'd almost reached the clearing.

The radio barked another string of words at him, which he again ignored.

Then a figure wearing camouflage clothing emerged from beside one of the trees, a pistol held in his right hand, but pointing at the ground, and his left hand raised.

Obediently, Bronson slowed down the BMW slightly and dipped the lights. He lifted the Walther off his lap and rested the end of the suppressor on the door, aiming the weapon at the man as the car approached him.

The figure stepped forward a couple of paces, then seemed almost to recoil as a spark of recognition crossed his face. Immediately he began to raise his pistol, but Bronson was a whole lifetime faster.

He adjusted his aim slightly and squeezed the trigger of the Walther. The pistol coughed in his hand, the suppressor doing its job, and the man beside the car fell backward, the front of his camouflage jacket suddenly turned crimson.

Bronson didn't wait around. He flicked the lights back

to high beam and floored the accelerator pedal. The BMW leaped forward, tires scrabbling for grip on the loose and rutted surface of the track. There was no point in him watching his mirrors, because the night behind him was impenetrably black, and the first warning he'd have if he was being shot at would be the arrival of the bullet.

Instead, he just concentrated on covering the ground as quickly as he could, trying to increase the distance between him and the other man—or other men—in the clearing.

A sudden flash of light from the track behind him caught his eye. Then he heard the bang of a gunshot, the noise echoing all around him. It sounded like a pistol, in which case, unless the man firing it was an Olympic-standard shot, Bronson had nothing to worry about. Few people can hit even a large stationary target with a pistol at much more than twenty yards, and he reckoned he'd already covered well over fifty. Another shot rang out, then a third, but all missed the BMW.

Now he was almost at the end of the track, trying to work out whether to turn left, which would take him past the front of the house, or right, to follow the Röthen road, which he knew curved around in a large loop to join the road he'd driven down to get to Spreenhagen earlier that day.

Then the choice was made for him.

As the BMW bounced over the last of the rough ground where the track intersected with the tarmac road, Bronson glanced to his left and saw headlights coming down the drive from the house. It looked as if the man with the radio hadn't just been trying to contact the driver of the BMW, but had raised the alarm in the house as well.

It took only a second or two for Bronson to figure the angles. If he went left, the other car would be out of the drive and blocking the road long before he could drive past the house. Going right was the only viable option.

As soon as the front wheels of the car reached the tarmac, he swung the steering wheel around to the right and accelerated as hard as he could.

Then he heard the unmistakable hammer of an automatic weapon from somewhere behind him, and realized that the men in the clearing hadn't just been carrying Walthers or Glocks; at least one of them had a submachine gun or an assault rifle. Through the open window of the car, he heard the sound of bullets ripping through the undergrowth and thudding into the trunks of trees that he was driving past, and which now provided a sort of natural bulletproof shield on his right-hand side.

At short range, pistols worried him, but automatic weapons were in a different category and added another layer of danger to the situation. And it also concerned Bronson that the men from the house were apparently happy to fire such weapons despite the certainty that other residents in the area would hear the noise, and most likely immediately call the police.

But that was the least of his worries.

The Röthen road was narrow and, as Bronson already knew, full of twists and turns as it made its way back toward the main road down to the southwest, but that was the way he was going to have to go because of the car that, he could now see in his rearview mirrors, had left the driveway to the house, and was swinging around to the right to follow him.

He was driving a strange car, with the steering wheel on the wrong side, along a road he didn't know, pursued by men who he guessed knew both the area and their vehicles intimately. The one single advantage he had was that he'd been trained as a Class 1 police driver, and that meant that he knew how to handle a car at almost any speed.

The first part of the road was virtually straight, with just a very gentle left-hand curve in it, and he kept the power on as he steered the BMW through it. The lights of the pursuing car were visible in his mirror, but he had been able to swing right as soon as he left the track, whereas the other vehicle had possibly stopped to block the road before beginning to chase him, so he had a very slim lead over it.

In a matter of seconds, Bronson saw the first of the bends, where the road swung left almost in a right angle around another property, looming up in front of him. He hit the brakes hard, hauling the speed down as he shifted the gear lever from fourth directly to second. Slow in, fast out—a basic rule of high-performance driving.

He clipped the apex of the corner and the moment he saw the clear road ahead he accelerated again, swinging the car into the following right-hand curve.

Another sharp left-hand bend appeared in front of him, Bronson trying to read the road as he concentrated on getting as much speed as he could out of the BMW. He was still in second gear, which was probably right, and again he hit the brakes hard before powering around the curve.

The main beams of the headlights showed him that the road was straight, at least for a couple of hundred yards, and he took full advantage of the fact. Another gentle curve to the left was followed by a sharp left-hand bend, and then another straight, this one much longer, and he managed to get the car traveling at well over seventy miles an hour before the next bend in the road. That bend swung through almost ninety degrees, and had a couple of junctions on it as well.

He'd been checking his rearview mirrors, and the lights of the pursuing car were still with him, but they didn't seem to have gotten any closer. He estimated that it was still at least two hundred yards behind him, a slim enough margin. He accelerated around the bend and into another straight, and at the end of that he could see the signs indicating that it was a T-junction. This time, he knew he had no option about which way to go. He had to get away from the area of Spreenhagen as quickly as he could, and that meant a right turn, to head northwest.

He was hampered by the fact that he had neither a map nor a satnav in the car. Or, to be exact, he didn't know if he had either, and he certainly didn't have time right then to look. He was having to rely on his memory, what he recalled of the journey he'd done the previous day, and he just hoped that would be enough.

He knew that part of the Berliner Ring lay somewhere over to the west, and getting on that and simply driving as fast as he could was one option. A second choice would be to find a town or village somewhere on the road and lose the pursuing car in the streets, maybe by stopping in a car park or a side street and hoping that the pursuers drove on. The third option was the riskiest, and definitely the last resort: let them get close enough for Bronson to mount his own ambush on some quiet road.

He reached the T-junction, flicked off his headlights as he approached, so that he could detect the lights of any vehicles on the road he was about to join, saw nothing, turned the headlights back on, and braked hard again, changing down as he did so. Then he clicked the steering wheel to the right, simultaneously lifted his foot off the brake pedal and back onto the accelerator. The back end of the BMW slid out in a power slide with a squeal of tortured rubber, and the car fishtailed down the road as he straightened up.

Now he knew he had a good chance of losing the following car. The road was virtually straight and had curves rather than bends, the surface was better, and it was much wider than the Röthen road. He still had a good lead, at least three hundred yards now, he estimated, because of the speed he'd managed to achieve on the section before the T-junction. Then he realized he'd done better than expected, because the pursuing car's headlights only appeared in his mirror as he reached the bridge across the river, and that meant a lead of over half a kilometer, more than five hundred yards.

There was a tiny village named Spreeau, little more than a hamlet, a short distance beyond the bridge, but he didn't even attempt to slow down, just kept the BMW running as fast as he possibly could. He was doing an indicated one hundred and forty kilometers an hour—

over eighty miles an hour—as he drove out of the northern end of the village, and knew immediately that he simply had to outrun the pursuit, because the road ahead was arrow straight as far as he could see, and that meant that if the men chasing him didn't see his taillights, they would know that he'd stopped somewhere.

He simply had to rely on speed, and he just hoped that, whatever the pursuing car was, the BMW he'd stolen would be faster.

There was no other traffic on the road, in either direction, which was both a blessing and a curse. Other cars would have slowed him down, certainly, but at night, just as in the dark all cats look gray, all cars look alike, and he could have tried to lose himself in the traffic. He continued accelerating hard, the BMW easily traveling at well over one hundred miles an hour, his concentration absolute.

The headlights appeared behind him under a minute after he'd cleared the end of Spreeau, but it was immediately obvious that he'd managed to increase his lead even further. Either their car was slower than the BMW or he was simply outdriving them.

The sign for a roundabout appeared suddenly out of the dark, and Bronson started to slow down, looking out for the road sign that he knew would follow. He glanced quickly at it, saw that the Berliner Ring was indicated over to his left, and continued slowing down as the roundabout came into view. Again, he flicked off his headlights as he approached, checking for other traffic. No other lights were visible, and instead of going around the obstruction, Bronson simply eased the car over to the opposite side of the road and took the left-hand exit, saving a few precious seconds.

Again, there was no traffic, and Bronson was able to extract every last scrap of speed from the BMW as he headed for the autobahn interchange. The pursuing car was now so far behind him that he knew the men in it would be completely unable to see which direction he turned at the junction. He was hoping that he'd find somewhere to tuck the car out of sight just before the junction so he could make sure that whatever direction they turned, he would go the opposite way.

And here the road helped him. Although it was wide and fast, there were numerous curves and the land on both sides was heavily wooded, which meant that once his car was around one of the curves, he would be lost to sight for anyone following him.

Another road sign told him that he was approaching the autobahn junction, the road at that point swinging to the left in a gentle curve, and a further sign warned of a left-hand junction. Bronson braked gently but firmly, ensuring that the car's tires left no marks of rubber on the road that could alert the men in the following vehicle, and as soon as he saw the junction ahead, he swung left off the road and into the entrance of a small industrial estate. The road was comparatively wide, and he was able to swing the car around in a U-turn so that it faced back toward the main road.

He pulled the BMW to a stop at the edge of the road, switched off the lights, pulled on the handbrake and lowered the window on the driver's door. There were trees over to his right—the whole area seemed heavily forested—

which would prevent his car being spotted by any approaching vehicle on the main road, but the area to the west of him was comparatively clear, and he could actually see the autobahn junction about eight hundred yards away down a completely straight road. As long as his pursuers didn't guess that he'd pulled off the road, he knew he'd be able to see which direction they turned.

And although the roads he had driven on so far had been devoid of traffic, he'd already spotted several vehicles on the Berliner Ring, which would further confuse the pursuit.

Moments later, he heard the sound of a powerful engine running at high revolutions, and a black Mercedes saloon swept past the junction where he was waiting and powered on toward the autobahn interchange.

The car's brake lights flared into life as the vehicle reached the junction, and Bronson could imagine the conversation taking place inside. Reduced to its barest essentials, it was a simple choice: left or right?

The Mercedes came to a complete stop, engine idling, in the road a few yards short of the entrance to the northbound slip road. Then the motor roared again and the car lurched forward, past the slip road and on toward the southbound carriageway.

For about five minutes, Bronson just sat in the driver's seat staring out at the autobahn junction over to his left. He had always been taught never to assume anything—he remembered an old adage that one of his sergeants had frequently trotted out during his time in the army: "assume makes an ass out of u and me"—and because he hadn't actually been able to see the Mercedes heading south on the autobahn, he didn't know that was where it had gone. It was possible that the car had stopped just out of sight, and that the occupants were looking back, in the direction they'd come, in case he'd managed to fool them.

He thought the possibility was remote, but still he sat there, just in case.

Then he turned on the ignition of the BMW and checked that all the instruments were giving correct readings. He climbed out of the car and made a quick visual check of the tires—what little he could see of them in the dark—because they would obviously have suffered from the treatment he'd given the car during the pursuit. But they were intact and, as far as he could see, they had plenty of tread left.

The glovebox of the vehicle produced nothing particularly helpful, apart from a map book and the car's handbook written in German, but tucked under the driver's seat Bronson found two full boxes of nine-millimeter ammunition. The other thing he found, which particularly pleased him, was a built-in satnav. He changed the language to English, which took him a couple of minutes, and then used the map book to pick a destination at random—a satellite town to the east of Berlin—and plotted a route to it. He needed somewhere quiet where he could park the car while he slept inside it, and he needed to talk to Angela.

Bronson drove back onto the main road and then took the slip road leading to the northbound Berliner Ring. The dashboard clock told him it was after two in the morning, but still there was quite a lot of traffic on the road, an almost equal mix of cars and trucks.

Twenty minutes later he pulled into a heavily wooded area beside a lake, switched off the engine and closed his eyes.

32

24 July 2012

Marcus Wolf's cold blue eyes bored into the face of the man standing in front of him.

"And then, Oskar, you simply let him get away." His voice was low and laced with barely contained fury.

The man shook his head, but didn't reply. He knew this was an argument that he couldn't win.

"There were three of you, armed with pistols and a submachine gun, and he"—Marcus pointed at another man slumped in a chair by the wall of his office, a man bent forward and clutching his stomach—"was in the pursuit car. And still the Englishman managed to get past the three of you. Not only did he get past you, but he killed Pieter and stole a car. It was a complete shambles."

Wolf fell silent and picked up a SiG semi-automatic pistol from the desk, hefting it in his right hand. As he did so, the two men in front of him visibly tensed.

"We do not tolerate failure in this organization, but we

are now so close to the final act that every man must pull his weight. Too many of our men are deployed elsewhere for me to be able to afford the luxury of simply shooting you both. You're lucky, because you have one more chance. So get out of here, find Bronson, and kill him."

"He could be anywhere by now," Oskar objected. "Where do we start looking?"

"You're beginning to try my patience," Wolf said. "Use what brains you have. You know which car he stole, so the first thing you do is call up one of our contacts in the Berlin police and request that a watch is started for that vehicle. Make sure that whoever you talk to understands that this is an unofficial request. I definitely do not want Bronson apprehended by the police."

Klaus Drescher, who was sitting in an armchair to one side of Wolf's desk, made a suggestion.

"Don't you think it's possible that he might simply have headed for the Channel ports, to get back to England?"

Marcus Wolf shook his head.

"There's only one possible reason why he would have been hanging about near this house. He knows that the pistol and the film we took in the cellar are enough to hang him, and I've no doubt that he was hoping to somehow get inside this house and recover that evidence. He didn't manage it, but that doesn't mean that he won't try again, so I think he'll still be somewhere here in Germany, working out a way to achieve that objective."

"He'd be mad to try it again, surely?" Drescher said.

"I think he'd be mad not to. One thing Bronson has already shown us is that he's capable and resourceful.

He's been inside this house, and I expect that he's got a good idea of the way the security systems work. He's probably hoping that we'll leave the place unoccupied so that he can try to break in."

"But we're not going to do that?"

Wolf shook his head.

"Of course not. Or not until we head for London, and by then it'll be too late."

"Suppose he goes to the authorities? He might decide to take the chance, to try to argue that he was forced to kill Polti."

"What information can he take to the authorities? He knows nothing. Our hands are clean. We are all respected businessmen and citizens of Germany; he is a proven killer. And I'm quite certain that Bronson will be desperate to avoid coming to the attention of the police in either Germany or Britain. I still think he'll be somewhere in this area. And I want him found and killed."

Drescher nodded. "You're probably right, but finding him won't be easy."

"I didn't say that it would be. I just want it done."

Wolf switched his attention back to the man standing in front of him.

"Do you understand? This is positively your last chance. If you can't do this, don't bother coming back here because if you do I will kill you myself."

Oskar nodded, turned away and walked out of the study, his companion hobbling painfully along behind him.

"Do you think they'll track him down?" Drescher asked.

"They'd better. I want Bronson dead."

"But suppose that they can't find him? He could be almost anywhere. What then?"

Wolf shook his head and smiled grimly.

"Whether he's alive or dead won't make the slightest difference to our operation. There's nothing that one man—that any man—can do to stop us now."

33

Bronson woke, stiff and cold and aching, just after six in the morning. Dawn had already broken, the first pale streamers of the rising sun spearing slim shafts of light through the trees, and birds were greeting the new day with a medley of songs.

He opened the door and stepped out of the car, stretching and straightening his aching back, and for a few moments just looked around him and listened. He appeared to be entirely alone. He could see neither houses nor other cars, and no signs of walkers either.

He walked the few yards to the shore of the lake, bent down and splashed water onto his face. It was so cold it almost seemed to sting him, but it very effectively completed the process of waking him up. He had nothing to eat or drink in the car, and he badly needed both a cup of coffee and some food; he was ravenously hungry.

He also needed to decide what to do next. Getting

back into the house near Spreenhagen would be impossible now. Marcus and his men knew that he hadn't trotted back to London as he'd been instructed, and they would be even more alert than before to the presence of any intruder. He had no idea what would eventually happen about the undercover policeman he'd killed and the unarguable forensic evidence he'd been forced to leave in the house and, because he could do nothing about that situation, he tried to dismiss it from his mind.

He also didn't know if he'd killed the man who had tried to stop his car near the clearing the previous night, but he certainly wasn't going to lose any sleep over him—if he hadn't shot him with the silenced Walther, he knew beyond any doubt that the man would certainly have shot him. In that situation, it was kill or be killed.

But the bigger question, the one that really worried him, was what Marcus and his men had planned for London. Exactly what was the "lantern bearer" that he'd mentioned? What could it do? And why was a group of reborn Nazis trying to mount a terrorist attack on Britain's capital city?

Bronson glanced at his watch. It was too early to ring Angela, but he turned the phone on anyway and deselected the "silent" option, just in case she decided to call him. Then he fished out the map book, opened it at the page that showed the area to the east of Berlin, and for a few minutes just stared at it. He knew exactly where he was, but he had absolutely no idea where he should go next, or what he should do.

His mobile phone suddenly burst into life, the speaker playing the opening bars of "The Ride of the Valkyries," and he made an immediate note to change this for something less offensive—or at least something more modern—as soon as he could. Bronson's musical taste had stalled somewhere in the mid-seventies, and his CD collection was almost exclusively rock 'n' roll.

Without even looking at the screen, he knew it had to be Angela, simply because nobody else knew his number.

"Chris? Thank God. I've been trying to call you for hours, but your bloody phone has been switched off all night."

"I know," Bronson replied. "I had no option. It was—"

"Tell me later," Angela interrupted. "Listen. Thanks to Steven, I think I know what *Laternenträger* refers to, and it's not good."

"What is it?"

"I'll tell you when I see you. That's what I was really ringing you up for. I'm in a taxi heading for Heathrow; I'm booked on the morning Lufthansa flight to the new Brandenburg Airport in Berlin. The flight gets in at about ten, and I expect you to be in the arrivals hall no later than quarter past, and pleased to see me."

"I'm always pleased to see you, Angela. You know that. But I don't think you coming out here is a good idea. I'm involved with some really dangerous people."

"I always thought you were quite dangerous, Chris, and I'm sure you can take care of yourself, and take care of me as well. Anyway, I'm coming, because you're going to need my help to sort this out. I'll see you at the airport."

And with that, she rang off.

Bronson stared at the phone in his hand, then shrugged and put it on the seat beside him. In truth, he was pleased that Angela was flying to Germany. He was sure that whatever information she'd discovered would help point him in the right direction, and it would be really good to have her around. He just had to make sure that he kept her well away from the clutches of Marcus and his gang of homicidal thugs.

He looked at his watch again. He had hours before she landed, plenty of time to find somewhere, some quiet café, where he could buy breakfast, and then make his way to the airport, which he located quickly when he looked again at the map. It was in the Schönefeld district, just a few miles almost due south of the center of Berlin.

A thought struck him, and he realized that there might be something else he could do at the Brandenburg Airport while he was waiting for Angela to arrive. He smiled to himself, then started the BMW, bounced over the uneven ground where he'd parked for the night and got back on the road.

Two hours later, having breakfasted cheaply and copiously at a small café on the outskirts of Hoppegarten, and still well before Angela's flight was due to touch down, he drove into the long-term parking area at Brandenburg. He knew he was only going to be there for a short time, but he was looking for something very specific, and he thought that that parking area represented the best chance he had of finding it.

On the way to the airport he'd stopped at an out-of-town shopping center, where he'd found a large hardware store. He'd bought a pop rivet gun with a selection of rivets and washers; a hand drill and half a dozen drill bits, including a countersunk bit; a plastic vehicle cover; and finally a basic toolkit.

All he needed now was to find the right car.

The long-term car park was the usual multi-story structure, each level covered by a single surveillance camera, which meant Bronson would need to be careful where he parked and what he did, to avoid attracting attention. He drove slowly up to the third level, then slowed down even more as he started looking for another black BMW 3-series. He had plenty of choices. He counted over twenty such vehicles as he drove through the car park, but he needed one that looked clean, which would suggest that it had been parked recently and implied that the owner wouldn't be back to collect it for at least a few days.

He found what he was looking for on the fourth floor. A black BMW parked next to a Mercedes van, which shielded the car from the unblinking eye of the surveillance camera at the other end of that level, and with a vacant parking space nearby.

Bronson reversed the car into the vacant slot and waited for a few moments until the Mercedes saloon that had been behind him as he drove up the ramp passed him and continued up to the next level. Then he climbed out, checked that he was unobserved, and opened the trunk of his BMW. He walked across to the back of the other parked car and looked down at the number plate. As he'd expected, it was secured in place by two rivets, one at either side.

He walked back to his car, removed the hand drill from the trunk, inserted the countersunk bit in the chuck and tightened it firmly. He returned to the other vehicle, watchful that nobody had spotted him, then bent down, placed the point of the drill bit against the first rivet and started turning the handle. The bit was brand-new and made short work of the aluminum rivet, and in less than thirty seconds he was able to repeat the treatment on the second rivet. The moment the number plate came free, Bronson stood up, walked back to his own car and put the plate into the trunk.

Then he walked over to the front of the other BMW and repeated the process. In less than two minutes, he had both number plates stored in the trunk of his own car, and a minute after that he'd covered the other vehicle with the plastic weatherproof sheet, which would hide it from view and prevent anyone spotting the missing number plates.

He locked his car, leaving the weapons hidden under the seat, and set off for the lifts and walkways that gave access to the terminal buildings.

Thirty minutes later, he was sitting by himself at a table in one of the cafés in the arrivals hall, a cup of coffee in front of him, and a one-day-old copy of the *Daily Mail* in his hand. Beside him was a plastic sports bag containing a designer-label washing kit—the only one he'd been able to find—a couple of shirts and a selection of underwear, all of which he'd bought at the shops in the terminal building, because he'd needed to replace the bag and clothes he'd had to abandon in the Hyundai. He'd also found a twelve-volt universal phone charger for use in a car, and that was in the bag as well.

Angela's flight arrived on time, and Bronson stood up,

grabbed his new bag and walked over to greet her as soon as he recognized her in the stream of passengers entering the hall.

Bronson moved quickly through the melee of people, reaching her side before Angela even saw him. The moment she did, she lowered her bag to the floor and hugged him tight.

"I've been so worried about you," she whispered. "I've had the police round twice, looking for you, and I swear that at least once somebody followed me to work."

Bronson nodded. "I'm not surprised. I left Britain under something of a cloud, and a warrant's been issued for my arrest."

"Then you really are in trouble, aren't you?"

"More than you can possibly imagine, for a whole bunch of different reasons. I'm really pleased to see you, but I'd still rather you were safely back in London."

"It's too late for that. I'm out here now, because I decided I couldn't stay away any longer. Besides, I think you need my help."

Bronson smiled at her. "You know," he replied, "I think I probably do. I realized this morning that I had no idea where to go or what to do next, so I hope you really have got some information about this 'lantern bearer' thing."

"I have," Angela said, "and I'll tell you all about it in the car on the way to Ludwikowice. You've got a car, I hope?"

Bronson looked puzzled. "Yes," he replied, "I've got a car. But what—or where—is this Ludwig-whatever place?"

"It's in Poland," Angela replied, "and it's where I hope we might find the answers to a lot of questions. It's certainly the place where the story of the 'lantern bearer' began."

Twenty minutes later, they were sitting side by side in the BMW, and Bronson had just finished programming the built-in satnav with Ludwikowice as a destination.

"It's over two hundred miles from here," he said, as the satnav finished its computations, "so it'll take us most of the day to get there."

He started the car and a couple of minutes later the barrier in front of them lifted and they drove out onto the exit road from the airport.

"We'll get a few miles under our belt before we stop for something to eat," Bronson went on. "So you've got plenty of time to tell me exactly what you're talking about, and why this Ludwig place is so important."

Angela leaned back in her seat and relaxed. "You'll notice," she began, "that I haven't asked you how come you're driving around in a BMW—a make of car I know you detest—on Berlin plates, or why there's the butt of what looks to me like an automatic pistol poking out from underneath your seat."

"It's a long story," Bronson replied, "and thank you for reminding me about the plates. I need to fix those as soon as I can. And it's not so much BMWs I dislike—it's the particular collection of arrogant and incompetent idiots who always seem to end up driving them."

"What do you mean by 'fix'?"

"You'll see."

Once they'd cleared the airfield, and had passed the

intersection between the E36 and the Berliner Ring, Bronson turned off on the L40 toward Ragow and pulled into the first deserted turnout he saw. There, while Angela stood beside him, looking and listening for cars or pedestrians, Bronson quickly and efficiently swapped the registration plates on the BMW, tossing the originals over a hedge and into the adjacent field.

"Because of what you've just done," Angela said, "may I assume that you've borrowed the car we're traveling in, using the term 'borrowed' in its loosest possible sense? That we are, in fact, driving around in a stolen vehicle?"

"You assume correctly," Bronson replied, getting back in the car and restarting the engine. He didn't know what contacts Marcus might have with the Berlin police—if he had any contacts at all—but he knew that changing the plates would make it a lot more difficult for anybody to track him as they drove across Germany. Unless somebody checked the chassis number of the BMW, it would appear to be entirely legitimate, at least until the owner of the car in the long-term parking at Brandenburg Airport returned from wherever he'd flown to and blew the whistle.

"I've been very patient," Bronson said, as he swung the car around in a U-turn to head back the way they'd come, "and you've been very mysterious. So why don't you tell me exactly what you've found out about the 'lantern bearer.'"

"Right," Angela replied. "Since you called me, apart from running around most of London trying to find different places to call you from—calls you never actually answered, I'd like to point out—about all I've done is research, following on from everything that Steven told me. It has been," she added, opening her handbag and taking out a small notebook with a dark blue cover, "grimly fascinating. First of all, have you ever heard the German terms *Wunderwaffen* or *Vergeltungswaffen?*"

Bronson shook his head. "No, I don't think so. What do they mean?"

"The word '*waffen*' translates as 'weapon,' so '*Wunderwaffen*' means 'wonder weapon' and '*Vergeltungswaffen*' translates as 'vengeance weapon.' Originally the *Wunderwaffen* were supposed to be various types of tactical battlefield weapons, while the *Vergeltungswaffen* were much more powerful strategic theater devices, but these days the term *Wunderwaffen* is often applied to both types of weapon. You probably know that toward the end of the Second World War the Nazis were desperately trying to find some kind of weapon or tactic that would turn the tide and force back the Allied advance, and keep the Russians off their backs."

Bronson nodded. "I know they developed jet engines for their fighters, and of course there were the V1 and V2 missiles that they fired at London. I suppose they were classed as 'vengeance weapons,' because of the 'V' designation?"

"Exactly. But the Nazis had far more interesting and exotic devices up their sleeve. Their problem was that by that time they'd lost air superiority in the skies over their own country, and the Allied bombing raids were doing enormous damage to their airfields and especially to the factories that were turning out military hardware. But one of the odd things about this period of the war was that despite all this bombing, Germany's war production actually continued to increase."

"I didn't know that," Bronson admitted. "How did they manage it?"

"It was all down to a man named Albert Speer."

"I've heard of him. He was one of Hitler's ministers, wasn't he?"

"You're right. In nineteen forty-two he was appointed Minister of Armaments and War Production, and as Allied bombs rained down on Germany night after night, he came up with a radical solution. Because the factories on the ground were no longer safe, he decided to move them. But instead of simply relocating them to other parts of Germany, he put them underground."

"Underground? That must have been an enormous job. You mean the Germans dug tunnels?"

"It was a huge undertaking, without question, but it wasn't the Germans who were doing the work. Because of the concentration camps, they had an enormous force of slave laborers—hundreds of thousands, even millions, of people, who could be quite literally worked to death in the most appalling conditions. And as soon as one man died, they simply dragged in another and forced him to take his place. They didn't need to supply safety equipment or proper clothing or masks or anything. In many of the construction sites, the SS doctors estimated that a fresh concentration camp prisoner would have a working life of as little as six weeks, working twelve-hour shifts with the most basic possible rations of food and drink. In several cases, according to the testimonies of the handful of people who managed to survive, prisoners were marched into the tunnels and only left them when they died, their bodies hauled out and dumped in a mass grave."

"Horrendous," Bronson muttered, "simply horrendous." He'd decided not to mention what he'd seen at the house—the chilling sight of Marcus in full SS regalia—for the moment.

"It was," she agreed, her voice bitter, "but it was also very efficient, and the Nazis were nothing if not efficient. Working prisoners to death not only meant that their construction projects proceeded quickly, but it also saved them the price of a bullet or the cost of a canister of poison gas."

"So how many of these tunnels are you talking about?" Bronson asked.

"It was one of the largest projects in the history of mankind," Angela replied. "Nobody knows for sure exactly how many underground facilities were built, or even planned, but even before the end of the war the Allies knew of at least three hundred and forty underground sites and, according to the records recovered after the end of the conflict, over four hundred sites had been given code names. But in fact there were far more than that. Plans held in the German Ministry of Armaments referred to some eight hundred plants in all. Work on them started in the summer of nineteen forty-three, when Allied air raids began inflicting enormous damage on Germany, and Albert Speer gave the go-ahead for the project, with Hitler's blessing.

"I suppose it's also worth saying that the idea of having underground facilities wasn't exactly novel. From as early as the mid–nineteen thirties, the Nazis began creating massive oil and fuel tanks underground. One of these—it's near Bremen—is still in operation today. There are eighty tanks there, each made of high-quality shipbuilding steel surrounded by a concrete jacket about a meter thick. Each tank holds four thousand cubic meters of fuel. They're absolutely massive."

"Well, underground storage tanks are quite common, and have been for many years," Bronson commented. "When you're dealing with potentially explosive liquids, burying them is often quite a good plan."

"I know. But actually the tanks were only a very small part—though an important part—of the project. The biggest and most significant plants were those used for manufacturing, rather than just for storage. The Nazis built an underground aircraft factory at Kahla in Thuringia, using foreign slave laborers who worked twelve-hour shifts and who were told when they arrived there that they would be worked until they dropped dead. That place was used to manufacture the Messerschmitt Me 262 jet fighter, and the plan was to build twelve hundred aircraft there every *month*, a huge output that absolutely could have turned the tide of the Second World War. That one factory, if it had reached full production, could have produced enough aircraft to drive the Allied bombers and fighters from the skies of Germany. The intention was to create almost twenty miles of tunnels inside the mountain, with four huge subterranean halls, covering around twenty-seven thousand square meters, where the actual manufacturing would take place. By the end of the war, almost half of the internal construction had been completed, and the first aircraft took off from Kahla in February nineteen forty-five. And it was, as I said before, very efficient. The aircraft were assembled in the halls, then they were taken out of the mountain through the tunnels, hauled up to the top in a sloping elevator, and would then take off from a runway the Nazis had constructed on the top of the mountain. Luckily for us, only a few of these Messerschmitts were completed and flown away, so they never became a major threat to Allied aircraft."

Bronson took his eyes off the road for a second or two to glance across at Angela.

"That's huge. Was that the biggest underground factory?"

Angela shook her head. "No, not by a long way, and some of them are still in use today. In Baden-Württemberg, down in the southwest of Germany, there's a town named Neckarzimmern. There's been a gypsum mine there since the early eighteen hundreds, over one hundred meters below the banks of the Neckart River. It was used as a dynamite factory in the First World War, and then after nineteen thirty-seven it became an ammunition dump. The various shafts inside it were expanded to accommodate its new role. Today, it's a subterranean town. There's a road network almost thirty-five kilometers long in there, and the various caverns occupy about one hundred and seventy thousand square meters of space. In nineteen fifty-seven, units of the German armed forces were first stationed there, and today over seven hundred people work underground, in the tunnel system, supplying parts and repairing equipment for the German army."

"Okay," Bronson said, "I understand that the Nazis turned into moles and burrowed into the hills and mountains, or rather their slave laborers did on their behalf, but you still haven't told me why we're heading for the Polish border, or what the 'lantern bearer' has to do with any of this."

"Patience, Chris. To fully appreciate what I'm going to tell you about that, you need to understand a bit more about the Nazi secret weapon program, the *Wunderwaffen*. We talked about the so-called 'vengeance' weapons, the V1 and the V2. The V2 was developed by Werner von Braun at Peenemünde, though it wasn't at first called that—it was designated the A4—and the first examples were ready for testing by early nineteen forty-three, and the weapon became operational in the summer of 'forty-four. The first V2 hit London on the seventh of September that year and after that the rockets became fairly regular and most unwelcome visitors to the capital. What's not generally known is that this missile wasn't built by the Germans, though it was undeniably designed by them."

"What do you mean? They contracted the work out?" Bronson asked.

Angela shook her head. "No, nothing so civilized. When American troops reached a town named Nordhausen in the Harz Mountains in mid-April nineteen forty-five, they found a concentration camp there named Mittelbau-Dora. The few inmates who were still alive— the vast majority who hadn't been executed by the Nazis before they left the area had simply starved to death— told the Americans about tunnels in the nearby mountain and a top secret missile factory deep underground where they'd worked as slave laborers of the SS. The American troops were shocked at what they found, but in fact the Allies already knew about it.

"In August nineteen forty-three, after the Royal Air Force bombed Peenemünde, the Nazis had transferred their missile production to Nordhausen. Some ten thousand slave laborers from the Mittelbau-Dora camp were forced to start digging tunnels into the mountain to accommodate the new production lines. For obvious reasons, we don't know the exact numbers, but it's been estimated that around three and a half thousand workers died in the first few months from pulmonary diseases, starvation, exhaustion and maltreatment by the SS. Some of them almost certainly simply froze to death.

"In all, the Nazis had allocated an area of about six hundred thousand square meters for the production of the V2 missile, and set a target of one thousand missiles per month, a theoretical output that they thankfully never achieved. We do know that in April nineteen forty-four the factory produced four hundred and fifty missiles, but that was one of their best months ever. Most of the time, production was badly delayed because the German scientists at Peenemünde kept altering the design and making changes. And as a result of that, more than half of the rockets that were assembled were not fully operational and either never reached their intended targets or simply blew up on the launch pads. But the missiles themselves were constructed by specially selected prisoners, who assembled them from some forty-five thousand different components. The sad reality is that most of the V2s that landed on London and caused such destruction to the city were actually built by people—Poles and Jews and others—who we would have considered to be our allies. Of course, they had absolutely no option. If they didn't do exactly what they were told, they would be summarily executed by the Nazis."

Bronson didn't respond for a few moments, as he tried unsuccessfully to imagine what it must have been like to be forced to assemble weapons that you knew, without the slightest shadow of doubt, were going to be used to kill members of the only nation likely to rescue you from imprisonment.

"That's horrendous," he said again.

"You know, almost everyone who has read anything about the Second World War knows about the V1 and the V2, but hardly anybody has ever heard of the V3."

"You'd better include me in that," Bronson said, "because I've never heard of it. What was it? Another type of rocket?"

Angela shook her head. "No. It was something much simpler, but arguably even more dangerous than the other two 'vengeance' weapons. It was known to the Germans as the England Cannon or Busy Lizzie, and it consisted of five batteries, each containing twenty-five high-velocity cannons that were designed to fire shells up to one hundred and twenty miles."

"Jesus," Bronson muttered. "If they'd ever got that working, from the right location it could have flattened London."

"It did work and they had the right location. It was a small French village near the English Channel coast named Mimoyecques. Luckily for all of us, the British government found out about it in nineteen forty-four. The Nazis had built an underground facility for the production, and also the operation, of the weapon. But this time, instead of relying on the natural defenses of an existing mountain, they had to build their own mountain, as it were, because the terrain around there is fairly flat. So they constructed a reinforced concrete roof that was five meters thick, and walls that were almost equally massive. On the sixth of July nineteen forty-four, aircraft from 617 Squadron—you'd know them better as the Dambusters—attacked the site with twelve-thousand-pound Tallboy bombs. They were one of the first of what are now called 'bunker-busters,' and one bomb went straight through the concrete roof and exploded inside the facility."

Bronson nodded. "And I suppose that was more or less that," he said.

"Yes. It was obviously the right decision in the circumstances, and it was a fine piece of precision bombing. What worried the British government at the time, quite apart from the possibility of a constant stream of high-explosive shells landing in and around London, was that they suspected the Nazis might be prepared to fit the shells with chemical or biological payloads. After all, they were very experienced by this time in the use of lethal gases. Zyklon B gas had been supplied to the Buchenwald concentration camp early in nineteen forty, and to Auschwitz in September of the following year. Oddly enough, its principal use was for delousing in an attempt to control the spread of typhus, but fairly soon it started to be used as the principal agent to solve the Nazi's Jewish problem. The gas had also been used as early as nineteen twenty-nine, but in America, not Germany, for disinfecting freight trains and sanitizing the clothing of Mexican immigrants.

"But Zyklon B wasn't what the British were worried about, because it only works effectively in a confined and unventilated space, like the Nazi gas chambers. Toward the end of the war, the German chemical company IG Farben moved into another underground facility named Falkenhagen, about ten miles northwest of Frankfurt, near the Polish border. Believe it or not, some of the British records concerning this place are still classified, even today, but it's fairly clear that the facility was intended to produce a brand-new and much more lethal type of weapon: a nerve gas. This new concoction was named sarin, which can't be seen, smelled or tasted. The lethal dose is tiny: one droplet on the skin will cause death in about six minutes. Zyklon B was just as lethal, but took up to twenty minutes to do its job. Luckily, the war ended before large-scale production of sarin, or any other of what you might call the 'new generation' nerve agents, like tabun, could start."

Angela looked up from her notes for a moment and stared ahead at the road that was unwinding steadily in front of them.

"Where are we now?" she asked.

Bronson glanced down at the satnav display.

"About halfway there, I suppose," he replied. "As soon as we see somewhere we like the look of, we'll stop and buy ourselves some lunch. Right, I think I understand the kind of things that the Nazis were working on toward the end of the Second World War, but I still have no idea about the significance of the 'lantern bearer.'"

Angela smiled at him, but without any humor in her expression. "Ah, yes," she said, "the *Laternenträger*. Now that was something completely different."

34

Half an hour after they'd spotted a roadside café that looked clean and welcoming, they were back on the road again, and Angela continued telling Bronson what she'd discovered.

"It's not clear exactly when this particular Nazi project was conceived," she said, "but from what I've been able to find out, it looks as if sometime in mid–nineteen forty-one an unidentified German scientist came up with a theory that was sufficiently interesting, and presumably already sufficiently well-developed, for the Nazi leadership to allocate development funds to it.

"What is known is that in January 'forty-two, a brand-new project code named *Thor*—or possibly *Tor*, meaning 'gate'—was created, under the leadership of Professor Walther Gerlach, a leading German nuclear physicist. The project was under contract to the *Heereswaffenamt Versuchsanstalt*—that roughly translates as 'Army Ordnance Office Research Station'—number ten, and was a part of the Nazi atomic bomb project. The operation functioned as a single entity until August of the following year. Then the project was divided into two separate parts, and the code name *Tor* or *Thor* was replaced by two other names: *Chronos* and *Laternenträger*. Depending on which source you look at, by the way, *Chronos* could either be spelled with a 'C' or a 'K,' as *Kronos*, and that could be significant."

"Okay," Bronson replied. "I already know what *Laternenträger* stands for, but what about *Chronos*? Is that Latin for 'time,' perhaps? You know, like in 'chronometer'?"

"Almost. It's actually Greek, but you're right: the word does mean 'time.' Some researchers who've investigated this project have come up with some fairly unlikely conclusions about what the Nazis were trying to achieve. They looked at the code names—*Tor* and *Chronos*, 'gate' and 'time'—and presumed that the purpose of the project was to build a time machine, or maybe come up with a device that could somehow be used to manipulate time."

"I see what you mean by 'unlikely.'"

"Exactly," Angela agreed. "The chances of the Nazis actually managing to get anywhere with a project as futuristic as time manipulation well over half a century ago are pretty slim. And the other fairly obvious counterargument is that, even if they had, by some miracle, devised a way of altering time, it's difficult to see how that could possibly have helped the war effort. What they really needed were weapons, guns or rockets or bombs, stuff like that, to achieve superiority on the battlefield or in the air, and that was what all their other secret projects, all their various *Wunderwaffen* programs, were designed to create. Personally, I think it's most likely that the code words were randomly generated, and had no direct connection with the projects they were linked to. And that brings us neatly to our mystery weapon, *Charité Anlage*, the Wenceslas Mine and *Die Glocke.*"

"Now you've lost me," Bronson said, pulling out to overtake two slow-moving cars. "Charity what?"

"Charité Anlage," Angela repeated, "aka *Projekt SS* ten forty. It was a massive operation, beginning in June nineteen forty-two, and required the German company AEG to supply huge amounts of electrical power. It may even have been a joint project with Bosch and Siemens. According to one source, the entire venture was officially named *Schlesische Wekstätten Dr. Fürstenau*, presumably because for a time it was based at Ksia̢z̄, also known as Fürstenstein Castle, a thirteenth-century castle at Silesia in Poland."

"But what did it do?" Bronson asked.

"I'm coming to that. First, we need to go back to the nineteen thirties, before the war started. In nineteen thirty-six, a German scientist named Dr. Ronald Richter performed some experiments using electric arc furnaces to smelled lithium for U-boat batteries. Almost by accident, he discovered that by injecting deuterium into the plasma, into the arc, he could create a kind of nuclear fusion. Or at least, that was what he claimed.

"His work was to some extent complementary to that being undertaken at around the same time by Professor

Gerlach, who had been involved in the creation of plasma by utilizing the spin polarization of atoms since the nineteen twenties. To me, it looks as if this entire project was conceived by Gerlach, who apparently convinced the Nazi high command that he could build a device that could transmute the element thorium into uranium, most likely using beryllium as a source of neutrons. Now you can really appreciate the significance of at least one of the code names, because I believe that it wasn't called *Projekt Tor*, but *Projekt Thor*, a reference to thorium, and nothing to do with any kind of a gate."

Angela glanced across at Bronson to make sure that he was still paying attention. He was.

"To me, as a nonscientist, the next step in the chain of logic seems to make sense. The Nazis were having a lot of trouble trying to get sufficient supplies of heavy water out of Norway, and they hadn't got many other potential sources. I think they turned to Gerlach and his theoretical machine for converting thorium into uranium—uranium that could then be used to produce plutonium to create a nuclear bomb."

Angela glanced back at her notebook to refresh her memory.

"There are a few more facts that I've been able to turn up but, as you'll obviously appreciate, some of the information is pretty sketchy, just because of the circumstances and what happened at the end of the war. It seems there were at least two important laboratories involved, one at a town named Leubus—its modern name is Lubiaz—in Silesia, and another at Neumakt—which is now called Sroda Slaska—to the east of Breslau or Wroclaw. I mentioned *Die Glocke*, and this device was at the very heart of the project. The German name means 'the Bell,' and was apparently inspired by a poem penned by a man named Friedrich Schiller, entitled the 'Song of the Bell,' which describes the forging of a great bell from metal of extreme purity. I'm sure the Nazis would have loved the mystical overtones of this idea, creating a perfect device from perfect material, much as they were trying to do with the huge and diverse population of the European countries they had conquered.

"The other reason for the name was because the device apparently looked very much like a large bell. Again, it depends upon which source you refer to, but it seems that *Die Glocke* was partly built at the laboratories in Leubus and Neumakt. The main part of the unit was a contrarotating centrifuge, and that was fabricated in Germany, at Dessau, by a company named BAMAG: the Berlin Anhaltische Maschinenbau AG.

"The obvious question is: did it work? Well, it did do *something*, that much we're quite sure of. And, if it did work, how did it function? Were the Nazis able to produce uranium in this device? Nobody knows the answer to that specific question, and there are various ideas about its form and function. This isn't my area of expertise, obviously, but I've looked at various theories suggested by people who seem to know what they're talking about."

Angela turned to a fresh page in her notebook and read from her notes: "The most plausible suggestion is that the device was a plasma induction coil, which worked by using the two colocated contrarotating centrifuges to spin mercury in a powerful magnetic field. This would cause a thing called a toroidal plasma to be created. Compounds of thorium and beryllium would already be in position in the core of the centrifuge, held in position in a kind of jelly made from paraffin. The thorium would then be bombarded by neutrons stripped from the beryllium, and this bombardment would result in the creation of uranium." She looked up. "That was the theory, as far as most researchers have been able to deduce. But I have no idea if it's scientifically plausible, or even possible, because nobody, apart from the scientists and technicians who worked on it, ever saw it."

Bronson glanced at her. "You mean, they didn't find it after the war?"

Angela shook her head. "No, but that's another story, and we're not there yet. First, you remember that I told you the *Thor* project was divided into two?"

"Yes. The new ones were called *Chronos* and *Laternenträger.*"

"Exactly. And I also said that there was some dispute over the spelling of the word *Chronos.* One reason for this is that *Kronos* spelt with a 'K' is a classical name for Saturn, and the shape that a toroidal plasma would assume is much like that planet, a central core containing the compounds of beryllium and thorium, with the plasma forming a ring around the outside. To me, that just seems too deliberate a name to be coincidental.

"There are a few other things we know about *Die Glocke.* It was obviously reasonably portable. After it was manufactured, it was taken to yet another of the Nazis' underground complexes at an airfield to the west of Breslau. That was on the first of November nineteen forty-three, and as far as I can gather it first became operational in May nineteen forty-five, with catastrophic results. According to one set of records, seven scientists were responsible for conducting that experiment, and five of them died shortly afterward from what appears to have been a massive dose of radiation poisoning. The following month, or possibly in July of the same year, they held a second test run, when the scientists were wearing protective clothing, but again some deaths—we don't know how many—occurred soon afterward.

"But by this time, the Soviet forces were beginning their inexorable advance toward Berlin, and in November nineteen forty-four the device was moved to the tunnels that lie under Fürstenstein Castle, along with the scientists who were still working on it. But even that proved to be only a temporary relocation and a month later, on the eighteenth of December nineteen forty-four, the Bell was moved for the last time within Europe, to the Wenceslas Mine, near the village of Ludwigsdorf, which is now known as Ludwikowice."

"Which is where we're going," Bronson commented.

"Which is where we're going," Angela echoed.

"But I thought you said that it wasn't there—this bell thing, I mean. You said it wasn't found at the end of the war."

"That's exactly what I said," Angela agreed. "Nobody knows where *Die Glocke* ended up. On either the seventeenth or the eighteenth of April nineteen forty-five, the device was removed from the tunnels of the Wenceslas Mine. It was taken to a nearby airfield, loaded onto a six-engined Junkers Ju-390 transport aircraft, and simply vanished. There were a couple of reports from South America that described sightings of an aircraft that could have been the Junkers, but to the best of my knowledge after April nineteen forty-five, the bell itself—*Die Glocke*—has never been seen.

"And that's why the fact that this German named Marcus used the word *Laternenträger*, which is meaningless in almost any other context, set my alarm bells ringing. If his group has managed to find *Die Glocke* and get it working, there's at least a possibility that it could be used to create a genuine nuclear weapon, though that would involve a lot more than just a centrifuge, or, at least, a kind of dirty bomb that could kill by irradiation or by dispersal of radioactive particles."

Angela glanced at Bronson.

"And that's why I came out here, so that I could tell you everything I know, everything that I've managed to find out about it, and hopefully between us we can find some way of stopping him from deploying it. I know the Olympics start in just two days, but unless we have some idea about what this weapon is and what it can do, I don't see how we could convince anyone in London that there was a real and believable threat to the city. And the Wenceslas Mine was the last place that *Die Glocke* was known to have been operating, so that's where we need to start looking."

35

25 July 2012

Klaus Drescher knocked on the door of Wolf's study and then walked in.

"I've had a call from Oskar," he said. "I think he was afraid to call you."

Wolf grunted his displeasure. "I presume that he has failed to find Bronson?"

"You assume correctly," Drescher confirmed. "He did as you requested. He organized a watch through the local police, for both patrol cars and surveillance cameras, but so far there has been no sighting of either the car or Bronson. Of course, that situation might change at any moment."

"I hope that's not all Oskar has done."

"No. He's organized three teams, a driver and an observer in each one, and they've been on the road almost continuously, searching the area around this house and steadily moving further afield. They've seen absolutely no sign of Bronson or the car, and I think they're running out of ideas."

Wolf nodded but didn't reply for a few moments. Then he glanced up at Drescher.

"I suppose there's one other possibility that we haven't considered. I still don't think Bronson would have returned to Britain. I've given Georg details of the car so that he can put the team in place at Dover, at the ferry port, and also at the exit from the Channel Tunnel. They've seen nothing so far. So if Bronson isn't somewhere near this house, trying to work out how to get inside it, and he hasn't crossed the Channel back to England, there's only one other place that he might have gone."

Wolf gave a rueful smile before he continued speaking.

"And it could be my fault," he added.

"What do you mean?" Drescher asked.

"After the execution, I talked to Bronson for a few minutes before my men drove him back to the station car park. I mentioned the *Laternenträger* to him, just in conversation, and I know that he noticed it, because he asked me what the word meant."

"But that's ancient history, and not really relevant to what we're doing."

"I know," Wolf agreed, "but if Bronson decides to investigate the meaning of that word, we both know what he will find out. Enough has been written about *Die Glocke* for him to discover what happened at the Wenceslas Mine in nineteen forty-five. And if he decides to try to pick up that trail, he might think that a visit to the site where it all began would be a good place to start."

"But there's nothing there," Drescher objected.

"We know that, but Bronson doesn't. I think it's worth a try. Give Oskar a call and tell him I have new orders for him. He's to keep two of the teams searching in this area, but he himself is to proceed at once to Ludwikowice and check the Wenceslas Mine. And if Bronson is there, the mine can become his tomb."

36

25 July 2012

Bronson was staring ahead through the windscreen of the BMW. What had started out as a simple but irritating case of vandalism and damage in northeast London had suddenly taken on a nightmarish quality. Not only was Bronson himself in deep trouble, abandoned by his superiors in Britain and with a warrant issued for his arrest on firearms charges, but he was also guilty of two killings, one the murder of an undercover German police officer.

But even that paled into insignificance compared to the threat to London that Angela had just outlined. If she was right, and he had the uncomfortable feeling that he couldn't fault her logic or the conclusion that she had drawn, then they were facing the very real possibility of a terrorist attack on the streets of Britain's capital city to rival the 9/11 atrocity in New York. He had no idea how many people a dirty bomb could kill, but if the device were to be triggered during, say, the opening ceremony of the London 2012 Olympic Games, the death toll would be at the very least in the thousands, possibly in the tens of thousands.

And at that precise moment, he had no idea what he could do about it. He knew that if he contacted Curtis, or even went straight to Davidson, his claims would be dismissed as the ravings of a bent copper simply trying to save his own skin, because he would have absolutely no proof of any sort to back up a single statement that he made. He couldn't go to the German authorities because he guessed that by now the Berlin police, and possibly every force in Germany, would be looking for an ex-English copper named Christopher Bronson who was wanted for the willful murder of a policeman. They might already have a video film or still photographs of him committing the crime, and possibly also the Walther pistol with his fingerprints all over it.

It was looking more and more as if the only way that he could do anything about Marcus's nasty little plot was to somehow stop it by himself. Preferably with Angela's help, if she decided to stick with him. But even as that thought crossed his mind, he knew he was being unfair. The two of them had had their differences in the past, but their ultimate loyalty to each other had never been in any doubt, at any time. The one thing he was quite certain about was that she would stick by him.

Bronson glanced across at his former wife and smiled grimly. "You know that I'm always pleased to see you, and I hope the feeling's mutual," he began. "And we've had some interesting times together, tramping around the world trying to unravel ancient mysteries. But I have a horrible suspicion that right here and right now, we're both completely out of our depth."

"Never say die, Chris. If we can find out as much as we can about this man Marcus and what he might have planned, surely we can just go to the authorities here in Germany, and probably in Britain at the same time, and hand over everything to them? Provide them with the information and let them sort out the problem?"

For a couple of moments, Bronson debated telling her exactly what had happened to him since his arrival in Berlin, but then decided not to.

He shook his head. "It's not that easy, I'm afraid. I didn't tell you before, but I left Britain under a real cloud. I ended up firing a pistol at a van-load of police officers, and that's not a simple offense to walk away from. I'm not surprised you were being followed around London, because there's a real live warrant out for my arrest, and if they do catch up with me—cliché or not—they'll want to lock me up and throw away the key."

For a few seconds, Angela just stared at him, her face clouded with disbelief. "You did what?" she demanded. "Why the hell would you do something like that?"

Bronson shrugged. "It's a long story," he said, "and it's complicated. I believed there was a serious threat to London during the Olympic Games, and I simply couldn't convince any of my superiors that there was any truth in it. They were going to pull me off the case, and just mop up a small and insignificant bunch of thugs who'd been breaking a few windows in northeast London, and I knew that if they did that we'd never find out about the bigger plot until it was much too late. So I did what I thought was right, not what I was told to do."

"But shooting at your fellow officers? That's really serious, Chris."

Bronson nodded. "Tell me about it. Actually, I didn't shoot *at* any of them, only at one of the tires on the van they were driving, but that's probably splitting hairs. But I still believe I was right, and what I found out here has confirmed it."

"You mean the stuff I've told you about *Die Glocke*?"

"That, obviously, but now I know a lot more about Marcus as well. I was watching his house last night, and I saw him in his full jet-black regalia, along with a group of other men who were clearly his subordinates. He was dressed as a Nazi *Obersturmbannführer*, a lieutenant colonel, right down to the swastika on his left arm. I even saw the lightning bolt runes on his lapel."

Angela was silent for a few moments, then she shook her head.

"That's really nasty," she said. "The SS probably killed more people—mainly innocent people who couldn't fight back, in the concentration camps and elsewhere—than any other single unit of the Nazi armed forces. And they were heavily involved with *Die Glocke* as well. One thing I didn't tell you was that when the Bell and the equipment were taken out of the Wenceslas Mine, it was a special *SS Evacuation Kommando* that handled the operation."

"I've never heard of a unit like that."

"You won't have done," Angela replied, "because as

far as I've been able to find out, it was the only one ever
created. These SS men went into the mine, removed *Die
Glocke* itself and all the documentation, and selected
which scientists should accompany the device on its journey out of Germany. The rest of the scientists and technicians were executed on the spot."

Bronson nodded grimly. "I guess that's what you'd
expect of the SS—doing what they did best and keeping
up their tradition of slaughtering the innocents."

"That's one way of putting it."

"So you're sure that everything to do with *Die Glocke*
was removed from the mine? In that case, why are we
going there? What do you hope to find?"

"I don't know, but that place is the only firm lead we
have. Everything else I've told you has just been culled
from recovered documents and the recollections of the
very few survivors of that period of the war who were
vaguely aware of what was going on. That mine was the
last location where the device was known to be operating,
and I suppose I'm hoping we might find something there
that other people have missed."

Bronson looked at her for a second or two, then
turned his attention back to the road.

"According to the satnav," he said, "we'll reach the
Polish border in a few minutes, and I suppose we'll find
out fairly soon. Did you discover anything else about this
blasted Bell?"

"Only one thing, but it is quite significant," Angela
replied. "All Nazi projects and operations were given
code names, as we've already discussed, but they were
also allocated priorities that reflected their importance,

and that priority determined what resources they could command, and how quickly requests for additional men or equipment would be processed. From the very start, both *Projekt Thor* and the later twin projects of *Chronos* and *Laternenträger* were allocated the priority classification *Kriegsentscheidend*. That meant 'decisive for the outcome of the war.' It was the highest possible classification in the entire Nazi system. Guess how many other German *Wunderwaffen* projects shared that same classification?"

Bronson shook his head. "I haven't got a clue."

"The short answer is 'none.' *Die Glocke* was the single most vital project of any sort embarked on by the Nazis at any time during or before the war. If they could have got it operational, they obviously believed it was so important a development that it could literally have won the war for them."

"And that's why we have to find out whatever we can about it, because if Marcus has found the device and managed to get it working, I really think it's possible that he has a weapon that could be used to destroy a large part of London, perhaps rendering it uninhabitable for centuries to come."

37

The first thing Bronson noticed was that the road on the Polish side of the border was in a markedly worse condition than the same road in Germany. Whereas the German autobahn had been smooth and well-maintained, the Polish section resembled a construction site more than anything else. The surface was scarred by cracks, potholes and the uneven finish caused by numerous previous repairs, and in various places road gangs were working on sections of it.

The landscape had been generally flat, just grassy meadows interspersed by golden fields of corn and other crops, but as they approached Walbrzych the scenery began to change as hills, their flanks covered in trees, reared up in front of them.

"This whole area used to be part of Germany," Angela said. "It was a section of the Reich before the Second World War, and most of the people who lived here then were German-speaking farmers. And it was important during the war as well, because there were lots of coal mines here, and the *Wehrmacht* used some of them as production facilities and storage bunkers. I believe they even built some of the *Wunderwaffen* here, or at least some of their components, like bits of the V2 rockets."

"If there was so much military activity in this area," Bronson said, "there should still be some signs of it, some buildings or whatever left standing, maybe."

"Could be," Angela replied. "We'll soon find out. That must be Walbrzych right in front of us, so we're getting close."

The town was busy, the pavements thronged with pedestrians and the roads crowded with cars and vans, pickup trucks and buses. The BMW's satnav took them through a part of the city named Stary Zdrój, avoiding the town center, which would presumably have been even busier.

Once clear of the built-up area, they continued southeast, through the villages of Jedlina-Zdrój and Gluszyca, leaving most signs of habitation behind and cutting deep into the Polish countryside. In this part of Poland, the road ran very close to the border with the Czech Republic, for some distance almost paralleling it less than a mile away, before turning due east as it approached Ludwikowice K³odzkie.

This road was narrower and much more serpentine than they'd experienced before, and even the satnav seemed to be having trouble because many of the tiny villages, most of them little more than hamlets containing a handful of houses, weren't present in its database. But at least the compass incorporated in the unit told them which direction they were heading.

"We're here," Angela said, pointing to a sign on the right-hand side of the road that showed that they'd just entered Ludwikowice.

"Glad to hear it," Bronson replied. "So now where do we go?"

"I've got no idea. The underground facility is somewhere near here, and that's absolutely all I know. With a bit of luck, there might be a sign somewhere, or maybe we might even see the Henge."

"The what?" Bronson asked.

"The Henge. It's also known as the Flytrap, and it's a kind of circular reinforced concrete cage. There's a theory that it was used by the Nazis as a test facility for some sort of circular craft."

Bronson smiled at her. "You mean they were building flying saucers?"

She shrugged. "Nobody knows. They were certainly pushing the boundaries toward the end of the war, but I doubt if they'd managed to push them that far. And there is another explanation—a rather more mundane and plausible one—for the Henge."

"And that is?"

"I'll tell you when we've found it," Angela said.

Ludwikowice appeared to be a small but surprisingly long village, with buildings extending along both sides of a narrow road that didn't really seem to go anywhere. It looked as if somebody had built a house there years earlier, and then others had simply followed suit, the village growing in a haphazard and linear fashion.

They followed the main street, both of them looking down the infrequent side roads that appeared to lead up into the tree-covered slopes surrounding Ludwikowice, hoping for a road sign or some other indication that might point them in the right direction. But nothing looked particularly hopeful, and after almost two kilometers Bronson drove the BMW past a second sign that marked the far end of the village. He pulled the car to a stop by the side of the road and glanced across at Angela.

"The satnav isn't a lot of help to us now," he said, changing the scale on the map that was displayed on the screen. "Most of the roads that we passed in the village don't even seem to be marked, and there aren't any junctions shown on this road either, or at least, not for a few kilometers. Do you think we should go back and try one of the side turnings in the village?"

"I think what we need to do first is find somewhere to stay tonight," she said. "It's starting to get dark, and even if we did locate the road to the underground complex, it's too late to explore it today. But it's probably a good idea to go back and check those side turnings once more, just in case we see something that helps when we approach the village from this direction."

Bronson checked the road in both directions, then swung the car round and headed slowly back into Ludwikowice. But once again, neither Bronson nor Angela saw any signs that helped them, nothing that seemed to indicate where they might find the complex. At the end of the village, he turned the car round again and headed back through toward the east.

"You are sure it's here?" Bronson asked. "I mean, it's

not somewhere miles up in the hills and it was just named after the village because that was the closest inhabited location?"

Angela nodded. "It's here. The Nazis needed road access to deliver concentration camp workers to the site, plus all of the mechanical equipment and explosives they used to extend the passageways. And there was even a railway line from the complex to the nearest airfield."

Bronson pulled the car to a stop and looked again at the screen of the satnav.

"There's a railway line marked on this," he said, pointing at an area to the north of the village, where a black-and-white dotted line was shown, running almost parallel with part of the road. "Even if the complex was served by a spur from an existing railway line, we can be pretty certain that the underground facility had to be somewhere near that line; otherwise they'd never have bothered providing rail access. So that at least narrows the search area."

They set off again, driving slowly back through the village, this time looking out of the windows to their left. Yet again they reached the end of the village without spotting anything that seemed helpful.

"This is hopeless," Angela said. "We'll just have to come back in the morning."

"Do you know much about road construction?" Bronson asked. "Have you ever noticed a difference between the two inside lanes and the outside overtaking lane of a motorway?"

Angela stared at him.

"I have absolutely no idea what you're talking about."

"Then let me tell you a story. Sometimes on motorways you can see two grooves on each of the inside carriageways. They mark the track followed by articulated lorries and heavy goods vehicles, which use only those lanes, where the weight of the vehicle has actually compressed the tarmac very slightly. Because HGVs don't drive in the outside lane, you don't see the same pattern of use there."

Angela didn't respond, just continued to stare at Bronson, but her growing irritation was only too apparent.

"Now, what you've told me about this underground complex the Nazis built suggests they probably had a fair amount of vehicular traffic, a lot of it no doubt heavy lorries. They obviously wouldn't have built a multi-lane highway to get from the village to the complex, because that would have taken too long and might also have been spotted from the air by Allied reconnaissance aircraft. So they would have constructed a single-track road."

"If you don't get to the point pretty damned sharpish, Chris," Angela snapped, "I'm not necessarily going to be responsible for my actions."

"I have, sort of," Bronson replied. "The point is that tarmac is a very good building material for roads. You can pour it continuously, which means no joins, and it gives a very smooth surface. But it has problems. It can be attacked by hydrocarbons—especially petrol, diesel and motor oil—and the surface is fairly soft. The last thing the Nazis would have been concerned about was the quality of the ride on the road up to the complex. So they wouldn't have built the access road with a tarmac surface. They would have used concrete, because it's a whole lot tougher, much easier to lay because they can do it in convenient-sized chunks, and it won't soften in sunlight or be affected by chemical compounds. About the only thing that does damage concrete surfaces is freezing, if there are gaps that water can get inside and then expand when it freezes. That can crack off chunks of concrete, but if it's laid properly in the first place it's not a problem. And that's why you normally find that runways and taxiways on airfields are constructed from reinforced concrete."

"So?"

"So two of the access roads that we've just passed aren't surfaced in asphalt like all the others. They're built from concrete, and to me they look old."

Angela snapped her head round and looked back toward the village they'd just driven through.

"You could have given me the short version," she said. "Which side of the road were they on?"

"The north side, where the railway line is. As far as I could see they were the only two in the area, and I reckon they're definitely worth a bit of investigation."

"I agree. We'll come back here in the morning, and see what we can find in daylight. But we also need to buy some torches and other stuff before we start trying to crowbar our way inside that mountain."

Angela paused and looked at Bronson for a few seconds.

"Occasionally, Chris," she said eventually, "you surprise me."

38

Finding a hotel in the nearby town of Nowa Ruda didn't prove to be a problem, and they picked a small establishment tucked away in a side street, where Bronson hoped nobody would spot the stolen plates on the stolen BMW. The following morning they had a large breakfast in the hotel dining room to set them up for the day, then climbed back into the car and headed north, through the suburbs of Drogoslaw, and the completely unpronounceable Zdrojowisko.

Bronson stopped in a garage on the outskirts of Nowa Ruda and topped up the tank of the BMW. The garage's kiosk was well stocked, and as well as fuel he bought enough packet food and drink to last for two or three days, plus half a dozen flashlights and plenty of spare batteries, and a couple of sets of disposable mechanic's overalls. Lying on a dusty shelf at the back of the garage shop, he also found a guidebook for the area. It was written in

Polish and German, and had been published about fifteen years earlier. He wasn't sure exactly how much use it would be to them, but he decided to buy it anyway.

When he got back in the car, he passed the book to Angela, who began looking at the text and having a stab at translating some of the German with the aid of a small dictionary she took out of her handbag. After a few minutes she closed the book and leaned back in her seat.

"There's a map in it but it isn't a lot of use," she said. "I don't think it's to scale, and there's very little detail on it, but there is some information about the underground complex. Apparently some of the tunnels are now owned by private individuals, and one or two are even open to the public."

"I doubt very much if those tunnels are what we're looking for," Bronson said.

"True enough. According to the documents I've looked at, the entrances to the area where the Bell had been installed were blown up by explosive charges when the complex was abandoned. But it's a huge complex, covering almost thirty-five square kilometers, and I've no doubt that there are dozens or even hundreds of tunnels and chambers in it that are still completely unexplored."

A few minutes later, Bronson flicked on the turn signal and turned the car off Ludwikowice's long main street and onto the first of the concrete roads he'd spotted the previous afternoon.

"Here we go then," he said.

The road was fairly narrow, perhaps eight or nine feet wide, and made up of a series of single concrete elements, each of them about six feet long. The car's wheels made a rhythmic thumping sound as they crossed the joints between the blocks.

"The surface isn't in bad condition," Bronson remarked, "bearing in mind it's probably been here for over sixty years."

The road climbed slowly away from the village, the slope gradual as it wound its serpentine way into the hills, and Ludwikowice quickly disappeared from view behind the car. Bronson kept the speed right down, ever conscious of the possibility of hitting a broken block or fallen tree.

Part of the way up the slope, and about six hundred yards from the main road, he drew the car to a stop and pointed.

"I was right," he said, pointing ahead through the windscreen. "This road was definitely built by the military. That looks to me like an ammunition bunker."

On one side of the road a spur led to a massive round-topped concrete structure built into the tree-covered hillside. The entrance, obviously originally protected by a heavy steel door, was wide-open, the surrounding concrete discolored and heavily overgrown as nature slowly and inexorably reclaimed the land.

"It's pretty creepy," Angela said, staring into the black oblong of the open doorway. "I'm kind of half-expecting to see a Nazi soldier walking out of there any minute."

They continued a little further up the hill, but it was soon clear to both of them that wherever the Henge they were looking for was located, they were nowhere near it. All they found were low-lying structures made of reinforced concrete and in good general condition, apparently further storage facilities, dug into the ground.

"In the photographs I've seen of it," Angela pointed out, "it looks as if it's built on a plateau, or at least on a patch of level ground." She gazed out through the windscreen at the tree-covered slope in front of the car. "There's no sign of anything like that here, unless the Nazis lopped off the top of the hill."

Bronson nodded.

"I think you're right. Let's head back down to the village and try the other concrete road."

Ten minutes later, with a distinct sense of déjà vu, Bronson slipped the car into first gear and again began climbing up the concrete slope of the hill, this time on the opposite side to the road that had terminated near what he'd supposed were ammunition bunkers. Almost as soon as they left the main road, the trees crowded in, the green canopy almost meeting above the road, shutting out the daylight.

Angela had opened up the guidebook again, and was looking at one particular section of it, which dealt with the German occupation of the area.

"I don't know if it's relevant," she said, "but there's a passage here which refers to a building erected in this area during the Second World War—if I'm translating the German correctly, that is—but it's obviously not the Henge. It's described as the *Fabrica*, which I think means 'factory.' There's a picture of it as well, and it just looks like that—like a factory, I mean—the walls still standing but the roof collapsed. Maybe it was bombed by the Allies."

After about one kilometer, they quite suddenly drove out from the forested terrain they'd been following and into a wide valley.

"That's better," Bronson said, blinking in the sudden daylight.

Although there was nobody in sight, it was immediately obvious that this area was being worked. There were piles of tree trunks, presumably felled from the forest, and the tire marks of heavy vehicles were clearly visible on the fairly soft ground on one side of the road.

"There's some logging going on," Angela said, and then pointed over to one side. "I think we might be on the right track this time," she added, "no pun intended. That's a deserted railway line."

Bronson looked where she was pointing, toward the northern end of the valley, where the railway track disappeared into the tall grass and undergrowth.

"You said there was railway access," Bronson said. "If we just follow that track, we might find the place at the end of it."

He steered the car over toward the railway track, which ran more or less down the center of the valley. It obviously hadn't been used for years, because the rails were caked with rust and had grass and stunted bushes growing between them. Over to their left, a few of the outlying houses of Ludwikowice were visible, standing above a reinforced concrete wall some forty or fifty feet high, which marked that edge of the valley. That supporting wall clearly dated from about the same period as the ammunition bunkers, from the looks of the concrete. The wall also bore signs of additional structures, mainly small rusted patches and protuberances that might originally have been the anchor points for hooks or the like, their purpose unknown.

The valley floor was still fairly open and level, the BMW bouncing over the uneven ground but having no trouble moving forward through the long grass and around the occasional clumps of small bushes that grew near the railway track. In the distance, over on the left-hand side of the valley, Bronson could see a group of small trees, and it looked to him as if the railway line passed fairly close beside them, while the slopes on both sides were quite heavily wooded.

A few minutes later, the car bounced past the group of trees Bronson had spotted. Just beyond them, the valley opened up even more. On the left they could see a few more of the houses at the edge of Ludwikowice, but their attention was drawn immediately to a huge building, deserted and derelict, standing right in the middle of the clearing.

"That's the *Fabrica*," Angela said, as Bronson stopped the car a few yards away. "I recognize it from the picture in the guidebook."

It was big. A two-story structure, the upper floor apparently with a much higher ceiling height than the ground floor. The roof had obviously collapsed long ago, and the outer walls showed signs of damage by either a fire or perhaps even an explosion, pieces of old blackened wood visible among the heaps of bricks and masonry that surrounded the structure. The grass and vegetation growing over and around the building suggested old, rather than recent, damage.

"Maybe we should follow the railway track," Bronson suggested, pointing over to the east of the clearing.

He steered the car in that direction, and within a few

seconds found an unpaved path that had clearly been used by vehicles at some time, because it was wide enough for even a tractor to pass along it and drive through the clumps of bushes and trees. Then the path Bronson was following vanished, and he drove the car onto a large reinforced-concrete open space, maybe originally used as a parking area, and there, at the end, stood the Henge.

The structure was huge, and bizarre. More than anything else, it resembled a concrete cage, vertical pillars arranged in a circle and topped with equally massive horizontal bars, like some modern but marginally more delicate version of Stonehenge.

"I've never seen anything like that before," Bronson muttered.

"People claim that it's unique," Angela said. "It's known as either the Flytrap or the Henge, and nobody knows for certain exactly what it was used for. There's the suggestion that the Nazis had designed some sort of circular aircraft, and that the structure was used as a kind of containment area to support the vehicle during testing. There are huge ducts under the Henge, which were probably used to run power cables up to whatever was inside it."

She paused. "That's one explanation."

The way she spoke made Bronson look at her.

"And the other?" he demanded.

"All you have to do is look at it from the other direction," she said. "Because, actually, you have seen something like this before."

Bronson shook his head. "I haven't," he insisted. "I'd remember if I had."

He looked back at the structure. There were eleven columns in all, evenly spaced, and it was about thirty yards across, he estimated, which meant a circumference of roughly ninety yards.

"The clue is those bolts you can see on the top of the circle of concrete above the pillars," Angela said.

Bronson looked where she was indicating, and could clearly see a heavy-duty bolt sticking upward directly above each of the vertical columns.

"Some people have theorized that they were used to support something being tested inside the Henge, but that doesn't really make sense. If that were the case, surely the bolts would have been positioned on the inside of the structure, not on the top. Because the Germans stuck the bolts there, I think it's reasonable to assume that they intended to attach something to the top of the Henge, or actually did so."

"Like what?" Bronson asked.

"Like a sheet-metal cylinder."

"What?"

"I think the simplest and most logical explanation for the Henge is that it was the base of a power station cooling tower, the same sort of structure you'll see at any power station today. Think about it: the *Fabrica* is only a few dozen yards away, and was obviously manufacturing something— nobody knows what—but it would definitely have needed a source of power. And some parts of the Wenceslas Mine produced coal, so there was a fuel source nearby."

Angela paused and pointed at some concrete blocks that lay on the flat land below the slight rise where the Henge was positioned.

"I believe that if you'd visited this plant during the Second World War, you'd have seen a coal-fired power station running down there, on those foundations, with the cooling tower right here. Cables would have been run in underground conduits from the power station over to the *Fabrica* building, and that would be the obvious explanation for something that is otherwise almost inexplicable."

Bronson nodded. What she'd said made sense—certainly much more sense than any suggestion that the Nazis had developed and been test-flying some kind of saucer-shaped craft. That, he believed, could not have been kept secret during, and certainly not after, the war. Somebody, somewhere, would have seen something or even taken a picture of it.

"So do you mean we're just wasting our time here?" he asked.

"Definitely not. I'm reasonably certain I know the exact purpose of the Henge, but the Bell is something else. And, actually, if I'm right and the Henge *was* a power station cooling tower, that reinforces the story of *Die Glocke*, because every account of its operation stresses the fact that it needed huge quantities of power."

Bronson nodded.

"So where do we go now?" he asked.

Angela pointed downward.

"According to the few surviving records, the Henge was built on the hillside almost directly above the chamber where *Die Glocke* was positioned. That's also the reason for the ducts various people reported. They just had things the wrong way round. The ducts did carry power cables, but the power wasn't being sent from the Wenceslas Mine *up* to some futuristic craft being tested inside the Henge, but from the power station up here *down* into the cave to power the Bell."

"So somewhere around here there has to be a way into the caves in the ground we're standing on?" Bronson suggested.

"Exactly. So let's go and find it."

39

It had sounded easy enough when Bronson said it, but finding their way into the cave complex of the Wenceslas Mine proved to be far more difficult than either of them had expected.

One of the first and biggest problems was simply finding any trace of the mine entrance because of the considerable growth of trees, bushes and undergrowth that had occurred over the decades. The shape of the ground had been softened and altered by weathering and the passage of time, and although they were able to use the railway line as a guide—because Angela had discovered that during the war a spur had linked the mine entrance to the main line—it still took them over half an hour to find anything that even resembled a mine entrance.

And when they did find it, it wasn't much help.

"There's an entrance over here," Angela called out. "At least, I think it's an entrance."

Bronson trotted over to where she was standing.

At first sight, what she was looking at didn't appear much different to the rest of the rock face. They had been searching in the area between the remains of the railway track and the plateau upon which the Henge stood, studying a fairly steep slope about thirty feet high. It was mainly rock, except where rough grass and the occasional stunted bush grew in the cracks where there was just enough soil for the roots to gain purchase. At the foot of the slope, large boulders and smaller rocks lay scattered on the ground, where they'd fallen over the centuries.

"Where?" he asked.

Angela pointed.

"This section looks a lot more tumbledown than the rest of the slope," she said, "with more vegetation growing all over the rocks. And there's a concave area just above it, see?"

Once she'd pointed out the visual clues, Bronson could absolutely see what she was driving at. He nodded slowly.

"You could be right," he said. "If this was once a tunnel, a natural or man-made entrance, and it was blown up, this is pretty much what you'd expect it to look like, over half a century after the event."

For a few moments they just stood there, staring at the rock face.

"You told me that the Nazis had destroyed the entrance," Bronson said.

Angela nodded. "That's in all the contemporary reports that I've managed to track down. When the special *SS Evacuation Kommando* arrived here, they removed

Die Glocke and the documentation, killed everybody who wasn't vital to the project, then blew down the entrance tunnel. And that," she added, "is what I think we're looking at."

"I presume they were in a hurry," Bronson said. "They must have known that the Russian advance was only a matter of days, maybe even hours, away."

"Probably, yes. What's your point?"

"I don't know too much about mining or underground facilities, but I do know that a supply of fresh air would have been essential. And I think that it would be normal practice to have more than just one source."

"You mean they might have destroyed the entrance used by people and vehicles, but they wouldn't have had time to blow up all the ventilation ducts?"

"Exactly." Bronson nodded. "This was a huge complex—you said it covered over thirty-five square kilometers—and to keep that kind of area livable in, they would have needed plenty of sources of fresh air."

"So all we have to do is find one, I suppose. But at least we now know we're looking in more or less the right place."

They separated again, and this time they started looking higher up the rock face, because logically the air vents would have been placed high enough to avoid animals taking refuge in them, and where undergrowth would not interfere with the flow of air. And the Nazis had repeatedly demonstrated to the world that they were logical. Implacably evil in their intentions, but supremely logical and efficient in the implementation of their intentions.

Once again, it was Angela who spotted what they were looking for. About fifty yards from the dynamited entrance to the cave, under a natural overhang about ten feet off the ground and almost invisible in the shadow cast by that overhang, she saw a dark shape, not a perfect circle but too regular to be a natural opening in the rock.

Bronson pulled on a pair of overalls, handed a second pair to Angela, and checked that his flashlight was working.

"Do you really think you'll need that in the cave?" she asked, pointing at the butt of the Walther that he'd tucked into the waistband of his trousers.

"Not really," Bronson replied, "but you never know. I think they have wolves in this part of the world, and maybe bears as well. I'd hate to get inside the tunnels and find that I'd arrived in a wolf den just in time for lunch."

"Good point. What about me? I have shot the odd pistol in my time, you know."

Bronson fished the Llama .22 out of his trouser pocket and handed it to her.

"It's loaded, with one round in the chamber, and the safety catch is on, so just click it off, point and then shoot. But only if you have to. I doubt if one of those bullets would stop a wolf, and all it would do to a bear is just piss it off, really badly, so let me do the shooting if we meet anything like that."

"Fine with me."

Bronson again checked the flashlight he was carrying, confirmed he had spare batteries for it and for the second, smaller flashlight in his pocket, then scrambled up the rock face to the opening. The hole itself was about three feet wide, and appeared to have been chiseled out of the rock, because he could see the unmistakable marks of picks or chisels on the stone.

He crawled a few feet into the narrow tunnel, then turned round and waited for Angela to follow him, extending his hand to help her as she neared the entrance.

"This is definitely man-made," Bronson said, pointing at the tool marks.

Angela shivered slightly. "It gives me a funny feeling, seeing something like this, knowing how it was constructed, and knowing that the men who were forced to dig this out of the rock were probably dead just days later."

There wasn't anything Bronson thought he could say in reply to that, so he just shook his head, switched on his flashlight and shone the beam down the tunnel.

Then the two of them began making their way, slowly and cautiously, along the horizontal shaft that had been cut through the rock and into the side of the mountain.

40

The shaft was fairly easy to negotiate, being wide and unobstructed apart from a few stones and bits of rock that had fallen from the roof over the years, and it wasn't even particularly long. Bronson estimated they'd covered only about twenty yards when the beam of his flashlight suddenly no longer showed the sides of the shaft, but a heavy-looking lump of rusty machinery.

"Stop where you are," he murmured to Angela. "There's something blocking the duct."

He crawled forward a few more feet until he could clearly see what it was.

"It's a fan," he said. "I'll need to shift it before we can go any further."

He reached out and gave the rusted lump of machinery a push. It moved very slightly, but he knew he didn't have either the strength in his arms or a fulcrum that he could use to shift it. He'd have to use his feet.

"Can you take this torch?"

Bronson passed it back to Angela, then awkwardly turned completely around in the tunnel. He braced himself with his arms against the side of the duct, then drew up his legs and kicked out, his feet hitting the fan squarely near its center. There was a sudden squeal of tearing metal, but the obstruction stayed in place. Bronson moved slightly, then kicked out again.

This time, whatever was holding the fan gave way, and it tumbled out of sight, landing with an echoing crash somewhere beyond.

Angela shone the flashlight over Bronson's body. The worked stone sides of the ventilation duct stopped a couple of feet ahead, and beyond that was an inky blackness, part of a stone wall visible some distance away.

Bronson repeated the maneuver, turning himself round so that he was facing the open space ahead of them. Then he slid forward the last few feet until his head and shoulders projected beyond the end of the duct. He shone the flashlight downward, the beam revealing a level floor of hard-packed earth on stone and the crumpled remains of the fan.

"The floor's about six feet down," he said, his voice echoing in the confined space. "I'll go first."

"No bears or wolves, I hope?"

"Not that I can see, no."

Bronson maneuvered himself awkwardly for the third time, turning round so that his legs dangled over the edge, then lowered himself with his hands, dropping the last couple of feet.

"Just come straight out," he told Angela. "I'll take your weight."

Angela crawled forward, glancing with interest around the chamber, then stretched out her arms toward Bronson, who grabbed her shoulders and eased her body forward out of the shaft, then lowered her to the ground to stand beside him.

"What is this place?" she asked, unconsciously lowering her voice to a whisper.

"I don't know. There doesn't seem to be anything in it, so maybe it was just a storage room, something like that." He aimed the beam of the flashlight toward the center of the ceiling, where a rusty electrical fixture dangled. "It had a light once," he added, "as well as that fan, so I'm pretty sure we're in the right place. It must be a part of the Nazi underground complex."

He switched the beam to the wall directly under the opening of the vent and noticed that there was a power socket attached to the stone, and a cable ran from it to the fan he'd kicked out of the duct.

Bronson led the way toward the doorway on the opposite side of the room and shone the flashlight into the space outside. A corridor, hacked through the rock, extended in both directions.

"Left or right?" he asked.

"Doesn't matter. We'll probably need to go in both directions. For now, go left. That'll probably take us back toward the dynamited entrance, and we can get our bearings from that."

As they walked down the corridor, Bronson stopped suddenly and shone the beam of his flashlight down at the floor.

"Tire marks," he said. "Not a modern tread pattern,

obviously, so they clearly brought the odd vehicle in here. Maybe to take away the Bell just before they blew the entrance, or maybe just to deliver supplies."

He shone the flashlight at the walls. "It's not very wide, but I guess a small truck could get down here. The tunnel's pretty straight, as far as I can see."

They walked on, and within a few dozen yards they found the entrance. Or what was left of it. The damage on the inside of the complex mirrored what Angela had noticed outside. A massive pile of boulders, rocks and rubble completely blocked the tunnel. Whoever had blown the entrance had made a competent and comprehensive job of it.

"That seems clear enough," Angela said. "This was what the reports described, so somewhere down there"— she pointed back the way they'd come—"is the chamber that was used as the test facility for *Die Glocke*. All we have to do now is find it and learn what we can from whatever's left there."

"Right," Bronson said, and led the way down the corridor, the beam of his light playing over the walls as he walked.

There were numerous openings on both sides of the corridor, all either without doors at all or with doors that were standing wide-open. Some of the rooms had clearly been used as offices, equipped with desks and chairs, and each time they looked into a room and saw anything in it, they stepped inside to investigate.

In several rooms the chairs had toppled over, evidence of a hasty departure or possibly caused by the blast wave of the explosion that had sealed the tunnel entrance. In some, dust-covered paper littered the floor and covered the desks, but Angela scarcely gave it more than a cursory glance.

"Isn't it worth checking some of these documents?" Bronson asked.

Angela shook her head. "If I was a German-speaking historian specializing in the Second World War, it might be, but my guess is that most of this stuff will just be routine administration, orders for food or fuel or equipment, that kind of thing. Anything that was important to the project would have been taken away with the device itself."

The papers were generally speaking in good condition, probably because the interior of the mine seemed very dry—certainly there was no smell of damp, and the walls were dry to the touch. The edges of some were chewed, evidence of rats or mice, or maybe even insect activity.

Bronson wasn't sure that Angela was right about the papers. They knew that the Germans had left the place in a hurry, believing it would soon be overrun by Allied forces, and in those circumstances he thought it was possible, maybe even probable, that important papers might have inadvertently been left behind. But he also realized that as neither of them spoke German, they would be unlikely to recognize any significant documentation unless they spent hours doing translations.

And he knew that they didn't have the time to spare.

"So what are we looking for, exactly?" he asked.

"To be perfectly honest, I don't really know," Angela replied. "I wanted to find the chamber where the Bell was operated, because I thought if we could take a look at the controls and instrumentation they used to operate it, we might get a better idea about what it was supposed to do."

That made sense to Bronson.

Moments later, the beam of his flashlight fell on a door that was closed. In fact, it wasn't just closed, it was bolted shut. Two large bolts, the steel almost an inch in diameter, had been driven home into sockets set into the rock around the door.

"That's different," he said, pointing.

"That could be it," Angela said, and strode across to the door.

Bronson seized the top bolt and tugged at it, but it didn't move.

"I think it's pretty much rusted in place," he said, handing his flashlight to Angela and changing his grip.

With both his hands tugging on the bolt, it did move. Not easily, and not far, but he knew it was only a matter of time. He wiggled it back and forth, each movement freeing it a little more, until after a minute or so, with a final defiant squeal, it slammed back as Bronson's efforts at last pulled it free of the socket.

"One down," he muttered, and grabbed the second bolt.

For some reason, that was easier to move, and in a few seconds Bronson was able to grab the edge of the door and swing it open.

Angela sniffed as the door swung open, and an unexpectedly familiar scent wafted out of the closed room.

"It smells almost like a church," she said. "Old stones. Old stones and something else."

The beam of Bronson's flashlight, a circle of brilliant white light in the blackness of the room, played over the walls and then dropped down to the floor. At first, Angela couldn't make out what she was seeing: the floor was covered with what looked like ragged, frayed and torn clothing interspersed by a confused tangle of white and brown shapes.

Then she caught her breath as she realized what she was staring at. The floor was carpeted with old corpses. A mass of rotten clothing from which skulls and bones, some showing white, others with brown and mummified skin and flesh still adhering to them, projected. She'd seen bones and bodies before, like everybody who trained as an archaeologist or in any of the related disciplines. But this was a sight she knew she would never forget.

"Oh, dear God," she murmured, her voice choked with emotion. "So the reports were right. They couldn't take all the scientists with them, so they massacred them to make sure they kept their mouths shut." She closed her eyes for a moment, then looked again at the scene in front of her. "There must be at least twenty or thirty bodies here."

"Old stones—and old bones," Bronson agreed.

41

The white light of the flashlight flickered again over the confused tangle of bones and flesh and clothing.

"Most of them look as if they were shot in the head," Bronson suggested, "so maybe the SS just locked them in here and then sent in a couple of men with pistols to do the job. No—" he broke off. "I'm wrong. See that piece of wood over there?"

He pointed to a spot near the center of the room, and Angela nodded.

"I'm pretty sure that's the handle of a German stick grenade, what our boys used to call a potato masher. They must have made them all wait in here, then lobbed in a hand grenade or two, waited for the bang and then gone back in to finish them off."

"Callous bastards," Angela muttered, as she recovered her composure. "These people were almost certainly Germans, German scientists, working for the Third Reich and most of them probably even supporting Hitler. And this is the payoff they got for their loyalty and dedication. I can't even begin to comprehend the mindset of the kind of people who would do this."

"In the end," Bronson said, "it might have just been a case of simple logistics. They might have only had enough space on the aircraft for a dozen or so people, plus the Bell. And they were probably desperate to prevent any documentation or—worse—any of the people involved in the project from being captured by the Russians or any of the other Allied forces. The fastest, easiest, cheapest, most efficient, and above all the most certain, way to ensure that that couldn't possibly happen was to kill them all."

He paused and ran the beam of his flashlight around the room.

"It's difficult to tell how many bodies are in here," he said, "but I think it's more than twenty. My guess is that there are at least thirty, maybe forty of them. I suppose you could say that it's just another example of Nazi efficiency. When you link that to their total disregard for human life, you get a pretty frightening combination. The only good thing is that we now definitely know that we're in the right place."

Bronson pushed the door closed on the silent room and its long-dead occupants and slid home one of the bolts to secure it.

"Can you imagine what those poor souls must have felt like," Angela said, her voice quiet and subdued, "locked in that room and probably knowing that they had just minutes to live? Wondering if they would be shot

or bayoneted or simply left there to die of thirst and starvation."

"At least it was quick," Bronson muttered, "but they
probably died screaming in terror. Those that survived
the blast of that grenade would have been begging for
death. The explosion in that confined space would have
done terrible things to their bodies. So I hope their souls
found some peace."

Angela dabbed at her eyes with a tissue and glanced
over at his dark shape as they walked down the corridor
together, heading further into the mine.

"That's very deep for you, almost religious," she said.
"You feeling all right?"

"Yeah. It's just that it's one thing to read in a history
book that the Nazis killed God knows how many millions
of people, and you completely understand that on an in-
tellectual level, but it's just facts, you know, just numbers.
But then, when you actually see the bodies—or rather the
bones—it brings it home to you. I've never seen hard and
unarguable evidence of a Nazi atrocity before. It just
makes everything so much more real."

"Yes. And those poor souls wouldn't even have been
listed among the dead. That was a secret atrocity, if you
like, one nobody was ever supposed to know about. It
makes you wonder how many other piles of bones are still
out there somewhere, in some underground chamber or
wherever, waiting patiently to be found so that another
unfinished chapter about that war can finally be completed."

Their lights danced ahead of them as they walked
steadily down the corridor, the beams illuminating the

bare stone walls and the concrete floor. They passed numerous chambers, all of them, with the exception of the charnel house they'd investigated, with their doors standing wide-open. They looked in every one, but saw only a virtual repeat of the first few offices they'd checked: papers scattered everywhere, chairs and desks displaying signs of a hasty departure.

The only rooms that were different were a canteen or dining room, the chairs and tables thick with dust, a serving counter at one end, and a couple of washrooms—male and female—equipped with sinks and toilet stalls.

Then Angela spotted another closed door—in fact, a pair of double doors—though these weren't bolted, just pushed shut.

Bronson pulled them open, and they found themselves looking down a separate wide passageway that led off the corridor they'd been following. At the far end, facing them, was a further pair of double doors, standing slightly ajar. On the left-hand side of the passageway were two more doors, and another one was set into the right-hand wall.

"You said the Bell was pretty big," Bronson remarked, "so maybe that's the chamber it was positioned in, down at the end of this corridor."

"Could be. Let's take a look."

Angela strode down the passage, Bronson right beside her. At the end, he pulled the doors open and they stepped into a chamber that was completely different from any that they'd seen before.

It had a significantly higher ceiling than all the others they'd explored, probably twelve or fifteen feet above their heads, and was almost circular. But that wasn't what made them stop in their tracks. Almost directly in front of them, a pair of skeletons lay against the wall, the bones in two untidy heaps below the numbers "3" and "4" that had been painted on the wall.

"What the hell happened here?" Angela asked.

"I've no idea," Bronson replied, striding across the room to examine the grisly remains. He stared down at the skeletons. Some connective tissue and tendons had survived, along with a few patches of skin, and on one corpse part of the skull still bore skin and a few strands of fine wispy hair. Rusty chains dangled above them from rings secured to the wall.

"I don't know who these two were," he said, glancing back at Angela, "but they were chained up here."

He pointed to one of the dangling chains, at the end of which was a handcuff, one skeletal wrist still secured by it. The corpse's other arm had apparently dropped free of its steel support at some point after the victim's death.

"And they were probably naked," he added, "because I can't see any evidence of clothing anywhere near them. Some of their skin has survived, so if they had been wearing clothes, I would have expected some scraps to still be visible. From the look of the pelvis region, I'd say they were both male. Other than that, I've got no idea what went on in this room."

He shone his flashlight at the walls, which were different from those in the rest of the complex, and not just because they were circular.

"That's odd. Why did they line this chamber with bricks? Weren't the stone walls enough?"

"Obviously not."

Angela walked over to a section of the wall well away from the two skeletons and examined the brickwork carefully. She tapped one of the bricks with her fist, then rubbed the surface with her fingertip.

"I'm not a bricklayer, obviously," she said, "but I don't think these are normal bricks, not like the ones we use today, anyway."

Bronson had also been looking at the bricks, and nodded agreement.

"You're right," he said. "They've got a kind of glaze on them."

He took out his multi-tool, opened the knife blade and scratched the surface of a brick.

"It's not made of the usual material either. In fact, I think they're probably some sort of ceramic."

"Ceramic? Why would they need to line the chamber with ceramic bricks?"

"Against excessive heat, maybe. The underside of the American Space Shuttle has a layer of ceramic tiles on it, to protect it against the heat of re-entry into the atmosphere."

Bronson paused and shook his head.

"No, that doesn't make sense. If the Bell was generating so much heat that it was damaging the walls of this chamber, it would also fry anybody in here."

"According to the reports, several of the scientists on the project died."

"Yes, but it can't have been from heat. If that had been the case, those two skeletons"—he pointed at the opposite wall—"wouldn't be here. To damage the walls would mean it would have to get as hot in here as in the incineration chamber in a crematorium, and all that would leave would be a couple of piles of dust and ash. No, it wasn't heat they were worried about. It was something else."

"Radiation, maybe?" Angela suggested.

"That sounds a lot more likely to me, though I have no idea what kind of radiation would need ceramic bricks to absorb it. And maybe they didn't know either."

"What do you mean?"

"Whatever happened in this chamber was brand-new technology. As far as we know, nothing like the Bell had been constructed before, so they were treading completely new and unknown ground. Maybe they realized it was radiating something, and using ceramic bricks was their first attempt to contain it. If they'd been able to continue their research, they might have eventually switched over to lead sheets or to something entirely different."

"Maybe." Angela didn't sound convinced. "Or perhaps they knew exactly what they were doing. Don't forget that this project was the brainchild of one of Germany's leading physicists, Walther Gerlach. He was a full professor, and his work on the behavior of atoms in a magnetic field was part of the founding science of quantum physics. He was a smart man and he surrounded himself with an equally smart team."

Bronson grunted and glanced round the chamber again. In the center of the floor was a tangle of power cables. If their theory was correct, this would have run from the coal-fired power station they guessed had been built above the complex, somewhere near the Henge. He settled the beam of his flashlight on a long horizontal glass window that was the dominant feature of one wall.

"I suppose the control room was probably behind that," he suggested.

They walked out of the circular room and pushed open the door, which gave access to the chamber on the other side of the glass—glass that had a peculiar greenish glow in the light, and which was obviously at least a couple of inches thick.

Where the large chamber had been almost bare, this room was equipped with banks of instruments, dials and switches, clearly designed to control whatever experiments had been conducted on the other side of the glass viewing pane. Swivel chairs were ranged in front of the control panel, and there were other dials and switches on the back wall.

Angela shone her flashlight at the markings still visible on the various controls, then took a compact dictionary out of her pocket and began jotting down notes in a small book.

"Anything useful?" Bronson asked after a few minutes.

"Sort of, yes," she replied.

She pointed at two dials set side by side and more or less in the center of the panel.

"The legend above these decodes as 'centrifuge,' and the dials seem to be intended to record the speed of rotation. *Die Glocke* apparently contained two counterrotating components—one inside the other, according to this schematic drawing—but the numbers don't make much sense. The dials are labeled from zero to ten, and they're both red-lined at eight, and I suppose that could mean eighty, eight hundred or maybe eight thousand."

"Actually," Bronson said, "centrifuges generally have a very high rotation speed, so it could even be *eighty thousand*. Anything else?"

"There are power meters and switches, that kind of thing, but nothing that seems to measure the output of the device, or give any hint about what it was supposed to do or generate. As far as I can see, all these instruments just controlled or measured the power input and what the device was doing."

"Maybe what it did wasn't something they could measure using instruments."

Angela nodded.

"That would make sense, actually. The most persuasive suggestion I read was that this thing was supposed to turn thorium 232 into protactinium 233 or maybe even straight to uranium 233. This isn't my field of expertise, obviously, but from what I read, protactinium is highly toxic and very radioactive. Nasty stuff, in short. There was another suggestion that the Nazis could use the same technology, and the same device, to convert uranium 238, another isotope of the element, into plutonium. And with enough plutonium, they would have been able to build a nuclear bomb."

"That's the nightmare scenario, isn't it? But I wonder how close the Nazis really were to succeeding. After all, the Americans' Manhattan Project cost tens of millions of dollars in the nineteen forties, which would be billions today, employed the best scientists and engineers they could find, and by the end of the war they'd only managed to build two working weapons, of two different types. And both of those were incredibly inefficient in terms of yield. I read somewhere that the Hiroshima bomb only used a tiny percentage of the fissile material in the warhead, maybe as little as six hundred milligrams."

"It did the job, though," Angela said.

"Definitely. That was enough to give it a yield of about fifteen kilotons. Do you really think that the Bell could have produced uranium or plutonium?"

"We know it didn't produce enough to let them construct a nuclear weapon, but that's not what worries me. Whatever *Die Glocke* was capable of doing back in the nineteen forties, we do know that it was almost certainly producing copious amounts of radiation, and that was probably what killed the German scientists working on it, and of course also murdered any test subjects they had chained to the walls of the chamber when they switched it on.

"From what I've been able to find out, the device probably generated extremely powerful X-rays when it was running, as a part of the transmutation process when a plasma was created. That would be enough to kill anyone nearby, but not necessarily very quickly. But for thorium to transmute into uranium it has to absorb additional neutrons and protons, and the Nazis probably used beryllium oxide as the source of these particles. That means the device would also have generated beta radiation—the emission of protons."

"I don't really need a lesson in nuclear physics, Angela," Bronson said. "Just tell me if X-rays and beta radiation would have been enough to kill people near the device."

"Almost certainly, and probably to kill them quickly and unpleasantly. Some reports refer to the flesh of the test subjects liquefying."

"So forget the possibility of the Nazis manufacturing uranium or plutonium. Just running this thing would be enough to generate lethal radiation. What we're looking at here is a kind of sophisticated dirty bomb, but instead of the particles of radioactive material being blown in all directions by explosive charge, in this case they would presumably be emitted in a continual stream for as long as the device was running."

"Yes. And there's something else we need to remember."

"I know," Bronson said, "and that was what it could do in the nineteen forties, when it had only just been developed. Wherever the Bell went, and whoever took it, they've had seventy years or so to refine it and get it right. And that's really bad news."

"I think we—" Angela began, then stopped abruptly as Bronson put his finger to his lips. From somewhere in the tunnel system he'd just heard a sudden thump or bang, as if a large object had fallen over.

Then they both heard a faint metallic clatter. Sounds echo in confined spaces, and it was impossible to work out exactly where the sound had come from. But there was no mistaking what it meant.

Someone else was in the mine with them.

42

"One more thing, Klaus," Wolf said.

The two men were sitting on opposite sides of the desk in the study, and had been going over the final sequence of events that would culminate in the completion of the operation. These particularly concerned the actions that were to take place in London when the device was first positioned and then activated using the built-in timer system. Marcus himself was going to supervise and initiate this final phase. It was his destiny. He would be fulfilling the wishes of his long-dead grandfather, and realizing the dreams of all the members of *Die Neue Dämmerung*, members both alive and dead, who had worked together over the decades to bring this triumph for the Fatherland to its climax.

"Yes?"

"I'm still worried about Bronson and what he's doing. If he was still in the vicinity of Berlin, somebody—either the police or our men—would have seen him, and there's still been no word from Oskar, I suppose?"

"Nothing so far," Klaus replied.

"Do you know where he is now?"

"He'd just crossed the border into Poland the last time he called; he hoped to reach the mine within two or three hours."

Marcus Wolf nodded.

"I suppose Bronson might be there, but I'm beginning to wonder if we've read him wrong, and if he might be trying to get back to Britain. That doesn't bother me, but I'm getting slightly concerned about making sure that the lorry crosses the English Channel as soon as possible. The ferry ports and the Channel Tunnel terminal are obvious choke points, and the last thing we want is for the truck carrying the weapon to be stuck on the wrong side of the Channel."

"That makes sense," Drescher replied. "What would you like me to do about it?"

"Contact the team driving the vehicle and tell them to get across the Channel as soon as they can, and then to find somewhere they can park, somewhere no more than an hour's drive from London."

"No problem." Drescher took his mobile phone out of his pocket and dialed a number from memory.

43

Bronson stepped soundlessly across to the partially open door. He eased it a fraction wider and for a second or two just listened.

Then he pushed it closed and looked back into the control room, the flashlight beam flitting around the room as he searched for a hiding place, for somewhere that Angela would be safe.

"Who is it?" she whispered.

"I don't know," Bronson replied, just as quietly, "but somehow I don't think it's some guy doing a guided tour of the mine. It's most likely one of Marcus's men, and it sounds as if he's right down by the entrance, probably where we got in."

"They followed us here?"

"I doubt it. I think it's just Marcus covering all the bases. He and his men will have been looking for me ever since I shot my way past them at the house outside Berlin. He'll have the British gang watching out for me, and if I'd been him I would have sent somebody here, just in case. The only clue he let slip was the expression 'lantern bearer,' and he must have known that that would only make sense in the context of the Wenceslas Mine. If they've spotted the car outside, they'll know I'm inside, somewhere. But what they can't know is that you're here as well, and I'm going to make sure that that doesn't change. You have to get out of sight."

"And then what?" Angela demanded, her voice low and urgent.

"Stay hidden and stay quiet. I'm armed, and I have one big advantage. I don't have to go searching for them, because they'll come looking for me."

"You mean you'll kill them?"

Bronson looked at her pale face, barely visible in the gloom of the chamber, his flashlight pointing at the far wall, his fingers partially obscuring the lens to cut down the light.

"If it comes to that, yes," he replied. "These men are utterly ruthless—I've seen that for myself, at first hand—and they have absolutely nothing to lose. Whoever has followed us inside will be carrying weapons—they've been sent here to kill me. I have no doubt at all about that." Bronson smiled briefly. "So we'll just have to make sure that they won't succeed."

He turned away from Angela and checked the room once again. Apart from directly behind the door, which was hardly a suitable hiding place, the only possible place of concealment was a cupboard with double doors built into the rear wall. Bronson strode over to it and pulled both doors wide, hoping that it wouldn't be fitted with shelves or stuffed with equipment that would take time to remove.

In the event, it was virtually empty, just a few printed forms and other pieces of paper lying at the very bottom of the cupboard.

"Can you fit in there?" Bronson asked.

"Yes, but I really don't like this."

"I'm not wild about it myself, but right now I don't see another option. Just stay in the cupboard and wait until it's all over."

"Just a minute," Angela interrupted. "Are you sure that these people don't know about me?"

"I don't see how they can, so that's why you need to stay hidden. If they don't know you're here, they won't be looking for you."

"So use me. We've got to find out what they've got planned for London. If they think they've got you cornered, maybe you can get some information from them that will help. I've still got your pistol, so I can be your insurance policy."

"That only works in bad movies," Bronson objected.

But then there was no more time for talking or planning, because they both heard the door at the end of the short passageway swing open, the unused hinges creaking a warning, saw the faint glow of a flashlight down the corridor, and then heard the sound of footsteps drawing steadily closer.

Bronson extinguished his own flashlight and, moving only by feel, ducked down behind the end of the heavy steel control panel, taking the Walther pistol out of his pocket as he did so, and quickly attaching the suppressor.

He could hear the man—only one man, he guessed, much to his relief—more clearly now, as he proceeded in a methodical fashion to clear each room as he reached it, exactly the way Bronson would have done if their situations had been reversed. And then the man stopped outside the door of the control room, presumably listening for the slightest sound that would confirm the presence of his quarry.

The door swung wide, kicked open, and the interior of the control room was filled with light as the man switched on a powerful lantern that he was carrying in his left hand. In his right he held a Heckler & Koch submachine gun.

Bronson registered all this in a split second as he crouched down low, peering around the base of the control panel and aiming the Walther.

But before he could pull the trigger, the intruder must have spotted either Bronson's face or the pistol, because he immediately squeezed the trigger of the submachine gun and sent a lethal stream of nine-millimeter bullets toward him, the noise of the burst deafening in the confined space.

Bronson ducked back into his rudimentary shelter, bullets ricocheting off the steel plate and stone floor and howling around the room, almost as dangerous to the shooter as to the man he was aiming at.

Bronson risked another quick glance, guessing that the man's next move would be to step inside the room and widen the angle so that he'd be able to see his target properly. The glare of the lantern was blinding, and Bronson could see nothing behind it. But he knew where the man had to be, so he adjusted his aim slightly and then squeezed the trigger.

The Walther kicked in his hand, but the only sound the weapon made was a flat slap, followed by the metallic noise of the slide being forced backward by the recoil, the ejected case clattering onto the stone floor, and a fresh round being loaded into the breech.

He had no idea whether he'd hit his target, but because the man made no sound, Bronson assumed that he'd missed. Semi-automatic pistols are notoriously inaccurate, even in experienced hands.

But then there was another shot, the crack of a small-caliber weapon, and immediately Bronson heard a howl of pain from the intruder, followed by the sound of something heavy and metallic falling to the floor. No way was he going to stand up to see what had happened, but he still needed to know the situation. He reached up and placed his flashlight on top of the metal control panel, aimed it more or less at the door of the room, and switched it on. At the same time, he ducked down again, aimed the Walther around the corner of the control panel directly at the lantern, and squeezed the trigger.

Immediately, the room plunged into relative darkness, and there, illuminated by the much weaker beam of Bronson's flashlight, he saw the intruder for the first time, and recognized him immediately as one of the men he'd seen—what felt like months ago—in Marcus's house in Germany. At his feet lay the Heckler & Koch, and he was clutching his stomach with both hands, his face ashen with pain.

Aiming the Walther straight at him, Bronson stood up

and moved forward cautiously. In the light from the flashlight, he could see that the front of the man's one-piece overall, somewhat similar to the ones he and Angela were wearing, was soaked in blood and, even as Bronson stepped near him, the man abruptly tumbled backward, falling limply to the floor like a marionette whose strings had suddenly been cut.

Bronson picked up the submachine gun and slung it over his shoulder, then stepped backward a couple of paces and glanced over to his right, toward the cupboard where Angela had taken refuge.

"Angela, are you okay?"

The cupboard door swung open and she peered out, her eyes moist in the dim light, her body trembling with shock.

"I just meant to frighten him," she said. "I thought if I—"

"You did a lot more than frighten him," Bronson said.

"I just pointed the gun at him and pulled the trigger."

Bronson didn't reply, just took the second flashlight from his pocket, switched it on and stepped forward to where the man lay writhing on the floor, a low moan of agony escaping his lips.

It probably wasn't a fatal wound, especially from the low-powered .22 pistol, but from what Bronson knew of gunshot injuries, the stomach was one of the most painful places to be shot.

"Do you speak English?" he asked, staring down at the man who'd tried to kill him.

The wounded man nodded slightly.

"A little," he said, from between clenched teeth.

"We can get you a doctor," Bronson said, as Angela walked across the room to stand beside him. "But first there's something we need from you."

The man didn't respond, just stared upward, his eyes flickering between the two of them.

"We need information. First, did Marcus send you?"

The man seemed to be considering his answer for a few moments, then he spoke.

"Yes."

"Good. That's what I thought. Now, we need to know what he's got planned for London. Is he intending to mount a terrorist attack on the city?"

Again the man stared at them, then his face contorted into a kind of smile, and he laughed shortly. Then he coughed, and a fine mist of blood shot out of his mouth and sprayed down the front of his overall. It looked to Bronson as if the bullet Angela had fired had done a lot more damage than he'd first thought.

"Well?"

The man shook his head.

"Terrorist attack, no," he said. "Vengeance attack, yes."

"What's the difference?" Bronson asked. "And why 'vengeance'?"

"Terrorist attack kills people, destroys buildings. Two, three years, is forgotten. Vengeance attack destroys city."

Bronson felt the hairs on the back of his neck start to rise.

"But why? Why attack London?"

"For vengeance. I told you."

"Yes, but vengeance for what?"

The man looked puzzled.

"You do not know?"

Bronson shook his head.

"For the Reich that never was. For our Führer who was killed."

"The Thousand-year Reich that lasted less than a decade?" Angela snapped. "And Hitler committed suicide. He didn't even have the courage to face his enemies and die in combat."

"You are a liar," the man said simply, another cough spraying more blood over his clothing. "Our Führer fought gloriously to the very end. Our Fatherland should have been victorious. There would be no Jews, polluting the nations of the world. We would have abolished homosexuals, and made sure that the Arab nations knew their place."

Bronson glanced at Angela and shrugged. He'd been right: the group Marcus had apparently founded wasn't neo-Nazi. It was the real thing, a dyed-in-the-wool recreation of a part of the awesome military machine that had so very nearly conquered the whole of Europe.

"That sad old Aryan dream," Angela said. "Didn't any of you see the irony? You were being led toward this ideal of a nation of tall, attractive, fair-haired, blue-eyed people by a short ugly man with black hair and brown eyes, who wasn't even German. Who was also mad, by the way."

The wounded man stared at her, then coughed again, producing still more blood.

"So your foul little group is intending to do what Hitler couldn't manage? You're going to try to destroy London?" Bronson asked.

"Yes."

"With the *Laternenträger*?" Angela asked.

The man looked surprised, but nodded slowly.

"So what will it do?" Bronson asked. "How does it work?"

Again an expression of amusement crossed the man's pain-ravaged face.

"You do not know?" He laughed shortly, then coughed again. "You will find out," he said. "The whole of London will find out."

"When?"

"When the Rings of Olympus fly over London. When the eyes of the world are staring at our symbol for the Games. When the—"

Then he gave a shudder and emitted a gasp, almost, it seemed, of surprise, and lay still, his eyes wide-open and his mouth forming a silent "O."

"Is he . . . ?" Angela asked.

"He's dead, yes," Bronson replied, checking the man's neck for a pulse. "I think that bullet must have hit his lungs, maybe some other organs."

Angela stared down at the corpse.

"I've never killed anyone before," she said, a quaver in her voice. "I didn't even mean to do it."

Bronson wrapped his arm around her shoulders. "It wasn't your fault," he said, "but I'm glad you shot him. If you hadn't, I might be dead now and I don't like to even think what he'd have done to you if he'd found you. As I told you, these people play for keeps."

Angela looked away from the body, and took a step backward.

"So now what do we do?"

"I don't think there's much else we can learn here," Bronson replied. "We still don't know exactly what the Bell does, but at least we know that Marcus's group intends to attack London with it—or maybe with a modified version of the device—so that's where we need to go, as soon as we can."

He searched the body, removing the dead man's wallet, all the ammunition he was carrying and his backup weapon, a nine-millimeter Walther P99.

They took a last look round the room, the light from their flashlights reflecting off the dusty dials and controls, then stepped over the corpse and made their way back down the stone corridor, retracing their steps toward the chamber where the ventilation shaft terminated.

In the chamber, Bronson looked around for something to stand on. He could hoist Angela up to the entrance to the shaft, but he knew he couldn't just jump or climb up to the opening himself. There was nothing in the room, but they'd found plenty of offices, equipped with chairs and desks.

"Hang on for a second," Bronson said. "I'll just get a chair or something."

He left Angela standing in the doorway, walked down the corridor to the nearest office, grabbed one of the chairs and walked back. He placed it against the wall, stepped up onto it and looked along the ventilation shaft, staring toward the welcome sight of the fresh air outside.

It would feel good to be out of the mine, Bronson thought, away from the old bones and the long black shadows of evil cast by the Nazis.

But as he looked down the ventilation shaft he realized that there was one question he hadn't asked the man who'd attacked them.

Because he'd just seen another shadow, a shadow that had nothing to do with his imagination. Somebody—or something—had just walked across in front of the opening, and that action had faintly disturbed the light shining down the shaft. It could have been an animal, perhaps, or even somebody from Ludwikowice out walking in the hills, but Bronson didn't believe that for a moment.

The man Marcus had sent hadn't come alone. A second man was waiting outside the mine.

44

"What is it?" Angela asked.

"Quiet," Bronson muttered. "I just saw something. I'm certain there's somebody outside, walking around near the ventilation shaft. I don't think our deceased friend was working alone."

"Oh my God. Is there another way out of here?"

"I doubt it very much, and even if there is, it could take us days to find it. We don't have any choice: we have to leave this place the same way we entered it."

"But if you're right," Angela said, her voice rising slightly with fear, "whoever's out there will shoot us down the moment he sees us."

"I know," Bronson said. "That's the problem. Either we have to take him out of the equation before we leave or we have to somehow convince him that we're not who he thinks we are."

For a few seconds he considered the problem from a

tactical point of view. As long as they stayed inside the mine, they were invulnerable, because the only way the man outside could attack them would be by coming through the ventilation shaft himself, and a man—even a heavily armed man—stuck inside a stone tunnel was a sitting target. Unfortunately, precisely the same argument applied to Bronson if he tried to crawl along the ventilation shaft and then shoot down the man waiting outside. He couldn't possibly cover the distance from the chamber to the end of the shaft in silence, and the man would be waiting and alert when he finally reached the outside opening. To do that would simply invite a bullet through his head.

Then he glanced down at the overalls he was wearing, and a slight grin appeared on his face.

"What?" Angela whispered.

"I think I know how I can make this work. You'll have to stay here and wait for me. And don't argue. There'll be shooting, but if it goes according to plan, I'll call you to come out as soon as I've taken care of the problem outside."

Angela looked at him in the gloom of the chamber and shook her head.

"Just be careful," she said.

Then she took a couple of paces forward, wrapped her arms around his shoulders and kissed him full on the lips.

Bronson responded immediately, holding her tight and stroking her blond hair back from her forehead.

"I don't think I've ever said it enough," he said, his voice thick with emotion, "but I've always loved you."

"I know you have. Now stop fannying about and get us out of here."

Bronson smiled at her, nodded and turned away. He climbed up onto the chair and looked down the ventilation shaft. There was now no sign of movement, no subtle changes in the amount of light visible, but he knew what he'd seen. He took the Walther out of his pocket and screwed on the suppressor. He also checked that he had the Heckler & Koch submachine gun with him, but removed the magazine and tucked it into one of his pockets. That weapon would play a crucial part in his plan to ambush the man outside.

Bronson was gambling on the fact that he was dressed in a very similar fashion to the German who'd attacked them inside the mine, and that one man wearing a set of dark blue overalls and emerging feetfirst from a stone shaft should look very similar to any other man doing the same thing. The submachine gun should help to complete the deception.

He made no attempt to be quiet. In fact, he deliberately knocked the butt of the Heckler & Koch against the stone wall of the ventilation shaft a couple of times as he climbed up into it. He was sure that the noise of the shots would have been audible outside the mine, though the sound wouldn't have traveled very far, so the waiting German—and Bronson was hoping that Marcus had sent only two men to the Wenceslas Mine—would be expecting his colleague to reappear at any moment.

As Bronson made his clumsy way backward along the ventilation shaft, the Walther pistol tucked into his pocket and the submachine gun clutched in his left hand, he heard the man outside call out to him in German. He just grunted in reply, feeling with his feet for the end of the shaft, because that was when his plan would succeed or fail.

Then his left shoe scraped over a rocky lip and he felt a faint breath of wind through the thin material of his sock. And then someone tapped his shoe twice. The second man was obviously waiting right beside the entrance to the ventilation shaft, and that was exactly where Bronson wanted him to be.

He maneuvered slightly in the confined space, and slid the unloaded Heckler & Koch down his body, butt first, until it projected out of the shaft, and then just held it there for a few moments, waiting for the other man to take it.

Seconds later, he did so, and that gave Bronson just the opportunity he needed. By handing over the weapon, he hoped he'd convinced the man waiting outside that it was his colleague emerging from the tunnel, which should mean that the second man was now holding the unloaded submachine gun—without the magazine just a useless lump of metal—instead of whatever weapon—possibly a pistol—that he was armed with.

Time was now of the essence. As quickly as he could, Bronson wriggled backward out of the shaft, keeping his face turned away from the other man.

Then he heard a disturbingly familiar sound—the series of metallic clicks made when the magazine is inserted into a submachine gun and the bolt is pulled back to cock the weapon—and he guessed that the second German had just converted the Heckler & Koch back into a lethal weapon by attaching a new magazine. At close quarters, his Walther pistol would be no match for that weapon.

He had seconds to react.

Bronson scrambled the last couple of feet out of the tunnel and down the rock face, keeping his head facing away from the other man the entire time. In one fluid movement, he dropped to the ground, drew the Walther pistol with its cumbersome suppressor from his pocket, slipped off the safety catch and whirled round to face his opponent.

The German—and Bronson was relieved to see only one man facing him in the small clearing—was looking straight at him, the submachine gun held in both hands, the barrel pointing directly toward him. Something must have alerted the man, perhaps the color of Bronson's overalls, or simply his failure to reply to his questions as he'd emerged from the shaft. Whatever it was didn't matter. But it left Bronson with absolutely no choice about what to do next.

He altered the aim of the Walther fractionally, pointing the barrel at the center of the man's chest, and squeezed the trigger.

Only in films can somebody shoot a weapon out of another person's hands, or bring someone down with a well-placed shot to a leg or arm. In a real-life firefight, soldiers, policemen and bodyguards aim for the center of mass, the middle of the torso, because that's where a bullet wound is most likely to incapacitate and, given the inherent inaccuracy of pistols, that also increases the chances of the bullet hitting the target.

Good shots are born more often than they're made, and Bronson had always been good with weapons.

The flat crack of the silenced pistol echoed off the rock face, and before the German could squeeze the trigger of the submachine gun, the nine-millimeter copper-jacketed bullet slammed into his chest. The shocked expression on his face told its own story, and without a sound he simply fell backward, the Heckler & Koch dropping to the ground beside him.

Bronson strode across to where he was lying, the aim of the Walther never varying for an instant, pointing directly at the fallen man. He stopped beside him and looked down, but it was immediately clear that he wouldn't need a second shot. There was remarkably little blood from the wound because the bullet had clearly ripped apart the man's heart, and he had effectively been dead even before his body fell.

Bronson replaced the Walther in his pocket, slung the submachine gun over his shoulder and looked around. There was no sign of anybody else in the area, and the single shot he'd fired would not have been audible for more than a few dozen yards, thanks to the efficiency of the suppressor.

The best place to put the body was undoubtedly inside the mine, but Bronson knew that that simply wouldn't work. Trying to lift up the man's literal deadweight to force it down the ventilation shaft and into the chamber would take too long, and might not be possible at all, even if Angela helped him. And he didn't want her to be traumatized any more than she was already. After all, she'd just shot and killed a man inside the complex, and was still in shock. Disposing of another dead body was something he wasn't prepared to even contemplate putting her through.

There was plenty of undergrowth around the rock face, long grass, bushes and shrubs, and even a narrow crevice not far away that he thought would be big enough to conceal the corpse. Bronson bent down beside the man and searched his pockets. He removed his wallet—to make identification a little more difficult when the police were finally summoned by somebody who'd noticed the smell of decomposition—a set of car keys, a box of nine-millimeter ammunition, and another Walther pistol in a belt holster. He was acquiring quite an armory.

Then he grabbed the man by his heels and dragged him across the level ground toward the crevice he'd noticed. He stopped beside it, laid the body parallel to the opening, and simply rolled it down into the crevice. He tossed a few broken branches and other debris over the corpse, completely concealing it from view. With any luck, it would be several days before anybody discovered the body.

Bronson walked back across the clearing to the end of the ventilation shaft, climbed up the rock until he could shine his flashlight down it, and called out to Angela.

"Can you climb on the chair and follow me out?" he asked.

Her face, pinched with concern, appeared at the end of the shaft.

"Are you okay?" she replied. "What happened?"

"I'll tell you later. Now, we need to move. The clock's running and we have to get back to London as quickly as we can."

Thirty minutes later, they drove back down the track toward the main road and the village of Ludwikowice, but this time in a different car. The keys Bronson had taken from the pocket of the dead man had fitted another BMW, a big four-by-four, which he'd found parked about fifty yards away from the vehicle he and Angela had arrived in. Bronson wasn't sure how long it would be before the owner of the BMW he'd stolen the registration plates from alerted the police, but it seemed prudent to change vehicles. The one thing he was certain about was that neither of the men who'd driven the four-by-four to the mine would be able to report its theft.

And there was another reason as well. When Bronson had opened the trunk to transfer their bags to the second vehicle, he'd discovered that the trunk lid of the new car had been modified, the plastic covering over the inside of the metal fitted with two concealed catches and a hinge. When it was opened, padded recesses were revealed, clearly designed to hold a pair of submachine guns, a couple of pistols, and half a dozen boxes of ammunition. The only reason he'd discovered the hiding place was that the cover had been opened by the two men to access their weapons when they arrived at the spot, and they hadn't replaced it fully. One MP5 was still in place: obviously the men had decided to carry only those weapons appropriate for their task.

Bronson had tucked the pistols, the submachine gun and the ammunition into place and snapped the cover shut. Once in place, there was no external indication that the trunk lid was anything other than absolutely standard.

As he drove away, he reflected that he and Angela were almost certainly better armed than the occupants of any police car in any country in the world, with a total of two submachine guns and four pistols, including the Llama, which was now tucked away in Angela's purse, and the second Walther pistol, the silencer still attached, hidden— but within reach—underneath the driver's seat.

At the end of the road, Bronson swung the BMW to the right, heading west, back toward the German border. They had a long way to go to get to London, and he knew that time was running out.

What Marcus's man had blurted out as he lay dying in the Wenceslas Mine meant that the attack on London was imminent. The one event of the Olympic Games that would be sure to attract publicity from around the world was the opening ceremony, scheduled for the evening of the following day. And that, Bronson guessed, was when the attack would take place. Not only would that mean Marcus's vengeance attack on London would be witnessed by the whole world, but because of the popularity of the event, it would also result in enormous casualty figures.

Whatever Bronson and Angela did, they simply had to stop this catastrophic attack from taking place.

The only problem was, right then, Bronson had no idea how they were going to achieve that.

45

"One thing that man said still puzzles me," Angela said, giving a slight shiver as her mind replayed the events that had taken place a few hours ago in the darkness of the Wenceslas Mine.

They'd crossed back into Germany without any problems, and Bronson was simply following the instructions given by the satnav, which was taking them along the fastest possible route to Calais.

"What's that?" he asked.

"That remark he made about 'our symbol for the Games.' I presume he meant something German, but nothing about the Olympics has any link with Germany, surely? I mean, the tradition goes back to ancient Greece, doesn't it?"

Bronson glanced at her and gave a smile. Then he shook his head.

"What?"

"It's not often that I know more about something than you do," he said teasingly. "And you know my dislike of all forms of organized sport. So it's actually rather odd that I do know something about the Olympics. In fact, I know several things about the Games that most people don't, but it's all information I acquired by accident. A couple of months ago I was involved in a surveillance operation that went absolutely nowhere because we had the wrong information, and I spent a couple of nights sitting in the bedroom of a house on a small estate, waiting for a phone call that never came. The only books the owner of the place possessed were about sport, and the only one I found even halfway readable dealt with interesting facts about the Olympic Games."

"And?"

"And the symbol of the Olympic Games—the famous Rings of Olympus—which most people seem to think was created by the nation that invented the concept, i.e., the ancient Greeks, wasn't."

"Wasn't what?"

"Wasn't anything to do with the Greeks, ancient or modern. The design came from the fertile brain of a French aristocrat named Pierre Frédy, better known as Baron de Coubertin, who's usually considered to be the father of the modern Olympic Games. He created the symbol in nineteen twelve. The design of five interlocking rings, colored blue, yellow, black, green and red on a white background, was intended for the World Congress of nineteen fourteen, but that was suspended because of the First World War. It was later adopted for the Olympic Games. And there's no truth in the idea that each ring represents a continent. In fact, de Coubertin chose the colors because they appeared on all the national flags of the world."

"Fascinating," Angela muttered, but the tone of her voice caused Bronson to glance across at her. "And that has what, exactly, to do with Germany?"

"Nothing, directly," Bronson admitted, "but the German propaganda machine virtually took over the symbol and used it to glorify the Third Reich in the run-up to the 'thirty-six Games, and afterward. I think that's why that German used the expression "our symbol"—it was so closely linked with the Nazi party. The Berlin Games were hugely important to Hitler, and he and a man named Carl Diem were largely responsible for creating two Olympic myths that endure to this day.

"The first relates to the Olympic Rings. Hitler was determined that the Games should put Germany, and especially the Nazi party, in the center of the world's stage, and also establish a kind of link with ancient Greece, with the nation that had founded the Olympics, because Hitler apparently believed that the Greek civilization was a kind of ancient version of the German Reich."

"That man brought a whole new breadth of meaning to the word 'deluded,'" Angela said.

"Exactly. So Carl Diem traveled to the sanctuary of Apollo at Delphi, where the oracle was supposed to have lived, and which was also the site of the Pythian Games, the forerunners of the Olympics. He ordered a stone altar to be constructed there—it included the interlocking rings symbol and was to be used as part of a torchbearers' ceremony for the Berlin Olympics to be held in Greece.

Once the ceremony was over, the altar was left at Delphi and more or less forgotten about. Then a couple of British academics visited the site in the late fifties, found the stone and assumed it dated from the earliest days of the Games, and claimed it established a link between the ancient Greek contests and the modern Olympics. Some history books even today quote this 'evidence' as proof that the symbol originated about three thousand years ago. In fact, of course, Carl Diem's Stone, as it has become known, was just an inspired piece of Nazi propaganda."

"I didn't know that," Angela said.

Bronson nodded. "Not many people do," he replied. "I think the majority still believe the symbol is as old as the Games. But that wasn't all Carl Diem did. Hitler also wanted to emphasize the superiority and purity of the Aryan race, so athletes representing Germany were chosen as much for their appearance as for their abilities. He wanted every major event to be won by a German, and for every one of those Germans to fulfill the fair-haired, blue-eyed Aryan ideal. The torch relay, carrying the Olympic flame from Greece to the host country, is now an important part of the Olympics, but again it was invented by Carl Diem. There was no such event at the original Games, though a flame was kept burning throughout the ancient events to symbolize the theft of fire by Prometheus from the god Zeus. The modern concept of the Olympic flame was introduced in nineteen twenty-eight at the Amsterdam Summer Olympics, but the torch ceremony was Carl Diem's idea. To reinforce Hitler's message, every one of the German runners who transported the flame almost two thousand miles from Greece to Berlin fitted the Aryan mold."

"Again, news to me," Angela said. "How come you remembered all this?"

"I've got a retentive memory, and all the misunderstandings fascinated me. And there's something else," Bronson went on. "Bearing in mind what we've managed to discover, there's an odd link between the nineteen thirty-six Games and what's happening now."

"What?"

"There was a bell at the Berlin Olympics as well. It was another Nazi innovation, a bell that was supposed to sound to summon the youth of the world. It weighed over thirty thousand pounds, carried the usual mix of symbols, including the Olympic Rings and the German eagle, and was positioned in a bell tower at the western end of the Olympic stadium, a tower almost two hundred and fifty feet tall that could be seen from most of Berlin."

"Is it still there?"

"Yes, but it's pretty battered. The tower was set on fire after Berlin eventually fell, and a couple of years after the end of the war it was demolished by British engineers. The bell tumbled down from the top and hit the ground so hard that it cracked. A few years later it was used for target practice to assess the effectiveness of antitank ammunition, and today it's down at ground level outside the stadium, slowly rusting away."

Angela nodded. "And now we have to stop a different kind of Nazi bell from sounding," she said.

"That's a very good way of putting it," Bronson replied.

Then he lapsed into silence as the enormity of the task facing them began to sink in.

The only thing they knew for sure was that the target was going to be the London Olympic Games, but they had no idea how Marcus and his men intended to deliver the weapon, how big it was or what was needed to trigger it. They now knew the approximate dimensions of the original Bell, the one that had been tested and developed in the Wenceslas Mine, but it was reasonable to assume that, if some group of renegade Nazi scientists had been working on the device since the end of the Second World War, the overall miniaturization of electronic components would have allowed them to greatly reduce its size, and instead of trying to find something the size of a small car, like the original Bell, a modern version of the device might fit inside a suitcase, and be considerably more difficult to locate.

The old cliché of trying to find a needle in a haystack barely began to hint at the degree of difficulty facing them, and a sudden wave of despair flooded through Bronson.

Moments later, he realized that Angela's thoughts must have been running along a very similar track.

"Chris, we don't have any option. There's no time left. We have to involve the authorities, the London police or somebody," she said. "There's no way the two of us are going to be able to find this thing, and even if we did, I don't know how we could possibly stop it. You've told me about Marcus, and it's pretty obvious he's a driven man, not to mention completely ruthless. The fact that he sent those two men to the Wenceslas Mine to kill us is proof enough of that."

Bronson nodded, his hands involuntarily clenching the rim of the BMW's steering wheel.

"I know. All we've managed to do so far is discover the bare outline of this plot, literally at the eleventh hour, and it's obviously just the culmination of a long process that he's been planning for years. He must have devised a way of getting this weapon into one of the Olympic venues, or very close beside it, and I'm still certain that he intends to trigger it tomorrow, during the opening ceremony. The problem is that I don't think I'll be able to convince anyone in the Met that I'm doing anything other than trying to avoid my own arrest.

"I mean, who in their right mind would believe that we've uncovered a plot by a group of reborn Nazis to take revenge on Britain for the destruction of the Third Reich by using a weapon that was developed in the Second World War and looks like a bell and might even be a small nuclear device?"

"I don't know how we're going to do it, Chris," Angela said. "Just the two of us, against whatever organization Marcus has put in place, and with you being hunted by the British police at the same time. And all we know—all we think we know, to be exact—is the time of the attack and the target. And even that's a pretty big place."

46

26 July 2012

The telephone call to the Metropolitan Police went pretty much as Bronson had expected. He'd turned off the motorway and stopped the BMW in a quiet Kent village to use a public pay phone, and got through to Bob Curtis almost immediately. But as soon as Curtis realized who he was talking to, his voice changed.

"Right, Bronson," he said—the use of Christian names now seemed to be off the menu—"I'm taping this call and as soon as we've got your location from the computer, Davidson will be sending out the cavalry. You are so deep in the shit that you're going to need a scaffold tower to climb out of it. What the hell have you been doing?"

"And good afternoon to you, too, Bob. I reckon the trace will take no more than three minutes, but I'll be off the line in less than two. You don't need to talk, just listen, because this is serious."

With one eye on the second hand of his wristwatch, Bronson told Curtis what he'd discovered in Berlin and at the Wenceslas Mine, and what he believed the German terrorist group intended to do at the opening ceremony of the Olympic Games.

"And you've got proof of this, obviously," Curtis said, when Bronson finished, "otherwise you wouldn't be wasting my time telling me."

"Of course I can't prove it," Bronson snapped. "What are you expecting? A signed note from Marcus—and I've found out who he is, by the way, or at least where he lives—saying that he intends to blow up half of northeast London?"

"Yeah, well, that's the thing, isn't it? It's all too little, too late, and far too bloody vague. Sounds to me like you've been reading too many thrillers, my friend, and you're trying to create a smokescreen you can hide behind. The best thing you can do is stand right where you are until the patrol car gets to you, and then come in quietly."

"That comes from Davidson, doesn't it?" Bronson asked. "He's not going to listen to anything I say, is he?"

"You got that right."

"Okay, then, Bob. I've got a piece of advice for you. You've been taping this call, so I suggest you make a copy of that tape and stick it away in a safe place somewhere, so that when northeast London goes up in flames you can tell the official inquiry that I gave you fair warning. That way, at least you can save your own skin, even if Davidson fries for it."

For a moment, Curtis didn't reply.

"You're that certain?" he finally asked.

"I'm that certain," Bronson replied, and hung up the phone.

As he drove out of the village on one of the minor roads, heading more or less west toward London, Bronson spotted a Volvo police car traveling in the opposite direction along the main road, at speed, lights flashing.

"That'll be the cavalry," he remarked to Angela. "I don't think Bob Curtis believed a word I said to him. I was right: we're on our own."

"Suppose I called the police?" Angela asked. "Or even the newspapers?"

"I doubt if the police would listen to you. You're tainted because of your association with me. They'd just assume I'd prompted you to tell them the same story. If you went to the newspapers they'd note down what you told them, but before they did anything else they'd talk to their friendly Media Relations Officer at the local cop shop. He'd do some checking before he gave the go-ahead to print anything, and the result would be the same: your name would be mud because of me. And if by some miracle a newspaper reporter *did* believe you, and thought the terrorist threat was real, the paper still wouldn't run the story because the police would tell them not to, to avoid panic."

"Like that strange American expression: we're between a rock and a hard place," Angela said. "Time's running out because the opening ceremony is tomorrow evening. What do we do now? What *can* we do?"

"Two things," Bronson replied, sounding suddenly determined. "In fact, three things. First, tomorrow you don't go to work at the British Museum, but stay in your apartment, because I want you well out of harm's way. I'm pretty sure the target will be the opening ceremony, but we don't know how big or powerful the device is, and if it is some kind of a dirty bomb, the fallout could spread for a long way. In Ealing, you should be safe enough."

"What about you? You won't be hiding away somewhere, will you?"

"No, but that's my job. I have to do whatever I can to stop this attack, and if I don't have to worry about your safety, that'll make things easier for me."

Angela shook her head, but didn't argue the point.

"You said there were three things, so what else will you do?"

"I'll be making a phone call to a friend, because I'm definitely going to need help on the ground. And then I'm going undercover again."

"Not to that same group?" Angela sounded alarmed.

"No. I mean deep undercover. I need to be able to move around the Olympic complex without anybody seeing me, or at least without taking any notice. And there's one group of people that almost everyone ignores, who can go wherever they want without anyone bothering them."

"Who? Policemen?"

Bronson smiled at her.

"No," he said. "Almost the exact opposite, actually."

47

The following morning, just after five thirty, Angela drove the BMW four-by-four east out of London to pick up the M25. The plan she and Bronson had come up with was of necessity simple. She'd just dropped him off in northeast London, where the streets were still largely deserted, and was going to drive out of the city on the M11 motorway as far as Stansted Airport. There, she'd leave the BMW in the long-term car park, where a vehicle on foreign plates would be less likely to attract attention, and hire a car.

She knew it was possible, or perhaps probable, that her credit card purchases were being monitored by the police, in case she led them to Bronson, but he was miles away so it really wouldn't matter if she was stopped and questioned at the airport. And she had all morning to complete the transaction.

In the event, nobody—neither the Avis booking clerk

nor a couple of patrolling police officers bristling with weapons and body armor who were lurking nearby—took the slightest notice of her, and twenty minutes after she'd handed over her credit card, she was driving back down the M11 toward London, in a one-year-old Ford Focus.

And worrying about Bronson.

Bronson was cold and, he hoped, invisible. He certainly thought he looked the part. In a restaurant, nobody really notices waiters—they're just members of staff who take orders, deliver plates of food and clear the tables. On the streets of London, and most other capital cities, the homeless and the beggars are the nonpeople, shapes hunched in doorways or lying on cardboard, perhaps with a plastic cup in front of them holding a few low-value coins. But for the most part, people notice them but don't see them, averting their eyes or stepping around them. And that's what he was counting on.

He hadn't shaved for a couple of days—not a deliberate or planned move, just dictated by the circumstances and their movements in Germany and Poland—and his face was grubby with what looked like ingrained dirt, an effect it had taken him some time to achieve. He was wearing the oldest pair of trainers he owned, dirty and torn jeans, a hooded sweatshirt and a camouflage-pattern jacket that he thought he'd thrown out years ago. Angela had recovered all of those from Bronson's house in the early hours of the morning, but only after they'd spent twenty minutes making absolutely sure that the property wasn't under surveillance. He also had a battered rucksack that contained a handful of chocolate bars, cans of soft drink, a couple of sweaters, Angela's mobile phone, which was switched off, and the silencer and spare magazines for the Walther. The pistol was in his pocket, just in case. Beside him was a grubby old sack, inside which were the two Heckler & Koch submachine guns and extra magazines, each wrapped up in a couple of old sweaters and a tattered blanket.

At that moment he was sitting in the doorway of a small office building about a quarter of a mile from the stadium in Stratford where the opening ceremony was due to start early that evening, and trying to decide what to do next. He was also still wondering what Marcus had planned, because the one thing that was already abundantly clear was that getting anywhere near the stadium, even as a pedestrian, was as near impossible as made no difference.

Getting close with a vehicle, and especially a vehicle big enough to carry an object even half the size of *Die Glocke*, was simply a nonstarter. Every street Bronson had tried to walk down was cordoned off, steel barriers placed across the entrances preventing access to any unauthorized vehicles, police officers in attendance, as they'd probably been for days. And already, despite the early hour, the whole area was starting to come alive.

There were people everywhere, walking to and fro, cameras clicking as they took photographs of each other, sometimes posing in front of the Olympic advertising slogans, information boards and illuminated displays, which listed the timetable of events. Establishing shots, Bronson supposed you could call them, for the myriad picture collections they were obviously intending to compile of the event. There was a huge buzz of excitement in the air as people realized that the time for the Games had finally come, and that the greatest sporting contest in the world was about to be held in Britain's capital city.

Bronson had been moved on twice by regular police officers and once by a community policeman, and every time he'd kept his head down and simply complied, weaving his way through the crowds of people as he looked for another quiet spot where he could sit down and wait. The doorway of the office building he was occupying wasn't ideal, but he knew that he needed to stay in that vicinity, so it would have to do.

He wriggled about, trying unsuccessfully to get comfortable; cardboard may have provided some insulation against the cold seeping up through the paving slabs, though he wasn't convinced about that, but it did nothing to cushion his body.

People walked past him, none making eye contact and most stepping well away from him, to the other side of the pavement, as if being homeless was a contagious condition. Then one man didn't. He was tall and solidly built, but very scruffily dressed. He had the air of a man looking for something. Or someone.

When he saw Bronson half-lying in the doorway, he crossed the street and walked over to stand beside him. Then he prodded the recumbent figure with the toe of one grubby sneaker.

"You look like shit," Dickie Weeks said, looking down at him.

"That's the general idea, Dickie," Bronson replied. "You don't look that sharp yourself."

"Blending in, mate, blending in. I'm feeling charitable. Fancy a cuppa?"

"Thought you'd never bloody ask."

Bronson climbed slowly to his feet—even the comparatively short time he'd been sitting on the pavement seemed to have driven a chilling ache through his bones—and the two men walked away down the road.

"You must know a good café," Weeks said, "you being a street person and all that. Job not going so well, is it?"

"Give it a rest, Dickie," Bronson snapped. "This is serious."

They walked into a café that was little more than a glorified snack bar, Bronson attracting hostile glances from several of the men sitting there, but his bulk was obviously sufficiently intimidating to prevent anyone saying anything to him.

"Tea?" Weeks asked.

"Coffee: hot, black and strong," Bronson replied. "And a bacon sarnie if your funds will stretch that far."

While Weeks strode across to the counter, Bronson walked over to a table in the far corner, as far away from everyone else as possible, pulled out one of the chairs and sat down, his back to the window.

As he did so, two men at another of the tables stood up and walked out, one of them glancing across at Bronson with a disgusted expression as he reached the door.

A couple of minutes later Weeks walked over to him, carrying two chipped mugs, and sat down facing him.

Bronson wrapped his hands around the mug, relishing the warmth of the china.

"I asked for it extra strong," Weeks said, "which means you've got two spoonfuls of instant in there instead of only one. Breakfast'll be along as soon as they've found a pig to kill. So," he lowered his voice slightly, "what the hell's going on here, Chris?"

"First, thanks for that Llama. It got me out of trouble once, and saved my life as well. I'll be keeping it."

Weeks nodded. "I take it somebody who was walking around the place now isn't?"

"If you mean did I use it to kill someone, the answer's yes. Or, to be exact, I didn't pull the trigger, because somebody else did, but there is a body out there with a traceable bullet in it. Not that anyone's ever likely to find it."

Weeks nodded.

"Glad it worked for you," he said. "But that's not why you asked me to meet you here. And it doesn't explain why you look like you're auditioning for a part in a low-budget zombie movie."

"Long story," Bronson replied, then broke off as a grossly overweight man, wearing a grayish apron decorated with an interesting and comprehensive selection of stains, only some of which appeared to be from food, waddled across to their corner and deposited two plates on the table in front of them.

"Bacon butties," he announced, in case either man didn't recognize the greasy offering he'd presented, then returned to his position behind the counter.

Bronson looked at the roll, butter oozing from all sides and a couple of bits of bacon sticking out of one end. He lifted off the top half of the roll, applied a liberal helping of brown sauce from the encrusted plastic bottle on the table, then picked up the roll and took a bite. It tasted wonderful.

"Right, Dickie," he said, and outlined what had happened to him since the two men had last met.

Weeks sat in silence, listening intently and eating his way through his own bacon sandwich. His eyes widened as Bronson described the events in the Wenceslas Mine, and he even put down his mug at one point.

"Bloody hell, so Angela shot the bastard? Good for her. Hey, are you two an item again, or what?"

"More or less, I suppose, but that's not really too important right now."

"Sorry, you're right. So what do you want me to do? And what happened to the MP5 that German comedian was toting?"

Bronson nodded toward the sack lying on the floor beside him.

"It's in there," he replied. "In fact, there are two of them, plus three Walther pistols, one of them with a proper suppressor."

"You're selling them?" Weeks asked, his professional interest clearly aroused.

Bronson shook his head.

"Help me sort out this mess and you can have them as a gift," he said.

"That's a deal. Now, you've told me what happened, but I still don't know what you expect me—or you, for that matter—to do about it. All you think you know is that this bunch of German thugs will be trying to attack northeast London, probably during the Olympic opening ceremony, which, I'd like to remind you, will be starting in less than twelve hours. But you don't know what the weapon looks like, or even what it does. It could be some kind of dirty bomb, a straight explosive device, or even— and I really hope you're wrong about this—a pocket-sized nuke. That's the worst-case scenario, because the yield from even a suitcase nuke like the Russians developed would be enough to flatten a large part of this area."

"You know more about this kind of stuff than I do," Bronson said. "What was the yield of those weapons?"

"Nobody knows for sure, but the best estimates suggest around a hundred kilotons, one hundred thousand tons of TNT equivalent. Put one of those babies in the ground floor of Centrepoint and light the blue touch paper, and all you'd be left with would be a bloody great hole about a mile across and full of rubble."

Bronson shook his head. "I didn't know they were that powerful," he said.

"But that's a nuclear weapon," Weeks reminded him, "designed for use by the Russian special forces, the *Spetsnaz*. We still don't know what this Bell thing is supposed to do. Or how big it is, or where they intend to place it."

"That's the trouble. All I do know is that Marcus and his cronies clearly have an agenda, and the core of their plan involves launching a serious attack on this part of London. Before the German who Angela shot in the mine finally died, he told me it wasn't a terrorist weapon or a terrorist attack they were launching. He described it as a 'vengeance weapon,' like the V1 and the V2, and that's what worries me the most. Whatever the Bell was designed to do, even back in the Second World War, it was still capable of killing people. I told you about this chamber in the mountain, a chamber lined with ceramic bricks—"

"That could suggest it produced radiation," Weeks interrupted. "The Nazis might have been experimenting with different materials to try to contain it. And I have a feeling that ceramic materials are used for shielding in some parts of modern nuclear power stations, but don't quote me on that."

"Anyway," Bronson continued, "we know for a fact that whatever it produced was lethal in nineteen forty-five, and since then this bunch of brand-new Nazis have had about seventy years to get it right, to miniaturize it or increase its yield or do whatever else they wanted. I think we have to assume that this weapon represents a clear and immediate danger to London."

"And you can't go to the police because . . . ?" Weeks asked.

"I've tried," Bronson said resignedly. "And I got the run-around, just as I expected, because of what's happened. What the Met wants is to see me sitting in a cell facing firearms charges. Trying to get them to look beyond that is almost impossible. That's the police mentality, I suppose. Arrest somebody for whatever offense they're known to have committed, and take no notice of the bigger picture."

"So it's all down to you and me?"

Bronson nodded. "There are no more strings I can pull, nobody I can talk to who will take me seriously, and even if I knew somebody who had the kind of clout we'd need to get this area thoroughly searched, I haven't got a shred of evidence to support what I believe is going to happen."

"You're not exactly filling me with confidence here," Weeks said. "This Olympic site is huge, and the weapon could be anywhere. Oh, and by the way, access to the site is severely restricted, so if you had some idea about getting inside and looking for the Bell there, that isn't going to happen."

"I don't think we need to get inside the Olympic Park or any of the stadiums," Bronson said. "Like you said, access is very restricted, and it has been since pretty much the start of the construction. And today nobody's getting anywhere near it without a ticket, and certainly not in a vehicle. I don't think that Marcus and his pals would have been able to get a device positioned inside a building on any part of the Olympic complex. Don't forget, all the reports about the Bell emphasized that it needed huge amounts of power, which would mean more than just plugging it in to a wall socket, and I can't think of any way that they could have arranged to get the device installed and provide a dedicated high-voltage power supply to it."

"Depends on how competent the architects and builders were, I suppose. But on the other hand, the builders would've been working to detailed plans, so if the device wasn't on the plan, it probably wouldn't have got installed. So you're probably right."

"And there's another thing," Bronson went on. "It wasn't so much something that Marcus said, more the way that he said it. When I was with him in Berlin, I got the distinct impression that the device was on its way here, not already in position, which has to mean they'll be putting it somewhere outside the complex. That means in a vehicle or they're going to get it into a building near the site."

For half a minute or so, the two men ate and drank in silence, then Weeks glanced out of the window, put down his mug and looked at Bronson.

"What?"

"Anybody know you round here?" Weeks asked.

"Not really. That group I was supposed to infiltrate was based in this area, but that's all. Why?"

"Because when we arrived in this exclusive establishment, two men got up and left. One of them is now standing on the opposite side of the road looking this way, but I've no idea where the second one's gone. I've never seen either of them before, so it looks to me as if they recognized you, and I wouldn't mind betting we're going to have company any time now."

Bronson turned round slightly in his seat so that he had a view of the street outside. The figure Weeks was talking about was leaning against the wall of the building opposite, a cigarette cupped in his left hand, staring across toward the café. Bronson had a good memory for faces, and now that he could see the man clearly, he recognized him immediately. He'd never spoken to him, but he'd been one of the group at the warehouse when Bronson's true identity had made the news.

Weeks was right. Bronson had no doubt that within a few minutes Georg or some of his men would be arriving, and because of what had happened in Germany and Poland, their response to his presence in the area would be violent, and possibly fatal.

"Well spotted, Dickie. We need to get out of here, right now. You reckon there's a back entrance?"

"Bound to be," Weeks said, standing up. "There'll be a backyard or something."

The two men walked across to the counter, lifted the flap and stepped behind it, to the immediate and very obvious irritation of the proprietor, who stepped over to block their path.

"You can't go through here. It's private."

"Get the hell out of my way, fat boy, unless you really like hospital food," Weeks said, lifting a large clenched fist to the man's face.

For a second or two, it looked as if the café owner was going to try his luck, but then he shook his head and stepped to one side.

Weeks led the way through the back room, like the rest of the café a dark and grubby space, the shelves lined with tins and packets, a couple of fridges and a large freezer humming away in one corner, toward the rear door.

And as he opened it and stepped outside, Bronson realized what should have been obvious to him from the first. The only reason the man would have had for standing in plain view on the opposite side of the road in front of the café was to alert Bronson to his presence, and force him to pick another, less public, way out.

In fact, the man had been acting like a sheepdog, driving the sheep—Bronson and Weeks—exactly where he wanted them to go: out of the café through the back entrance.

Because the moment they stepped outside and the door clicked shut on the latch, Bronson saw a group of five men waiting about twenty yards away, covering the only exit from the narrow alleyway.

48

Bronson knew immediately who they were, not least because the man he knew as "Mike" was standing in the middle of the group, a satisfied smile on his face.

"You might have fooled Georg, but I had you sussed from the start," he snarled. "You fed us a long line of bullshit, but all the time you were just another bloody copper. And now you're going to get what's coming to you."

The other four men were carrying short lengths of timber, less obvious weapons than baseball bats, but just as effective in the right—or rather the wrong—hands.

But before any of them could move, a deep chuckle sounded beside Bronson as Weeks took a step forward.

"That's the problem with some of you north London villains," he said. "You talk too much, and you don't think things through."

Unhurriedly, he reached inside his jacket, extracted a

Colt 1911 semi-automatic pistol, cocked the weapon and aimed it straight at Mike.

Beside him, Bronson took out the Walther and mirrored his actions.

Mike's mouth opened and closed, but no sound emerged. The other men had frozen in place the moment the pistols appeared.

"We don't have time to mess with you today," Weeks said, "so you're quite lucky, really. Why don't you just take your bits of carpentry away with you and do something useful with them, like build a table. But if we see you around here again, we'll make sure you don't bother us—or anybody else—ever again. Now get the hell out of here."

But as the five men turned to leave, under the silent threat of the two pistols, Bronson raised his other hand.

"Hang on a minute," he said.

The group stopped as one and turned back to him.

"It's just a question," Bronson said. "Do you know what's going to happen at the opening ceremony of the Games today? What Georg has got planned, I mean?"

Mike shrugged reluctantly.

"He's organized a massive demonstration for this evening," he said, "right in front of the cameras. That'll get the message out to the biggest number of people possible. Then he'll pay us off, and that'll be it."

"And that's all?"

"Yes."

Bronson shook his head.

"He's fooled you all. You won't get paid. In fact, if you're in this area, you'll probably end up dead. He's smuggling a massive bomb here, and he'll trigger it during the ceremony. That's what all this has been about, right from the start."

"Bollocks," Mike snapped. "Georg is an environmentalist. He's making a stand against overdevelopment, and especially against overdevelopment for sport. He's committed to a nonviolent approach."

"Glad to see that you remembered the official message," Bronson said. "But don't forget you killed that nightwatchman. That was hardly 'nonviolent,' was it?"

"That was an accident. We didn't know he had a weak heart. Apart from that, all we've done is smash up machines and try to disrupt things."

"Just following Georg's instructions?"

Mike nodded.

"What Georg has been telling you is exactly what he thought you wanted to hear," Bronson said. "You've been causing trouble to suit his agenda, and to divert attention away from his real target. If he'd told you that the other part of the group, the people in Germany, were planning on blowing up half of northeast London, you wouldn't have helped him, would you?"

"No, of course not."

"Well, welcome to the real world, Mike, because that's his actual agenda. What you got involved with is a last gasp of Hitler's Third Reich, if you like. Georg's German friends have decided that the London Olympics will provide the ideal opportunity to finish off what the Nazis started with their V1 and V2 weapons. Their aim is to destroy as much of London as they possibly can."

Mike just stared at him.

"Bollocks," he said again. "You're making this up."

"Why would I bother?" Bronson asked. "I'm just giving you a reality check, and a warning about what's going to happen."

"You're serious, aren't you?"

"Deadly," Bronson replied.

Mike glanced around at his companions, all of whom looked somehow uncertain, so clearly Bronson's words had had an effect on them.

"If you're right," Mike said, "if this isn't just more bullshit, I mean, what the hell can we do about it?"

It looked as if Bronson had suddenly acquired a somewhat unexpected group of allies. But the reality, he knew, was that there was very little they could do, except keep their eyes open. So that was what he suggested.

"All we know is that the device they're intending to position here is probably fairly bulky, and we think it'll be arriving in a vehicle, possibly to then be unloaded and placed inside a building, just because it's likely to need a main power supply. So keep your eyes open for anything like that."

Bronson jotted the number of Angela's pay-as-you-go mobile phone on a piece of paper, walked across to where Mike was standing and handed it to him.

"If you see anything, anything at all," he said, "call me, and then call the police."

Mike looked at him, and nodded.

"I heard the cops were looking for you—for real, I mean. Is that true?"

"Yes. Right now, I'm deep in the shit because they don't believe that there's any threat to the Games. That's why I'm dressed like this."

Mike nodded again, then turned to leave the alleyway. Then he turned back and looked at Bronson again.

"I think you ought to know," he said, "that when Tom spotted you and your mate in that café, we told Georg about it. He told us to rough you up a bit, break one of your legs and leave you here. So he's probably coming along pretty soon to finish the job. Might be useful, knowing that."

Bronson nodded. "Thanks, Mike," he said. "It is. Now you'd better make yourself scarce."

As soon as the men had disappeared from view, Bronson turned back to look at Weeks, who was holstering his pistol.

"Not exactly what I expected," Bronson said.

"What about this Georg bloke?" Weeks asked. "Think he'll turn up here looking for you?"

"Probably," Bronson said, "and that might be as good a lead as we're going to get."

He pointed further down the alley.

"There's an open yard or something down there. If you take one of the Heckler & Kochs, you can cover me from in there. I'll just lie against the wall here, and I'll have the Walther right beside me. But don't shoot unless you have to, because firing that MP5 will alert every copper in the area. This Walther's silenced, so let me take care of this German bastard."

Weeks took one of the MP5s out of the sack, checked it, took a spare magazine, and then walked away down the alley. In seconds he was out of sight, but Bronson knew he would be watching what happened from his hidden vantage point.

Bronson took the Walther pistol out of his pocket, checked it and then screwed the suppressor onto the end of the barrel. Then he lay at the edge of the alley, resting his back against the wall, his legs stretched out in front of him. He tucked the pistol almost under his right leg, where it would be immediately to hand, but at the same time invisible to anyone passing. Not that they'd seen anyone else in the alleyway—apart from Mike and his cronies—since they'd stepped into it.

He didn't have long to wait.

About a quarter of an hour after Bronson had taken up his position, his left leg twisted awkwardly under the right, as if it was broken, two men turned into the alleyway from the adjacent road and walked steadily toward him. Recognizing them wasn't difficult. The slight figure of Georg was quite unmistakable, and the last time Bronson had seen the taller man walking next to him was in the concrete-lined cellar at Marcus's house outside Berlin.

"This is a surprise, Bronson," Georg said, stopping beside him. "Got a bit of a problem walking, have you?"

Bronson didn't reply, just looked up at him. He was actually in some pain, just because of the awkward position of his leg.

"I think you might have seen Gunther in Germany," Georg said, gesturing to his companion. "He certainly remembers you. Quite an impressive piece of shooting, he told me."

"Just get on with it, Georg," Bronson snapped.

"You've got the *Laternenträger* here already, I suppose, and I'm the last loose end you need to tie."

The German nodded, reached into his pocket and took out a small semi-automatic pistol. He took his time, extracting the magazine from the butt and then replacing it before taking a compact suppressor and screwing it on to the end of the barrel. The second man already had an automatic pistol held casually in his hand, but no suppressor.

"I need to know," Bronson said. "It is here? Is it ready to be triggered?"

Georg glanced up and down the alley, making sure that they were still unobserved, then nodded again.

"It's not here yet," he said, moving his pistol until it pointed at Bronson, "but it will be arriving later this morning as the final part of the operation, far too late for the authorities to do anything about it."

"Somebody might spot it," Bronson said. "It might never reach London."

Georg smiled bleakly.

"That's not going to happen. Nobody will be able to stop it, and we already know exactly where it will be positioned. We have a reserved spot, as it were, because we've been planning this for five years, ever since the city was chosen to host these Games, in fact. And the best bit is that we won't be blamed for what's going to happen. In fact, when it's all over, people will see that we were right all along. And because of the timing, it will literally be a broadcast that the whole world will see. And now it's time for me to do you a favor. I'm sure your leg is hurting quite badly, so I'm going to relieve your pain, permanently."

Timing, Bronson knew, was everything. He lifted his left hand slightly, and moved his right hand until he was touching the butt of the Walther.

"Actually, it's not really hurting at all," he said. "And thanks for the information."

He twisted slightly sideways, and instantly brought up the Walther to point straight at Georg.

Shock flared across the German's face at Bronson's totally unexpected action, but he was committed, and both men knew it. Georg squeezed the trigger of his weapon, but even as he did so, Bronson fired.

The nine-millimeter bullet from the Walther slammed into the German's chest, knocking him backward as his pistol discharged harmlessly, the bullet ricocheting off the wall several feet away from Bronson. The reports made by the two silenced pistols would have been barely audible outside the alley.

Instantly, Bronson shifted his point of aim to the other man, who was quickly recovering from his surprise at the turn of events, and was already bringing up his own weapon to fire at Bronson. Again, there was no option. Bronson pulled the trigger a second time, the flat slap of the detonation echoing from the alley walls, but probably not audible in the street outside.

The second man tumbled backward and crashed onto his back on the stone floor of the alley.

Bronson climbed to his feet and stepped forward, but one look was all he needed to tell him that both men were dead, which absolutely wasn't the result he'd been hoping for. If he could have taken Georg alive, he might have found out enough about the plot to take to the authorities. But obviously that wasn't going to happen now.

Weeks stepped up beside him and looked down at the two bodies.

"Shame," he said. "I heard him say something, but I guess it wasn't enough."

"Not really. All I know is that the device isn't here yet, but it's due to arrive this morning. I suppose that's some help, just not very much."

Weeks nodded back toward the yard where he'd been concealed.

"We can put them in there," he said. "Somebody'll find them today, I guess, but at least that'll get them out of sight for a while."

Bronson picked up Georg's pistol, slipped it into his bag, and then searched the body, removing his wallet and everything else the man was carrying, while Weeks did the same thing to the other corpse.

A few minutes later, the bodies hidden out of sight in the yard, Bronson and Weeks walked out of the alley and headed toward the main road.

49

The moment they stepped out of the alleyway, Bronson saw a distinctive white car approaching, the lights on the roof bar flashing blue and red as it carved its way through the traffic. Unusually, the officers hadn't turned on their siren; for most villains engaged in the perpetration of a crime, the noise simply acted as a two-minute warning and allowed them to make good their getaway before the police arrived. And on this occasion, Bronson would have appreciated that warning as well.

"Someone must have heard something, or even seen something," Weeks said. "We can't afford to get caught with these weapons on us."

"You got that right. Just keep going. They might not be looking for us."

"Yeah, and I still believe in Father Christmas."

The police car powered past them, the driver giving the traffic his full attention. But his companion, sitting in the front passenger seat, was scanning the faces of the people on the sidewalk. For the briefest of instants, he locked eyes with Bronson, and almost immediately the brake lights of the vehicle flared into life as the driver dragged the car to a stop.

"He's made us," Bronson said, breaking into a run.

"Only you, actually," Weeks said, matching Bronson's stride.

"You're guilty by association. Welcome to the club."

The sidewalks were quite busy, shoppers wandering to and fro with their usual scant regard for anyone or anything around them. Bronson and Weeks were forced to dodge and weave their way through the crowds, angry shouts and spilled shopping lying in their wake.

Bronson risked a quick glance behind them. The two police officers were pounding along in pursuit, people moving quickly out of their way. One of them had his hand to his collar and was speaking into his microphone, obviously calling for backup. Somehow, they had to stop the two officers, or at the very least slow them down.

Weeks clearly had the same idea, and pulled the Colt 1911 from its holster. Without breaking stride, he swung his right arm around to point behind him, glanced quickly backward and then pulled the trigger.

The bang of the forty-five-caliber cartridge firing was shockingly loud, the report echoing from the buildings on either side of the street. Instantly, screams and shouts of alarm followed, and all around them people either dropped to the ground or ran for cover.

"You didn't hit anyone, I hope," Bronson said, panting from the exertion.

"Just scared them. Well above their heads."

Bronson glanced back again. The two police officers were a lot further back, Weeks's use of his pistol obviously having shocked them.

"They'll keep coming, you know," he said. "And by now they'll have a couple of ARVs heading this way as well."

"I know. But my motor's parked a couple of streets away. Once we get to that, we're out of here."

Weeks led the way down a side street, then took the first junction on the left. The moment he reached the building that stood on that corner, he stopped, took out his pistol and waited. Within a few seconds, the two police officers appeared, still running, albeit slightly more slowly than before. Weeks waited until they'd covered a few yards, then stepped into plain view, lifted the pistol and fired another shot. The bullet slammed into the wall of the house a few feet above their heads, and both men instantly dropped to the ground.

"Breathing space," Weeks said. "And now they know I'm not firing blanks either."

At the end of the next street, Weeks took out his remote control and pressed two buttons in sequence. Fifty yards ahead, the hazard lights flashed on his Range Rover, followed almost immediately by the welcome sound of the engine starting. The two men reached the car, pulled open the doors and jumped inside. Weeks released the handbrake, pulled the automatic transmission lever into drive, and powered the heavy car away from the parking space.

As the Range Rover accelerated down the road, the police officers appeared again, their approach clearly much more cautious. But they were still following.

"Do you think they got the number?" Weeks asked, punching buttons on the built-in satnav.

Bronson pulled on his seat belt, then turned round in his seat and looked back at the two men.

"I don't know. But they'll have a good description of the vehicle, and that might be enough."

As soon as he could, Weeks turned off the road, Bronson now using the satnav to pick a route that would take them away from the area as quickly as possible.

"We'll need to lose the car and these clothes as soon as possible," he said.

"Not a problem. We'll head out into Essex, find somewhere there."

"I've got a better idea. Keep heading down this road. At the end, take a left turn and then follow the signs for the M25. At the junction, go west. We'll go to Angela's flat in Ealing and sort ourselves out there." He paused for a moment, then chuckled. "I suppose one good thing is that Stratford will now be swarming with armed police looking out for anything suspicious, which is pretty much the result I'd hoped to achieve when I told the Met what I thought was happening."

But when Weeks braked the Range Rover to a stop at the T-junction, both men knew that getting out of the area wasn't going to be anything like as easy as they'd hoped.

Weeks spotted the flashing blue and red lights in his rearview mirrors. At almost the same moment Bronson saw a Volvo estate car approaching the junction from the right, traveling very fast.

"I think that's an ARV," he said, gesturing toward the Volvo.

"Then let's hope they don't spot us," Weeks said.

Seconds later, before Weeks could pull the Range Rover out onto the main road, a siren on the Volvo began sounding, to move traffic out of the way, and then it slewed across the road, stopping right in front of Weeks's car, blocking the way.

50

"Hang on," Weeks snapped.

He swung the wheel of the Range Rover hard over to the left, shifted the transmission into reverse and backed up a few feet, until the rear of the four-by-four slammed into the front bumper of the car immediately behind them. The driver sounded his horn in a loud, continuous and clearly angry blare, which Weeks completely ignored. He spun the wheel to the right, engaged drive and floored the accelerator pedal.

The two-ton car hit the left-hand rear of the Volvo just as the two front doors were opening. The impact turned the Volvo violently on its axis. The passenger door instantly slammed shut while the other gaped wide, the black-clad figure of the police driver visible in the opening, struggling to stay in his seat.

Weeks kept the power on, forcing the police car out of his way. Metal ripped and tore, tires howled as the tarmac road surface ripped rubber from them, and pedestrians on the sidewalks watched the unequal contest in open-mouthed amazement. He shunted the Volvo over to the left, keeping the wheel of the Range Rover hard over, all four tires smoking and leaving black streaks on the road, forcing the other car back against the curb. There was a sudden explosion as the right-side rear tire of the police car blew, forced off the rim by contact with the curb-stone. People scattered in all directions.

"That'll do," Weeks said, straightened up his car and accelerated rapidly down the street.

"That's probably buggered up your no-claims bonus," Bronson observed. "Did you damage this car?"

Weeks shook his head. "Unlikely," he replied shortly. "I've got bull bars on the front, and the chassis and suspension have both been uprated and strengthened. I like this car. In fact, I need to do something about that, right now."

He punched buttons on the center console and a ringing tone sounded in the car's stereo audio system. Then a disembodied voice announced: "Police."

Weeks grinned at Bronson and immediately launched into an urgent description of having left his car outside a newsagent's while he went inside to buy a paper, and of seeing two men jumping into the vehicle and driving off.

"Then," he continued, "these two bastards rammed one of your jam sandwiches and then buggered off down the street. You need to stop them, mate. That bloke who nicked my motor is bloody mad."

He finished off with the registration number of the Range Rover and his personal details, then rang off.

"You think that'll work?" Bronson asked.

"I dunno. I thought it was worth a try. Muddies the waters a bit, anyhow."

As soon as they got out of sight of the damaged Volvo, Bronson directed Weeks down side roads to get them away from the area as quickly as possible, and they neither saw nor heard a police car for several minutes.

"I reckon we've lost them, but they'll have a chopper up any time now, so we need to lose this motor pretty soon," Weeks said.

"Best place is a multi-story," Bronson said. "You're invisible as soon as you drive inside, and there's always some car there that you can jack. I should know—I've investigated dozens of car thefts from places like that."

Five minutes later, Weeks drove the Range Rover into a car park on the edge of a shopping center, and headed for the up-ramp. Bronson crouched down in the front seat so that he would be invisible to the unwinking eye of the security camera covering the entrance, and Weeks made sure he kept his left hand over his face as he took the parking ticket.

He drove the Range Rover up to the fifth floor, where there were far fewer cars, most shoppers obviously preferring to find a parking place on one of the lower levels. He stopped just as he reached the floor and then maneuvered the car until it was directly underneath the camera that covered that parking level, felt in the door pocket and pulled out a pair of insulated pliers, which he handed to Bronson.

"Snip the coax on that camera," he said, gesturing upward.

Bronson climbed onto the hood, stood up and cut the lead in two where it entered the camera.

Weeks parked the car on one side of the level, then they both checked the other vehicles there. The obvious choice was an oldish Ford, the newer cars having far more sophisticated antitheft systems, and in under ten minutes Weeks had the door open and the engine running. They transferred all their possessions to the new vehicle, then drove off down the ramp. They stopped beside a payment machine on the second floor, and Bronson got out to pay the charge on the ticket Weeks had taken about a quarter of an hour earlier.

"That's a deal," he said, when he got back into the car. "The first half hour is free."

As they exited, Bronson again ducked down out of view of the camera, and Weeks hid his face as he fed the ticket into the slot.

Weeks drove the car with care, not out of respect for the vehicle, or for the person they'd deprived of it, but simply so as not to attract any attention. The car didn't have a satnav, and so they had to rely on the road signs to find their way. But that wasn't difficult.

Just under an hour after Weeks had started the engine on the Ford in the car park in northeast London, he and Bronson were stepping inside Angela's apartment, having dumped the Ford a few streets away.

"I've been watching the news," she said, as the two men walked in. "A pair of thugs driving a Range Rover rammed a police car near the Olympic stadium, then got away. Know anything about that?"

"It was just a bit of a fender-bender," Weeks replied. "Nobody got hurt. You're looking well," he added.

A smile flitted across Angela's face for a period best measured in milliseconds.

"Thanks," she said, "and so are you. So what's going on, Chris?"

Bronson provided her with a highly edited account of what had happened in London that morning, avoiding any reference to the killing of Georg and his anonymous companion.

"Based on what we've found out," he finished, "it looks like the device will be arriving this morning, but we still don't know how it's being transported or where it will be positioned. But it is definitely coming."

Angela shook her head.

"I really hoped we'd got it wrong. So what can you do now? Is there any point in calling the police again?"

"Probably not," Bronson replied. "I still don't know what it is that they could do, even if they took me seriously. The area was swarming with police even before we had our little traffic accident, and my guess is that there are probably about double that number around Stratford by now. Granted, they're not looking out for some kind of a nuclear device shaped like a bell, but they will have their eyes open."

"And I suppose you two are going back?"

It was actually less a question than a simple statement, and the two men nodded in reply.

"Yes," Bronson said, "but we need to change our clothes, so that we look different."

"And what can you hope to achieve, just the two of

you, if hundreds of police officers and the troops and everyone else can't stop this weapon being positioned?"

"I don't know," Bronson replied, "but we have to try. We might see something, or hear something, that makes sense to us but which would mean nothing to anyone else."

Angela nodded. "You have to do what you can, I know. Right, Dickie, the bathroom's through there if you want to clean up, and if you go into the bedroom you'll find a bunch of Chris's clothes in the small wardrobe. You look as if you're about the same size, so help yourself."

"Wear smart casual, with a jacket," Bronson instructed.

Weeks nodded, but didn't respond. While he was out of the room, Angela made coffee for the three of them.

"Is there anything I can do?" she asked.

"Not really," Bronson replied, "unless you can work out how Marcus is planning on getting the Bell into the heart of the Olympic site. I told you I saw Georg today—"

"You told me less than half the story, but I really don't want to learn any more," she interrupted.

"Yes, point taken. The thing is, he was in no doubt at all that they'd manage to deliver the device. He was certain they'd have no trouble getting it into position. In fact, he talked about having something like a 'reserved space,' as if he had a ticket to the opening ceremony."

"That doesn't make sense," Angela said. "All access is going to be strictly controlled, for obvious reasons. The last thing London wants is a repeat of the Munich Olympics, only a hundred or a thousand times worse. Every spectator is going to be checked, and probably have to walk through a metal detector or body scanner, and the amount of vehicular traffic allowed anywhere near the stadium is going to be incredibly limited, and checked just as thoroughly. Are you sure he didn't mean they'd already got it into position? Into a reserved space, or whatever?"

Bronson shook his head.

"That's not what he said, and I'm certain that's not what he meant. There's something we're missing here, some loophole Marcus has obviously identified and is going to exploit. I was even wondering if he had some plan to get the device onto an underground train or into a sewer somehow, but I just don't see either of those options working, for a host of basic logistical reasons."

Angela nodded, then leaned forward as another thought struck her.

"There's another factor. If he's been planning this for years, he can't have worked out a way to beat the security system London's put in place to safeguard the Olympics all that time ago, because it probably wasn't even finalized until quite recently. So it must be something else, something fundamental, that we're just not seeing."

The door opened and Weeks appeared, wearing blue jeans and a white open-necked shirt, both garments fitting him reasonably well. He had a light jacket slung over his shoulder.

"Bathroom's free," he announced, then sat down and picked up his mug of coffee.

Twenty minutes later, Bronson emerged similarly dressed, his growth of stubble removed, his hair combed.

"Right," he said, "we need to go. We'll have a bag each, because we need somewhere to store the hardware, and a couple of sets of vests and caps I borrowed a while ago."

"Vests?" Weeks asked.

"Yes. If we find something, we're going to need to be able to move fast. I've got two sets of police baseball caps and overvests in my bag. Undercover officers use them when they need to identify themselves to the public. You just pull them on over your shirt. They aren't Kevlar, just nylon, but those, and the caps, might help us pass for real coppers if we have to."

"You are a real copper," Angela pointed out.

"I was when I started this caper," Bronson replied, "but I have no idea what I am right now. I don't even know if they're still paying me."

He picked up the keys for the car Angela had hired, a nicely anonymous means of transport that wouldn't ring the alarm bells in any police car they passed, and turned to leave.

"If you have any brain waves, give me a call on the mobile," Bronson said. "Otherwise, I'll see you later."

51

Bronson and Weeks gave up looking just after four that afternoon, having achieved absolutely nothing.

They'd driven around all the Olympic sites in Angela's hired Ford, and seen all of the security precautions at first hand. Whole streets had been cordoned off by linked steel barriers, effectively turning the various sites into islands within the suburban environment. Police officers, many of them armed, were manning the barricades, their numbers supplemented by vast hordes of civilian staff. Troops were on the streets as well, providing an impressive extra level of security, and Bronson knew that Typhoon fighter jets had been stationed at nearby airfields, Royal Navy ships were moored in the Thames, and surface-to-air missile batteries were positioned and on alert around the city. London was protected by an impressive ring of steel, but he knew that these defenses would be completely and utterly useless if the weapon was already inside the city. And that, he thought, was the appalling reality of the situation.

Pedestrian access was rigidly controlled, and neither he nor Weeks could see any possible way that anybody without the correct ticket was going to get anywhere near the stadium. And certainly no unidentified vehicle carrying a weapon, disguised or not, would have been allowed access to the area.

They'd concentrated on the main stadium, the site of the opening ceremony, which was also where the most restrictive security precautions were in force, for obvious reasons. They'd driven around it twice, following a tortuous route through the side streets, but keeping as close to the stadium as they could. Then they'd parked the car and walked pretty much the same route. But there were no gaps in the security cordon, no places where even an agile man would be able to get through the barriers and into the stadium, and certainly no points where a vehicle could be driven through.

The only other possibility was that the Germans were planning a kind of suicide attack, driving a heavy truck through the barriers and then detonating the device once the vehicle had finally been brought to a stop. But that didn't seem likely—suicide attacks just weren't a part of the German national psyche.

But Georg's words still echoed in Bronson's memory. The German had been so certain, so sure, that Marcus's foul plan would reach fruition. And in the circumstances of their confrontation that morning—when Georg had obviously believed that Bronson was going to be dead in seconds—there had been no reason for him to be anything other than truthful.

*   *   *

The streets were already packed, throngs of people streaming toward the venue, the cafés doing a brisk trade, and a tremendous buzz of excitement in the air. Even getting near the stadium was difficult because of the crowds, and it soon became clear that seeing any unusual activity would be virtually impossible. Above them, helicopters buzzed around, some police aircraft, but several emblazoned with the logos of television channels.

"I think we've blown it," Weeks said, as he and Bronson stood on a street corner watching a long line of people queuing to gain entrance to the stadium. "Wherever the device is, either it's in position already or it's not going to make it."

"I'm sure it's here," Bronson replied, finality in his voice, as he gestured at the continuous activity in front of them. "Marcus would have known it was going to be like this. He must have anticipated it, and somehow worked out a way to get around it. Or through it."

Weeks shook his head. "I don't see how. And you said Georg claimed the device would be arriving today, maybe even while we were here on the streets. That seems a hell of a lot more unlikely. I mean, they weren't letting anything through, as far as I can remember, apart from what you'd expect—police cars and so on." He paused. "They couldn't have got it into a cop car, could they? Or a police van?"

"I doubt it. Even a police Transit might be a bit small to cope with the Bell, unless Marcus and his cronies have devised some way of really miniaturizing it. And even if they did manage to do that, it would probably still need a large power supply unit, so that might mean several generators in the vehicle as well as the device itself. It would have to be a small truck at the very least. There just has to be a loophole, something that we're missing."

Weeks looked at him.

"Is there any point in you surrendering yourself to the plods?" he asked. "If you were in custody you could explain what you and Angela discovered in Germany and Poland. That would at least identify the threat and they could blanket the area, looking for the device."

Bronson shook his head.

"I'd do that in a heartbeat if I thought it would help," he said, "but I know police procedures. I'd be arrested, charged, and then stuck in the cell somewhere while they decided who was going to interview me. By the time I could get to speak to anyone in authority who had a bit of brain, the Olympic opening ceremony would already have started, and it would be far too late to do anything. In any case," he added, waving his arm at the police and troops who were in position further down the street, "the area is already stuffed full of armed men who've been briefed to watch out for trouble. What good would another five hundred coppers do?"

Weeks nodded, the cold reality of Bronson's logic making perfect sense.

"Then we really are screwed," he said. "The best thing we can do is get the hell out of here, before Marcus lights the blue touch paper."

"I can't do that. If that Nazi bastard could devise a way of breaching this security, then we have to be able to work out how he's done it. How could he get a truck through this lot without it being stopped and searched?"

Bronson broke off as his phone rang.

"It's Angela," he said, recognizing the number.

"Chris, I'm watching stuff on the TV," she said. "All the preparations for the opening ceremony. They're switching between shots from the helicopters and the cameras on the ground, around the stadium and inside it. And I've been thinking about what you told me. When that man in the mine said 'when the eyes of the world are staring at our symbol for the Games' we got sidetracked by thinking about the Olympic Rings, but what if he accidentally let another clue slip? What if the 'eyes of the world' meant a TV camera?"

"They're showing an aerial view now," Angela went on. "The stadium is enormous, and it's already full of people, and there are huge crowds outside. I don't know how you can hope to see anything with that mob blocking the area. There are buildings all around it as well, and I suppose that the weapon could be in any of them. And all the trucks are there, too."

Bronson stiffened as Angela finished speaking.

"Trucks? What trucks?"

"They're all lined up outside a massive building near the stadium. Hang on a minute. The cameras on the helicopter are just covering that area now. They've all got logos on their sides."

For a second or two, Bronson just stood there, the mobile phone pressed to his ear as his brain processed what Angela had just said. And in that instant, everything fell into place. It was the only scenario that made sense, the only answer that worked for all the questions.

"Angela, you're a genius. That has to be it. Call the police. Call Curtis, tell him who you are and tell him there's a bomb in one of the television outside-broadcast lorries at the Media Center. If he won't listen, dial triple nine and give them the same message. And I think I might know which van it will be in, too."

Bronson told her his idea and gave her Curtis's direct line and mobile numbers, then rang off.

"The TV trucks?" Weeks asked.

"It must be. They're big enough to hold the device, and because they're designed to operate out in the field, either they can be plugged in to external power supplies or they carry their own generators."

"But they can't just have mocked one up. They must have documentation that authorizes them to be here. Do you mean Marcus and his men faked all that?"

Bronson smiled grimly. "I doubt it," he said. "More likely he identified a small television company that was sending just one lorry and stopped it on the road some-where. He'd have pulled out the crew, killed them and dumped their bodies, and then he and his men would have loaded the device into the back of the truck and taken their places. They'd have arrived here in London with the right documentation, and been directed to a prebooked location. That has to be what Georg meant when he said they had a 'reserved spot.'"

"And," he added, "it also adds another dimension to his remark about them not being blamed for the attack. I didn't understand it at the time, but he said 'when it is all over people will see that we were right all along.' I'd bet anything that the truck we're looking for will belong to an Israeli television company."

Bronson glanced at his watch.

"And we've got less than half an hour to find it and defuse the Bell and stop the greatest carnage London has ever seen."

52

27 July 2012

Weeks shook his head.

"I thought all the media coverage was being handled from inside the Media Center, or whatever it's called," he said, "not from outside-broadcast lorries."

"As far as I know it is," Bronson replied, already heading down the road. "But the building just provides the transmission facilities—studios and so on. All the broadcasters—and I'm sure I read somewhere that they were expecting about twenty thousand people all together—would have brought their own equipment, cameras, microphones, recording gear and so on. That's what would be in the lorries."

"And Marcus and his merry men would have wanted to delay their vehicle's arrival until the last minute, just in case anybody spotted anything odd about it?"

"That's about the size of it. That'll be why it was programmed to arrive today. Even if it had been scheduled for an earlier arrival time, I'm sure they would have faked a breakdown or something on the journey to delay its arrival. So if I'm right at least we know what we're looking for."

The International Broadcast Center, a huge multistory building three hundred yards long and over one hundred yards wide, was positioned in the Main Media Complex in the northwest corner of the Olympic Park. It had been designed from the outset to be a state-of-the-art media center, able to cope with the transmission requirements of journalists of every nation, beaming reports to a worldwide audience of up to four billion people.

Just like the rest of the Olympic Park, access to the building was strictly controlled, but that wasn't a problem because they didn't need to get inside it. The one thing Bronson was certain about was that Marcus wouldn't have risked trying to get the Bell inside that, or indeed any other, building, because there was simply no point. Leaving it in the truck was the ideal solution, as long as the device had adequate power supplies, and that could presumably be supplied by a plug-in mains feed, maybe supplemented by onboard generators.

"Where is it?" Weeks asked, striding along beside him. "Where do we have to go?"

Bronson pointed down the street.

"We carry on down here and then take that road over there. That should take us in the right direction."

He glanced at his watch. It was already nearly seven in the evening. The start of the opening ceremony was imminent, and the German terrorist group would be triggering the weapon at any minute. They could clearly hear the sound made by the thousands of spectators in the main stadium, a dominating and undulating buzz, like the noise of a colossal beehive. The stands there would be full of people, including the Prime Minister and most of the country's senior politicians, the upper echelons of the military, leading businessmen and a host of other dignitaries from Britain and around the world. For almost the first time, Bronson fully appreciated the magnitude of the catastrophe facing the country if the device was triggered.

The death or incapacity of the people in the stadium would not simply be a humanitarian tragedy of epic proportions; it would cripple the country for decades to come. The government would fall, businesses would collapse, and the country could even be bankrupted by the financial cost of repairing the damage and the compensation that would have to be paid. The deaths of so many foreign dignitaries would produce international condemnation. Britain would become a pariah on the world's stage, reviled by every nation for having permitted such an event to occur. The glory of the Olympics would in an instant be transformed into the greatest catastrophe of modern times.

And it wasn't just the rich and powerful who would suffer, Bronson knew. Countless thousands of ordinary people, from most of the nations of the world, would also perish. All around them, the streets were choked with people on their way to the stadium or perhaps just attracted by the sense of excitement that pervaded the area. Bronson looked at the sea of faces, at their eager expressions of hope and expectation, and knew that in minutes—if he and

Weeks didn't manage to do something about it—most of them could be dead or dying.

"Down here," he said, and led the way down another street, pushing through the crowds that clogged the pavement.

Simply getting through the press of people was difficult enough, because they were moving against the flow, away from the stadium, and the two men had to rely on their bulk to shift people out of the way. But within minutes it was clear that they weren't going to make it in time. They had to do something else.

"Here," Bronson instructed, and turned off the pavement into a gap between two buildings.

"What?"

Bronson didn't reply, just opened the bag he was carrying and pulled out two black nylon vests with the word "police" printed on them, front and back. He had also brought along his utility belt, which he buckled around his waist. Both men put on black baseball caps, again bearing the word "police," on their heads. The final touch was the sunglasses, which rendered their eyes completely invisible.

Weeks checked his MP5, then slung the weapon across his chest and stood waiting as Bronson looked him up and down. His own Walther was in a belt holster.

"It should be a ballistic vest, obviously," Bronson said, "and you should have a utility belt, but otherwise it looks quite convincing. I think the British public's got used to the sight of Heckler & Koch submachine guns on the streets, which isn't necessarily a good thing. Now let's get going."

Faced with the sight of two grim-faced and heavily armed police officers, who were clearly in a hurry, the crowds parted easily in front of them, and Weeks and Bronson were able to run along the pavements almost unobstructed. A couple of times they were forced to detour down less crowded streets simply because of the mass of people virtually blocking the more direct route.

"That's it, right ahead," Bronson panted, as a huge building came into view.

He and Weeks slowed down to a jog as they approached the structure, both men looking for the first sign of the trucks that Angela had seen on her television screen. "Over there," Weeks said, pointing.

To one side of the building was a large open area where rows of broadcast trucks had been parked, presumably after whatever equipment needed had been removed from them. Bronson and Weeks strode across to the high wire fence that enclosed the parking lot and walked steadily along beside it, looking carefully at the parked vehicles.

Around them, crowds of people ebbed and flowed, and above everything else the noise of the thousands of spectators talking and laughing and arguing provided a constant soundtrack.

"Remember we're looking for an Israeli TV truck," Bronson said, peering through the fence.

"There are still a hell of a lot of them here."

"I didn't say it was going to be easy."

There were dozens of trucks parked in rows, many with unfamiliar registration plates and bearing logos for TV stations neither man recognized. Large satellite dishes were mounted on the roofs of the majority of the trucks, but most were folded down because the crews would be using the on-site facilities to relay the events being filmed in the stadium direct to the studios in the country where their TV stations were based.

Bronson and Weeks walked down the side of the fence, looking closely at every single truck as they passed it, alert to anything unusual or suspicious but, as far as they could tell, all the vehicles seemed to be legitimate. Several had their doors open as technicians and other staff bustled purposefully about, getting a few last items of equipment as the media circus prepared for the imminent opening ceremony.

"This is hopeless," Weeks muttered, as they strode past yet another group of lorries. "There are just too many of them."

Bronson shook his head.

"I don't believe that Marcus is planning a suicide trip, for himself or for any of his men, so what we're looking for, I guess, is a lorry that looks more or less the same as the others, but is probably locked and with nobody working anywhere near it."

"Okay," Weeks conceded. "I suppose that does narrow the field slightly."

Bronson shook his head again. "We're not going to achieve anything wandering about out here," he said. "We have to get inside this compound right now, find the truck and work out how to stop the device from being triggered."

He pointed at a set of gates wide enough for a truck to pass through easily, gates that were of course closed, and beside which was a smaller pedestrian gate set into the boundary fence, with a booth containing the security checkpoint beside it.

"Just follow behind me," Bronson said, "because I've got a warrant card, and that should be enough to get us inside."

Half the skill of being an impostor is attitude. People judge others by their bearing, by the way they walk or the way they talk, and Bronson and Weeks knew this as well as anyone. So as they approached the entrance to the compound where the trucks were parked, both men adopted a slight swagger, trying to exude confidence. They weren't the only armed police in the area. Several pairs of officers were patrolling different parts of the Olympic Park, and that should also help them reach their objective.

The civilian staff member manning the entrance in a glass-fronted booth looked up as they approached.

Bronson stepped forward and held up his warrant card, Weeks right behind him, and strode up to the barrier.

"Let us through," he instructed.

"What's the problem, officer?"

"I didn't say there was a problem," Bronson replied.

"But we already have a police patrol covering this area. An unarmed patrol," he added.

"And now you've got an armed patrol as well, okay? Nobody told you to expect us?"

"No."

"So after you've let us through, you'd better check with whoever your supervisor is and find out who needs a swift kick in the nuts."

The civilian gave a resigned nod and gestured for them to enter.

The two men strode on without a backward glance, crossed over to the parking area and then started working their way down between the lines of trucks.

"There's something else that might help us," Bronson said. "As far as I can see, none of these trucks are connected to external power, because the crews are using the built-in facilities in the media center. Before the Bell can be activated, it'll need some form of power supply, so if you see a lorry that's got a generator running, that could be it."

And almost immediately, they found one. And the truck seemed to fit the bill in other respects as well. It had a Star of David painted on the side, was somewhat battered around the edges, and had the name of a television station that neither Bronson nor Weeks had ever heard of handwritten on the side panels. And from inside there was a distinct noise of some kind of a motor running.

"God, I hope this is it," Bronson said. "Cover me, will you?"

Weeks stepped back a few paces and leveled his MP5 to cover the side of the truck over to Bronson's right.

"Ready."

Bronson nodded, readied his own weapon, then stepped forward and rapped smartly on the double side doors of the vehicle.

To his surprise, one of them opened almost immediately, and a man wearing blue jeans and a white shirt peered out.

"Hello?" he asked.

As soon as the man spoke, and Bronson could see into the truck behind him, he knew that it wasn't the vehicle they were looking for. It was very obviously full of recording and other equipment, and he could now identify the noise he'd heard as a heavy duty air-conditioning unit, maybe with worn-out bearings.

Bronson looked at the man for a few seconds, then turned away, gesturing for Weeks to follow him.

"Wrong one," he muttered.

He walked back to the end of the parked truck and turned right to continue the search.

53

"Damn it!" shouted Bronson. "Keep looking. I'm certain it'll have generators running inside. And the doors will probably be locked, because the weapon must be triggered by some kind of timing circuit."

"I've got it," Weeks nodded. "Bit of a bloody needle-in-a-haystack job, though. There must be hundreds of trucks here."

That was a slight exaggeration, but there were a *lot* of trucks in the park.

They walked along the first double row of trucks side by side, looking at every vehicle they passed, searching for any that met the rough criteria Bronson had specified.

"Hang on a second," Weeks said, as they reached the end of the row. "All these lorries are parked in a kind of herringbone pattern."

"Yes." Bronson nodded. "So what?"

"So if that bloke Georg was telling the truth, and the

truck only arrived today, it's probably been parked in one of the spaces off the central avenue. It can't be in any of these other rows because those vehicles are boxed in by the trucks behind them."

"Bloody good thinking, Dickie," Bronson said.

They jogged over to the center of the truck parking area and started heading back the way they had come, checking the vehicles on both sides of them as they did so. They had almost walked back as far as the closed entrance gates before either of them saw anything that looked like a possibility.

And then it wasn't something they saw, but rather something they heard.

Bronson stopped short and raised his hand. Even over the all-pervading noise of the crowds of people that surrounded the Media Center, he'd heard something distinctive: a deep rumble, overlaid with a higher-pitched mechanical noise, like a small petrol engine running at constant power. He turned his head to the left and right, trying to identify the source of the noise.

On the opposite side of the open central avenue was yet another of the heavy trucks, an articulated unit, the sides bearing logos that identified the vehicle as belonging to Karel TV in the Czech Republic, and a quick glance at the registration plate confirmed the truck's origin.

"Dickie," Bronson called, pointing across to the truck and starting to move. "Over there."

Weeks trotted across the tarmac, following Bronson.

"You reckon this is it?"

"Maybe. There's an engine of some sort running in this truck," Bronson said as he stopped beside the truck and looked at it critically. "And there are closed padlocks on all the doors. You wouldn't normally leave a generator running and then lock up the vehicle. This could be the one."

"I thought you said it would be an Israeli truck?"

"I did. And I got it wrong, okay? I suppose the Israelis would have sent their trucks by ship. It's only just dawned on me."

"Right, then. Let's get inside it and find out."

They had no bolt-cutters to remove the padlocks, but Bronson thought a nine-millimeter bullet or two would be just as effective.

He stepped forward, drew his Walther and aimed the pistol at the padlock that secured the side door of the truck. He fired at virtually point-blank range at the body of the padlock, which simply blew apart under the massive impact.

But before Bronson could do anything else, he heard the sound of another shot, very close by, and turned quickly to see Weeks tumbling backward, the MP5 dropping from his grasp. And at the rear of the truck, a man wearing overalls was taking aim at Bronson with his pistol.

Instinctively, Bronson dropped the Walther, and dived sideways, rolling across the ground while simultaneously bringing his Heckler & Koch up to the aim.

The man fired twice, both shots cracking through the air somewhere above Bronson.

Then Bronson opened up with the MP5, a double tap followed by another. At least one of the bullets hit the man in the stomach, and he screamed as he fell to the floor, his weapon dropping to the ground.

Bronson glanced over at Weeks, who lay unmoving on his back a few feet away. Then he ran across to the injured man and seized his weapon. The man was whimpering with pain, but there was nothing Bronson could do for him, or for Weeks. His first priority had to be disarming the Bell.

He presumed the injured man was one of Marcus's men, left to guard the vehicle and ensure that nobody interfered with the countdown to the triggering of the weapon.

The noise of the shots had reverberated from the sides of the vehicles parked all around, and the sound made by a submachine gun firing is very distinctive. Bronson knew that he'd soon be surrounded by armed police officers. He had to confirm that this actually was the truck containing the weapon as quickly as he could because if he'd gotten it wrong it would be too late. The opening ceremony would be starting in less than five minutes.

He glanced behind him: a uniformed police officer was running from the compound. The alarm had already been raised, and within minutes the area would be swarming with police. Time was running out.

He took another glance around him, just in case there were any other armed men lurking in wait, then strode back to the side door of the truck, pulled it open and climbed inside, holstering his pistol as he did so.

It was immediately obvious that this vehicle was very different from all the others he'd seen inside. There was no sign of any recording equipment or the spare parts and cables and lights and microphones Bronson had glimpsed in other vehicles. All that was in it were three large petrol-powered generators in locked steel cages, their motors running, exhaust pipes running up to the roof, and armored power cables vanishing beneath the floor of the truck. Beyond them, the rest of the truck was blocked off by a steel partition with a single door set into it. The door was also made of steel and protected by a combination lock.

Set into the partition was what looked like a viewing panel, a slab of heavy glass secured inside a steel frame. Bronson walked across to it and peered into the second compartment.

He'd never seen anything like it.

In the center of the hidden space was an object that looked remarkably like a bell, mounted on a steel framework. It was about five feet tall and perhaps three feet in diameter, made of some kind of metal that appeared bluish in color in the dim light. From the base of the object, a mass of cables extended vertically downward, disappearing below the floor.

On one side of the truck was a control panel, further armored cables snaking from it under the floor and presumably connected to the object that lay behind the steel partition.

He'd found the weapon, but Bronson had not the slightest idea how to disarm it, or even how to get inside the locked inner compartment.

He pulled out his mobile phone, dialed 999 and told the operator who and where he was and that he needed a bomb-disposal expert there, fast.

In the background he could hear the scream of sirens, and a few moments later distorted and amplified voices as officials apparently tried to initiate an orderly evacuation of the area. That was far too quick to be in response to his call, and he guessed it was because of the shooting a few minutes earlier.

Bronson ignored the noises outside as he struggled to make sense of the control panel, trying to work out what the various cables did, but his efforts were hampered by his lack of knowledge about the type of weapon he was dealing with. And, of course, by the fact that he knew almost nothing about bomb-disposal tactics.

The only thing he could tell for sure was that there was some kind of timing circuit incorporated into the control panel, because right in the center of the instrumentation was a digital counter, which was ticking off the seconds. At that moment, the number stood at one hundred and ninety-one—just over three minutes. He pressed buttons, but nothing happened. Then he spotted a keyhole on one corner of the panel, which presumably locked the controls.

As he stood there, staring down, he felt a sudden waft of air, and a narrow beam of light illuminated the interior of the truck.

"It's too late now, you know," an unpleasantly familiar voice said, from behind him.

Bronson whirled round, his hand dropping to his Walther, but he was too late.

Marcus stood at the back of the truck, having presumably released the padlock that secured the rear doors and climbed in that way. His own pistol was pointing straight at Bronson.

Bronson knew that if he tried to draw his Walther, or reach for his MP5, he'd be dead in less than a second. At that range, Marcus couldn't possibly miss.

"The timer's just passed three minutes, Marcus," he said. "I would have thought you'd be miles away by now. Or are you planning on waiting around for the bang?"

The German shook his head, then laughed shortly.

"You really don't have the slightest idea what you're dealing with, do you? This isn't a bomb, you bumbling idiot. It's something far, far worse. But luckily it'll have no effect on me. Or on any of my men."

That wasn't what Bronson had expected at all.

"So what is it? And how come you're immune?"

Marcus shook his head.

"You'll find out. And don't bother trying to do anything about the timer, because you can't. Everything's armored and protected, so unless you've got something like a thermic lance to cut through the cables, there's nothing you can do to stop it. And even then, it only needs the power supply for a couple of minutes after it's triggered, because then the reaction becomes self-sustaining. So there really is nothing you can do."

Bronson stared at him. What the German had said made a horrible kind of sense. It looked as if the *Laternenträger* was indeed a kind of lineal descendant of the Nazi's *Die Glocke*, miniaturized, improved and refined. That probably meant it was the worst possible kind of dirty bomb, or rather something like a rogue nuclear reactor that would spew out lethal radiation for as long as it was working, turning northeast London into a desolate wasteland that would make the area around Chernobyl seem like a paradise.

And if Marcus and his men were immune, that could mean only that they knew the type of radiation the device would produce, and had taken drugs to neutralize its effects. Bronson had a vague recollection of antiradiation drugs from his time in the army, and he recalled that iodine could be an effective treatment in some circumstances.

"I could kill you right now, I suppose," Marcus said, "but that would just deny you a lot of suffering, so I won't. You shot my man outside in the stomach, and he's dying slowly and in agony, so I think it's only fair that you should enjoy the same kind of death."

Marcus lifted the pistol and took careful aim.

54

Bronson tensed, knowing that now he had to reach for his pistol, because he had nothing left to lose.

But before he could move a muscle, two shots rang out and the German seemed to crumple to the floor of the truck.

Bronson swung round to see Weeks framed in the side door, the Heckler & Koch MP5 held steady in his hands.

"I thought you were dead," Bronson said.

"I deal in illegal weapons, Chris. Wearing a Kevlar jacket under my clothes is second nature to me. The bullet just knocked the wind out of me, and my chest'll be bruised for weeks. Is he the last of them, do you think?"

"I bloody hope so."

Bronson turned back to the control panel as Weeks hauled himself up inside the truck.

The timer now stood at fifty-seven seconds.

"We need bolt-croppers or something like that, to cut the cables that power the device," Bronson said.

His voice radiated the tension and resignation he was feeling. Because at that moment he believed Marcus was right, that there really was nothing they could do to stop the Bell.

"There are police cars and a fire engine heading this way," Weeks said, peering out of the open rear door.

"Yes," Bronson said, because now he could hear the sound of the sirens getting closer. "But will they get here in time?"

"Can you shut it down from here?" Weeks asked, stepping over to the control panel.

"Not without the key that unlocks the controls, and probably not even then. The key," he repeated.

He ran over to Marcus's body and swiftly searched it. He pulled out a bunch of keys, but as soon as he looked at them he knew they were house keys or similar, and he slipped them into his own pocket. But around the German's neck he found a chain with a single key attached.

Bronson ripped off the chain, ran back to the control panel, stuck the key in the lock and turned it. Immediately, the various controls lit up, but Bronson could see nothing that looked like an abort switch.

The timer reached seventeen seconds.

He pressed a couple of buttons experimentally, just to do something, but to no avail.

At fourteen seconds to go, a figure in army uniform climbed into the truck through the rear door.

Weeks covered him with his MP5, but the man ignored him and strode forward.

"Russell. Bomb disposal," he announced. "What have you got?"

"Do you speak German?" Bronson demanded.

"A little, yes."

"Good. There's twelve seconds to go and the control panel's unlocked."

The army officer stepped over to the control panel and looked down at it, his lips moving silently as he rapidly scanned the illuminated labels.

"Right," he said, and pressed two buttons simultaneously. "That should be the abort," he said.

Then he frowned, because the counter was still unwinding and a message had popped up in an alphanumeric display.

"It's asking for the abort code," Russell said. "Do you have it?"

Bronson and Weeks just stared at him.

"I said: do you have the code?" Russell repeated.

"No," Bronson replied.

Russell's face seemed to age five years in an instant.

"Then we're buggered," he said.

55

The three of them stared at the timer in horrified fascination as it counted down to zero.

Then a new message appeared in the display.

"That says that the actuating sequence has begun," Russell said, in a small voice.

Bronson strode across to the viewing pane in the steel partition and looked into the other compartment.

The Bell was in motion, the outer shell beginning to rotate slowly, a faint whine just audible through the steel wall.

"It's started," Bronson said.

"Did Marcus tell you what it did?" Weeks asked.

Bronson nodded, but then, as a pale violet light suddenly became visible in the viewing port, the color deepening with each passing moment, a sudden thought struck him.

"Lateral thinking," he exclaimed. "After two minutes,

that thing becomes self-sustaining. We've got to cut the power to it right now."

"But we haven't got any bolt-croppers," Weeks pointed out, "and the cables are under the floor."

"I know," Bronson said, seizing his MP5, "so we have to hit the generators. Blow their fuel tanks. Stop them operating."

"That's bloody brilliant."

Russell ran for the door as Bronson and Weeks aimed their Heckler & Koch submachine guns at the fuel tanks of two of the petrol-driven generators.

The interior of the truck echoed to the sound of machine-gun fire as the two men, standing side by side, opened up with their weapons, firing short bursts. The bullets ripped through the two fuel tanks, sending petrol flying through the air, the fuel splashing down onto the hot engines below. In moments, the petrol ignited with a heavy "whump" and that end of the truck turned into hell on earth, blazing fuel igniting everything flammable.

The heat was intense, and the oxygen was being sucked out of the air Bronson and Weeks were breathing. They needed to get out. But the third generator was still running, still supplying power to the nightmare device inside the locked compartment, and both men turned their weapons on it.

As they did so, both the other generators died, the fuel in their carburettors exhausted. Again, fuel spewed everywhere as the third fuel tank ruptured, but the blaze ensured that it was ignited immediately. Maybe that tank held more than the others, or there were other supplies of fuel there they hadn't spotted, but for whatever reason the third petrol explosion was both louder and more powerful than the other two, blowing Bronson and Weeks off their feet.

"Let's get out of here," Bronson said, helping Weeks stand up again.

They staggered to the rear doors of the truck and jumped down to the ground, both blackened and barely recognizable as human beings. And at that moment something else—perhaps another can of petrol—blew up in the truck behind them with a deep booming sound.

All around the vehicle, police officers and firemen were assembling, the latter preparing their firefighting equipment, though it was already clear that little inside the truck would survive the blaze.

Then there was a scream from inside the truck, and Marcus, his clothes sodden with blood, flames licking around his limbs, stood framed in the rear doorway, silhouetted against the blaze like some devilish creature from the pit, his pistol in his hand as he looked for a target.

Bronson and Weeks acted as one, swinging round and aiming their MP5s at him. The four shots sounded like two as they simultaneously each fired two rounds.

Marcus tumbled backward into the flames, the pistol falling from his hand to land on the ground outside the truck. And he didn't move at all as the raging fire began to consume his body.

"Christ, I thought he was dead," Weeks said.

"Well, he is now," Bronson replied.

"Do you think we stopped it in time?"

"I have no idea, but I suppose we'll soon find out."

Bronson glanced around him at the circle of faces that surrounded them.

"I think it's time we made ourselves scarce," he said. "At least I've got an excuse for wandering about carrying a submachine gun, but you should definitely get the hell away from here."

Weeks nodded, then walked over to Bronson and pulled a couple of clear plastic evidence bags from one of the pockets on the other man's utility belt. He strode over to the blazing truck, picked up the pistol Marcus had dropped and slipped it into one of the bags. Then he made his way back to Bronson, a somewhat bemused smile on his face.

"Give me the other pistol," Weeks said. "Might as well try to pick up some stock while I'm here. And carrying these two weapons will give me an excuse to get out of here."

Bronson grinned at him, pulled the Walther he'd taken off the German out of his belt and handed it over. Then he felt inside his trouser pocket, took out the keys for the hire car and gave them to Weeks as well.

"You've got a bloody cheek, Dickie, but actually that might work. Whatever happens, give me a call and I'll do what I can."

Weeks walked briskly away from the truck, a police officer on a mission, and the circle of people parted silently to let him through.

Bronson smiled at his retreating figure, then turned back to stare again at the burning truck. Then he was conscious of a couple of people approaching him, and swung round to meet them. Neither Bob Curtis nor Detective Inspector Davidson looked particularly pleased to see him.

56

9 August 2012

"Sit down, Chris."

Bronson took a seat in front of the superintendent's desk and waited.

"You're fully recovered, I hope. Smoke inhalation can be dangerous, and I can see that your hair and eyebrows suffered a bit."

Bronson nodded.

"I'm fine, sir, really. And the checks for radiation sickness came back negative as well."

"Good. Now, there's good news and bad news, like there usually is. The good news is that the boffins have finally finished picking over what was left of that burned-out lorry in the Olympic Park. Your instinct was right. Because you managed to stop the generators delivering a current to the Bell only a few seconds after it was activated, the two contrarotating cylinders never reached a sufficiently high speed to start a sustained reaction."

The superintendent paused and glanced down at the notes on his desk.

"Now, I don't pretend to understand the science behind it, but it seems that when it was originally constructed—when the Nazis built *Die Glocke*, I mean—it was intended to act as a kind of nuclear reactor, to transmute thorium into uranium or possibly uranium into plutonium, as part of the German atom bomb project. And we now know a bit more about what's happened since then. The Met police arrested half a dozen other Germans who were clearly involved with this plot and a couple of them have been quite forthcoming. According to them, at the end of the last war, the Nazis managed to fly the original Bell, and the most important scientists involved in the project, out to South America. It looks as if Marcus Wolf's grandfather was the officer in charge of that evacuation, and he and a bunch of other renegade Nazis, who were certain that Hitler had been right all along, decided they'd use the Bell to take revenge on the rest of Europe. The problem they had was that it took them a lot longer, decades longer in fact, to produce a fully functioning and miniaturized version of the weapon.

"And they also changed the way it worked from the original. Marcus Wolf's Bell was only ever intended to produce radiation. Massive amounts of lethal radiation. If you hadn't stopped it, I have been assured by the scientists who've looked at it, a circular area covering over one hundred square miles would have been so badly contaminated that nothing would be able to live there for a minimum of fifty years. The estimates of the immediate death toll don't run into the thousands. They run into the tens of thousands, possibly even higher, and an incalculable number of people would have suffered from cancers and other diseases caused by radiation sickness of various sorts.

"It was an outstanding piece of work, and I'm only sorry that Detective Inspector Davidson—I'm sorry, I mean the former Detective Inspector Davidson—was so dismissive of the information that you provided to him and his officers. He's already been suspended and will probably be dismissed from the force, and there will be a commendation for you in the near future, I imagine. The other evidence that has emerged from this operation is that Marcus Wolf—which does actually appear to be his real name—was a very professional operator. As well as the technical expertise he and his men showed in the construction of this nasty weapon, he had even managed to arrange for Israel to take the blame. I fully accept your view that Wolf was a Nazi, in the proper sense of that word, and he genuinely believed that the Jews were responsible for most of the ills of the world. What we think he was hoping for was a backlash against the state of Israel once his plot had succeeded.

"What he'd done was prepare forged documentation that would apparently show that the device had been developed and positioned by a radical Egyptian terrorist group, but which would, on closer examination, prove to have been the work of rogue elements within the Israeli Mossad secret service. It was, if you like, a forgery within a forgery. But thanks to the information you've provided, identifying the real culprits has not proved difficult."

The superintendent paused and smiled at Bronson.

"And the bad news, sir?"

"There have been a number of questions raised about the weapons you and your companion were seen to be carrying, and later using, in the Olympic Park. You've also failed to identify your companion. Your statement that he was a former army colleague presently seconded to the Special Air Service, and that he supplied the weapons you used, appears to be without foundation. Or at least, the army has so far failed to identify anyone who meets those criteria."

For a few seconds, the superintendent simply stared at Bronson. Then he nodded and continued.

"We will be taking the pragmatic view here, Chris. Because you managed to foil this plot, no action will be taken over any perceived firearms offenses that you and your companion may seem to be guilty of. As I'm your superior officer, all inquiries into this matter will eventually arrive on my desk, and I am prepared to provide evidence that the weapons were issued to you by the Kent Police, and that your companion was an undercover officer employed by this force who can't be identified for security reasons."

Bronson breathed a sigh of relief. Because of what had happened, he hadn't expected to encounter any problems over his somewhat unorthodox handling of the situation, but it was good to have this confirmed.

There was only one other matter that was gnawing at his conscience. Two days after the incidents in the Olympic Park, he and Weeks had traveled by car to Berlin, used the keys Bronson had removed from Marcus's body in the truck, and thoroughly searched the German's house.

One of the keys had opened a safe in a bedroom, hidden inside a wardrobe that contained only Nazi uniforms. Inside that safe they'd found several hundred thousand euros, which they'd split between them as unofficial payment for the job they'd done in London, a Walther pistol and a DVD.

Bronson had played the first few seconds of the DVD to make sure it was the correct one, then removed it and the pistol. On the way back across the Channel on the ferry, he'd cut the DVD into a dozen pieces and tossed them all over the side rail, and then dropped the component parts of the Walther into the sea, one at a time.

But that still left the killing of the undercover police officer to be addressed.

"And the other matter, sir?" Bronson asked.

"Ah, yes. That's caused a bit of confusion, actually, but the Berlin police were very helpful. They still don't know why we needed to know about an undercover police officer named Herman Polti, but they did check their records for us. And that's a puzzle, really, because not only could they find no trace of an undercover officer by that name, but they also could find no serving police officer anywhere in the Berlin force called Herman Polti. So I don't know where you got your information from, but it appears to be completely inaccurate."

The superintendent paused again, and looked speculatively across the desk at Bronson.

"They did do a wider check, though, and the name cropped up on one of their databases. A week or so ago, shortly after you went undercover in London, actually, the body of a man named Herman Polti was found in woodland on the eastern outskirts of Berlin. He'd been shot in the chest, and the corpse showed unmistakable signs of having been brutally tortured."

Bronson sat forward in his chair, hanging on every word.

"But he wasn't a policeman. Quite the reverse, in fact. Now that we've managed to identify Marcus Wolf as the ringleader of this plot, we've also been able to trace many of his associates. Herman Polti was one of those associates, and he was also wanted by the Berlin police in connection with at least two robberies and three murders. He was, in short, a career criminal who seemed to have thrown his lot in with Wolf. Who killed him, and who tortured him, are two mysteries that we may never solve. It's possible that someone from his past life caught up with him to exact revenge, or perhaps Marcus Wolf discovered he was playing both sides against the middle and had him executed. We don't know, and frankly we don't care."

Bronson didn't even realize he had been holding his breath until he exhaled.

"Thank you, sir," he said, getting to his feet, "for everything."

The superintendent smiled.

"Actually, I think it's the other way round," he said. "I don't care what you're working on now, just clear your desk and take some leave. You've earned it. I don't want to see you back here for at least two weeks. If Angela's still speaking to you, take her somewhere hot. Just not the Berlin area. It's possible some of Marcus Wolf's friends might still be on the loose, and I'd hate you to meet up with them."

Bronson nodded.

"I hadn't planned to go back to Germany for some time," he said. "Maybe never. There's something about that country that I don't like. Probably just too many echoes of the past."

AUTHOR'S NOTE

Olympic Myths

There are a lot of misconceptions about the Olympics in general, and about the 1936 Berlin Olympics in particular.

One myth that has endured to this day is that Adolf Hitler deliberately snubbed the hugely successful black American athlete Jesse Owens. In fact, no such thing occurred. All the evidence suggests that Hitler actually admired Owens, and that the feeling was mutual. In reality, Hitler was told by Count Henri de Baillet-Latour, the then president of the International Olympic Committee, that as the Führer was a guest at the Games, he would have to either congratulate all of the winners or none of them. Hitler's schedule—he was, after all, running Germany at the time—did not permit him to attend every event, and so after the first day he congratulated none of the athletes, white or black.

This myth was perpetrated long after the Olympics were over by, among other people, Jesse Owens himself, and it wasn't until 1965, almost thirty years after the Berlin Olympics, that Owens finally admitted in an interview that there was no truth in the story whatsoever. Owens had become a popular public speaker in the interim, and had told and retold the story of the alleged snub simply because, as he put it in his own words: "Those stories are what people like to hear, so you tell them."

Right from the start, the Berlin Games were mired in both controversy and myth. During the opening ceremony, the British team's military-style "eyes right" as they strode past Adolf Hitler in the viewing stand was watched in stony silence by the German spectators, and the refusal by the American team to lower their flag as they passed the Führer was greeted with whistles and catcalls of disapproval by the German crowd.

In fact, it was touch and go whether the Americans would send a team at all: in 1935 the Amateur Athletic Union of America voted to participate in the event by the slimmest possible margin of 58 votes to 56.

When the German team, five hundred strong and wearing white military-style uniforms, marched into the stadium at the end of the parade, there was no doubting the feelings of the spectators. After greeting the German competitors with a roar that seemed almost to shake the very fabric of the stadium, the crowd burst into an impromptu rendition of the chorus of *Deutschland Über Alles*, the German national anthem.

When the parade was complete, Hitler made one of his briefest speeches ever—just a single sentence to officially open the Games—and then a recording of a special greeting from Baron Pierre De Coubertin, the founder of the modern Olympics, was played over the public address system. When that was complete, twenty thousand homing pigeons were released, all except one returning to their owners. That single dissenting bird took up residence in the stadium and was seen on a daily basis throughout the Games.

Immediately after the opening ceremony, a single runner, a twenty-nine-year-old blond-haired and blue-eyed athlete named Fritz Schilgen, entered the arena. Schilgen was carrying a flaming torch in his right hand, holding it high above his head. He paused for a bare second as he entered the stadium, apparently shocked into immobility by the deafening noise of the spectators, then ran down a long flight of steps that led to the track itself. The sound died away almost to nothing as he ran the entire length of the arena, staying on the track, the torch still held high, then ran up a set of steps at the opposite end of the stadium, where a large steel cauldron stood waiting. He paused for a moment, then plunged the burning torch into the top of the vessel. The fuel in the cauldron caught fire immediately, the flames dancing high above his head.

Again the crowd roared approval. The XI Olympiad, the Berlin Games, as much a propaganda exercise for the ruling Nazi regime as a sporting event, had finally started, and at the same time at least two enduring myths had been created.

The orders given by Adolf Hitler had been most specific. The Berlin Games were to be the most impressive and memorable that the world had ever seen. Preparations had started years before, overseen by a remarkable, imaginative and very talented individual named Carl Diem.

Diem hadn't just organized the building of the stadia and tracks and swimming pools and accommodation and all the other facilities essential for the conduct of the games themselves. Acting on Hitler's most specific orders, and letting his imagination run wild, he had gone further. Much, much further.

He had visited Greece, the home of the original Olympic Games, two years before, and had come up with the idea of creating a symbolic pageant that would imbue the Berlin Games with a sense of the history and traditions of the ancient Greek event. That might have been enough, but he was a lot more ambitious than that. Instead of just trying to replicate some of the historical details of the original Games, he decided to invent history. And he did it so well that two of Carl Diem's fabricated "traditions" would be used in every subsequent Games.

The ancient Olympics were dedicated to the Greek god Zeus, whose statue, originally one of the Seven Wonders of the Ancient World, had stood at Olympia, and the place had then given its name to the Games. Diem discovered that in the original Olympic Games a flame was burned to commemorate the legend of the theft of fire from the gods by Prometheus, and that gave him the idea for the torch relay from Olympia to the city hosting the Games, a ritual that had never taken place previously.

The carefully orchestrated procession began on the last day of June 1936, in the ruins of the Temple of Hera at Olympia in Greece, the site of the ancient Olympics. A troupe of fifteen young women, clad in white robes to symbolize virginity, and working under the direction of an apparent "high priestess," kindled this first modern Olympic flame by using a specially designed parabolic mirror to focus the rays of the sun onto twigs gathered from nearby trees.

To further reinforce the image Diem was trying to create, the flaming torch was then carried to the Acropolis in Athens for a special invocation, and handed to the first of the runners who would carry it to Berlin. Then it was taken to the ancient stadium at Delphi for a modern re-creation of Diem's idea of what an ancient Greek ceremony might have been like.

Central to this event was what looked like a centuries-old three-foot-tall stone altar with the now-familiar design of five interlocking rings chiseled into its surface. But this wasn't old. It had been especially prepared for this one event, another product of Diem's fertile imagination, and yet another of his ideas that was to become a part of the ancient Olympic myth.

So firmly entrenched did the idea of the "Rings of Olympus" become that about two decades later, when a group of British researchers visited Delphi and found the carved altar stone there, they recognized the ring design and immediately proclaimed that they'd discovered an incontrovertible link between the ancient and modern Olympics. Some apparently authoritative history books still include a reference to this ancient stone and the Olympic tradition. Public humiliation and embarrassment for the researchers followed shortly afterward when it was revealed that the ancient stone, this "millennia-old altar," was just a clever piece of twentieth-century Nazi propaganda.

The flaming torch was then relayed along the 3,422 kilometers through Greece, Bulgaria, Yugoslavia, Hungary, Austria and Czechoslovakia to the Olympic stadium in Berlin by specially selected runners—chosen as much for their Aryan appearance as for their abilities as athletes—each of whom carried the flame for a single kilometer before passing it on to the next man, culminating in the lighting of the first ever Olympic flame by Fritz Schilgen.

The Wenceslas Mine and *Die Glocke*

The Wenceslas Mine is real, and all the available evidence suggests that it was the final home in Europe for the experimental object that became known as *Die Glocke*, the true purpose of that is still uncertain, though the idea that it was some kind of generator to produce radioactive material is as plausible as any other suggestion.

The description given in this novel of the circumstances of the creation of the Bell, of the science behind it, of the events leading up to the abandonment of the Wenceslas Mine, and of the subsequent fate of the device, are as accurate as it's possible to be at this remove. It is also a fact that the development of *Die Glocke*—whatever its true purpose—was of the utmost importance to the Nazi regime. As far as my research has been able to show, this project was the *only* clandestine development operation ever to be allocated the priority classification *Kriegsentscheidend*, meaning "decisive for the outcome of the war." This was the highest possible classification in the entire Nazi system, which guaranteed that whatever supplies, equipment or personnel were required for it would be provided as quickly as possible.

One confirmation of this is that when, as the Russian forces drew ever closer to the German borders in April 1945, a request was made by the German high command in Berlin for the use of one of only two Junkers Ju-390 aircraft so far constructed to assist in the evacuation. One of these precious aircraft was under the control of General Hans Kammler, the man in charge of the operation in the Wenceslas Mine, and he refused to release the aircraft on the direct orders of Hitler, because the evacuation of *Die Glocke* had a higher priority. This is somewhat astonishing in military terms, that one single secret project could have acquired a greater importance than the evacuation of the entire German high command.

The three sightings reported in the book, of the aircraft being seen in Bodø and South America, are unconfirmed, but the choice of the Argentine as a destination for the device would seem to be plausible, again for the reasons outlined in this book.

But wherever it went, and whatever it was designed to do, the ultimate fate of *Die Glocke* remains as shrouded in mystery today as it was in 1945.

About the Author

James Becker spent more than twenty years in the Royal Navy's Fleet Air Arm. Throughout his career he has been involved in covert operations in many of the world's hot spots, including Yemen, Russia, and Northern Ireland. He writes action-adventure novels under the name James Barrington and military history under the name Peter Smith in the UK.

Also available from

James Becker

THE NOSFERATU SCROLL

Bohemia, 1741: A noble lady is laid to rest—with
her heart cut out and a covering of heavy stones.
Whatever it takes to keep her from rising from
the grave...

Venice, 2010: While on a much-needed vacation,
Chris Bronson and Angela Lewis discover a
desecrated tomb containing a female skeleton and a
diary that is centuries old. Scribbled in Latin, the
pages tell of a scroll that holds the key to answering
an ancient secret. Soon, the bodies of young
women begin surfacing, all killed in a ritual
manner. When Angela vanishes, Bronson is drawn
into the hunt for a demented murderer who
torments his prey on the eerie Isle of the Dead—
and into a deadly conspiracy hundreds of years in
the making.

Also available from

James Becker

NATIONAL BESTSELLING AUTHOR
OF *THE FIRST APOSTLE*

THE MESSIAH SECRET

Assessing the contents of a lavish English estate,
museum conservator Angela Lewis discovers a crate
full of sealed pottery jars—one of which holds a
parchment which describes the life and times of
Jesus of Nazareth.

For Angela, the find is a miracle—a written
reference to Jesus outside of the New Testament.
But herdiscovery draws her and her husband,
Chris, into a centuries-old race for the truth that
they may not win...or survive.

S0327

Also available from

James Becker

THE MOSES STONE

An ancient code...
A sinister secret…
A deadly chase for the truth.

In Morocco, an English couple discovers a clay
tablet covered in ancient writing. One day later,
they are dead.

Called to North Africa to investigate, detective
Chris Bronson follows a trail of clues that plunge
him into a mystery that has gone unsolved since
biblical times. For the stone he must find is older
and far more dangerous than he could ever
have imagined...

**Available wherever books are sold or at
penguin.com**